John,

You're good a ......y proyer.

Let me know at what point you have this one figured out.

And thanks for your support.

John
(E. Rocco)

Altomare

Change For a Dollar

Change For a Dollar

John E. Rocco

ISBN: 1974665348
ISBN 13: 9781974665341

Prelude

The boat lurched erratically through the dark, murky water, made frigid but not yet frozen, by the unseasonably cold fall weather. The lone rower struggled, breathing hard, winded from half carrying, half dragging his lifeless cargo the forty plus yards from the house to the boat. He paused briefly, sucking in the cold night air. Was he far enough out? Hard to tell.

The sand bar extended about 30 yards from shore before it dropped off. It certainly seemed like he had gone that far. Then again, he might be rowing at an angle, not straight out.

Scudding dark clouds made the sky starless and moonless, yielding little help. And he had turned out all the lights at the house. He shrugged, realizing that he probably wouldn't be able to judge the distance even if it were broad daylight.

He decided to row a bit farther. There was no reason to rush and even less reason to take unnecessary chances.

A minute later he was confident he had gone far enough. Resting the oars, he reached down and grabbed the body under the armpits. He heaved, straining mightily, and finally managed to maneuver the corpse into a sitting position on the side of the boat. Then, with a final effort, he pushed the body overboard, making a huge splash that soaked his face and jacket. Exhilarated both by the cold water and the completion of his task, he smiled broadly as the body sank to the muck and seaweed some thirty feet below.

As he turned the boat around for the row back to shore, he cast a backward glance at the drop spot, still smiling.

"See you later, bitch," he said.

1

My late night dinner at Giovanni's didn't turn out exactly as planned. One of my favorite Italian restaurants, Giovanni's is on Detroit's southwest side and I eat there often. Especially when my caseload is lean. The excellent food and a pleasant conversation with Frances, the proprietor, always put me in a good mood.

Carlo, an authentic Italian waiter, had just delivered my linguini with clam sauce, smiling something in Italian that I pretended to understand. As I lifted my glass of grappa for a sip, a shout pierced the air.

"Pietro! Look out!" It was Frances.

Startled by the warning, I almost dropped the glass, but managed to set it down with minimal spillage. I looked up just in time to see an enormous man close in on my table. I recognized him immediately. Stu Gotts, one of local bookie Lorenzo Nematotta's muscle men. He could have been Primo Carnera's cousin.

"You're late for your meeting with the Toad," he growled, not as menacingly as I would have expected. "Don't do nothing funny and nobody won't get hurt." He gestured as though he had a gun in his jacket pocket.

I refrained from pointing out his triple negative as my instant rush of adrenalin slowed down to a drip. Not wanting to make a scene in the restaurant, I calmly acquiesced and got up.

"Okay Gotts. Let's go. No need for any violence." I didn't bother to mention that I was keenly aware he could rip my limbs off.

As he grabbed my arm and guided me past a few dozen inquisitive faces, I looked back longingly at my untouched plate of pasta. Frances stood there, a confused expression on her face. I gave her a quick head-shake. Don't worry. It's no big deal.

Outside, the evening was cool. Threatening clouds obscured the moon and loud rumbles of thunder and flashes of lightning foretold an imminent storm.

"My car's right over there," I offered. "Can we drive separately?"

"What are you a comedian? You think I would trust you to do something like that? Besides, we ain't driving. We're walking.

Halfway down the block, the deluge hit. Gotts steered me through a battered screen door. I thought it was to get out of the rain, but we continued up a flight of stairs and into a medium-sized office with a couple of doors that probably led to closets or a wash room. I immediately recognized it as one of the Toad's phone rooms, a place where his clientele phoned in their bets. And there was the Toad himself, a broad smile on his face.

"Pietro! Paesano! Come stai?"

"Va fa, Nematotta." I did know a little Italian.

"Pietro, no need to be profane. This is just a friendly get together."

"Friendly? You call yanking me away from dinner because I'm late for some non-existent meeting friendly? We never had any appointment."

Actually, I have nothing against bookies and gambling. I play the horses a little myself. All right, more than a little. I just don't like Lorenzo Nematotta.

Gotts, who still had my arm, looked surprised. "You mean there wasn't no appointment? So how come ..."

"Shut up Stuart. You just do as you're told and keep your big mouth shut."

At that moment, Gotts did just the opposite. He opened his big mouth. To sneeze. As he instinctively released his grip to cover up, I slid around in front of him and delivered a sharp knee to his groin. In spite of what should have been great pain, he reached for me with a snarl. I ducked out of reach just in time and he grabbed air instead.

2

I hit the steps running and took them three at a time, which is no easy feat going down. But, when you're being chased by Stu Gotts, speed is of the essence. And discretion is the *only* part of valor. Two yards from the bottom, my foot caught something in the darkness and I went airborne. Not exactly the way I wanted to increase my lead over Gotts, who was coming down in a more gingerly fashion, one hand over his damaged crotch. I threw my hands out to break the fall, sprawled and slid across the short landing and crashed into the already battered metal bottom of the door leading out to Fort Street.

I scrambled up and ran outside, sensing a nasty scrape on my left knee and feeling a knot forming on my forehead. Fifteen yards down the sidewalk, I heard Gotts banging through the door, already breathing hard. Stu was clearly not into physical fitness.

The rain was coming down hard as I sprinted back past Giovanni's Ristorante and toward my new '93 Saab 9000 CSE Turbo. Okay, I bought it used, but it was only two years old and still looked and ran like new. Looking back, I noticed that Gotts showed no sign of a limp. Fortunately, I had put a little more distance between us. But he had a lot of momentum, and I knew he wouldn't give up the chase very easily.

I reached the Saab, glancing back again as I unlocked the door. Stu seemed confused. He stopped and looked around, then started running back the way he had come. I hopped in, keyed the ignition, and unlike those predictable scenes in the horror movies, the engine immediately roared to life. I let out a shiver of relief, flicked on the lights and wipers and squealed a U-turn out onto Fort Street doing 40.

As I turned right, I caught sight of Gotts getting into his biggest fringe benefit, an Eldorado Brougham. He was parked across the street and closer to the intersection than I. He headed straight for his car when he saw me go for mine. I guess he wasn't as confused as he looked.

Eluding him wasn't a problem. When the turbo kicked in, old Dago Red packed enough punch to outrun his Caddy, which was more powerful, but far less maneuverable. What concerned me was the fact that Stu knew where I lived. And I knew he would do anything necessary to bring me back for my on-again, off-again meeting with Nematotta.

It was a matter of honor to Stu. He didn't want to lose face. On the other hand, I didn't like being forced into an appointment I had never made in the first place, or being dragged out of a restaurant in the middle of a meal. *Before* a meal, actually. And Giovanni's linguine with clam sauce is … well, to die for.

3

Traffic was light. Probably because it was raining and it was 11:30 on a Thursday night. All the normal people were either in bed or watching the late show. The fun lovers were still getting dressed for a night of clubbing. I kicked the speedometer up to 55 and beat the red light at Oakwood Boulevard by a nanosecond. I took a hard right that felt like it might have been a three-wheeler. Maybe even two. Split seconds later, Gotts ran the red without slowing down, doing maybe 70. He had noticed that traffic was light too.

We were now in Melvindale, a small suburb southwest of Detroit, and the home of my high school alma mater. It didn't make me feel any better. Gotts was closing ground fast, either unaware that we were about to pass the Melvindale police station or not really giving a damn.

It didn't matter. The police station flew by, a dim beacon in the darkness, oblivious to our passing. The patrol boys were probably discussing the wet driving conditions over a coffee at Frank's Grill, home of the best chili in town and the world's only surviving six-plays-for-a-quarter juke box. I caught the light at Allen Road in mid-green, went on for a few blocks, and then took a sharp left at Hanna, my right rear wheel tattooing the curb.

Through the rearview mirror, I saw Gotts screech past the side street. I was near the end of the block before he was able to straighten out and pick up the chase. Now the rain was really coming down. Even with my wipers going full blast, it was difficult to see. If there was a moon out, it was hidden by the storm clouds, and this was an old neighborhood with lots of big trees hanging over both sides of the narrow street. The scene was the very definition of pitch dark.

I didn't know what the hell I was going to do about Gotts. He was being annoyingly persistent. As my mind raced for a solution, a bright flash of lightning briefly lit up the sky and gave me an idea.

Halfway up the next block, two cars were parked directly opposite each other. I slowed down for a few seconds to let Gotts get just close enough. Then I flicked off my lights, stood on the accelerator and prayed. He stayed right on my tail. Good. I could faintly make out where I thought the cars were ahead. I sensed more than saw two darker masses in the black. I steered straight at the one on the right, and then swerved at the last possible instant. My lithe Saab made it through; Gotts' clumsy Caddy didn't.

I'll give the guy credit, though. He saw what was happening and tried to steer clear. But he had too much speed and too little time to succeed. His efforts did avoid a dead-on rear-end collision, but the crash was still as loud as thunder as his right front fender crunched the left rear of the parked car.

My lights still off, I stopped and looked back. There was no apparent movement. But the Caddy was definitely damaged; the windshield broken. I didn't know if Gotts was hurt, or how badly. I suspected his head may have gone through the windshield, but I wasn't about to stick around to find out. Porch lights were starting to come on.

I made a left at the next side street and flicked my lights on as I turned onto Allen Road. Carefully observing the speed limit, I made my way to the Southfield Freeway and headed north toward Southfield.

To my office. And my home.

4

The rain slackened considerably by the time I pulled into the driveway in front of my two-story bungalow on Ten Mile Road. By the looks of the pavement and grass, it hadn't rained nearly as hard in my neck of the woods, about fifteen miles northwest of Melvindale. I got out, activated my alarm and locked up. On the way in, I picked up the mail and tossed it on a chair.

I use the first floor of my bungalow as an office. It's very simple. In the "business" area, which used to be the living room, there's a desk, sofa, custom-built record case, television, filing cabinet and a couple of chairs. A reference library, my computer, and a big worktable occupy a former bedroom. And in the kitchen, which I essentially use for storing boxes of junk, I also keep a refrigerator and cabinets well stocked with drinks and snacks. And there's a john I still use as a john.

Oh, I keep the kitty litter in the kitchen too. My two orange tabbies, Nehi and Nesbitt, have free rein of both floors, but they aren't allowed to do their business in my living quarters upstairs. And the computer I referred to as mine is used at least 50 percent of the time by my nephew Gianni. The kid is 10 years old and he's somewhat of a computer whiz.

Me? Sometimes I have trouble turning the thing on.

I flicked on the light in the kitchen, chose a Leinenkugel from my gourmet beer selection and suddenly realized my head and knee were both throbbing. I took a deep slug, decided it wasn't going to be enough, and grabbed a can of Point for later. The Leinenkugel was in a bottle.

I mention that because I consider myself an expert on beer, and in my expert opinion, it doesn't much matter if your beer comes in a bottle or a can. Good beer is good beer. Period. But a dark bottle, brown or green, does keep beer fresher much longer than a clear bottle. That's why I never buy beer in a clear bottle.

I limped back into my office in severe pain, paused at the wall selector of my antique Wurlitzer, which was upstairs, and punched in a few tunes to help me forget the bruises: "Shortnin' Bread" by Paul Chaplain and the Emeralds, "Peanut Butter" by the Marathons, and "Blueberry Hill" by the immortal Antoine "Fats" Domino. I enjoyed putting "theme" medleys together.

Paul started wailing, coming through my less than top-of-the-line speakers a bit on the tinny side. The good speakers were upstairs, hooked up as auxiliaries to the jukebox. I picked up the mail and plopped down on the sofa. Horizontally.

It looked like the usual junk. Mr. Pete Pepper (or current resident) 18765 Ten Mile Rd., Southfield, MI 48076. Of the seven pieces, only two weren't immediate throwaways. My August bank statement (it was late October), and a solicitation from a sports advisory service that guaranteed 65% winners betting college and pro football. I popped the tab on the Point and set the tout service literature on the desk to give to my friend, Lou Bracato. Then, grabbing my bank statement, I hobbled up the stairs as Fats was climbing Blueberry Hill on his quest for a thrill.

He was sounding better with every painful step as I entered the range of my Fisher speakers in the living room. The full glory enveloped me just as the song ended. I filed the August statement underneath the September statement, which I had already received. I make it a habit to keep all my personal stuff filed upstairs; everything to do with business, I keep downstairs. Not that I'm a particularly neat or meticulous guy. I just like to follow all the IRS guidelines. And, as a private investigator, I like to take full advantage of the fifty percent business deduction I was taking on the mortgage payment.

Just as the Wurlitzer clicked off, the phone rang. I glanced at my watch. 1:15. Way too late for a client. But it could be one of my good friends, Lou Bracato or Lefkowitz Turner. Or even my brother's widow, Marianne. I took a long pull of Point and picked up the phone.

It was Nematotta.

"You're a bad boy, Pietro," he taunted, in his whiney voice. Shit, he *sounded* like a toad. "You hurt Stuart. He's gonna be real mad when he gets out of the hospital."

Gotts' full name was Stuart Gottschalk. I guess Stu Gotts made him sound tougher. Not that he needed any help.

"Listen, Nematotta. I'm sorry about Stu. Really. I just did what I had to do."

"Pietro. You didn't have to hurt him. He was just running a simple errand for me. Why do you refuse my hospitality?"

"Hospitality?" I asked angrily. "You call pulling me out of a restaurant and dragging me over to your dump of an office hospitality? If you have a problem with Lou Bracato, settle it with Lou Bracato."

"This has nothing to do with your slimy friend Bracato. So the weasel owes me a dime and a half. I'll get it. And I sure don't need your help. I wanted to see you on another matter completely." The Toad seemed to be getting mad too.

"Yeah? What kind of matter?"

"A business proposition."

I had to stifle a laugh. "With a heavy-duty collector like Gotts, why do you need someone like me?"

"Goddammit," he shouted. "You still think I'm small time, don't you? You think bookmaking and loans are all I do? That's just the tip of the glacier, you asshole. You'd shit your pants if you knew the size of the organization I'm building."

"Oh yeah? What kind of organization?"

"It ain't something I can talk about over the phone. That's why I wanted to meet you at my office. And, by the way, that place where Stu brought you is just a phone room for my Southwest Detroit clients. I got three or four nice places all around town. Including a new executive suite right there in Southfield."

"Look, Lorenzo. I'm flattered. But there's no way I can do business with you. Any kind of business."

He mumbled something in Italian, too fast for me to catch. I can only understand a little anyway, but I'm sure there was a curse or two buried somewhere in his words. Then he continued in English, obviously struggling to control his violent temper.

"Listen, Pete," (not Pietro?) "I'm asking you as a Paesano. We're almost family, me and you. My father, may he rest in peace, and your grandfather were the best of friends. Giovanni Pepperini used to treat me like a son. To this day, I still send him a card every year on his birthday. Doesn't that mean anything to you? Can't you do me a favor for old time's sake?"

He was right. The two men had been close friends. And they were both resting in peace. But Giovanni Pepperini, my grandfather, was still alive, living in an apartment for the elderly in Wyandotte. Luciano Nematotta, on the other hand, was resting permanently. He had died in prison serving a life sentence for the least violent crime he had ever committed. Tax evasion.

I stayed silent for several seconds to give the impression I was thinking it over. In fact, I had already decided to meet with him. If he had an office in Southfield, he had business in Southfield. And he might let something slip that I could pass on to my friend Lieutenant Harvey Steinberg of the Southfield Police. I liked to deposit favors whenever and wherever I could. You never knew when you were going to need to make a withdrawal.

"Alright, Nematotta. You got to me with that one. I'll meet with you on one condition. But it can't be until sometime next week. I'm on a pretty hot case," I lied.

"Anything. You know how the Toad hops when he can do something for a friend."

"Don't get carried away. I said I'd meet with you. Not hold hands and go steady."

"So what's the condition?" he asked. He didn't seem even slightly offended by my little jab.

"Gotts. I want you to keep him off me. No retaliation for tonight."

The Toad laughed. "Is that all? Shit. I thought maybe you wanted me to forget Bracato's fifteen hundred. Don't worry about Gotts. That's already taken care of. You have my word he won't touch you. Besides, if anything happened to you now, you got about thirty witnesses from the restaurant."

I still wasn't convinced. "How do you know he'll listen to you? How do you know he even heard you? What kind of condition was he in?"

"Pietro, don't worry," he said in soothing condescension. "Look. I know Stuart ain't the brightest man in the world, but don't you or nobody else ever doubt his loyalty. When the Toad speaks, he hops. Or don't hop, as the case may be."

Christ. Two toad hoppers in five minutes. "Okay, if you say so. But you didn't tell me how he was."

"He'll be out in a few days. Doc Owens is taking good care of him over at Oakwood Hospital. Got a couple of busted ribs, a few bruises here and there and a nice gash on his forehead. Hell, he came out better than the windshield." He let out a cackle that actually could have passed for a toad laughing.

I was only slightly relieved. "Good," I told him. "I'm glad it wasn't more serious. I mean it. God knows it could have been."

"Not to worry. You should go see him at the hospital. Tell him yourself."

"Are you serious?"

"Yeah! He'd like that. All he could talk about was the neat stunt you pulled on him. He was pissed off about it, but he was really impressed too. So am I, Pietro. I could use a guy like you in my organization."

"Alright. Maybe I will stop by. But I've already got a job that keeps me busy enough. I don't have either the time or inclination to work for you."

"We'll see. I'll talk to you next week and we'll set up a meeting, okay?"

"Okay, Nematotta. Goodnight."

"Ciao."

5

I drained the last drops of the Point on my way to the bathroom. I ran a hot bath and surveyed my own injuries. The knot on my forehead seemed to have peaked at an inch and a half and was definitely in recession; and there was some skin missing from my knee. They both still hurt, but the prognosis was rosy. And I was sure as hell a lot better off than Gotts.

I lowered myself into the tub and pain stabbed through my knee for a few seconds, and then subsided, numbed. I got flat on my back, put a washcloth compress on my knot, and did some serious thinking.

What the hell was Nematotta up to? Why would he have Gotts pull me out of a restaurant in public? Why did Giovanni's, my favorite Italian restaurant, have to be located a block down from the Toad's bookie parlor?

Why couldn't Gotts have waited until I was finished with my meal? I guess the only way of answering the first question was to meet with Nematotta. That, I would do.

As for Gotts, maybe he was acting on his own initiative, exceeding the limits of Nematotta's instructions in order to impress him. God knows I sure wouldn't have gone with him if he had just asked me. Even if he had said please. The other questions would probably never be answered. I smiled as I thought of a fifth question that definitely would be answered the next time I went to Giovanni's. Did anyone pick up my check?

I dried off, feeling much better. Physically, at least. Mentally, I wasn't so sure. But I didn't want to deal with it now. I walked into the living room with a towel around my waist and punched up a Marcels medley on the Wurlitzer: "Blue Moon," "Heartaches" and "Melancholy Baby."

The voice of lead singer Cornelius Harp was quite distinctive. Listening to him reminded me of the time, right after college at Michigan State, that Lou and I were going to make a million dollars syndicating an Oldies radio show.

Right after *my* college days, that is. Lou joined the army after high school, then, when he was discharged, got a job at the pari-mutuel windows at Hazel Park Race Track before eventually winding up in advertising.

We were going to call the show *Two Wops Playing Doo-Wops.* We even put together a couple of demo shows, one of which prominently featured the Marcels. All we ever got was a bunch of polite rejections. Amazingly, none of the stations we sent the tapes to ever suggested we change the name of the show. And today, of course, the Oldies format is big in virtually every major market in the country. Maybe we were ahead of our time.

I bomp-bomp-bomped along with Cornelius as I went into the kitchen and grabbed a can of Walter's, another of my favorite brews. Where would I be without those wonderful independent breweries of Wisconsin? The only problem was, I couldn't get Wisconsin beer that often. I should be rationing it more carefully. Mix in a Bud here and there.

That's not a putdown of Bud, by the way. I like it a lot. It's the one beer that's consistent no matter where you get it. Detroit Bud tastes just like St. Louis Bud. And St. Louis Bud tastes just like Los Angeles Bud. Foreign beer? Forget it! As far as I'm concerned, it's a myth. What everybody seems to think is that "heavy European flavor" is often nothing more than varying degrees of skunkiness. At least, that's my take on the situation.

Beer has to be fresh to be at its best. How can beer that sits in an overseas warehouse, comes over on a slow boat, sits in an American warehouse, gets shipped to a distributor on the outskirts of town, and then trucked to Freddie's Party Store be fresh? Simple. It can't be. Give me a good old fresh domestic beer anytime, preferably a local one.

I finished my last swig of Walter's just in time to sing the final melancholy baa-beeee with Cornelius and suddenly realized another good thing about beer. It made me tired. I trashed the empty and walked into the bedroom, my knee feeling better with every step. I hopped into bed and buried my forehead into the coolness of the pillow. I wanted to sleep, but the conversation with Nematotta kept playing in my head. I started to roll over, then stopped suddenly. Only now did his metaphor butchery register. Tip of the *glacier*?

When sleep came, I was smiling.

6

The petite redhead was gesturing for me to come toward her. She was exquisitely beautiful, an opinion made stronger by the sight of her full, pink-tipped breasts, proudly visible through the clingy, diaphanous gown. She sat seductively, on the edge of the bed, everything about her saying, "I want you."

I walked toward her, as totally aroused as I was naked. Just as she loosened the tie at her throat and the gown slid to the floor, an alarm went off. No, it wasn't an alarm. It was ...

The telephone! I groaned, rolling over toward my nightstand. The cheery green digits on the clock radio said 6:09. I was just aware enough to know that it meant a.m., and the realization made me groan even louder. Rising anger pushed aside some of my grogginess. I jerked the receiver out of the cradle and shouted.

"Goddammit, Nematotta! You said you'd call me next week!"

"Pete." It wasn't Nematotta. The voice was vague, weak, like the speaker was as dazed as I had just been. Or maybe drunk.

"Pete ... George ... I ..."

Suddenly, it registered. It was George Gianotti. An old friend from Michigan State. He was a year older than I and had gone on to get a law degree from Wayne State while I pursued my Bachelor's in Criminal Justice. He was a very successful attorney who, over the years, had sent a fair amount of business my way. And I knew he didn't drink. At least he didn't in college, and if you didn't drink then, when?

"George! What is it? What's going on? Where are you?" Suddenly I was fully alert.

"Her ... her husband ... killed ..." The words came out slowly, painfully. Then a groan. Far more sincere than mine had been a few minutes earlier. I felt a prickle run up the back of my neck. I was scared, my whole body instantly cold and clammy.

Something was definitely wrong. George was in trouble, maybe hurt, probably both. I heard him groan again; but it wasn't just a groan, it was a half-scream, tinged with terror. It became a full scream, a shriek, and I heard a sickening thud, like the sound of something solid striking a skull. And another thud, louder, like it could have been a body falling to the floor.

Then, I'm quite sure, I heard breathing. Just for a few seconds. Just before someone hung up the phone.

7

I called Harvey Steinberg. Detective Lieutenant Harvey Steinberg, Southfield Police. I could imagine Harv's groaning and swearing as he looked at his clock. But I didn't care. After six rings, he finally answered.

"Yeah."

"Harv, it's me, Pete."

"Pete, it's 6:15 in the morning, Harv." He was mocking me. But he didn't sound angry.

"Harv, I think something just happened to George Gianotti. Something bad. Hell, I think he may have been killed."

"Whoa! Slow down. Hold on a minute. Who's George Gianotti? Oh, it's that lawyer friend of yours, ain't it. So what makes you think something's wrong here, huh?"

I told him about the call.

"Holy shit! He didn't say where he was? What did he mean by `her husband killed'? Her husband got killed? Or her husband killed somebody? And who the hell is her?"

"Christ, Harv, let's worry about George first. What do you think we should do?"

"Just a second. Let me think." He covered the mouthpiece and yelled for his wife to make some coffee. Apparently, she was an early riser.

"Listen," he continued. "Let's just be calm. Be rational. Maybe he's okay. If so, he'll call you back. He may be trying to call you now. Call his wife. Maybe she can tell you where he was. I'll assume worst case and put out a BOLO. And see how quick we can get something on that phone call. You just go on about your business. And don't worry. Yet. I'll call you as soon as I find out anything. You do the same. Alright?"

If Harv was trying to calm me down, he did a good job. Right up until he said "yet." I did my best to sound relieved anyway. "Yeah, okay, Harv. Thanks. I'll talk to you later."

I hung up, hoping George would call back.

He didn't.

8

Something brushed against my leg and I froze. It was Nehi, my longhair orange cat; Nesbitt was a shorthair.

Christ, I was edgy. I needed some caffeine. I put on a pair of shorts, some cheap briefs that an even cheaper aunt had given me for Christmas which, believe it or not, were left-handed. Nehi rubbed me again. I picked him up and carried him into the kitchen.

Nesbitt was already waiting by their food dishes, letting me know I had forgotten to fill them up before I went to bed. I set Nehi down and started brewing some coffee. While it was dripping, I opened a couple cans of Amore and fed the boys. Well, they used to be boys. Maybe it was guilt that led me to feed them fine Italian cuisine like Amore.

I felt I should call Maria Gianotti, George's wife, but it was probably too early. Besides, George might call me back any minute, so why call and worry her needlessly before I knew anything for sure. I went downstairs and got the morning paper instead.

I generally only read two sections of the paper. Sports and business. But don't get the mistaken impression I'm shallow; the comics are usually in the sports section.

It only took a few minutes to check my stocks. Most of them were listed on the NASDAQ and the majority were up a few nickels and dimes. Funny how so many advisors tout the blue chips and warn of the dangers of speculating in so-called penny stocks. Maybe someday, when I get tired of doubling and tripling my investments, I'll wise up and buy blue chips too. But not someday soon.

Caffeine is supposed to be a stimulant, but after one cup, I was starting to settle down. Maybe it was all in my head, but I felt calm, relaxed. I was able to shuttle my concern for George to another part of my mind. There was nothing I could do for him now anyway, so I did my best to preoccupy myself with daily routine.

I got a free refill of coffee and punched an instrumental medley into the Wurlitzer. Usually, this time of day, I'd be listening to *Fun with Dick and Tom*, a popular oldies format show peppered with the antics of a couple of disc jockeys I had met through Lou. He frequently used them to record radio commercials.

But today, I needed the calming influence of the Royaltones, a local group that had some regional hits in the early sixties. They were great tunes; hard driving rock and roll. It was a shame they never made the national charts.

As the sax on "Flamingo Express" roared, I settled into my recliner and got down to serious business. I was surprised to see that the Lions were only getting three points against the Vikings. It should have been three touchdowns. I made a notation in the little notebook I always carry.

Nothing else looked very interesting. Which was fine because I didn't like to bet too heavily early in the season anyway.

This was just the appetizer, though. I turned to the Hazel Park Race Track entries to check the morning lines. Lou, Lef and I were going this evening. I had been watching a pacer named Hollow Promise who had bad racing luck for five straight races. It happens. Last time out, he was absolutely locked in on the rail and had a ton of pace left with nowhere to go. I was delighted to see that he was tabbed at 7 to 1 on the morning line.

Forty-five minutes and three more cups of coffee later, I finished studying the entries and reviewing Thursday night's results. I didn't pay much attention to them, however. It had been raining hard Thursday night. And form goes to hell on a muddy track.

9

Maria Gianotti answered the phone on the second ring. I had cleaned up the coffee stuff and was counteracting the caffeine with a cold can of Point. Her quick hello caught me in mid-gulp.

"Hi, Maria. It's Pete Pepper. I'm an old friend of George's from college." I had only met Maria on a few occasions. She was a real dark-haired Italian beauty. I wasn't sure if she'd remember me.

She did. "Oh, hi Pete. How you doing? George isn't here."

"I know," I replied, then caught myself immediately. "I mean, I didn't think he would be. Do you know where he is?"

"You might try his office. Have you called there?"

"Yes," I lied. "They said he wasn't in."

"Well, he's probably on the way in. He could have stopped for a cup of coffee. Heck, he could've stopped for a lot of reasons."

"Yeah, uh ..." I was having a hard time getting to the point. "Listen, uh, how long ago did he leave for work?"

"I don't know."

"Oh. He left before you got up?" I played it dumb. I knew she was going to tell me he hadn't come home last night. Strangely, she didn't sound even slightly worried.

"I don't know." She was suddenly cooler than one of the Toad's glaciers.

"I don't understand ..."

"Pete, George and I are separated. We've been separated for three weeks."

"Oh." I was shocked. "I'm sorry. I didn't know."

"I'm not sorry," she said, but her tone said otherwise. "We were two people who just happened to live in the same house. He never ... Look, Pete. This just isn't something I care to talk about right now. Okay?"

"Of course! Hey, I didn't mean to come off like I was prying or anything. It's none of my business if you don't want it to be. I'm just interested in finding George. Do you have his address? Phone number?"

She gave me his address; an apartment in Troy that he took in order to be closer to his office. She said he had misplaced his cell phone and didn't know if he had a new one yet. Nor did she know if he'd had a landline installed, which probably meant he didn't.

"Pete, what's going on here? What do you mean you want to 'find' George? Is he lost?"

I hadn't planned on telling her, but I couldn't lie. So I told her about the call, but said only that he had hung up suddenly. I didn't mention the screams and the thud.

"Maria, do you have any idea where George may have been?" I continued. "Do you know if he was working on anything out of the ordinary?"

"Well, that time of the morning, he certainly should have been at home." She said it like she was scolding him. "But I guess he was somewhere else, because if he had a new cell phone or home phone, he would have called me with the numbers by now. We're separated, but we're still ... friendly. I talked to him Wednesday at the office. In fact, he came by Wednesday evening. Just to pick up some winter clothes. He still has a lot of things here. What's he working on? Hmmm. Yes! He did mention something about a will. He only brought it up because it was so weird."

"What will? What was weird about it?"

"Let's see, what was that name? Bradshaw? Yes. I think it was Emily Bradshaw. Or very close to that. She's a rich old lady who lives out in Belleville somewhere. I think George said she was changing her will to cut out her husband. Something like that."

"That's weird?"

"No, not that part. *She's* weird. Emily Bradshaw. I mean, she has all this money and she never goes anywhere. A total recluse."

"Anything else?"

"Gee, Pete, it was just idle chatter. I wasn't taking notes."

"Do you remember if George said anything about why she didn't go out? Was there a medical reason, for example? Is she an invalid? Confined to a wheelchair, or something?"

"No. He didn't say. At least I don't remember." Then she changed her tone. "Pete, why are you asking me all these strange questions? Are you telling me everything you know? Are you sure George is alright?"

I debated carefully before replying. And lost the debate. "Look, Maria, I'll be totally honest," I said, not being totally honest. "I am a little worried. It just seems strange that he didn't call back. But there could be a thousand reasons."

"Give me a couple."

"Well," nothing came to mind immediately, but I cleverly stretched out the word and continued as though it were the same thought, "It's fruitless to speculate. But don't worry. I called Harvey Steinberg, a detective friend with the Southfield Police. If anything strange is going on, he'll get to the bottom of it."

"If you called the police, you're a lot more concerned than you're letting on."

"Just a necessary precaution. But, yes, I am a bit concerned." I still couldn't force myself to tell her about those terrible noises before someone hung up the phone. Someone besides George for sure.

"Maria, I'm going to do some checking around too. Do you mind if I stop by this afternoon? Maybe you can remember more of what you and George talked about on Wednesday."

"If you hadn't asked me, I was going to ask you to come over."

"Alright. Should I call first?"

"No. Just come by whenever. I'm not going anywhere."

"Okay. Look," I said, trying to be casually comforting, "I know this is easier said than done, but just go ahead and do whatever you were going to do. Try not to worry about George. It won't do anything but upset you. Hope for the best."

I wasn't very convincing.

"Thanks, Pete, I'll be fine."

She wasn't either.

10

I took a shower, shaved and got dressed. Another can of Point didn't do anything to ease my apprehension, so I punched out a Bobby Darin medley on the jukebox and sat back in my recliner. Bobby always cheered me up. One of the great voices and talents of our time. And I didn't think so just because he was Italian.

I had lost my father twenty-six years ago, when I was nine. Two years ago, I lost my brother Domenic. And the day after he was buried, my mother took enough sleeping pills to put her to sleep forever. (I found out later from my grandfather that she had attempted suicide when her first child, a son named Eugenio, was stillborn.) These were all deeply traumatic experiences, but I seem to have survived with minimal damage.

I lived through it all, and now had a relatively normal, often happy and usually satisfying life. In my opinion, at least. So relax, damn it. If you can survive the deaths of family, you should be able to handle the death of a casual friend. Calm down. Life goes on. Take the advice you gave Maria and do whatever it was you were going to do.

I was going to call Lou.

The readout on my VCR said 10:20. Just about the time for Lou to be rolling into his office. Lou was a copywriter at the Broderick & Stanley advertising agency, one of the so-called "hot shops" in town. Now there's a racket I'll never understand. Lou shows up when he feels like it, leaves whenever he wants to, dresses like a bagman and pulls down about ninety grand a year. Never mind that he loses a meaningful portion of it betting on sports and the ponies.

I called and was greeted by the voice of Irene, Broderick & Stanley's longtime receptionist. She recognized my voice immediately.

"Pete! How you doing, sweetie? When are you going to come by and see me again?"

"As a matter of fact, I'll be stopping by later today. Have to drop something off for Lou. Is he in yet?"

"Oh, yeah. He came in early today. Had a meeting with the old man." That was Bill Broderick, the agency's founder and chairman.

"Well, I'm planning on getting there just before lunch. Do you think he'll be out of the meeting by then?" Irene knew everything that went on in the agency.

"Hey, come on over right now, honey. They never had the meeting. Broderick forgot he had an early breakfast meeting with a potential client. He never came in; phoned Lou from the country club. Was he ever steamed! Lou, that is. Not the old man"

"I can imagine. Hey, I'd like to come over now, but I have some things to do first. Can you try Lou's line for me?"

"You got it, sweetheart."

Lou picked up on the first ring. "Yeah?" He wasn't a stickler on phone etiquette.

"Yeah, yourself. It's Pete."

"Hey! Pete-sa! What's shakin'?"

"You still on for Hazel Park tonight?"

"Does a dog do it doggie style?"

"Good. Want me to bring you a program? I'll drop it off before lunch."

"Yeah. Bring one for Lef, too. We're gonna shoot some Nerf basketball after work, then head out together."

"Okay. See you later."

"Ciao."

The scintillating conversational skills of a ninety-thousand-dollars-a-year copywriter. I'm definitely in the wrong business.

11

The phone rang again just as I was about to leave. I made a mental note to look into some AT&T stock.

"Pete Pepper Investigations."

"Hi, Pete. It's me." Me was Marianne, Domenic's widow, my sister-in-law.

"Oh, hi, Marianne. I was just leaving."

"I won't keep you. Just wanted to remind you about watching Gianni tomorrow. Just for a couple hours. I have to do some work for Father Wong."

"I remember," I lied. "What time was that again?"

"Late morning. Maybe noon. I'll drop him off if you like."

"Okay. Sure. I'll see you tomorrow."

"Thanks, Pete. You're a darling. Bye."

She hung up before I could reciprocate the sentiment. Not that I would have. I cradled the phone and thought about Gianni. My immediate reaction had been negative. This was no time to be babysitting a ten-year-old kid. I had some business to take care of on George's behalf. But the more I thought about it, the more positive I became. The kid was a real delight. Maybe seeing him was what I needed to get myself into a better frame of mind.

I turned on the answering machine and made it out the door without any further interruptions. I drove over to Freddie's Party Store and picked up three Hazel Park Harness Raceway programs. They were only a buck and a quarter at the track, but a buck seventy-five off-track. Another racket I should be in.

Every time I buy a program, Freddie asks me who I like. I told him about Hollow Promise and threw in a couple more: Neato Jet and Warp Factor Four.

On the way out, an incredibly buxom blond on the cover of a skin magazine caught my eye. For a second, I fantasized about giving in to Marianne's advances. Then my stomach growled and I thought about breakfast instead.

12

I'm a man of simple tastes. I can cook up some dazzling Italian dishes with the best of them, but I leave the gourmet stuff to the gourmets. Give me meat and potatoes and green beans and corn. Give me chicken fried steak and gravy and corn bread. Give me Vassili's breakfast special. Any day. Any time of day. Like right now.

Barb, my favorite day waitress, not to be confused with Wanda, my favorite night waitress, didn't even come over to take my order. She didn't need to. I had seated myself and was just finishing my cursory check of the first race when she walked over with a platter still steaming with three eggs over easy, a pile of hash browns and a rasher of bacon, whatever the hell a rasher is. I think the value of a rasher must fluctuate with the Canadian dollar or something, because sometimes it's four pieces, sometimes six or even eight. Being a health-conscious guy, I sent back the coffee and ordered a glass of orange juice. Better the coffee than the bacon.

"So, how's it going, Private Eye?" Barb asked, as she returned with the juice and a plate of rye toast.

"Not too bad. Just handicapping tonight's card. Big night out with the boys."

"Yeah? Anything look good in there?"

I toyed with the idea of introducing her to Freddie. "Nah, not too much," I told her. "There's a horse in the fifth that has a shot. Hollow Promise." I didn't like giving tips to waitresses. I was afraid they'd bet on them. Not that my tips were bad. I just didn't think that a hard-working waitress should be risking her money like that. Especially one like Barb, who had not one, but two out-of-wedlock children at home. Freddie, I didn't mind. He could afford to take the risk.

"Hollow Promise, eh?" She slipped her hand into her apron and came out with a ten-dollar bill. "Put it on the nose for me, and if that nag comes home, I'll make you a promise that ain't hollow." She looked me straight in the eye with a wicked smile and a wink.

I took the ten, laughing. "Okay, sweetheart. But you know I don't think ladies should gamble."

"Oh, I agree wholeheartedly." She smiled, turned and walked away with an exaggerated sway, then looked back. "*Ladies* definitely shouldn't."

I finished breakfast at the same time I finished checking out the fifth race. I had little doubt that Hollow Promise would win. Sometimes a horseplayer just senses these things. I wondered if maybe my sense was colored by wishful thinking inspired by Barb. But I knew it wasn't. I left seven dollars on the table to cover the breakfast and still leave enough for a fifty percent plus tip for Barb, hoping it would be small compared to the return on the other tip I had given her.

As I walked out the back door, Barb blew me a kiss from behind the counter. I almost drove back to Freddie's and bought the magazine.

13

Southfield's Civic Center is located at the foot of a street cleverly named Civic Center Drive. It was only about a mile from Vassili's, and coincidentally, about a mile from Broderick & Stanley, where I'd be going later. Among many other facilities, the complex houses the library and the police station. I had business at both.

The name Bradshaw rang a bell. I looked through some public records at the library and drew a blank. No wonder. They were Oakland County documents. Belleville was in Wayne County.

I was about to leave and go see Steinberg when I played a hunch. The Southfield Library had a number of online computer services available. One of them was specifically earmarked for accessing the archives of the *Detroit News*. Everything was conveniently catalogued. By subject. By name.

And, if you had a lot of time to kill, by date.

The setup was a beautiful tribute to modern technology and a sensible use of the taxpayer's dollar. I walked over to the computer section, sat at a terminal and called up the service. When it appeared on the screen, I punched in the name Bradshaw.

In about ten seconds a few dozen entries appeared on the screen. Most of them referred to a guy named Edward, who was apparently a resident of Belleville, a small town southwest of Southfield off Interstate 94. There was also a Bradshaw Enterprises and a Bradshaw Business Forms. No Emilies. Oh well, it was only a hunch.

Just for the hell of it, I typed in Pepperini. There was nothing at all. On the way out I stopped at the front desk, where my old friend Ruth Abraham was on duty. She had helped me locate some useful information on more than one occasion. Library Science wasn't my strong suit.

"Hey, Ruth, you ever heard of an Emily Bradshaw?"

She looked up from the newspaper she was reading, *The Jewish News.* "Emily Bradshaw. You mean the millionaire?"

"Yeah, I think so. What do you know about her?"

"Not much. She's a recluse. Inherited a few zillion from her father. Wilson Boggess was his name, I think. I seem to recall that he was an early investor in Ford. Made his fortune, built a huge mansion out in the sticks somewhere, rubbed shoulders with senators. Why?"

Not much? Sometimes I thought Ruth was plugged into the *News'* mainframe. "Oh, probably no reason at all. She may be involved in a case I'm working on. I'm really just killing time until lunch. Say, you wouldn't happen to know if she lives in Belleville, would you?"

"Belleville. Let's see ... yeah, I think so. That's sort of out in the sticks, isn't it? I remember reading somewhere that ... yes, she and her husband live in Belleville. He's in the import/export business, if I'm not mistaken."

Hmmm. Not bad for someone who didn't know too much. "Thanks, Ruth. You've been a big help. Want a winner at Hazel Park tonight?"

"No thanks. I have better things to do with my money."

"Okay. See you later."

She buried her nose back in the newspaper, gathering information for our next encounter.

I walked over to the police station. The desk sergeant, a young looking guy named Ferguson, said Steinberg wasn't in and didn't know when he'd be back. He offered to radio Harv if it was important. I told him it wasn't. And didn't bother to leave a message. If Harvey believed in cell phones, I would have just called him myself. But he wasn't ready to adopt any newfangled technology.

14

Broderick & Stanley occupied the top three floors of a modern steel and glass structure on Telegraph Road, a wide north-south thorough-fare that takes you all the way south to Raceway Park in Toledo ... if you were a real harness racing junkie.

I took the elevator up to the sixth floor, home of the Creative Department and Lou Bracato, ace copywriter and fanatic onomatoma-niac, which is sort of redundant. For those not inclined toward such sesquipedalian endeavors, that means he likes to use big words. He claims it's not to show off, but because he just loves words, and I can believe him, because a good part of the time, his vocabulary is liberally sprinkled with polysyllabic words I have to go home and look up.

It's generally only in private, when he and Lef and I get together that he launches into the obscure polysyllables. I have my own theory, though. I think that, subconsciously, he's trying to compensate for the fact that he never went to college. I've accused him more than once of not just *reading* the dictionary, but also taking notes.

I walked through the reception area, where Irene was busy jug-gling an overload of incoming calls. She smiled and waved me in. The Creative Department was a maze of halls and offices inhabited by a wild assortment of strange people dressed in colors like the flags of many nations.

After wandering for about five minutes, I convinced myself I was lost.

Strange. I must have been daydreaming; I had been here a hun-dred times before. How could I possibly be lost? I stopped a rather normal-looking young fellow whose only eccentricities seemed to be a pair of purple high-top gym shoes and a two-tone yo-yo he was walking-the-dog with down the hall. He said he didn't know any Lou Bracato.

Finally, down a short hallway I had probably passed three times, I spotted the big sign Lou has on his door: Department of Redundancy Department. What a wordsmith. He earns every cent of that ninety grand. Actually, I find the sign amusing and get a little chuckle out of it almost every time I visit Lou.

As I walked into his office, I nearly collided with a young woman rushing out. She was livid about something, and said "fucking picker," as she glanced back at Lou.

I couldn't resist taking a quick look at her. She was diminutive, as Lou would say, with short black hair. But it wasn't her 5-foot-3 or so fig-ure that caught my attention; it was her remarkably large chest. It had to be Jane Berkman, the incredible Foxy Loxie, as Lou referred to her in the many sexual fantasies he shared with his close friends. She was an art director who had started at B&S (or just plain B.S., as Lou liked to say) about six months earlier.

Lou didn't see me enter his office. His attention was focused on an old Easter basket full of Nerf basketballs. He seemed to be contemplat-ing their molecular structure. I sat down and watched him; an amusing sight. Lou was no more than five feet, seven inches tall and more than a little sensitive about it. He got feisty if you mentioned his slightly reced-ing hairline too. He was standing there with his back to me, a big unlit cigar protruding from his lips, eyeing the little hoop and net attached to his far wall. His right arm was cocked, forearm almost parallel to the floor, the green Nerf basketball nearly touching his right ear. He let it fly, about ten feet from the basket, and it arced through the net, a swisher.

He continued to pump them through, saying "one," "two," "three," with every ball that scored. I sat there silently, trying not to laugh at this highly paid professional, goofing off, in a pair of jeans so worn, his wal-let was held in by a criss-crossing of white strings that used to be a back pocket.

As he was about to launch his tenth throw, after sinking eight out of nine, I coughed loudly.

"Hey! Be quiet when I'm shooting," he yelled, missing the shot by a foot. Then he turned, not even slightly upset. "Oh, it's you. Got those programs?"

I handed him the extra programs I had picked up for him and Lef.

"So, was that the fabled Foxy Loxie?" I asked.

"It was indeed," he said. "Also referred to by some as the Nookie of the Year, although I'd wager that's based on speculation rather than personal experience."

"What did she mean by fucking picker?"

"Huh? Oh, that. She thinks she caught me picking my nose the other day."

"She *thinks* she caught you?"

"Yeah. I had my finger up my nose, but I was just trying to push a nose hair back in. Fucking thing was tickling the hell out of me. Drove me crazy."

"Yeah, right. Who hasn't done that before?"

"Seriously? You mean you've never had a nose hair stick out?"

"Yes, but I have this little pair of scissors I use to trim it."

"Whatever."

"Anyway, the Foxy Loxie looked pissed."

"She's a sore loser. I took her for five bucks and she goes storming out."

"You mean shooting Nerf baskets?"

"Hell yeah. She saw me in here practicing and asked if she could try. Next thing you know, we're shooting best out of ten for a fin. I beat her 8 to 1 and she gets all upset because I made her pay."

"Well, that isn't exactly gentlemanly."

"Gentlemanly? Hell, I offered her to go double or nothing!"

I smiled. "Yeah, you're right. She is a sore loser."

"Yeah, so how about you? Want to go best out of 10 for ten bucks?"

"At Nerf basketball? Hell no. I'd have no shot. You practically invented the game. Tell you what, though. I'll go you quarters on the elbow for ten bucks. Or dimes. Or pennies. You pick."

This was simply a game where you stacked coins on your elbow with your arm parallel to the ground, much like Lou's arm when he shot Nerf. Then you tried to catch as many as possible before they hit the ground. I was the local champion among my small circle of friends who competed in this yet-to-be Olympic event.

"And I'd have no shot at that," Lou conceded. "So let's just skip the fun and call it even."

"Okay. So what's the plan for tonight?"

"Oh, you mean the track? Uh, Lef's coming by around five thirty. We're gonna shoot Nerf for an hour or so, grab a bite on the way out and get there in plenty of time for the double. We'll meet you outside, by the horsemen's boxes, near the wire."

"You don't want to go together?"

"Well, Lef and I are going to hit the Iron Cage after and I thought you had to get up early to watch Gianni tomorrow."

I was astounded that he remembered. "Oh. Well, Marianne's not dropping him off until about noon. But I'm really not in the mood for topless terpsichore tonight." I liked to impress Lou with an occasional big word of my own. And I've never denied looking through the dictionary to find them.

He didn't acknowledge the word or my unintentional alliteration.

"Topless, my ass. Some of those babes take their G-strings off if there aren't any cops around."

"Yeah. Whatever. I'll just see you guys the track. Adios."

"You don't want to go have lunch?"

"Nah. I just had a big breakfast. Got a few things to do, anyway."

"Hell, maybe I'll just stay in, then. Work on the play."

One of the things I discovered about people in the creative end of advertising was that they all wanted to be doing something else. Directing movies. Drawing comic strips. Doing standup comedy. Lou wanted to be a playwright and a songwriter. I knew a little about his current stage effort. It was about a series of murders in an insane asylum. That sounds plausible on the surface, but he was making it a musical comedy called *Help! The Paranoids Are After Me!* As for the song writing, I actually liked one he had written called "Not Tonight, I've Got a Heartache." But for a guy who was a self-proclaimed rock and roller, most of his efforts seemed to lean toward country and western.

As I was about to leave, a tall thin guy with wire-rimmed glasses and less hair than Lou walked in. Steve Kidman. He was Lou's partner. An art director, like Jane Berkman. Except that he and Lou were Supervisors of a Creative Group. What an utterly fascinating business.

"So, did you ask him, Lou?" Steve was rubbing his hands in anticipation of something.

"Ask him what?"

"About Barbara Ann."

"Who the fuck's Barbara Ann?"

"The song, asshole."

"Oh yeah!" Now Lou seemed excited too. "Hey Pete, who did the original Barbara Ann? There's ten bucks riding on this."

I was a frequent arbiter of rock and roll trivia questions. A role I enjoyed. "The Regents," I told them.

"Horseshit!" Lou protested loudly. "It was the Beach Boys. I've got the damn record."

"You said the original. The Regents recorded it in 1961. The Beach Boys covered it in '66. You should know that one, Lou. Five Italian guys from the Bronx. Actually, I think only four were Italian. I don't remember what the fifth one was."

Lou was a fanatic Italian, even more so than I. The newfound knowledge seemed to soften the blow. Carefully avoiding any further damage to his pocket, Lou pulled out his wallet and handed two fives to Steve. "Ah, well. Easy come, easy go."

Steve made a big show of stuffing the fives into his wallet. He shook my hand and thanked me.

Lou gave me the finger.

I said goodbye again and left. By a much more direct route than I had come in.

15

Maria Gianotti's house was in West Bloomfield, about ten minutes from B&S. I made the mistake of going west on 13 Mile Road, which only has one lane in each direction. I got behind an old woman in a big Buick that apparently couldn't move faster than 25 miles per.

I wasn't in any particular hurry; Maria wasn't expecting me at any specific time. But I'm often impatient when driving and have a problem with people who I consider to be inconsiderate of other drivers. I mentally activated my dash laser, prepared to blast her into oblivion. Instead, I gave her a blast of my horn. She must have interpreted the loud honk to mean I thought she was going too fast, because she slowed down even more. So I blasted again and she responded by showing me the middle finger of her right hand, my second bird in less than ten minutes.

I was too amused to be mad. She continued along at a blazing 15 mph as we approached Inkster Road, and then floored it as the light turned yellow and left me stranded at the red. A real pro. I was giggling madly by now. The lady had spunk and more than a little admiration from me.

Nonetheless, I made a right at Inkster.

Seven minutes later, I pulled into Maria Gianotti's driveway. A long, semi-circular brick drive that led to a sprawling, modern split-level that must have had the boys at the mortgage company drooling. Maria opened the brass-knockered double door as I was carefully negotiating the steps. She was wearing a pair of those baggy shorts that look like a skirt and a tight, shiny-black top that did her ample breasts proud. I tried not to notice that she wasn't wearing a bra. It was hard.

"Hi, Pete. Come on in." She was smiling, apparently in a good mood. Her coal-black hair shimmered down to her shoulders. She smelled like she had just taken a shower. She turned, and I followed her into the family room, or whatever a couple without kids calls it. Her legs were long and lithe, her thighs and calves firm. If these were different circumstances...

"Have a seat and I'll get us a drink. What would you like?" Her sudden turn caught my eyes exploring her, but her expression didn't change.

"Uh, you have any beer?"

"Sure. Heineken? Guinness? Harp?"

Yuppie stuff. I should have expected it. If I can't have the good old local brew, the nectar of the guys, I don't want any. "On second thought, I'll just have a soft drink," I said. "If you have any."

"Of course. Just diet soda, though."

Soda? This is Motown, sweetheart. We call it pop. "Well, okay. I need to watch my weight, anyway." I laughed weakly.

She looked me up and down, but made no comment. "Make yourself comfortable. I'll be right back."

I watched her rump-bump into the kitchen and sighed down into an overstuffed easy chair covered with little blue and yellow flowers on a pale blue background. Not my taste, but I could tell it was expensive. I wiped a few droplets of sweat off my forehead and tried to look like I felt normal. Actually, I was a little uncomfortable. Okay, very uncomfortable.

"You want a glass?" Maria yelled from the kitchen.

"No thanks, I'll just drink from the bottle!" I yelled back.

She reappeared, sipping some frothy green stuff from a tall glass. I never could get into liqueur. "It's in a can," she said, handing me a white and brown can with the top already popped.

I read the label. Canfield's Diet Chocolate Fudge Soda. She was right. It wasn't pop. I took a slug anyway; I was hot and thirsty. And I was pleasantly surprised. "Hey, this is great! Where'd you get it?"

"Jane Broder. Her husband works with George. She brings it back every time she visits Chicago. Cases of it."

"Damn. It really tastes good."

"Glad you like it."

"Listen, Maria. I hate to change the subject, but we have to talk about George."

She set her drink down and her face suddenly went sad. "Something happened to George, didn't it Pete? I got a call from the Southfield Police. A Lieutenant Steinberg. He asked me a lot of questions. And George didn't show up for work today."

"I don't know, Maria. It's possible."

"He's not dead, is he? Please don't tell me he's dead." She stood up and started sobbing.

I stood, too, and she came to me, putting her arms around my neck, looking to be comforted. Or for the assurance I couldn't give her. I only patted her back, not knowing what else to do or say.

"Oh, Pete. What am I going to do? I still love him. We had problems, but I know we could ... would have worked them out."

"I don't know what to tell you, Maria. Something did happen to George. And yes, I think there's a chance he might be dead. Probably a pretty good chance. If so, I promise you I'll find out who did it. But let's not jump to any conclusions just yet, okay?"

"I'm sorry. I didn't mean to make a spectacle of myself." She didn't make any attempt to move away.

I did. I stepped back, put my hands on her shoulders. I looked into her tear-reddened, beautiful blue eyes and felt sorry too. Sorry for George.

"Maria, Harvey Steinberg is a friend of mine."

"Oh, that reminds me, he wants you to call him," she said softly. "I told him you were coming over when he called."

"Did he say where he'd be? I stopped by to see him earlier, but he was out."

"No. I just assumed he meant at his office. He said it wasn't urgent, though."

Yeah, it pretty much had to be at his office. Or his home. His refusal to buy and use a cell phone was a pain in the ass sometimes.

"Oh." I had been noticeably tense, digging my fingers into Maria's shoulders. Now I let go, relaxing. "Maria, did you remember anything more about that Bradshaw woman?"

"Do you think she has something to do with George's ... disappearance?"

"There's no real reason to think so. But it might be someplace to start looking for answers," I said, not explaining why.

"Well, I do remember a few more things. George talked about her from time to time. You asked me before if there was a medical reason why she stayed home. Well there is. At least, I think you'd call it medical. She has some kind of phobia. I can't remember the name. But it means that she's afraid to go anywhere."

"Yeah, I've heard of that. I don't recall the word, either. Anything else?"

"Well, George said she was really psycho about it. Not only didn't she leave the house, she didn't let anyone come in, either."

"George was able to get in, wasn't he?"

"He was an exception. He and a few other people, plus her husband, of course, were the only ones Emily Bradshaw has had any contact with for a long time."

"Who were the other people?"

"I don't know if George ever mentioned their names, but I think they were domestic employees of some sort. You know, like a gardener or a handyman, or maybe a nurse or secretary. Something like that."

I got out my notebook and made a few notations.

"Is that important, Pete?"

"Like I said, I have no idea. But I'll see if I can find out their names, just in case."

"You'll let me know if you come up with something significant, won't you?"

"Of course. And Harvey Steinberg will too. He's a good cop. He'll get some answers."

"Pete. Are you ... can I ... ?"

I knew what she was going to ask. "No. Not a chance. Anything I do on this case, I do because I want to. I'm not for hire." I winced inwardly at my elevation of the situation to a "case." Fortunately, she didn't react to it. She just reached out, grabbed my hand and squeezed it gently.

"Thank you, Pete. Thank you." She started to mist up, then just as quickly, brightened. "Oh! There's something I want you to have."

She ran into the kitchen and came back with the rest of the six-pack of the chocolate pop. I don't care what the label said.

"What do you guys call it when you drink one while you're driving?" she asked.

I smiled. "A road boy."

"Right. Here. Now you have enough road boys for a road trip."

"Thanks," I said, immediately popping the tab on one. "And thanks for taking the time to talk. If you need anything, or if you think of anything else that might be important, call me. Okay?"

"You mean about Emily Bradshaw?"

"About her or about anything George said that might give us a clue to where he was or where he is."

"I will."

"Good. Goodbye, Maria."

"Goodbye Pete. And thanks."

I made it home in seventeen minutes, twice turning down side streets to avoid Buicks.

16

I threw the mail, all junk again, on my desk and noticed I had forgotten to take the tout service literature to Lou. I picked it up; I'd give it to him at the racetrack. I heard a sound in my kitchen and saw Nesbitt scratching away in the litter box.

Upstairs, I popped a couple Buitoni frozen pizzas into the microwave. Pepperoni. What else?

I went into the bedroom, changed into a pair of jeans and a sweater. We were having a very cool October, so I pulled a medium-weight jacket out of the closet just in case. We Mediterranean types are a hardy lot, but it could get pretty cold if we stayed outside at the track like we often did, usually right at the finish wire. I grabbed my binoculars down from the closet shelf just as the oven beeped.

I detoured to the refrigerator to grab a Point, and then changed my mind. I wasn't quite ready to see if beer and chocolate mixed. So I grabbed a bottle of Calistoga mineral water instead. Just a hint of cherry flavor. Lou brought it back from the West Coast after one of his commercial shooting boondoggles. It was good.

I took one of the pizzas out of the oven; it was small, only about six inches in diameter. Then I went into the living room and called Harvey on his direct line at the office.

"Steinberg."

"Hi Harv. It's Pete."

"Pete. So you got the message. Understand you were by here earlier. Sorry I missed you. Out doing some nosing around. Talked to Owen Walters. We got lucky."

He paused, apparently waiting for a response, but I didn't quite follow what he was saying.

"Didn't you hear me?" he shouted. "We got lucky!"

"That's nice, Harv, but I'm not interested in your extracurricular sexual activities. What about George?"

"I'm talking about George, for Christ's sake!"

"Well, let's go over it again, only slower. I got lost during the part where you and Owen Walters picked up some chicks. And who the hell is Owen Walters?"

"Oh. Sorry. Walters is a buddy of mine over at the phone company. He checked out the call for me. It was quick and easy because it was made from a far zone. George Gianotti called you from Belleville ... "

"Let me guess," I interrupted. "From the residence of one Emily Bradshaw." I set the water down next to the pizza. I was shaking.

"I got it as the residence of a Zachary Bradshaw. But how the fuck did you know that?"

"I've been doing some nosing around too."

"Son of a bitch! Why didn't you call me? How do you like that? Jesus Christ!"

"Harv, I did call. But you were out. If you carried a cell phone like most other police detectives do ... "

"I got along all my life without one. Damn if I need one now."

"Whatever. Anyway, what about George? Any news?"

"Nothing yet. Shit. Well, what did you find out about Bradshaw?"

"You mean you didn't go there?" I was a bit surprised.

"I'm asking the questions, Goddamnit."

"C'mon, Harv."

"Yeah, I went there. Didn't find out anything. No sign of George. Strange one, that lady. All I could get out of her was that she hadn't seen her husband for two months. He's in the import/export business. Goes to Europe and the Far East all the time. She said he's never been gone this long before, though. Asked me to look for the son of a bitch."

"That's it? You didn't ask her about George?"

"Of course I asked her about George. She didn't know anything. Hell, it took me two hours to drag out what little I did get."

"I'm missing something here, Harv."

"Huh? Oh yeah, I forgot to mention. This lady was blitzed out of her Goddamn mind. Sporting one hell of a hangover. The shape she was in, General Sherman could have driven his army through her house last night and she wouldn't have known."

"Christ."

"So what did you find out, nosy?"

I told him what Maria had told me. "Think you can get the names of the handyman, maid and secretary and whatever else for me, Harv? They probably get paid by check. There has to be a bank record ... "

"I know how to do police work, Goddamnit! Sure. I'll check it out. Sorry, Pete. I ain't yelling at you."

"Forget it, Harv."

"Gianotti's wife hire you to look for George?" he neatly segued into a new subject.

"She tried to. I turned her down." I misled him with equal skill.

"Good. Stay out of it, Pete. Me and my boys will handle things. Capisce?"

"Yeah, yeah. But what are you going to do next?"

"I'm gonna go take a piss. But I'll keep in touch. And I mean it, Pete. Stay out of it. At least for now."

"Okay," I said.

But we both knew I wouldn't.

Other than driving out to the Bradshaw house, there wasn't much I could do right now. Anything I might get from a bank would have to wait until Monday. So I took the only logical course of action.

I finished my pizzas.

17

At 6:15, I gathered up all the necessities of a true horseplayer: program, pens, binoculars, notebook, cigars, matches and a Detroit Tigers baseball cap. Smoking cigars was something I had picked up from Lou. One night, a few years back, he offered me one of his stogies after hitting a trifecta for just over $700. I promptly hit the trifecta in the next race for $3,500. I've been taking cigars to the track ever since, although the ones I had tonight were relative cheapies. I kept my all-tobacco handmades at home and smoked them only on special occasions, like after a particularly outstanding meal.

On the way out, I emptied a couple packets of Tender Vittles into the cats' dishes. I noticed Nesbitt was still scratching around in the litter box. Poor guy. I don't know if he was constipated or had diarrhea. Either way, I felt sorry for him.

Halfway to the track, I realized I had forgotten the tout literature for Lou again. I could have gone back; it was only about a fifteen-minute drive to the track. But I like to get there early to watch the warm-ups. I've picked up many a winner by watching for and noting things out of the ordinary.

Equipment changes. The driver taking the warm-up instead of the trainer or an exercise boy. Unusually fast last quarters. Excessive sweating. Lots of little things that could add up to a big payoff at the windows.

Plus, this was Friday, which, along with Saturday is one of the best nights to win. Why? Because the better horses run on weekends and they run truer to form. Also because the crowds are bigger. Lots of people go to the track on the weekend for entertainment, not to make money like I do. The kind of people who bet a horse because of its name or pretty colored saddlecloth. And how many times have I heard people bet their kids' ages or birthdays in the gimmicks, especially the trifectas and superfectas? And especially on weekends.

No, I wasn't about to turn back.

I pulled into the horsemen's parking lot. The secret password tonight was Hollow Promise. I said it to Timmy, the money taker and he waved me in, nodding appreciatively. Our arrangement had made him a lot more money than it had saved me, even if he just bet $10 to win and place. Parking is only two bucks, but it's kind of an ego boost to get in free. And two bucks saved is an extra shot at the daily double.

I got into the clubhouse with my owner's pass, a $35 purchase from a trainer with out-of-town owners. At $3.50 a pop for the clubhouse, the pass paid for itself many times over.

I walked through the clubhouse and out to the horsemen's seating area, an open-air pavilion connected to the grandstand adjacent to the clubhouse. Ernie, the uniformed attendant, greeted me and escorted me to a seat right on the wire. I slipped him a fiver; partly a tip and partly to pay for the next night's program which he would bring me after the seventh race. I whispered Hollow Promise in his ear as he toweled my seat with a flourish. Pigeon droppings were one of the natural hazards of sitting outside at Hazel Park. Then I lit up a cigar, ignoring the groans of a couple nearby patrons, got out my Bushnells and went to work.

Lou and Lef missed the first race. So did I, by a nose. I had ripped up my ticket well before the official results were posted. I hadn't miscalled a photo finish in more than three years.

Six minutes before the second race, Lou made a grand entrance, with Lef trailing behind. Lou was doing his bugle version of the call to post and announced loudly to all who cared to listen, "The bettors are entering the track for the second race. Number one, Lou Bracato, a

$55 winner at Nerf basketball. Number two, Lefkowitz Turner, the vanquished." Then he noticed me. "Pete-sa! Don't you know it's dangerous to sit in the white seats?"

"Yeah, man," Lef tacked on. "You can't see the pigeon shit on the white seats."

They sat down next to me, oblivious to their own warning and to the obvious evidence that pigeons were indeed fauna native to the Hazel Park habitat. Lef looked disgusted; Lou sported a grin that touched his earlobes.

"That's a Goddamn pussy game," Lef snarled at Lou. "Play me on a real basketball court and I'll ream your ass blindfolded." He probably would, at that. Lef had been a member of the Oak Park High basketball team that went to the state quarterfinals his senior year. Those were glory days that still lived vividly in his mind. Lou was the equipment manager for the team Lou was still ribbing Lef when I excused myself to go bet Neato Jet, one of the selections I had given to Freddie. The line moved slowly, but I got my bet down just before the bell. Since I wasn't alive in the daily double, I put $20 to win and place on the Jet. I usually bet more, but I was just kibitzing. I was saving the really heavy stuff for the fifth.

I watched the second race on one of the color monitors near the windows; there wasn't time to get back to my seat. Neato Jet was third on the rail as they passed the wire the first time around. On a five-eighths mile track like Hazel Park, the horses start on the backstretch and cross the wire twice. It's the second time that counts. Entering the turn after the stretch, one of the trailers flew up on the outside and Neato Jet veered out to follow him. A good move.

They stayed that way until the turn for home, and then the Jet went three wide and got to the wire five lengths ahead of a fast closing Meigs Marauder. Neato Jet would move up in class in his next race and the comment would read "aired lesser," which means there was a lot of space between him and the rest of the field. He paid $8.80 and $6.40, a spectacular place price for a 3-1 shot. I cashed and went back to the seats where Lef was holding court with some teenage kids who worked the backside, cleaning stables and grooming horses.

Lef had his hands cupped around his mouth and was doing a much more creditable rendition of a P.A. announcer than Lou had done earlier.

" ... Lefkowitz 'Lef' Turner at center," I could hear him saying halfway down the aisle. "Leroy 'Slam' Duncan at forward. Irving 'Shoots' Toffel at the other forward. And your guards, Ralston Rackford and Rudy "Hanger" Zahn. Ladies and gentlemen, the Oak Park High starting five, Class of '79!"

The kids gave him a half-hearted round of applause and scattered. They had heard about the starting five of Oak Park High's state quarterfinalists many times before. So had Lou, but he liked to get Lef going.

"Hey Lef, what was the name of that sixth man?" Lou asked, winking in my direction as I approached. "The one you claim would have led you to the title, only he never played much?"

"You know his name, man." Lef wasn't in the mood to be ribbed.

"Yeah, but I don't think Pete ever heard about him."

Amazingly enough, I hadn't. "What sixth man?"

Lef looked at me suspiciously. "I never told you?"

"No. Honest!"

His suspicion turned into enthusiasm. "He was great, man. Probably the only guy on the team who could out jump me. Of course, he was taller than me, about 6-foot eight. He was from Israel. His father used to be a Cantor at my mom's synagogue."

The synagogue was Temple Shalom Abraham, and Lef's knowledge of Judaism wasn't casual. Although Lef's father was black, his mother was Jewish. And "was" is the key word. Her father disowned and rejected her for marrying a black man. Somewhat harsh in this rather enlightened age, but her father happened to be Rabbi Benjamin Geldman of Shalom Abraham. Sarah Turner and her infant son Lef were shortly abandoned by the father. But Sarah was a strong woman and raised her son well. And a strong schooling in Judaism was a part of that upbringing.

"So what was the guy's name?" I asked Lef.

He curled his lips in a big grin. "Avram 'Stretch' Marx."

"Christ. You may have lost in the quarterfinals, but you guys sure were state champs in the nickname department."

"Damn right," Lef agreed. "Anyway, ol' Stretch was a whiz. Really agile for a big guy. Good dribbler, too. And he had a hook like Kareem. You should have seen him tear it up in practice."

"But if he was so good, how come he never played?" It was the question Lef was waiting for.

"Couldn't!" Lef laughed. "His old man was Orthodox and wouldn't let him. Most of the games were on Friday night. He actually did play on a couple of Tuesdays."

I looked over at Lou who was chuckling. "Is he putting me on?" I asked.

"No. God's truth. I'm laughing because, today, Stretch is playing pro ball in Europe."

"His father lets him?"

"Well, they don't just play on Friday nights in Europe, but I'm sure it wouldn't stop Stretch if they did," Lou patted his hip pocket. "I'd renounce my faith for two and a half million a year. Wouldn't you?"

"How do you renounce atheism?" Lef wanted to know.

"I'm not an atheist," Lou protested. "I'm an O.A."

"Alright," I bit. "What's an O.A.?"

"Optimistic Agnostic. I have my doubts, but I hope I'm wrong. Either way, though, I consider myself to be a very spiritual person."

"Spiritual?" Lef said, in obvious disagreement. "The closest you ever got to being spiritual is when old man Broderick missed a meeting with you to go play golf and you said, 'I hope karma gets his ass.' That ain't spiritual, my friend, that's spiteful."

Lou just smiled, shrugged and raised his eyebrows.

I looked up just in time to see the starting gate rolling for the third race. "Well, guys, there goes the third. Did you come here to bet or discuss religion?"

"To bet!" Lou assured me.

"Right," Lef added. "The fifth race."

"Oh yeah? Who do you like?"

"Crooked Numbers. I got the word," Lou said, conspiratorially. "They added a little juice to his Lasix tonight."

Lasix is a legal drug given to horses that are prone to bleeding. It also has the effect of masking certain other drugs. The illegal kind.

"Lou, if you believe all the stories you hear, you'll go crazy. Somebody's saying something about every horse in the race. Look at the program. Crooked Numbers doesn't have a prayer."

"Hey, Cleon Able said they were shootin'."

Able was one of the many track blacksmiths and a part-time driver. He was a pretty honest guy from my experience. "Shootin' just means they're going to try to win," I said. "Actually winning is something else. Go ahead. Throw your money away, because nobody's beating Hollow Promise tonight."

"Hollow Promise? He hasn't done shit for two months."

"So go ahead and bet Crooked Numbers. Lef, you bet Hollow Promise."

"You sure, Pete?"

"I'm sure."

"That's good enough for me."

I made it a habit never to tell Lou or Lef what horse to bet. I'd say who I liked, but never touted. This was an exception. Lou buried his nose in the program until five minutes before the fifth. Then he left without saying a word.

Five minutes after the race, he returned, a sour look on his face. Hollow Promise had won for fun, paying $17.60, $5.80 and $4.80 across the board. Crooked Numbers went off stride out of the gate and was never in it.

Lou tore up his ticket into tiny pieces and watched them flutter to the concrete floor.

I looked at him, shaking my head. "Crooked Numbers?"

"Yeah, $55 to win," he said forlornly. Then he smiled and reached into his shirt pocket, pulling out another ticket. "And this one's $200 to win on Hollow Promise! Heeeeyaaaaah!"

Lef and Lou started slapping palms. High, low and in- between. It was quite a sight. A six-foot-six black giant and a little Italian dwarf.

"I took another look at the program and I liked him," Lou explained. "I just put the $55 on Crooked Numbers because it was Lef's money from Nerf."

Another reason Lou frequently loses. How many times have I heard guys say 'I'm playing with their money'? It's the attitude of a loser. If the money is in your pocket, it's your money. Period.

"Seventeen hundred and sixty bucks!" Lou exclaimed. "Hot damn!"

I was happy for him, but for a different reason. "Can I give you some advice on how to spend that money, Paesano?"

"How?"

"Pay Nematotta the fifteen hundred you owe him, then buy a few cases of Point and Leinenkugel."

"Nematotta! Shit! Yeah, I better settle with him before he gets after my ass."

"Not to mention mine." I told the guys about the Gotts episode.

"Consider it done, Pete. I'll pay him tomorrow. It's too much of a coincidence. I owe him fifteen hundred, I win fifteen sixty. It has to be a sign from God."

"If there is one," Lef chimed in.

We all laughed. "Alright you guys. The brew's on me."

We walked up to a refreshment stand and I bought three beers. Local, of course. I didn't mention it to Lou and Lef, but I had profited more than $5,000 on the race. My $100 across the board grossed $1,410. And I had five tickets on the trifecta, which paid $896 even. Total gross,

$5,790. Total invested, $450. Not a bad night, although I've had better here and there. I'd learned to keep my emotions in check.

Five years ago, two guys who had shared a winning ticket worth $9,000 plus, made the mistake of yelling and screaming "We won!" They also made the mistake of walking to the parking lot with the money in their wallets. To my knowledge, the police never found the killer or killers.

We finished our beers, chattering happily. Lou and Lef wadded up their cups and threw them at a trashcan ten yards away. I didn't hear the wager, but the cash passed from Lou to Lef.

They decided to hit the Iron Cage early. I walked out with them, satisfied with the night's profit and not concerned about the fact that Ernie would be looking for me with a program later. He could sell it and make another buck and change.

I teased Lef on the way out. "Hey, Lef. How come Ralston Rackford didn't have a nickname?"

"We called him Rack. I guess that was his nickname."

"Yeah, but it wasn't very colorful, like Shoots and Stretch and Slam."

"Hmmm, I never thought about it. He was just Rack to all of us guys." Then he brightened. "But his twin sister, man! She had a great name!"

"Nickname?"

"No. Regular name. First name."

"What was it?"

Lef was on center stage again. "Well, you know how the brothers and sisters got the unusual names. You know, like Toriano, Delacroy, Shawauna, Lavendella and like that. Well, Ralston's old man, his name is Garland, by the way, he raises dogs. Huntin' dogs. Like Pointers and Beagles and such."

"Anyway, ol' man Rackford, he's feedin' the dogs one day when he gets a call from the hospital that his wife had twins. The twins, of course, bein' Ralston and the sister. Never did hear how the ol' lady got to the hospital.

"So ol' Garland, he stops feedin' the dogs and crawls into his old Chevy, and I do mean crawl, because the door didn't work and he's got it tied shut with a clothesline, so he has to go through the window.

"And all the way to the hospital, he's pissin' and moanin' that his wife shoulda waited three more days, 'cause the baby – babies, actually – would've been born on his birthday. So he ain't payin' attention to his drivin' and the next thing you know the cops pull him over for makin' an illegal left turn.

"Now this one cop, he gets out of the car and walks over to ol' man Rackford's car, and when the other cop in the cruiser sees Rackford crawlin' through the window, he comes runnin' out, too. Even has his hand on his gun 'cause he thinks maybe they got a loonie or somethin'.

"Then the first cop, he asks ol' Garland for his license and Rackford can't find it. Doesn't even have a wallet. He looks in all his pockets, turns 'em inside out, and checks inside his beat up ol' Tigers cap. Then he sits down on the curb and takes off his shoes. By now, both cops are laughing their asses off.

"Well, finally, he takes off his socks, and there, inside his left sock, he pulls out this beat up, worn out, shriveled up piece of paper that's in shreds. Then he stands up with a smile and hands the license to the first cop who's now bustin' a gut tryin' not to laugh.

"They start talkin' and Rackford tells the cop that he's on the way to the hospital, that his wife just had twins. The cop congratulates him and says he can overlook the illegal turn under the circumstances, but then he says 'I'm sorry Garland, but I have to give you a ticket for a mutilated license.'"

"So now the ol' man jumps up and down, slams his cap to the ground and screams at the cops, 'Goddamn, it don't mutilate for three more days!'"

A roar of laughter broke out behind us. Lef had picked up a contingent of story lovers. None of us had noticed. Lef took a deep bow. "Thank you, thank you. I hope you'll all come back and see me next Friday night."

By now, we were all the way to Lou's car, a good fifty yards from where I was parked. I remembered something I had forgotten to ask Lou. "Hey, Lou, what do you call it when someone's afraid to leave their house?"

"You mean agoraphobia?"

"I don't know. That's why I asked"

"Yeah. It's agoraphobia. Which is actually the fear of open spaces, as I recall. Why?"

I didn't think the racetrack parking lot was the proper place to tell the guys about the situation with George. Although neither of them had ever met George, they knew he was an old friend from Michigan State. But, somehow, I couldn't hold back. I gave them the gruesome details of George's call and mentioned the subsequent phone conversation with Maria.

"Jesus, that's scary." Lef.

"What are you going to do?" Lou.

"I don't know. To be honest, I didn't even want to think about it tonight."

"Hey, if there's anything we can do," Lef offered.

"I'll let you know. Listen, you guys want some of my famous Italian cooking Sunday?"

They did.

"Alright, come on over, say around five or six. Maybe there'll be some news by then. If not, we'll just get fat together."

I started to walk away, then stopped. "Hey, Lef. You never told me Ralston's sister's name!"

He gave me a sly smile. "Hey, you're the investigator. Figure it out. I gave you all the clues you need."

"What clues?"

"The old man was feeding the dogs."

Somehow, the clues didn't click. "Yeah, well, thanks. I'll see you guys on Sunday."

"You coming out here tomorrow night?" I could tell by his tone that Lef wanted to.

"Nah. I don't think so. Maybe. I'll call you."

"Alright. Goodnight."

"See ya, Pete-sa. Thanks for the tip," Lou yelled from the driver's side.

"You're welcome. Goodnight."

I was half way home when it hit me.

Purina.

18

I've been a night person all my life. Rarely do I get to bed much before 1:00 or 1:30 a.m. If I'm not watching a late movie or handicapping the next night's Hazel Park program, I'm curled up with a good book and an oldies medley on the Wurlitzer.

Yet I usually rise and shine around 7:00 a.m. How does a 35-year-old body get by on five or six hours of sleep? I don't know. But I theorize it's because I maintain that rigorous schedule only during the week. On weekends, I sleep in. It's like I'm making up for the rest I didn't get the previous week and storing some extra rest for the upcoming week.

Whatever, it seems to work. Provided I get in eight or nine hours a night on the weekend. After all, the body has to have some time to produce melatonin. Or so a naturopathic doctor friend keeps warning me.

My phone rang at 7:00 a.m., three hours before the alarm was scheduled to wake me up. Nevertheless, I awoke instantly, fully alert. But it wasn't Harvey as I'd anticipated. It was Lou.

"Wake up call for room 18765."

"Lou! What the hell are you calling at seven in the morning for?"

"Lef and I wanted to see if you wanted to watch the Spartans tonight."

I did. "Yeah. Great. I forgot they were on the tube. What time?"

Lou put his hand over the mouthpiece and said something, apparently to Lef. Then the receiver must have slipped out of his hand because my ear was jolted by a loud crash.

"Pete, it's Lef. Kickoff's at 7:00. They're playing on the coast. Oregon State."

"Okay, I'll be there. What happened to Lou?"

"The phone slipped out of his hand. He's okay."

"What the hell are you guys doing up so early?" I knew the answer before the words were out of my mouth.

"Hell, we ain't been to bed yet. Lou sweet-talked one of the dancers at the Cage and we wound up going to an after-hours joint with her and a friend. Eldorado Club. Ever been there?"

"No. It's one of Nematotta's hangouts. The police are keeping an eye on it, by the way. If you ever go back, don't do anything foolish."

"I'll tell Lou."

"So the little guy finally got lucky, eh?"

"With a little help from the presidents."

"What are you talking about?"

"Well, let's put it this way. He ain't gonna be paying Nematotta *all* of that fifteen hundred. I figure maybe he's got a grand left."

"Aww, shit. Oh well. Look, I'm going back to bed. I'll see you tonight around seven."

"Okay. We're gonna grab some breakfast and then get some rest. Try to come by a little early if you can. I don't want you to miss a little surprise I've been working on for Lou."

I brightened momentarily. "Great. I'll get there a little early. Goodbye."

I hung up smiling. Lef loved to play practical jokes on Lou. One of his longest running tricks was sneaking into Lou's car late at night and sliding the seat forward. He made an extra key one day at lunch when he intentionally left his wallet in Lou's BMW and had to borrow the keys to get in. It irritated the hell out of Lef that Lou never mentioned the mysteriously recurring seat movements to anybody.

I got up, went into the kitchen and grabbed a Leinenkugel.

Five minutes later, I was back in bed, hoping to get back on schedule.

19

I should have known better. The phone rang at 8:22.

"Pete. Who did "Goodnight Sweetheart, Goodnight"? The one they always played at the high school dances?" It was Lou.

"The Untouchables."

"Thanks. You just bought my breakfast." Click.

Actually, several groups had recorded the song. But I knew it was the Untouchables' version they played at my high school dances. Who knows what they played at Oak Park?

I decided that getting more rest just wasn't in the cards. So I took a shower and got dressed. While I was shaving, I noticed the beginnings of a zit right on the tip of my nose. It could only mean one thing. I was going to be invited to a party. I soaked a cotton ball in some isopropyl alcohol and rubbed it good. The Pepperini version of Stridex. And a fairly effective zit prevention procedure. Christ! I hoped it wasn't noticeable the day before at Maria's. I didn't think so.

I put on some coffee, a blend I grind myself called hot buttered rum. Then I went down and got the morning *Free Press* to check the results of the races we didn't stay for.

Sure enough, Warp Factor Four won the ninth. He only paid $5.20, but that made me 3 for 3 with Freddie. You'd think he'd start giving me programs instead of charging me off-track prices.

I sat on the sofa and read the rest of the sports, noticing that Michigan State was minus seven and a half against the Beavers of Oregon State. They should cover easily. Then I checked the latest goings-on of Garfield,

Mother Goose & Grimm and Calvin and Hobbes. For those unfamiliar with the world of relevant literature, those are my favorite comic strips. After that, I must have fallen back asleep, because suddenly I was ten years old and surrounded by a bunch of screaming, taunting, nasty kids.

"Pepperoni nose!"

" Pizza face!"

"Pepperoni pizza!"

"Pete-sa, Pete-sa!"

They had me surrounded and were advancing on me slowly, wielding giant salamis. The taunts were redolent with the aroma of garlic as they closed in, salamis whizzing through the air all around my head. Then one particularly homely girl whose face was covered with ripe zits caught me over the right ear and I went tumbling to the ground, tears streaming from my eyes. Not from the pain, but from the agony of the terrible burden of being cursed with a name like Pietro Pepperini. Then I lapsed into unconsciousness.

The doorbell woke me up. I shivered myself into awareness, noticed by my watch that it was almost noon. I went downstairs, still shaking a little from the dream, promising myself I'd slug the next person who asked me why I used the name Pete Pepper professionally.

It was Marianne and Gianni.

"Hi, Uncle Pete!" Gianni reached up and gave me a hug. Ten year olds didn't kiss men.

Marianne did. On the cheek. "We didn't wake you up, did we, Pete?"

"Only for the third time this morning."

"What?"

"Nothing important. I got up early and I guess I dozed off reading the paper. Want some coffee?"

"No thanks. I mean, I do, but I don't have time. I'd better leave now or I'll be late for Father Wong."

"How is the Pontiff of St. Lucifer's?"

"Oh, he's fine. But I wish you wouldn't call him that. And it's St. Luke's."

"Come on, you know I'm teasing. I like the old coot." Father Wong was one of a kind. Even if he weren't a Chinese priest, he'd still be one of a kind.

"He's not an old coot, either!"

"Marianne, forgive me, for I have sinned."

She finally cracked a smile. "Oh, Pete. You're so funny. No wonder I love you so much."

I stiffened, but didn't say anything. We had been over this many times before. I let it go and smiled back at her.

"Well, I'm just a lovable guy. What time are you coming back?"

"About three or four. Is that okay?"

"Sure. Gianni and I'll have a good time. What do you want to do sport?"

"The computerrrr," he said, stretching the "r" as he disappeared into the workroom.

Marianne and I both laughed.

"Well, I'd better get going," she said. "I'll see you later." Then she reached over and kissed me goodbye. I accepted it on the lips. But only for the briefest instant.

"Take your time," I told her. We'll be fine."

20

Let me tell you about Marianne. She thinks she loves me. And maybe, just maybe, she does. But it doesn't matter. She was, is and always will be my brother's wife. End of story.

The irony is that, way back in grade school, I had an enormous crush on her. Along with every other red-blooded kid at Robert Oakman Elementary. Except that my crush lasted right into junior high. Which is about the time she began to notice that I existed. We even went out a few times, if meeting her at the Saturday matinee and buying her an occasional Holloway sucker constitutes going out.

Marianne Piccone. Her transformation from a cute little girl into a strikingly beautiful woman was something to behold. Only the "little" didn't change. Marianne was 5-feet, 2-inches tall and all of 95 pounds when she was a senior in high school. Today she's maybe 10 pounds heavier, but she's still a damn good-looking woman with a very desirable body. And don't think I haven't desired it on many occasions. But a man doesn't touch his brother's wife. Even if his brother is dead.

Why do I say she *thinks* she loves me? Because I don't believe a woman who's lost a husband knows her emotions for sure. When Domenic died, I was there. I comforted her, ran errands for her, took care of her son, and did virtually anything and everything that needed to be done for her. In short, I made things easy for her. Too easy, in retrospect. I let her get too dependent on me.

And, initially, at least, I think she mistook dependency and gratitude for love. Not that it mattered.

Here's more irony. I really didn't do anything for Marianne. I did it for Domenic. I loved my brother. I still think about him and the positive influence he had on my life. Our age difference – he was six years older than me – was great enough that we never really had any sibling rivalry. I emulated his every move. Listened intently to every word he said. And perhaps most important of all, he instilled in me a love of music. Many of the records I have today were originally his.

I learned so much from Domenic. And though he had it all over me in looks, in brains, in worldliness, he never, not once, ever talked down to me. His feelings toward me were the same as mine toward him. He loved me. He cared about me. He was, to use a cliché, one hell of a great guy.

I think Domenic always felt a little guilty that he married Marianne. After all, I was the Pepperini who discovered her. That summer he came home from Viet Nam, I was still dating Marianne. But not with any regularity. And, unknown to her, I was dating some other girls as well. Hell, I actually encouraged Domenic to ask her out. And once they got started, they became inseparable. By the time September rolled around, and I was shipping out to East Lansing, Domenic had gotten Marianne pregnant.

There was no scandal; they got married immediately. But there was shame. And the shame was that Domenic never went to college. Instead, he joined the Dearborn Police. I don't mean the job was shameful. Just that he never had the opportunity to do better. But, with a wife and a child on the way, he needed a job. And that was the job he got.

Ironically, the baby Marianne was carrying was stillborn. Domenic named him Eugenio after our own stillborn brother.

He could have gone to college then. But Domenic truly enjoyed his work. He got along with everyone. When you met Domenic, you knew after five minutes you wanted him to be your friend for life.

So he worked hard, advanced rapidly and saved money steadily. After five years, Domenic and Marianne gave it another go and Gianni was born.

A good cop. A sweet wife. A great kid. The All-American family. And they all lived happily ever after. Until a drunk, joy-riding teenager in a stolen car killed him.

We never talked about it, but we didn't have to. Domenic and I both knew that if anything ever happened to him, I'd take care of his family. It was a responsibility I took on willingly. Domenic and I had essentially grown up without a father. I would never let that happen to Gianni. And, just as much as I refused to be a husband to my brother's wife, I yearned to be a father to my brother's son.

That's not entirely true. Marianne's advances, her pleas for me to hold her and love her have taken their toll over the months since Domenic's death.

I do want to hold her and love her. Desire and lust have burned in my soul. But she is my brother's wife.

And I can't.

21

"Hey Uncle Pete, come here!" Gianni's voice wafted up the stairs as I was finishing feeding the boys. I went down to the workroom where he was seated in front of the computer.

"Look, I wrote you a poem," he said, with a shy grin.

I looked at the monitor and read:

I have an uncle. His name is Pete.
He treats me great. He's really neat.
He's the best uncle I ever had
I only wish he was my dad.

I fought back tears. "Hey, that's really good, Gianni."

"You really like it?"

"I like it a lot. Tell you what. Let's print it out so I can save it. Then we'll go grab some breakfast. Your Uncle Pete who's really neat would like to have some food to eat."

He laughed and clicked the printer icon. I pulled the sheet out, folded it and put it in my pocket.

Just as we were ready to go out the door, it opened and a bleary-eyed Lou Bracato walked in.

"Hey Pete. What's up? You got that tout sheet information you keep forgetting to give me?"

"Yeah, I have it right here. I thought you were going home to get some sleep."

"I'm on the way. Just thought I'd stop by and pick it up. Thought I might catch Marianne and say hi."

"She's already gone. You just missed her." I handed him the flyer and he squinted at it.

"Guaranteed 65% winners, $500 for the season, college and pro games. Hmmm. I got a couple of these offers at home too. One of 'em says they'll give you 60% winners and it's only $400 a season."

"College and pro too?"

"Yeah. Which one would you take?"

"I thought you said you had a couple offers at home. What was the other one?"

"No good. Only $195 a season and they didn't bother to mention a winning percentage. But I checked them out with a rating service and they've averaged exactly 34% over the last three seasons. Total waste of money."

"Well, then, if you plan to make at least five or six plays a weekend, 65% winners would probably net you more. What's another $100 if you're playing $200 or $300 a game?"

"Yeah, that's what I'm thinking. Guess I'll pop for the $500."

Gianni, who had been at the computer, but apparently following our conversation, didn't agree. "I wouldn't do that if I was you, Mr. Bracato."

"Huh? And why is that little man?" Shockingly, Lou didn't correct Gianni for his failure to use the subjunctive mood.

"Well, if you want the best *value*, like my mom always looks for, you should buy the one that's only $195. They only have 34% winners, but what you should do is bet the *opposite* of what they say. That way, you'll have 66% winners and pay, umm, $305 less. Theoretically speaking, of course."

Lou and I just stood there, looking at each other in wonderment. After a few seconds of silence, we both laughed simultaneously.

As we walked out to our parked cars, Lou reached into his wallet and handed Gianni a ten-dollar bill.

"Take this, Gianni, and treat your uncle to breakfast. He doesn't think too well on an empty stomach."

22

We entered Vassili's Restaurant through the back entrance. I didn't see Barb as we walked in, but two seconds after we were seated, she came running out of the kitchen, pumping her right fist in the victory sign.

"Good going, Private Eye! We won!"

"Did you ever doubt it?" I asked, peeling out $88 and handing it to her. Actually, I hadn't made the bet for her. I never do. I just make sure my own bet is big enough to cover any action I take out for other people. If the bet wins, I have plenty of cash. If it loses, there's no problem.

"Thanks. I can sure use this. Uh, we can discuss the other part of our deal some other time," she said, nodding toward Gianni.

"Whatever you say," I replied. I didn't really expect anything to come of it, nor was I going to let it. "I'll have the usual."

"And what about you, Gianni?" This wasn't his first trip to Vassili's.

"I'll have an artificial omelet." His eyes were sparkling with mischief.

"And what might that be?"

"Eggbeaters with Spam and Velveeta."

Barb didn't bat an eyelash as she pretended to write down the order.

"Right. And how about some instant coffee with Cremora and artificial sweetener? And maybe you'd like to wash it down with a glass of Tang?'

Now they were both laughing.

"No, I guess I'll just have some pancakes. And a glass of milk."

"Comin' right up, Tiger."

We ate in relative silence. Gianni was obviously very hungry. I was preoccupied, playing scenarios in my head about what could have happened to George at the Bradshaw house. Nothing played well.

I looked around the restaurant. It was a typical Saturday morning – afternoon, actually – crowd. And it was crowded. I recognized several faces, none of which I knew by name. There was a liberal sprinkling of newcomers too. A commotion up front caught my attention. A heavy-set guy and his equally corpulent companion were confronting Chris, who was doubling as a hostess and cashier. The guy was quite a sight. He packed at least 300 pounds into a colorful Hawaiian shirt, a pair of straw-colored Bermuda shorts, bright chartreuse socks, sans elastic, and a pair of black wingtip shoes that hadn't seen polish since the guy was skinny. His friend (wife?) had on a floral print smock that reminded me of the glider we had on the back porch when I was a kid. They weren't just out of style; they were out of season as well.

Other diners were beginning to notice the skirmish. Even Gianni looked up from his pancakes for a moment, sporting a milk moustache. But he quickly returned to his own skirmish. People near the battle scene were stifling snickers, some much more successfully than others. The guy was pointing to his ample chest and making a point to Chris. I couldn't make out what he was saying. Then a teenage girl in a red sweater shifted her position and I got a better look at the guy; a dead-on shot of his rear end.

Immediately, I realized what all the laughing was about. The guy's Bermudas were so worn, you could see right through them! And what you saw was a very large pair of boxer shorts covered with bright red polka dots. I almost choked on a bite of bacon.

Suddenly the guy put his left arm across his chest and arced his fisted right hand upward, perpendicular to the left. It was a gesture very familiar to me and virtually everyone else of Italian heritage. How many times have I seen it since my childhood? But this guy definitely didn't look Italian, which somehow, made it even more amusing. Turning and repeating the gesture to the rest of the audience, he stormed out the door, his companion following closely behind.

There was a surge of buzzing from the crowd; a few patrons even applauded. On the way out, I asked Chris what the disturbance was about.

"The jerk got teed off because I wouldn't give him the breakfast special for $2.89. The sign clearly says until 11 a.m. only. The hell with him!"

"Damn right," I said in earnest support. "He should take his two eighty nine and go buy a new pair of shorts."

"Yeah!" Chris concurred. "Bermudas *and* boxers."

Somehow she didn't notice that Barb had only charged me $2.89 for my breakfast. So I paid the tab and we exited quickly.

Gianni never made a move for the ten spot.

23

Instead of heading home, I drove north on Southfield Road. On a hunch, I wanted to do the obvious and check out George's apartment.

Traffic for a Saturday afternoon was unusually heavy, so I zigzagged east and north until I hit Sixteen Mile Road, which, honest to God, is also named Big Beaver. I took it into Troy, passing the law offices of Broder, Lerner, Roth and Calabrese. George's firm. Or former firm, as I feared.

It took me three passes to locate the entrance to George's apartment complex. It was one of those sprawling, low-rise developments set back off the main drag. No signs or addresses were apparent. Apparently, you just had to know it was there. It wasn't until I drove into a parking lot a mere eighty yards from the nearest building that I was sure we were where we wanted to be.

Golfview Gardens Visitors Parking, it said, without the benefit of an apostrophe. Then again, maybe it didn't need one. Gianni and I got out and took a shortcut across a vast expanse of weed-choked lawn that cut a good 30 yards off our trip. Along the way, we had to dodge several piles of circumstantial evidence that the locals were dog lovers. Luckily, we emerged in front of Building A. That meant Building C had to be close.

It wasn't. Building A sort of stood isolated from the rest. Like the apex of a triangle. The other 20 or so structures that comprised the complex were scattered randomly in its wake. After six tries, we had located R, T, L, O, M and B. But no C.

Then I spotted a pleasant looking elderly lady in black jeans and a hooded jacket working on hands and knees in a flower garden next to Building B. It looked like she was weeding, not planting. I put on a charming smile and approached her, intending to ask directions, but she beat me to the punch.

"Howdy there, young man! You, too, Sonny," she gummed in Gianni's direction. "Which building you gents looking for?"

"C," I said sheepishly.

"Yeah, yeah," she nodded knowingly, but gave no indication she intended to tell us where it was. "Say, either of you gents know anything about flowers?"

"They're pretty," Gianni offered.

"I took a little botany in college," I told her. "What do you want to know?"

She gestured to the bed, which ran for 40 or 50 feet along the length of the building and was maybe six feet wide. Several varieties of plants were in various stages of bloom. Or, to be more accurate, falling out of bloom.

"Well, I planted a lot of these gall-darn things from seeds," she said. "If they was all in bloom, I could probly figger out what they was. But, right now, I don't know if these critters right here is flowers or weeds. I don't want to pull out no flowers."

I looked at the critters in question. There were about three dozen of them, little purplish green plants that could have been flowers. But because they were scattered randomly rather than planted in an orderly fashion, I was putting my money on weeds.

"Aha!" I bluffed. "Have you ever heard of gazania?"

"Gazania ... ?" She tilted her hooded head toward the sky as if the answer were in the clouds. "Gazania. Yeah, I reckon I heard of 'em. Couldn't tell you what they look like, though. Are those gazanias?"

"Oh, no. Gazania are beautiful, colorful ground cover. They're pink or yellow, not purple. What you have there is often mistaken for gazania. In fact, some folks even call them false gazania. But they're weeds. Real name is chlamydia. Pesky little devils. Real hard to get rid of."

"Well, don't you worry none. No chlamydias are gonna get the best of me. I'll get rid of 'em, alright."

"I'm sure you will," I said, then changed the subject before I got in too deep. "Uh, you wouldn't happen to know which way Building C is, would you?"

"Of course I would! I live here, don't I? It's that one over yonder." She pointed to the twin of Building B, about 50 yards distant and let out a chuckle.

"Lots of folks get lost in here," she explained. "Visitors, I mean. Reason is, when this place was first built, there was just three buildings. A, B and C. If you look close, you can see that they're sorta in a straight line. The owners named them in the order they was built. All these other buildings came later. They started jammin' 'em in everywhere, destroying all the wide, open spaces and raisin' everyone's rent to boot. Heck, you never know what them guys are gonna do. Wouldn't surprise me none if they put up some more buildings over there on the dog walking area." She pointed to the area through which Gianni and I had taken our short cut.

"Yes, we're familiar with it," I informed her. "Definitely fertile ground for expansion."

"Well, anyway, that's your Building C over there."

"Right. Well, thanks, ma'am. We'll be on our way, then. We appreciate your help."

"And I appreciate yours! Chlamydia, eh? The name does sound familiar to me, now that I think about it."

I didn't want her to think too hard while we were still around. So I just smiled and headed for Building C.

"Goodbye," she said. "You and your son have a nice day, now. Ya hear?"

"Thanks. We will. Come on, son." I didn't even look at Gianni.

"Goodbye," Gianni smiled to the lady, as he ran to catch up with me.

I grabbed his arm and steered him toward the elusive Building C. After a few yards, I turned and looked back. She was just standing there watching us, her legs barely discernible from the rake she was leaning on. I couldn't resist.

"Be sure to dig 'em out by the roots," I shouted. "If you don't, they'll grow back."

She just smiled and waved.

24

Building C did look older than its neighbors. The bricks were a little more faded; the mortar a little more crumbled. We walked up a single concrete step to the sidewalk leading to the entrance. Inside, next to a bank of mailboxes, were a directory and a second door that led to an inner lobby with a few pieces of very used furniture. It was the kind of door that had to be buzzed from inside by a resident if you didn't have a key. I was confident I could pop it with a credit card, or use my picks if necessary. But either way was too risky. We were too much in the open. And it wasn't something I particularly wanted to do in front of Gianni. As I was pondering my options, the Good Humor man came to my rescue. The telltale jingling caught Gianni's ear too.

"Hey, look, Uncle Pete! Ice cream!"

"Hey! How about that? You know, I sure could go for a toasted almond Good Humor! How about you?"

His eyes widened. "Sure! It could be our dessert for breakfast!"

"Why don't you run and get us some? I'm a little tired from all that walking. I'll wait here." I fished a couple of singles out of my wallet and handed them to him, remembering that when I was a kid, they were only 35 cents.

He grabbed the bills and ran out the door to the truck, parked at the intersection of two of the narrow roads that laced the complex.

I went to work fast, punching the buzzers of all the residents of the third floor, which was the top floor. According to the address Maria had given me, George's apartment was on the second floor, so I didn't want to buzz anyone there. Or on the ground floor, either, for obvious reasons. After about 20 seconds, a tinny female voice asked me through the speaker, "Who is it?" Before I could answer, someone else buzzed the door open.

I stepped through and raced up the one-flight staircase, taking all eight steps in three strides. Quickly. Silently. It was a lot easier than going down. Then I skated down the carpeted hall to number 207 and flattened myself against George's recessed door, waiting for the inevitable. I didn't have to wait long.

"Who is it?" A man's voice drifted down from above. "Hello? Anybody there?" A brief pause. Then, "Goddamn kids," followed by a door slam.

I had palmed my credit card when I got the money out for Gianni. Now I was ready to use it. I grabbed the knob with my left hand and prepared to slide the card between the jamb and the latch. I never made it. The door clicked open. It hadn't been locked. I closed it, opened it again, left it slightly ajar and casually walked back down the stairs to the inner lobby.

I picked up a magazine from a table next to the beat-up old sofa and pretended to read it, trying to be inconspicuous. When I saw Gianni approaching with the ice cream, I put the magazine down, walked over and opened the door for him.

"Come on! In here," I smiled at Gianni. "Let's sit down and eat these first before we go up, okay?"

"Sure." He handed me my toasted almond and we sat on the sofa. If Gianni was surprised that I was already inside, he didn't show it. The ice cream had his full attention.

"My friend's in number 207," I told Gianni after we had finished and put the sticks into a floor model ashtray. "I haven't visited him here before. He just moved in recently."

"That's up on the second floor," he said, matter-of-factly.

I followed Gianni up the stairs. He walked straight to number 207 like George was his old friend, and knocked on the door. It swung open slightly.

"Look, Uncle Pete. It's unlocked. I didn't even touch the knob. Honest."

"Well, let's go in, then."

"You think we should?"

"Sure. George is a good friend. He's probably in the bathroom. We'll surprise him. I'm sure he wouldn't go away and leave his door unlocked."

The door opened on an L-shaped room. The large part of the L was the living room, the short part served as the dining area. I was sure the rental literature called it two rooms; but it was really just one. Furniture was sparse, but not cheap. Sofa, easy chair, TV, stereo, bookcase, table and lamp. There was a stack of record albums in front of the bookcase; a few CDs and books on the shelves. No pictures were on the walls. A small, round table and a single chair filled the dining area. There was no sign that anyone had occupied it recently.

A built-in counter separated the dining area from a small kitchen. A hall led past the kitchen. I could see three doors, all closed. I steered Gianni to the sofa in the living room.

"You sit here, sport. And don't touch anything. I'll be right back."

He sat.

I opened the first door on the left. It was the bathroom. Empty.

The second door was a small bedroom. It wasn't empty. It was cluttered with junk and boxes, just like my own downstairs kitchen and storeroom. But no sign of George.

That meant the door on the right was the master bedroom. I opened it. And immediately wished I hadn't.

George's body was sprawled across the bed, face up. At least, it used to be a face. He had been brutally, savagely beaten. Dried, caked blood obscured what was left of any facial features. I didn't care to look closely enough to determine if what I saw in his hair were bits of his brain.

There was no way you could identify the body as George by looking at anything above the neck. But I did recognize his Rolex watch. That still didn't make the body George's, but instinctively, I knew it was him.

I closed the door and hit the bathroom. "One toasted almond Good Humor, coming up!" a voice in my head said. It did, along with the remains of my breakfast special. I flushed the toilet, staggered back to the living room and collected Gianni.

"You okay, Uncle Pete?"

"Yeah. I just had to use the bathroom. Come on, let's go. We'd better get back before your mother does."

I didn't have the ambition to avoid the heavy traffic. It would have been a long ride home, regardless.

25

I deposited Gianni in front of the upstairs TV and turned on the Tigers game for him. I was pleased that he showed an interest in sports. It was a trait not usually associated with budding eggheads. And it kept him out of my way for a while. The Tigers were ahead 5-1 in the seventh, but the game was far from over. The Tigers' bullpen had a great talent for blowing late-inning leads. Lou referred to it as underperforming at the highest level.

I went downstairs to call Harvey. Surprisingly, I was very composed. It was a shock to discover George's body, especially in the condition it was in. But, in my heart, I had known he was dead; I was steeled for the confirmation. In my own way, I had already mourned. Or, at least, gone through whatever emotion is the equivalent of mourning when the deceased is really just a casual friend. I know there was some grief for Maria mixed in too. And certainly some of the scary notion that "it could have been me." In any event, it was over.

Harv answered my call immediately. He exploded the second he heard my voice. "It's about time you called back. Where the hell have you been?"

He caught me off guard. "What do you mean called back?"

"I've been trying to reach you for two hours. Didn't you get my messages?"

"No. I just got back. I haven't even checked my machine yet. You know, Harv, just because you don't like cell phones doesn't mean you can't call me on mine."

"Yeah, whatever. But I got some news for you. We've located George's car. You'll never guess where."

"Uh, Harv ... "

"Right in the fucking parking lot of his law offices. How do you like that? I bet the sonofabitch is off with a chick somewhere. A weekend of sex with an aspiring young law clerk."

"No, Harv. George won't be having sex with anyone anymore. He's dead. I found his body."

His first explosion was mild by comparison.

"What do you mean you found his body? Where? Didn't I tell you to stay out of this? Goddamnit, this is police work."

"It was in his apartment. On his bed. Somebody beat the shit out of him, Harv. He doesn't even have a face left."

My somber tone must have gotten to Harvey. He was suddenly calm, almost subdued.

"Jesus. I'm sorry, Pete. But something's screwy here. We checked his apartment last night. Nothing. And that was a good sixteen hours after you got his call."

"Well, he's there now. Whoever killed him must have taken him there some time between Friday night and Saturday morning. Possibly even in his car. His new apartment isn't very far from his office."

"Yeah, I know. We do a few things right around here every once in awhile."

"Don't be so defensive. Believe me, I wish that you had found him, not me."

"Right. Sorry. Look, you didn't move him, did you? You didn't touch anything?"

"Harv, I have a degree in Criminal Justice. Remember? Graduated with high honors. Of course I didn't move anything. I did touch something, though. The doorknob on his entrance door. And, oh yeah, I flushed the toilet. Sort of lost my lunch after I found him. But that's it."

"Shit. I hope you didn't cover up any prints. I'll send a crew over to check things out right away. And get hold of the coroner too."

"Harv. What about Maria? Do you want me to ... "

"No. I'll take care of it. It's ... "

"I know. It's police work."

"Damn right it is. And don't be a smart ass or I might think twice about pressing charges against you."

"Me? What for?" I was genuinely surprised.

"Breaking and entering. I locked Geroge Gianotti's door myself last night when we left."

26

Marianne showed up to get Gianni just about the same time the Tigers surrendered a three-run homer in the bottom of the ninth. It was their eighth loss in a row. I knew because Lou bet the Tigers, based on his theory that after seven straight losses, they were "due" to win. Poor Lou.

I reminded Marianne that I was cooking dinner on Sunday for her and Father Wong and casually mentioned that Lou and Lef might also be stopping by. She liked my cooking too much to object. Marianne isn't overly fond of Lou. She thinks he's the bad influence that got me started gambling. I never had the heart to tell her it was Domenic, who actually was an avid poker player in his spare time. But even though she doesn't care too much for Lou, she does enjoy it when Lou, Lef and I get together. She thinks we're very amusing.

Five minutes after I sent her and Gianni on their way, I stored a couple hours of rest.

27

I awoke at a quarter to six, freshened up and put on my Michigan State sweatshirt. It couldn't hurt.

I ate a couple of Buitoni pizzas while a special medley I put together for Lef played in the background. The highlights were "My Beloved" by the Satintones, which happens to be the first single released on the Motown label (#1000); "Come To Me" by Marv Johnson, reputed to be the first Motown release, even though it's on the Tamla label; and "I Found Myself A Brand New Baby", by Mike and The Modifiers, allegedly the first white group to record for Motown. This was on the Gordy label.

Lef loves music; possibly even more than I. And he is an absolute Motown fanatic. Looking back at our relatively short friendship, I'd have to say that music was definitely the glue that sealed the bond between us. And after the shaky start we got off to, God knows we needed something to help us.

I'll never forget the night we met. Neither of us will. I had just finished an informal talk on personal safety to a class at Lawrence Tech, a small college located at 10 Mile Road and the Lodge Freeway, barely a mile from my place. It was about 10:30 at night; the class was over at ten, but I stuck around to swap a few jokes with the instructor. It was late January. Colder than hell and snowing. Long, tall piles of old snow ran parallel to the rows of parked cars, left by plows scraping earlier snow-falls off the parking surface. Orderly rows of artificial Alps, just high enough to obscure the cars. That's why I couldn't see my car until I got to the row where I was parked. Not that it would have mattered.

I wasn't driving the Saab back then. It was a beat up old '74 Beetle. I was approaching it from the passenger side. Just as I was directly behind the car, Lef introduced himself. He had been crouched down on hands and knees on the driver's side.

He sprang up, scaring the hell out of me. His right hand was in his coat pocket, as though he were holding a gun.

"Don't move, man. Don't move an inch. Just slowly reach into your pocket and hand me your wallet."

Don't move? Hell, the only part of me that came close to moving was my bowels. I'm not exactly a small man. I'm 5-feet, 11-inches and around 190 pounds, depending on when I last ate pasta. But Lef dwarfed me. Although he was 6-feet, 6-inches, he easily appeared 7 feet tall to me.

"You're out of luck, buddy. I don't even have change for a dollar." Somehow, I managed a smile.

"This says you do, motherfucker. Now give me that wallet." He pulled his right hand out and pointed a small caliber revolver in the general proximity of the exact center of my forehead.

My brain was saying, "Yes sir. Here's my wallet. Take it. Take all my money. I think there's $100, maybe $200 in there. And how about if I write you a check for more?"

But my mouth said, "Why should I?"

Then my eyes told me why. Lef was shaking, and not from the cold. But he said, with just the right amount of menace, "I figure you owe it to me honky. I got it coming for 200 years of black suppression by the white establishment."

I suddenly got furious. Something in me snapped.

"Fuck you, you son of a bitch! I don't owe you a goddamn thing! My grandfather came to this country on a boat in 1930. With two hands and the clothes on his back. He was 22 years old and didn't even know what the hell a black man looked like. He wasn't responsible for slavery; he didn't have any prejudice. He was discriminated against back then just as much as you and your people are today. Maybe more. So don't give me that owe it to you bullshit. If you're still carrying a grudge, get your black ass down to Alabama and stick your gun in some Klansman's face. But right now, either get the fuck out of my way or shoot me and take the wallet off my dead body."

I don't know how I expected him to react to my outburst, but I sure as hell didn't expect him to cry.

But that's what he did. He started sobbing like a baby. After maybe ten seconds, he put the gun away and said, "I'm sorry man. I didn't mean it. Shit. The gun ain't even loaded. Honest. I'm sorry, man. I'm really sorry."

It turned out that Lef had lost his job that day. His car was repossessed and his rent already overdue. It was quite a sight. This six-foot-six black man towering over me, pouring out his soul. I did the only decent thing a man could do. I invited him for coffee.

We drove over to Leroy's Home Cooking, a 24-hour restaurant near his neighborhood, the Eight Mile/Wyoming section of Detroit. On the way, a CD that was already cued up in my car's player segued from a Jr. Walker & the All Stars instrumental into "Check Yourself" by the Temptations,

another early Motown release on the Miracle label. Lef couldn't believe it. It was a song he had been trying to locate for years. That a white man had even heard of it was astounding to him; but to actually own a copy and have it on a CD was far too much!

We sat in that restaurant for nearly three hours, talking about music, about Larry Dixon and Ernie Durham, two pioneering black disc jockeys in Detroit. We sang duets of dozens of Motown songs, much to the delight of the employees and other patrons in the restaurant, all of them black.

By the time I took Lef home, we discovered we had another common interest – harness racing. As I shook his hand that night, I gave him $150, all the spare cash I had. I didn't really care if he ever paid me back.

The next night, we went to the harness races at Northville Downs together and made about $400 apiece. He paid me back.

A few weeks later, Lou called me and asked if I knew anyone interested in driving a Federal Express truck. The guy who made pickups at Broderick & Stanley was moving to California. I mentioned Lef's name and told him he was a new friend. Lou nearly went crazy. He was intimately aware of Lefkowitz Turner and his basketball accomplishments at Oak Park High. As the team's equipment manager, Lou had become good friends with Lef and was sorry he had lost track of him. Shortly thereafter, Lef got the job he still has today. The three of us are still best friends. And to this day, I have never told anyone, especially Lou, the exact circumstances under which Lef and I met.

I finished my pizzas and washed them down with a can of Point.

Then I called Fluff, my local bookie. A much nicer man than Lorenzo Nematotta. The line on Michigan State had gone up from 7½ to 8, which meant if you bet State, they had to win by more than eight points. If they won by exactly eight, the bet was off. It was a tie, or a push, in the parlance of bookies. For me, the line moving up was a good sign.

Sports gamblers typically bet against a line move. There seems to be a popular misconception that the point spread means the odds makers believe the winning team will win by that much. But it's really the number they hope will get an equal amount of action on both sides. It sounds complicated, but when that happens – when the amount of money bet on State is the same as the amount bet on the opponent – the bookmaker is guaranteed to net 5% of the total amount bet. That's because losing bettors pay a 10% commission called vigorish or juice.

So if I bet $1,000 and win and Lou bets $1,000 and loses, he pays the bookie $1,100. The bookie pays me $1,000 and pockets $100, which is 5% of $2,000, the total amount bet. That's a very simplistic explanation; in actuality a bookie might have several hundred clients on any given day, betting on everything from sports to horses at stadiums and racetracks all over the country. I've even heard rumors that some gamblers are crazy enough to bet hockey.

So what do I mean by betting against a line move? I'll use the State game as an example. With the line at 7½, State would have to win by 8 for me to win. With the line moved to 8, they now have to win by 9, because they can't win by 8½. That's significant. Many bets are won or lost by 1 or even half a point. So the inclination is for bettors to take that extra half point and bet on the underdog, in this case Oregon State. That's betting against the line move.

I like to bet with a line move, because if it goes from 7½ to 8, it means the bookie wants you to take points. He needs more money bet on the underdog to even up the ledger and he entices you by giving you an extra half point. Sometimes it's even more. My logic is simple: If that's what the bookmaker wants you to do, do the opposite. State didn't just become another half point better than Oregon State; money moved the line. So I bet $300 on State minus the 8 and another $200 on over 44, which meant the total score of both teams added together had to be greater than 44.

My instinct told me it was an easy $500.

28

I pulled into the driveway of Lef's flat the same time that Lou's BMW pulled over to the curb.

We walked up together and were greeted at the door by Lef. He handed each of us a cold bottle of Colt 45 Malt Liquor. He still hadn't acquired my gourmet taste for local brews.

We plopped down on the oversized stuffed beanbag pillows Lef uses for furniture, nursing our drinks. The TV was already on, but it sure wasn't the football pre-game show.

"Holy shit!" I said. "What's that?"

Two naked women were on the screen, doing things to each other you don't usually see on television, even cable.

"It's a movie," Lef said, matter-of-factly. "*Nana.* From the novel by Emile Zola. It paints a rich tapestry of the socio-political mores and attitudes in 19th century France." He smiled, pleased at using big words in front of Lou.

But Lou wasn't impressed. "Looks like a rich tapestry of tits and ass to me," he retorted. "Not that I'm complaining. But let's catch the pre-game show, okay? They might give some scores I need."

With a stack of football parlay cards in his left hand, Lou reached for the TV remote with his right and switched to channel 7.

Lef shrugged, disappeared into the kitchen and returned a few minutes later, sipping a glass of wine. He placed a bowl of pistachios near Lou on the floor and winked in my direction.

The game went pretty much as I anticipated. State was up 27-7 with two minutes to go in the half. The real highlight of the first half was Lef's latest trick on Lou, which, of course, involved the bowl of pistachios.

Lou had virtually ignored them throughout the first quarter, concentrating instead on checking the progress of his football cards. When Lou finally reached for some pistachios, Lef caught my eye and motioned for me to watch. I did, not knowing what to expect.

Lou absent-mindedly grabbed a handful of the nuts, sifted through them and tossed them back in the bowl. His attention was still focused on the game. Then he grabbed another handful, sifted through them and, again, threw them back in the bowl. Over a period of about five or six minutes,

Lou did this several times as I looked on curiously and Lef was beaming, obviously straining to avoid laughing.

Finally, Lou realized what he was doing.

"Jesus Christ! Where the hell did you get these pistachios?" he bellowed.

Lef exploded into uncontrollable gales of laughter, bending over and holding his stomach as tears streamed down his face.

"What's going on?" I inquired with sincere innocence. I wasn't sure what Lef had done to the nuts.

"None of these fucking pistachios have a crack in them!" Lou yelled. "How the hell am I supposed to open them?"

I walked over and looked in the bowl. Every single pistachio in it was solid. Not even the slightest nail hold.

"I've been saving those suckers for six months," Lef explained. "I musta gone through 20 bags, savin' all the uncracked ones." He was still laughing like hell.

Lou didn't find the situation particularly amusing. "I know how we can crack them," he said. "By stepping on them!" Then he dumped the bowl all over Lef's tiled living room floor and proceeded to stomp the pistachios.

"Why not?" Lef giggled. "Good a way as any." He was too pleased with his caper to be even slightly upset at Lou's rudeness.

I left after the third quarter with Michigan State leading 34-7; confident I would win both bets. I did. Lou called me later with confirmation that State "palindromed" them, 41-14.

Lou, by the way, stayed at Lef's. The boys decided to stop by and see their friends at the Iron Cage again. They promised to stop partying in time to come over for dinner on Sunday.

29

When I got home I checked my machine for messages. There was one. Harvey Steinberg called and said to call back no matter what time I got home. It was five after ten, so I guessed that qualified.

He was in a mysterious mood.

"Pete, just how closely did you look at George's body?"

"Like I told you, Harv, not closely at all. I was maybe five feet away. The way he was positioned, his feet were closest to me. His head was at the foot of the bed."

"Well it sure was an understatement when you said somebody beat the shit out of him. And it was dead nuts right on when you said he didn't have a face left."

"What do you mean?"

"I mean that every single one of his teeth was missing. I mean that both his eyeballs were gone. That's what I mean."

"Jesus Christ!" I was stunned.

"And you know what that means, don't you?"

"What?" I was too dazed to think about anything but the incredible brutality of it all.

"It means that somebody wants to make it real hard to identify the body, that's what."

"What about fingerprints?"

"Burned off."

"I mean fingerprints in the apartment. Did you find any?"

"Besides George's? Two good ones. On the doorknobs. Just like you said. They were yours. Everything else was clean."

"Shit. What about Maria? Can she identify the body? Maybe he has a birthmark or something."

"Couldn't reach her. We're checking to see if she has relatives in the area. Might be spending the weekend with 'em. I'm sure not looking forward to having her look at the body. But you're right. There is something."

"What?"

"The body, whosoever it is, has webbed toes on the left foot. And right now, I'm guessing it isn't George Gianotti."

"Harv, it has to be George. The call. Those noises I heard ..."

"Think about it, Pete. What if my little theory about him messing around with some other woman is accurate? He stages the whole thing. Makes it sound like he's been killed, then offs some skid row bum, disfigures him, dresses him up in his own clothes and plants the body in his own apartment."

"But why? He was separated. He was free to mess around with anyone he chose to. Theoretically, at least"

"That I haven't figured out yet. But there could be a lot of reasons."

"Yeah. And it could be that whoever killed George is just trying to muddy up the waters too."

"It's possible. I admit it."

"Wait! The Rolex! George ... the body ... whoever it is, was wearing a Rolex."

"So you think that makes it George?"

"Well, would you throw away a $5,000 watch like that?"

"If I wanted somebody to think it was me, I would. But the reason I don't think it's George is, if I'm a killer and I kill a rich lawyer, why would I take his eyes and teeth and leave a $5,000 watch on his wrist?"

The thought struck me dumb. It didn't figure.

"I guess we'll know when we get Maria to identify the body," I said, my voice barely audible.

"Right. I'll let you know when that happens. Meanwhile, think about what I'm saying. See if you can't make it work."

"Harv, I can't believe George Gianotti is a killer. I just can't believe it."

The truth was, I didn't know what to believe.

30

Add one-quarter cup oil to sauce pan.
Cut 2 cloves of garlic in half and add to oil.
Cover with lid and brown.
Remove garlic when browned.
Remove pan from fire and add one large
can (28 oz.) Contadina sauce or puree
(always be sure to use Contadina, Pietro,
it's a good Italian company).
Return pan to flame and simmer for one half hour.
Then add one can (6 oz.) Contadina tomato paste,
stir in and cook for ten minutes.
Add one can (28 oz.) water. Use the empty
Contadina can, Pietro.

Also add one-half teaspoon of pepper, one-half
teaspoon of salt, one tablespoon of sugar and
2 bay leaves.
Cover and bring to boil.
Lower flame and simmer for 3 hours or until
the sauce gets thick the way you like it.

I looked at the crudely handwritten recipe card with tears in my eyes. My maternal grandmother, Teresa Pignanelli, had given it to me 20 years earlier. I was 15 at the time, spending the summer with her in

West Virginia. Her proudest accomplishments in life were learning to read and write in English and teaching me to cook.

I didn't really need to refer to the recipe; it was just a private ritual I went through every time I prepared one of the dishes she had taught me. The presence of the recipe card with her writing, and her rolling pin, a 25-inch-long piece of hickory doweling I had commandeered when she died, made it almost like she was there in the kitchen with me. Helping me along, making sure I browned the garlic enough, that the bay leaves were fresh, that I mixed the tomato paste in real good.

In fact, I had altered and embellished the recipe somewhat over the years. Today, for example, I was making a double batch, more than enough to serve the six I would be feeding. But I was using only about 48 ounces of water, not the 56 ounces my grandmother's directions called for. Using less water makes the sauce thicken more quickly, and I was in somewhat of a hurry.

Ordinarily, I love to cook. I find it not only relaxing, but also very challenging. Timing everything so it comes together. Browning the ribs. Making the meatballs. Rolling the dough. Cutting the fettuccine. Rolling and knurling the gnocchi. A good cook, according to Teresa, is always in motion, checking this, stirring that, tasting something else. And a good cook absolutely never leaves the kitchen until the meal is attractively displayed on the table, ready to be totally devoured. And I'm a good cook. At least that's the consensus of friends and family. But Teresa Pignanelli gets full credit for that. All I had to do was read her recipes. And I learned to read before she did.

Today, however, I wasn't in the mood to cook at all. So Marianne, Gianni, Father Wong, Lef and Lou would just have to settle for store-bought vermicelli. I just didn't want to commit to the two or three hours it would take to make fettucine or gnocchi from scratch.

I did force myself to brown a few pounds of country ribs, cut them up and add them to the sauce.

Then I made coffee and read the *Sunday Free Press*. I didn't make my usual Sunday morning trip to Vassili's for breakfast. I rarely eat breakfast – or lunch, for that matter – when I cook. Even store-bought vermicelli is great when it's topped with Salsa di Pignanelli.

31

At one o'clock, I turned on the football game. I didn't even have the desire to bet, although I felt strongly the Vikings would easily cover the 3-point spread over the Lions.

I glanced at the game, but didn't really watch it. I was still troubled by Harvey's theory. Troubled because I was beginning to believe it could be true. If old lady Bradshaw was blitzed like Harv said, George could have staged the call and she would never have known. But I still couldn't figure why.

Another thing started to bother me. Why would George call me? Why not the police? Or 911? That thought added a little more credence to Harvey's theory. But I guess we'd never know the answer.

It's not like George and I were bosom buddies. Sure, we were friends. But, since college, we probably hadn't seen each other more than a half dozen times. We'd talked on the phone more often. But we talked business. Rarely anything personal. Hell, I hadn't even known his marriage was in trouble. Wouldn't a guy tell a friend?

And yet I still felt I knew George well enough to be certain he wasn't a murderer.

Sorry, Harvey, I can't make it work.

But I can't be sure, either.

With three minutes to go in the game, the Lions and Vikings were tied 17-17. But the Vikes were driving. They had the ball at the Lions' 36, first down. It was just a matter of time. I watched the screen intently, waiting for the inevitable last minute touchdown that would send the Lions reeling in defeat once again. I had seen it happen time after time, season after season.

On third down and short, the Vikes' quarterback faked a handoff up the middle and arced a pass to the left sideline. The Lions' right cornerback came from nowhere, tipped the pass, caught it in stride and raced 76 yards untouched.

Final score: Lions 24, Vikings 17.

I was doubly elated. First, in spite of the fact I usually bet against them, I am a tried and true Lions fan. And, second, I *didn't* bet against them. It was, in a way, like I was $330 ahead. The $300 I would have lost had I phoned in my planned bet, and the 10% juice that Fluff – and all bookies – collect on losing bets.

I got up off the sofa, and imitating the interception, dashed into the kitchen untouched.

I checked the sauce, clanging the big metal spoon around the inside of the pot a few times. It was thickening nicely and the meat was falling off the bone. Perfect.

I scooped out a big hunk and broke my vow of hunger. Better than perfect. I decided to give the Wurlitzer a rest and put a Moody Blues album on my turntable. It was a kindness for Marianne. She loves them. I'm a huge fan, too, actually. Along with the Beatles and Cat Stevens, the Moodies are among the handful groups that I enjoy who came after what I consider to be the True Era of Rock & Roll, which I define as everything pre-Beatles. It's not that I don't like a lot of the more recent groups. I do. But for this particular occasion I felt the seventies and eighties stuff was appropriate.

Marianne, Gianni and Father Wong showed up a few minutes before five. Gianni, naturally, headed for the computer; the Father, Marianne and I went upstairs.

Marianne was delighted to hear the Moody Blues playing. Father Wong was disappointed that I hadn't been at Mass.

We sat around and chatted, waiting for Lou and Lef. When they hadn't shown up at a quarter to six, I started boiling the water for the vermicelli.

They finally arrived just in time to see the vermicelli reach al dente.

Dinner brought rave reviews, as usual. I was humbly proud and accepted the kudos with all the grace and modesty I could muster. It gets easy after a while.

Then Father Wong shattered my euphoria by going into a tirade against gambling. At first I thought Marianne had put him up to it, but I soon realized it was all a put-on.

When he was finished, Lou raised his hand.

I called on him. "Lou."

He stood up. "Father Wong, I sense that your anti-gambling fervor is sincere, and as a man who has occasionally made a wager, I have no alternative but to take it personally. I would like to point out, however, that you, sir, and your organization, are among the most flagrant violators of your alleged credo, and I must, therefore, brand you a hypocrite."

Father Wong stared at him, apparently without comprehension. "What you tark about? Speak Engrish."

I caught Marianne's expression out of the corner of my eye. She was smiling, obviously enjoying the impromptu routine.

"I am talking, my dear Father, about bingo," Lou continued.

"Bingo? You mean my dog or the Wednesday-night fundraisers held in the basement of the parish hall?" The Father was getting into it; his look of indignation was masterful. Bingo was his Chihuahua. He also had an Irish Setter named Gringo.

"I think you know exactly what I'm talking about," Lou shot back.

Lef was still scarfing down pasta and ribs, but following the conversation, at least with his eyes.

Gianni was finishing off a can of black olives, showing little interest in anything else.

"Well, if you mean my dog, he's feeling much better, thank you. And if you mean our weekly social gathering to raise funds for God's work, just exactly what do you mean?" Father Wong inquired.

"I mean that you are condemning me for doing precisely the same thing you're doing. Does not one of your parishioners receive a cash stipend at the end of each bingo game? And does St. Lucifer's, uh, Luke's, not withhold a portion of the take?"

"That's right. For God's work," Father Wong agreed.

"Ah, but that's exactly what happens in the case of pari-mutuel wagering. The, uh, parishioners of Hazel Park Harness Raceway purchase their tickets, just like yours buy bingo cards. The ticket either wins or loses, just like a bingo card. Horseplayers, just like bingo players, are risking money for the chance to win money. They're gambling, plain and simple. Those fortunate enough to win collect a cash stipend, and the state, just like the church, withholds a generous amount from the pari-mutuel pool to do politicians' work. All perfectly legal."

"Legal, perhaps. But not moral," Father Wong opined.

"Oh? I fail to see the difference between the two scenarios I just painted."

Lef nodded his agreement.

"Difference is simple. One is God's work. Other is not."

"Are you suggesting that skimming is acceptable if the church does it, and immoral if the state does it?"

"Not a suggestion. A fact."

"I see," Lou said, thoughtfully, rubbing his chin. "Can I surmise, then, that bingo is the one form of gambling that has God's approval?"

Lef and Marianne both laughed out loud. Even Gianni chuckled, projecting a fleck of black olive half way across the table.

"Oh, no. Bingo not the only form of gambling okay with God," Father Wong said. "He likes raffles, too."

That's the way it went for a couple hours. Lef and Marianne actively joined the conversation after Gianni went into the living room to color.

Few subjects escaped our acid wit and scathing commentary. Eventually, they noticed that I wasn't very much a part of it, and shortly after that, everybody left, obviously a little embarrassed.

Only Gianni was his usual exuberant self, proudly showing me the White Ninja Warrior he had colored, for some unknown reason, pink.

I was embarrassed too. I hadn't meant to be rude. I was amused by the repartee, but understandably, preoccupied thinking about George. And about what I was going to do next.

Two things came to mind. A visit to the Bradshaw residence out in Belleville. And a trip back to the library. A nagging voice in my head kept suggesting there was something at the library that I had overlooked. Experience had taught me to pay attention to such suggestions.

I cleaned up the dishes, rinsed them off and put them in the dishwasher. Then I grabbed a can of Leinenkugel to help the dilute hydrochloric acid in my stomach break down the complex carbohydrates of dinner.

In my bedroom, I took a science fiction paperback off my convenient bookshelf headboard. I made it through 40 pages before I realized I didn't give a damn if the Pardalians were obliterated by the Kachunga Horde before the Bobzakians arrived.

I put the book back, turned out the light, closed my eyes and waited for Monday's arrival.

32

I was having my morning coffee and reading the *Free Press* in my office. "Satisfied", a gut-wrenching rock-and-roll screamer by the Cashmeres, was rumbling along on the cheap speakers.

It was 8:30 and I hadn't slept well. Anxiety and two plates of pasta washed down with a brew aren't conducive to a restful night. Or maybe it was the prosciutto and melon appetizer.

At ten minutes to nine, the phone rang. According to my ad in the Yellow Pages, I didn't open until nine, but it probably wasn't a prospective client anyway.

"Pete Pepper Investigations," I said, just in case.

"Mr. Pepper ... "

It was a woman's voice, a bit on the husky side. Like someone who drank or smoked a lot.

"Mr. Pepper, my name is Emily Bradshaw and I'd like to hire your services."

I almost fell off the sofa. And I did spill my coffee. But I managed to keep my voice steady.

"Of course, Mrs. Bradshaw. What is it you'd like me to do?"

"Mrs. Bradshaw? Did I say my name was Mrs. Bradshaw?" She said it kindly; almost, but not quite, amused.

"Well, uh, no. I just assumed, that is, you are *the* Emily Bradshaw, aren't you? That would make you a Mrs."

She chuckled slowly. It sounded more forced than genuine.

"I don't claim any such notoriety, Mr. Pepper, but, yes, I guess I am *the* Emily Bradshaw. And it is Mrs. I suppose I should be flattered that you've heard of me."

"Well, to be honest, Mrs. Bradshaw, I hadn't heard of you until just recently."

"Well, good. I don't enjoy being flattered anyway. But, tell me, how is it that you came to hear of me?"

"From the wife of a friend. Maria Gianotti. Her husband is your lawyer. Or was, I'm afraid."

"I see. Well, I must confess that I've heard of you, too, Mr. Pepper. In fact, George Gianotti recommended you a few years ago when I was having some, shall we say, delicate problems with my husband. Please don't feel slighted that I didn't hire you then. I chose not to pursue the matter."

"Speaking of George Gianotti, Mrs. Bradshaw, did you see him last Thursday night. Or early Friday morning? She hadn't reacted to my mention that George *was* her lawyer.

"Hmmmm, now we have to probe into another delicate matter. A Captain Sternberg asked me the same question just the other day. In fact, he was here at the house."

"I'm aware of that. Harvey – and it's Lieutenant *Stein*berg, by the way – is a friend of mine. According to him, and the phone company records, George Gianotti made a call from your house early Friday morning. It would have been just after six o'clock."

"I'll be frank with you, Mr. Pepper. I have, shall we say, a slight drinking problem. My life has been less than idyllic despite the wealth, and sadly, I often turn to the bottle for companionship. I'm not proud of the fact, but I am too proud to deny it. Now, to get back to your question, I did have an appointment with Mr. Gianotti. Only he never showed up. He was due at seven in the evening. When he still hadn't arrived by ten, I went to bed with two close companions."

"I beg your pardon?"

"Mr. Gin and Mr. Vermouth, Mr. Pepper."

I smiled a big smile, not daring to laugh out of courtesy. I suddenly decided I liked Mrs. Bradshaw.

"Oh," was all I said.

"In any event," she continued, "when your Lieutenant Steinberg called on me, I told him essentially what I'm telling you. If George Gianotti did make a phone call from my house, and I'm not disputing that, he did so entirely without my knowledge. And he entered my house without my knowledge, as well."

"I see. Uh, did Lieutenant Steinberg mention that we suspect some foul play in this matter? That George may have been injured or even killed in your house?"

"Mr. Pepper, Lieutenant Steinberg would hardly have driven all the way out to Belleville if something weren't amiss. There is nothing unusual about making a phone call. Yes. He did tell me. In a very rude fashion, I might add. And I am appalled at the notion that so vile an act may have happened in my home."

"I am, too, believe me."

Her tone of voice suddenly changed; she was getting impatient.

"I don't mean to be rude, Mr. Pepper, but if you're through with your questioning, I'd like to get back to the reason I called."

"Oh. Of course. I'm sorry." I had been so involved in our conversation, I had temporarily forgotten she had called and asked to hire me.

"Mr. Pepper, I'd like you to find my husband, Zachary."

"Huh?" Another surprise.

"My husband, Mr. Pepper. He's been gone for more than two months. I want you to find him. Is that an unusual request?"

"Oh, uh, no. Not at all. I just assumed that your reason for hiring me had something to do with George. Please. Forgive me."

"Not at all, Mr. Pepper." She sounded a little softer, mellower. "Under the circumstances, I can see how you would make such an assumption. I'm sorry to disappoint you, but as far as I'm concerned, George Gianotti is a police matter."

I cracked another smile. How many times had I heard that from Harvey?

"Oh, I'm not disappointed. In fact, I'm ready to start right now. When can I come by and get some information about your husband. Zachary, wasn't it?"

"Well, if you're ready to start, why don't you – oh no, wait! No, I'm afraid today would be inconvenient. Could you perhaps drive out tomorrow, say about lunch time?"

I certainly could. She gave me the address and directions, and I jotted them down in my notebook.

"Thank you, Mrs. Bradshaw. Shall I call first?"

"No, that won't be necessary. Just come at your convenience. And by the way, Mr. Pepper, since you are so eager to begin, let's say you're on retainer as of right now."

"But my rate is two hun ... "

"Mr. Pepper, please. Allow me to get some enjoyment out of my wealth. I don't care to know what your rates are. Just bill me at the conclusion of your investigation and be sure to include today. Is that satisfactory?"

"Well, I don't want to seem ungrateful, but ... "

She interrupted again.

"Of course! How foolish of me. I can't expect you to work out of pocket for who knows how long. When you come tomorrow, I'll give you an advance of, shall we say, $5,000?"

I almost choked. I really liked Mrs. Bradshaw.

"Uh, yes. That's more than adequate, actually."

"Agreed, then. Until tomorrow, Mr. Pepper?"

I was about to hang up when I remembered something else I wanted to ask her.

"Oh, one more thing, Mrs. Bradshaw. Your husband is in the import/ export business, isn't he?

"Why, yes. He is." Very surprised.

"Could you tell me the name of his business?"
"Why it's Bradshaw Enterprises."
"Thanks, Mrs. Bradshaw. I'll see you tomorrow."
Bingo.

33

In my business, Monday is make-it-or-break-it day. Most of the things a private investigator gets hired for happen over the weekend. Runaway kids. Extra-marital hanky panky. Family squabbles too petty or personal to take to the police. When Sunday night rolls around and the "victim" realizes or suspects that something isn't as it should be, Monday is often the first chance he or she has to call for help. Over the years, I'd say that almost half of my jobs came to me on a Monday.

And this job, on this Monday, was one of the sweetest of them all. Financially speaking, of course.

I realized as I was sipping my last cup of coffee, that I might have sounded a little too enthusiastic to Mrs. Bradshaw. Of course, she had no way of knowing my enthusiasm was not so much because she had hired me, but because she had handed me the opportunity to question her and snoop around her house. I might be able to get a lead on what happened to George in addition to the scoop on Zachary. Sometimes it's too easy.

There was another angle that had me euphoric. I could now stay close to the Gianotti case under the guise of working on the Bradshaw case. And Steinberg couldn't do much about it. At least, not officially.

The five grand up front was nothing to sneeze at, either. I've made more on some jobs, even a lot more on a couple of insurance scams I uncovered, but five grand buys a lot of trifecta tickets. Or penny stocks. And those are the areas I rely on for a good portion of my income.

Yes, this was definitely a make-it Monday.

34

Ruth Abraham had her face buried in the morning *Free Press*. I walked by and she greeted me without even looking up.

"Hi, Pete. Where you going in such a rush?"

I pulled my notebook out and waved it at her. "Overdue book," I joked. "Gotta hurry. It was due in 1976."

She chuckled and muttered something into the editorial page that I didn't catch.

I went to the computer terminal and punched up Bradshaw. I keyed the cursor past all the Edward Bradshaw entries to the single mention of Bradshaw Enterprises. Then I pressed enter. Almost immediately the words appeared on the screen:

DETROIT NEWS...Sept. 22, 1982...C-16
ENTERPRISING BUSINESSMAN
IMPORTS GREAT WALL OF CHINA

Bradshaw Enterprises, an Ann Arbor-based
import/export company, has brought a piece of
Chinese history to America. Several hundred
pieces, in fact.

Owner Zachary Bradshaw, 53, of Belleville, recently
returned from a fact-finding mission as part of the
Tri-County International Trade
Commission, announced that he would soon

have various sized chunks of the Great Wall for
sale at his retail store in Ann Arbor.

Bradshaw pulled the "coup", as he called it,
when, during a meeting in Beijing, he
overheard one of the Chinese delegates mention
that the Great Wall was undergoing massive
repairs and restoration at Tsunhua, a small city
northeast of the Chinese capital.

"I immediately saw the vast commercial
potential of bringing back authentic pieces of
the Great Wall to the United States," Bradshaw
said. "Not only should the interest be great for
Chinese Americans, but to all Americans with a
penchant for history or the unusual."

When asked what someone would do with a
piece of the Great Wall, Bradshaw suggested
paperweights, doorstops, fireplace bricks, and,
with a laugh, added that they might be very
popular as "Oriental Pet Rocks."

The article went on to talk about the composition of the Great Wall,
a wild conglomeration of materials, but essentially granite and mud
bricks. I wasn't much interested in that part, but I found something that
might be useful in the photo that accompanied the article. It was an
apparently attractive young woman, apparently because the computer
image was about as sharp as a fuzzy Polaroid. Anyway, she was holding
a chunk of the Great Wall. The piece was about twice the size of an
everyday house brick. The caption said her name was Janice Vandever,
manager of the Bradshaw Enterprises retail store in Ann Arbor.

I motioned for the kid who was working at the library for high school
credit. "Need a hard copy of this article," I told him.

"Yes sir! Be right back." He disappeared to the centrally located printer and returned in a few minutes. "That'll be one dollar, sir."

I gave him two, with a smile. I was in a good mood, pleased that I might have a lead that could give me a jump on the Bradshaw case. I decided to take a leisurely drive in the country. To Ann Arbor.

Interlude

Janny Vandever sighed heavily. I've gotta quit this damn job, she told herself for at least the hundredth time. Old man Bradshaw is a real creep. Disappears for months at a time and leaves it all on me. Sales are down! Stay open later! Get out to the warehouse and put some new merchandise on the shelves! Why don't you get your ass back here and do it yourself, you asshole?

She knew there were some more of those pieces of the Great Wall of China somewhere. They were good sellers. But where the hell were they?

She got down on hands and knees and pulled a large piece of canvas away from a bottom shelf. Was that them? Yes! Finally! As she reached into the shelf and pulled out a large chunk, an unexpected noise startled her. She turned and rose, the piece of the Wall still in her hand.

"Mr. Bradshaw? Is that you? I wasn't expecting you back until next week."

"I just got back a little early, Janny."

"Oh. Well I ... what the hell?"

Shock, followed by panic as he emerged from the shadows and advanced menacingly.

"Oh my God! What have you ... ?"

But before she could say another word, his right arm lashed out and in one motion, grasped and guided the object in her hand, crashing it against the side of her head.

After, when he made it absolutely certain she was dead, he pulled three cylindrical objects out of his overcoat pocket and bent over the body. Rising seconds later, he arranged her clothing and covered her corpse with the canvas.

35

Ann Arbor is a lively college community some 40 miles west of Detroit. As much as I hate to admit it, since it's the home of the hated University of Michigan Wolverines, archenemies of the mighty Michigan State Spartans, it's a very pretty town. Unlike State, which has a sprawling, relatively modern central campus, the University of Michigan's campus is comprised of a great number of architecturally diverse and interesting older buildings. The campus is widely scattered, more or less integrated within the city itself. It's a nice effect. Somehow, I felt it would be less intimidating to a new student. Hell, I probably would have gone there myself, but State has a great program for Criminal Justice.

My drive out I-94 was uneventful. After a quick breakfast at Vassili's, I stopped at a Gas 'n' Go, gassed and went. It was 10 o'clock, which meant I had missed whatever rush hour traffic there was between Detroit and Ann Arbor. I really had no idea how many people made that daily commute.

At the 35-minute mark of my leisurely journey, I passed Belleville. I peered off southward, trying to envision the Bradshaw mansion, and made a mental note of the elapsed time. If I planned to make it for lunch, as Mrs.

Bradshaw had suggested, I would have to leave by about 11:15 to play it safe. Of course, lunchtime doesn't always mean high noon.

Taking the State Street exit off I-94, I drove almost to the campus before turning into a side street, where I pulled out my notepad to double check the Bradshaw Enterprises address. Actually, there were two. One was an office/warehouse on the north side of town; the retail store was on Main Street.

I pulled back on to the inappropriately named State Street and drove into the heart of campus, passing by the fabled Michigan Union. A few rights and lefts later, a city parking lot greeted me with a meter that still had 35 minutes on it. I got out, put in a quarter and cheerfully started walking the three blocks to where the store should be. My Monday luck was still holding.

The sidewalks were surprisingly crowded, mostly with students who either had very light schedules or were skipping class. I passed a restaurant where a large number of them seemed to be hanging out. I noticed the name, Nacho Mama, and cringed involuntarily. My constitution does not permit spicy ethnic food before noon. Not even Italian.

Bradshaw Enterprises was next door, but my luck ran out. It was closed.

I ducked into the restaurant and approached an attractive waitress whose co-ed days were at least ten years in the past. She gave me an expectant smile.

"Can I help you?" she asked.

"I hope so," I smiled back. Can you tell me what time Bradshaw Enterprises next door opens?"

"They're supposed to open at nine, but they haven't been open at all since, gee, last Wednesday or Thursday."

"Do you know why?"

"No."

"Hmmm. You don't happen to know a Janice Vandever, do you?"

"Janny? Sure. She has lunch here all the time."

"And you haven't seen her since sometime last week?"

"No. But she works at the warehouse every once in awhile. Could be there."

"Do you know where she lives?"

"Yes, but I don't know if I should tell you. Who are you?"

I reached into my pocket, took out my wallet and showed her my I.D.

"My name's Pete Pepper. I'm a private investigator. And I'm actually looking for Zachary Bradshaw. He's missing. His wife hired me to find him. I thought Janice, uh Janny, might be able to help me."

"That's the creep who owns the store next door."

"You know him?"

"Not really. But I do know that Janny doesn't much like him. Said he was real weird."

Interesting. Weird was the same word Maria said George used to describe Emily. Or maybe that was just her interpretation of what he said.

"I see. Well, will you tell me where Janny lives? I'd really appreciate it."

"I guess so. It's in the phone book anyway. It's 519 East Washington. First block off of State Street. Big green house that's been made over into a bunch of undersized apartments for students. Janny lives on the top floor."

"She's a student?"

"Gosh no. She's my age. She just lives there. You don't have to be a student."

She handed my I.D. back and I put it away.

"Thanks. You've been a great help, miss."

"Linda. The name's Linda."

"Right. Thanks, Linda." I turned to walk out, but Linda stopped me.

"Hey Pete. Why don't you see if Janny wants to have lunch? You can bring her back here."

"Hey, good idea," I lied. "I just might do that." Once I start lying, it's hard to stop.

36

The house was right where Linda said it would be, though calling it green was stretching it a bit. It was more like cream of khaki. Or maybe a few shades above the color of a spinach lasagna noodle. It took me a few minutes to figure out that the only way to the top floor, (it was a three-story house), was a narrow wooden stairway at the rear of the right side. I climbed the stairs with a firm grip on the handrail. Not just because they were shaky; my recent experience with stairs still had me a little edgy.

The door at the top wasn't locked. It led to a hall with a single door on either side. I hadn't noticed any resident directory in front, so I flipped a mental coin and knocked on the door to the right. Almost immediately, a sweet young thing answered. She was utterly naked, and one of those rare creatures we used to fantasize about when I was a teen-ager. A natural blonde.

"Who are you?" she inquired, demonstrating all the modesty of a chimpanzee at the zoo.

"Uh, excuse me, miss. I'm looking for Janny Vandever. I'm an old friend." Yet another lie.

"Janny lives across the way. My name's Gina. Gina Del Prete."

She actually pronounced it Praytay, the way it would be in Italian. "Del Prete, eh? Must be Northern Italian."

"Huh?"

"Southern Italians generally have dark hair."

Only then did she seem to be aware of her nakedness.

"Oh. I'm sorry. I didn't mean to embarrass you. I was expecting someone else." She didn't make any move to stop embarrassing me.

"I see. Well thanks for your help. I'll just mosey across the hall and see if Janny's in." I guess my expression made her think I thought she always came to the door nude.

"Hey! Really mister. Spike Davis will be here any minute. *The* Spike Davis."

My expression did my talking for me again. It was blank.

"Come on!" she said. "You never heard of The Nails? Rusty, Brad and Spike? They only sold out Hill Auditorium last Saturday night. It was a killer concert."

"Sorry, Gina. It didn't make the headlines in the *Free Press*.

"Whatever."

She shrugged, turned and walked back into her apartment, closing the door only slightly louder than normal.

I walked over to Janny's door, marveling at my incredible nonchalance in the face of nudity. Gina, who may have been somewhat immature in the intellect department, did have an extremely mature body.

I knocked, waited a few minutes and knocked again. Louder. Sadly, Janny didn't come to the door naked.

She didn't come to the door at all.

On the way down the narrow stairs, I had to squeeze sideways to let an incredibly thin and markedly unattractive guy get by on the way up. He kept his head down, apparently not even noticing my presence. His acne-scarred face had a vacant look.

"Hey, Spike," I yelled to him, "brighten up. You're in for a fun afternoon."

He just looked down at me and scratched his shaggy, unkempt hair. There was a lot to scratch.

37

Lucky Monday was rapidly turning into a big fizzle. I was zero for two, but still had a chance to pull it out in the bottom of the ninth. I drove over to the Bradshaw Enterprises address on the north side of town. A local oldies station on the radio made the drive a lot shorter than I would have liked. "Brand New Man" by Richard "Popcorn" Wiley, an unsung hero of the True Era who was better unknown as a songwriter, was blasting away as I pulled into the parking lot. It was a great song and Popcorn had a wonderfully lively and happy voice, so I stayed in the car until it was over. Only when I got out did it register that there were no other cars in the lot.

The building had a typical configuration. A one-story brick office in front connected to a two-story cinder block warehouse that stretched some sixty feet behind it. The whole complex was set in a clearing apparently cut out of a small forest of trees, mostly maples, and with just a few brownish leaves that hadn't yet joined their relatives on the ground below. A few weeks ago, maybe, they would have made a nice post card.

I tried the door to the office. It was locked. I circled the building to the left. The only door in the back was steel, one of those roll-up garage types. It wouldn't roll up. On the way back around, I stopped at my car and got out the briefcase I carry for occasions just like this. I casually sauntered back to the office door and did my best to look like a salesman. There didn't seem to be anyone around, but why take chances.

It took all of 12 seconds to get in with my credit card. No picks needed.

The office was empty. The single desk, apparently Janny's, had a vase of wilted flowers and a manila folder on it. I checked inside the folder. Invoices. I looked around for anything unusual, but nothing stuck out. In fact, it looked as though nobody had been using the office for a while. I guess that was unusual.

I went through the door at the back of the office and into the warehouse. It was dark. I found a bank of switches on the wall and flicked one on. A row of bulbs flickered to life overhead, the kind with the metal-cage fixture you usually find in an old gymnasium. They cast enough light to reveal that the warehouse was surprisingly neat. Long rows of shelves and racks, about ten feet high, ran parallel, from the front to the back.

A single aisle dissected them, perpendicularly. I walked across the front, looking down the rows. Crates and boxes of varying sizes were stacked in the racks as far as I could see. It was just what I would expect the warehouse of an import/export company to look like.

When I finally reached the last row, I spotted something out of the ordinary. A bulky shape in the shadows on the floor at the back of the building. I walked toward it, sorry that I hadn't turned on more lights, but my instinct told me not to waste time to go back and do it.

I quickened my step as I approached the shape, now obviously a large piece of old canvas. Olive drab. Or maybe green, if you asked Linda.

Something was under the canvas, and my nose gave me a clue before I reached down and flung it aside. It had to be Janny. I'm not a coroner, but I would have guessed that she'd been dead for several days, maybe weeks. Linda said she hadn't seen her for five or six days, so it fit. Janny was wearing a pair of blue jeans and a pink, short-sleeved blouse. Not exactly wearing the jeans, though. They were pulled down to her knees, along with her panties. The blouse was partially ripped open, revealing a white bra, still firmly in place. She was flat on her back, legs straight down and arms at her side.

She looked for all the world like she could be taking a nap, except that her head was caved in. Convincingly. An oversized chunk of brick was on the floor next to her body. From the Great Wall of China, if my guess was right.

With the canvas off, the stench was unbearable, but I wasn't going to make the same mistake twice. I bent down and did a quick check of the body.

When looking at her picture, I had thought she was attractive. She wasn't attractive anymore. Her skull was literally crushed, covered with dried, caked blood.

I straightened up, placed the canvas carefully over the body and shivered involuntary, relieved at the results of my cursory exam. Her teeth and eyeballs were intact.

Suddenly I jerked around and raced back down the aisle, now fully aware of why my instinct urged me to hurry. Silent alarm! I was certain of it. The police were probably on the way right now. I had nothing to fear except maybe a breaking and entering. But I was hired by Mrs. Bradshaw, and technically, had a right to be here. And I could always say the door was unlocked. Still, I had no desire to spend the rest of my day answering questions.

I heard the siren in the distance as I raced through the office and scooped up my briefcase. I had left it by Janny's desk when I looked through the folder. I made sure the door was unlocked when I closed it, then walked briskly to my car.

I was ten yards down the road when I saw the police car in my rear view mirror. I slowed down just enough to see it swerve into the parking lot and two policemen get out and run toward the building. I took a few deep breaths, trying to slow down my heart and accelerated out of there.

Back on I-94, heading east, I finally calmed down. Either the police hadn't noticed me, or they didn't connect me with the alarm. They obviously weren't chasing me. Hell, look at the bright side, Pepper. Now you don't have to call the police. They're already there. Of course, I still had to call Harvey.

The drive home took a lot longer than the drive out. No way was I going to go faster than 65.

38

I should have called Harvey immediately, but I had to take a few minutes to think. I had a Leinenkugel in my hand to help lubricate the gears. What the hell was going on? My reputation was above reproach, but two corpses in three days could raise your own mother's eyebrows. Harvey's were almost certain to twitch.

There had to be a connection between the two murders. At least, I thought so because of the similarities of the killings. Two pulverized skulls, one possibly by a brick from the Great Wall of China, the other by who knows what? Maybe a chunk of the Sphinx. But what was the connection?

Could it be Zachary Bradshaw? He certainly had access to both locations. Hell, they were both his locations. Maybe that was why he was missing. He killed George and Janny, not necessarily in that order, and went on the lam.

Wait a minute. I didn't know for sure, yet, if the first body was George. Harvey thinks it could be a John Doe, and George is on the lam. Ah, but did George know Janny? And what reason would he have to kill her?

Well, the Leinenkugel got the gears going, all right. I drained it and went to the phone. No reason to put it off any longer.

Harvey answered the phone like he'd been taking a correspondence course from Lou, "Yeah. Steinberg, here."

"Harv, it's Pete."

"Don't gloat, Pepper! So I was wrong." Harvey often spoke in mysterious ways.

"What the hell are you talking about?" I was mystified.

"The body. It was George. No question. We got a confirmation late this morning from Mrs. Gianotti. The foot. Unmistakable. Hell, I think she knew it was him before she even saw the foot."

"The foot? What do you mean?"

"Gianotti was pteradactyl. He had webbed toes on his left foot. Don't you remember? I told you that before"

"A pteradactyl is a pre-historic bird, Harv."

"Well some kind of fucking dactyl. What's the difference?"

"Right. Sorry. So, how'd she take it?"

"Pretty well, under the circumstances. She broke down when it was over, but she took it pretty well, I guess. Let me tell you something, Pepper. Knowing that someone is dead – someone you love – or even suspecting it, doesn't make it a damn bit easier to take when you find out for sure. Not one damn bit."

"I believe you, Harv," I said, sincerely. "I hope I never have to find out."

"Yeah, well. That's the way it goes, sometimes," he said, in a tone that was as close to compassionate as I'd ever heard Harvey get.

A sudden thought broke the brief reverie, "Wait a minute, where was Maria? Did she say?"

"Yeah. She was at her sister's in Cleveland. Nephew had an emergency appendectomy. Went to help out. Everything's okay."

Not everything, I thought. Not for Maria. "Oh," was all I said.

"Hey! Wait a minute yourself, Pepper! You didn't know about the positive I.D."

"Harv, I never said I did."

"Oh. So, you didn't call just to rub it in. Why did you call?"

"Well, uh, I have some more bad news, Harv. I found another body today. In Ann Arbor. A woman, late twenties, I'd say. Name's Janny Vandever. She worked for Zachary Bradshaw."

"Well, Jesus Christ! Ain't you the super snoop. What the fuck were you doing in Ann Arbor?"

"Just doing my job, Harv. Emily Bradshaw called me this morning. She hired me to find her husband. Remember? He's been missing for two months. Or I should say, he's been gone for two months. In his line of work, he's often gone for long periods of time. I guess it got to the point where Mrs. Bradshaw figured it was too long."

"My heart bleeds. So where'd you find her body?"

"At the warehouse of Bradshaw Enterprises in Ann Arbor. The girl worked at Bradshaw's retail shop on campus, but occasionally did some work at the warehouse. When shipments came in or went out, I'm guessing. Sporadically."

"Did you notify the Ann Arbor police?"

"Didn't have to. They arrived on the scene just as I was leaving."

"And something tells me you didn't stop to exchange pleasantries." Harvey spoke more with sarcasm than anger.

"You're sharp, Harv. No wonder you made Lieutenant so fast."

He ignored the jab. "You got a bad habit with locked doors, Pepper. Gonna get you in trouble some day."

"Harv, George's door was unlocked when I got there. That's a fact!"

"Yeah, yeah. Anyway, what about the girl?"

"Dead for several days, at least, maybe longer. And her head was caved in, just like George's."

"Just like George's? You mean ... "

"No," I interrupted, "I don't mean her teeth and eyes were missing. Just that she was struck on the head with a very solid object. And, in this case, I'm fairly certain that object was a brick from the Great Wall of China."

"Pepper, you are one strange son-of-a-bitch."

I told Harv about the article I'd found at the library. It seemed to soften his assessment of my heritage.

"Hmmm," he said, "that's a pretty strong link to Zachary Bradshaw. Of course, I guess anybody could have grabbed the damn thing just because it was handy. Was there a bunch of those bricks around?"

"I don't know, Harv. I didn't see any. The place was in pretty neat order. But the light wasn't real good. And I didn't hang around too long."

"Yeah, well I guess I'll call the Ann Arbor police. See what they've got. But have a listen to this. Bradshaw and Gianotti are in cahoots. They're bringing in drugs or stolen merchandise or something. Hell, they got the perfect cover. Anyway, this Vandever dame finds out about it somehow. She's working in the warehouse and sees something she ain't supposed to see. Bradshaw knocks her on the head. Then Gianotti and Bradshaw have an argument. Maybe about the split of the profits. Or maybe Gianotti gets scared and wants out when he finds out Bradshaw committed murder. Bradshaw invites him over, says let's talk about it, then nails Gianotti the same way he got the girl. Huh?"

"One thing, Harv. It was Mrs. Bradshaw who had an appointment with George, not Zachary."

"Hey, when opportunity knocks, what's the difference who made the appointment?"

"Could be, Harv. Lot of speculation. But I have to admit it's better than anything I've got. Not a bad theory. Not bad at all."

It suddenly dawned on me that Harvey and Lou had something else in common besides their brusque phone manners. Both were great theoreticians. Harv was always theorizing solutions to crimes long before the evidence was in. And Lou had a zillion theories about gambling. I think Harvey was right a little more often than Lou.

"Well, well, what do you know?" Harvey said, obviously pleased. "For once, you're not shooting your friend on the force full of holes."

"No. I'm not"

"Listen, Pepper, while you got me in a mellow mood, let me tell you something. I like you. I really do. I yell at you all the time. Rant and rave. You can't take it personal, okay? I do it more for effect than anything else.

I mean for the people around here. It's part of my image, you know? They expect me to be mean and tough, so I don't disappoint 'em. Follow?

You've done some things for me in the past and I've done some things for you. We're a good team. Sometimes I wish you weren't freelance. We could work together for real. But since we don't, I want you to do me a favor. First, keep your nose clean. I can't promise to protect you if you keep up with the breaking and entering. I'm not saying stop, just be careful. What I want you to do is, if you find Bradshaw – wait a minute, folks, I'm talking to Pete Pepper, here – *when* you find Bradshaw, point his ass in my direction. I want to ask him some questions. Okay?"

I was moved. This side of Harvey was a real revelation. "Christ, Harv," I said, "you don't have to ask that. You know I'll give you everything I find."

"Alright. Good. Keep me posted

"I will. And, Harv ...

"Yeah?"

"I love you too."

I hung up before he could propose marriage.

39

Generally, after a heavy pasta meal like I had the day before, I like to take it easy on the carbs and calories for the next few days. My breakfast at Vassili's had been toast and coffee. Now I was preparing the only other meal I'd have the rest of the day – a heaping helping of sliced melon and prosciutto, a spicy, dry-cured Italian ham whose flavor was magnificently magnified when mixed with a forkful of cantaloupe. The first taste hadn't reached my mouth when the phone rang.

I left the plate on the table and hurried over to the kitchen wall phone to answer. It was a woman's voice.

"Is this Pete Pepper?" she asked in a friendly tone.

"Yes it is," I replied. "And who is this?"

"Mr. Pepper, this is Denise Brown calling from WKWZ-FM. If you can answer our question of the day, you'll win two front row tickets to one of the hottest concerts of the year – Girls Without Dates, playing at the Pine Knob Music Theater next month. And since we haven't had a winner all day, you'll also win a complete set of the Girls' albums, including their latest, *500 Pounds of Chocolate*."

I thought I knew all the radio stations in and around Detroit; WKWZ was a new one on me; but then, new ones were popping up all the time. And I was always up to the challenge of a rock and roll trivia question, so I responded eagerly.

"Great, what's the question?"

"In the late sixties, a group called the Dellwoods had a one-shot hit record, and were never heard from again. For the prizes I just mentioned, Mr. Pete Pepper of Southfield, what was that song?"

I knew the answer immediately. The name of the song was "She Got a Nose Job," but it was never a hit. In fact, it was never released. The record, if you could even call it that, was a cardboard pullout from an old issue of Mad Magazine. My brother Domenic collected Mads and I'd always find them lying around the house. For some reason, I had torn the record out and added it to my growing collection of 45s. Except for me and my old girlfriend at Michigan State, I didn't think anybody in the world remembered it. We used to play it over and over, laughing and singing along together.

"Do you have an answer, Mr. Pepper?" the voice interrupted my thoughts.

And suddenly my thoughts realized the voice was familiar.

"Eva, is that you?" I asked, hopeful and joyful at the same time.

"Aw, shit!" she said. "How the hell did you know it was me?"

Eva, whose last name was Marino, occasionally sprinkled her sentences with cuss words.

"Because you and I are the only two people alive who remember the Dellwoods," I laughed. "Other than the Dellwoods themselves. Where are you?"

"I'm at the Michigan Inn. Doing some location scouting for a feature that's shooting in Detroit."

Eva had been a communications major at State. After graduation, she went out west, worked for a few ad agencies as a commercial producer, and then latched on to a job in the production department at Orion Pictures. It was a bittersweet parting when she left. We had been hot and heavy lovers in college, and I guess I had notions of eventually marrying her. I wasn't really shocked when she chose a career over me, but I was disappointed. Still, we remained close friends, kept in touch and occasionally met for a joint vacation, most recently in Las Vegas a few years back. And I still had hopes that we'd wind up together some day, with or without the benefit of marriage.

"Terrific," I said. "How long are you in town?"

"Hard to say. Maybe three or four days, maybe through the weekend."

"Well, we've got to get together," I said, with just a touch of apprehension. "Are you going to have any time?"

"As a matter of fact," she replied, "I was hoping maybe you could spend a few hours in my pants tonight."

My silence was broken by her raucous laughter.

"Uh, is that a joke?" I finally croaked.

"Well, why don't you invite me over and we'll find out."

"Great! Come on over. I'm free right now."

"Can't. Have to make some calls, set up some appointments. Can we meet for dinner later? Then go back to your place, of course."

"Damn. I wasn't planning to eat dinner tonight. But we can still go somewhere. You can eat. I'll have coffee, and we'll talk ... "

"Okay," she chimed in. "What's the name of that place with the veal parmigiana?"

"Giovanni's? Or do you mean Vassili's?"

"The one that's close to your place."

"Vassili's."

"Great. What time should I come by?"

"Whenever you're ready. I'll be here."

"All right. Pete, I'm really looking forward to seeing you," she said, seriously.

"And I'm really looking forward to seeing your pants."

40

Just as I lifted the prosciutto and melon to my mouth, the phone rang again. It was Harvey. And he sounded in a good mood.

"I forgot to ask you something, Pete. With all that sweet talk going on, it slipped my mind. How'd you like to go for a ride tomorrow?"

"Harvey! Are you asking me on a date?"

"Don't fuck with me, Pepper. I'm in a good mood. Don't ruin it."

"Sorry. Just kidding. A ride where?" I asked. "And when?"

"Tomorrow morning. To Belleville and environs."

I wanted to congratulate him on the big word, but I was afraid he'd consider it fucking with him. "But I'm already going to Belleville," I said instead. "I have a lunch appointment with Emily Bradshaw."

"Suit yourself. Just thought you might want to tag along. I'm going to see some people who might be able to help you find Zachary Bradshaw."

"You're kidding! Who?"

"Oh, Ralph Spaulding, Kay Kimberly and Edith Pringham." Harv was enjoying himself teasing me. I had never heard of any of them.

"And who might they be?" I inquired.

"Emily Bradshaw's gardener, nurse and housekeeper, respectively," he said.

"Three employees? I thought there were just two."

"You told *me* there were two. You were wrong. But your suggestion to check out the local banks paid off. Not that I wouldn't have done it without your input. The gardener and housekeeper have accounts at

Washtenaw Savings and Loan; the nurse at First National of Ypsilanti. And they all deposit checks signed by Emily Bradshaw, twice a month."

I thought about Harvey's offer. I definitely wanted to go. Hell, Mrs. Bradshaw said to come at my convenience. Maybe I could have a late lunch with her.

"You know damn well I want to go, Harv," I said. "What time are you leaving?"

"Oh, eight-thirty, nine o'clock"

"Alright, but we'll have to take separate cars. Do you mind?"

"Hell, no. The city pays for my gas."

"Okay," I said. "Why don't we meet at Vassili's for a bite first. Then I'll follow you."

"Sounds like a plan. But let's meet around eight if you want to eat first. I don't want to get out there too late and it's about a forty five minute drive."

"Thirty five," I corrected.

41

I hadn't taken three steps toward the prosciutto and melon when the phone rang again. This time, it was Maria Gianotti. She didn't sound well.

"Hi, Pete," she said, her voice a monotone.

"Hello, Maria. I'm so sorry about George. Sorry you had to see him like that. It must have been terrible."

"Pete, I want you to do something for me." She totally ignored my inept attempt at condolences. Or, more likely, she didn't even hear me.

"Of course, Maria. Anything. Anything I can do at all."

"George's funeral is Wednesday," she went on flatly, "I want you to go with me."

"Okay, I ... "

"I want you to come over and pick me up at 9:30."

"No problem ... "

"Then I want you to take me home after."

"Alright ... "

"And I want you to stay with me."

"Uh ... "

"Do you understand? I want you to be with me."

"Sure, Maria, I'll stay with you, but ... "

"Goodbye."

She hung up and I just stood there, dazed. For a good while. Do I understand? Well, I think I understand your intentions, Maria. They seem pretty clear. But I don't understand why.

Even when it's warm, prosciutto and melon is delicious. But somehow, when I finally finished, I had a really bad taste in my mouth.

42

I looked across the table at Eva, who was digging into the spaghetti that came as a side dish with her veal.

Chris had put us in a booth in a closed section. God, Eva was amazing! In some ways, she reminded me of Marianne. Eva had short black hair and she wore it close cropped. The way it framed her face, with her high cheekbones, aquiline nose and dark, mischievous eyes created an utterly remarkable effect. One moment you'd say she was cute and pixyish.

But, when you looked again, she'd be stunningly beautiful. Marianne wore her hair shoulder length and was a little taller, but they were both petite by anyone's standards. And the total package, in both cases, was extremely attractive.

There were even personality similarities, the most obvious of which, was a great sense of humor. They both loved to laugh, and did so at the slightest provocation. Eva had a sparkle in her eyes now as, between bites, she told me about the movie she was scouting locations for. Her demeanor underscored the one glaring difference between her and Marianne. Eva was much more outgoing, bubbly, vivacious. She could strike up a conversation with, and be comfortable around anyone, even a complete stranger.

Marianne lived in a shell by comparison. She only loosened up a bit when she was with someone she knew extremely well. Like me. And Father Wong. And maybe Lef and Lou, if I were present too.

It wasn't really fair to be critical of Marianne, though. Not for that particular aspect of her personality. Eva, after all, hadn't lost a husband. Nor did she have a young son to support. Circumstances like those can put a damper on anyone's outlook. I took a drink of my iced tea, and pointed a few understanding nods in Eva 's direction, hiding the fact that my mind had been wandering.

"Anyway," she said, after trying to describe the movie, "that's why I can't really decide if it's a drama or a comedy. I guess it's a little of each. What do you think?"

"I think you should start wearing a bra," I said, changing the subject to cover my lack of attentiveness.

She laughed, putting her hand to her mouth to keep spaghetti from flying out. "That's rich," she said. "You were the guy who encouraged me to go braless in college!"

"Yeah, but I had an ulterior motive then," I reminded her. "It made it much easier to get you naked."

She chuckled again. "That's right! You were the worst bra un-hook-er in the Big Ten."

"Big Ten, hell," I corrected. "The entire NCAA!"

She looked at me and winked as she took a bite of one of Vassili's crunchy breadsticks. "Well, look at the bright side," she said. "My being braless will help you get me naked faster tonight."

"Yeah," I agreed, "and if you don't cover yourself up better, I just might do it in here."

Eva looked down at herself, looked around and casually buttoned the top two buttons of her blouse with one hand.

We just sat there, looking at each other and smiling while she finished her meal. Neither of us said much, except with our eyes.

Later, when we left, I noticed Wanda, my favorite night waitress, giving me a dirty look from the kitchen door.

What her eyes were saying was unprintable.

43

We rode back to my place in silence. Eva was driving a rented Camaro. We had taken her car so she would be able to pull up in the driveway behind mine since she would be leaving in the morning before me.

At the top of the stairs, still 20 feet from the bedroom, we embraced. Our kisses earlier, when she came by before we left for Vassili's, had been quick, friendly. These were not. They were deep and lingering, what my brother Domenic used to call "gumswappers."

"Oh Pete," Eva said, when we eventually pulled apart, "that was wonderful!"

"It sure was," I agreed. "I love the taste of veal parmigiana."

She gave me a quick look, realized I was teasing and smiled.

"No wonder I miss you so much," she said. "I can't tell you how many times I've thought about ... what might have happened if I hadn't moved to California."

"Me, too," I said, putting my arm around her as we walked into the bedroom.

"It's just that, well, my career is important to me too. But I'm still not sure I did the right thing ... "

I put my finger to her lips. "It's alright, Emm," I said. Emm was short for Eva Marie Marino, my term of endearment for Eva. "We don't need to talk about it now."

But we talked about it anyway.

"It's funny," I went on, "but I honestly think that, if we were meant to be, we would have been."

"Or maybe we still could be," she said, removing her blouse, and unashamedly unzipping my fly.

"Well, we could sure give it a try for a night."

I sat down on the bed, kicked off my shoes and eased out of my slacks.

Eva, now completely unclothed, walked over to my dresser and turned on the small lamp. I smiled, remembering that she had preferred complete darkness. I liked full light. This was our compromise.

Shadows played across her body as she glided toward me.

"You know why I'm rubbing my feet on the carpet?" she grinned as she climbed into the bed next to me.

I smiled back, nodding, and we both said it at the same time.

"Ecstatic electricity."

44

I have never considered myself a great lover. Maybe it's because I'm not a casual lover. At least not anymore. As a teenager, I suppose you could say I was indiscriminate, but after college, or, more precisely, after Domenic's death, sex lost much of its appeal to me. I suppose the real reason was Marianne. While something in my moral fiber would never let me sleep with her, something else kept me from sleeping with anyone else. Guilt, I guess.

Not that I was celibate. Not at all. With a friend like Lou Bracato, a man obsessed with sex in general and breasts in particular, it's difficult to keep your thoughts always pure. But, I had to really know a woman, had to have serious emotional feelings toward her, before I would make love to her.

And I use those words intentionally. Make love. Not have sex. Not hop in the sack. Not screw. Not fuck. Not have a one-night stand.

Make love.

And there weren't many women in my life I really wanted to make love with. Least of all Wanda, who, in fact, was the last woman I, uh, had screwed.

Eva was such a woman, though. And on this particular night, I wasn't just a great lover. I was a magnificent lover. *We* were magnificent lovers. The sensitivity, the electricity, the ecstasy was incredible. It was surely sex as God had intended. For no pleasure since the beginning of Creation could have been greater than what we shared that night.

45

At about four in the morning, when the pent up lust of two years apart was sated, we sat on the sofa, still naked. Eva was sucking on one of those feminine designer cigarettes, just like in the movies. I was watching her, puffing on an all-tobacco, long-filler, hand-rolled Honduran, one of my special stock for occasions like this.

As a fitting tribute to our recent activity, I had punched in a selection of Marvin Gaye and Smokey Robinson tunes on the Wurlitzer. Nehi and Nesbitt were curled on the floor in front of the jukebox, purring along when a song came on they especially liked.

Stubbing her cigarette out in my crystal cigar ashtray, Eva stretched languorously and brought her hands down across her breasts.

"Tell me the truth, Pete," she smiled, "do you think my boobies are too small?"

I looked her in the eye and then down at her breasts. They weren't large; in fact, they were smaller than Marianne's. At least, they appeared to be. I have never seen Marianne's bosom unencumbered by fabric, but if her bikini was honest, she was a little larger. Eva 's breasts were beautiful, however. Perfectly symmetrical, well shaped, and capped with oversized, protruding dark brown nipples that I have always found exciting. As for size, though, I guess they were what a men's magazine caption writer would call "perky."

I pulled the cigar out of my mouth and slowly blew the smoke at the ceiling. I rubbed my upper lip with my free hand and gave Eva a look as though I were choosing the words for my answer very carefully. In fact,

I was. Eva was not an "anything-more-than-a-handful-is-wasted" kind of girl.

"What kind of a question is that?" I stalled.

"I just want to know what you think, that's all," she responded, batting her eyelids.

I shook my head. "Emm," I said, "all I can tell you is that I think they're beautiful. I love them just the way they are."

She gave me a dubious pout. "You can love boobies this small?"

"Sweetheart, I don't love them because of their size; I love them because they're yours."

I was pleased with my spontaneous answer; I thought it was a good one. It was certainly an honest one. She didn't seem to be so sure.

"So you won't come out and say they're not too small."

"I thought that's what I was saying," I said. "They're not too small. Connie and Libby are perfect."

"Oh my God" she said, laughing. "That's what you used to call them in college! Connie on the right and Libby on the left. Remember? You actually had to explain to me the Connie was short for conservative and Libby for liberal."

"Still my favorite girls in the whole world."

"Well, what would you say if I told you I've been thinking about getting implants?"

I looked her straight in the eye and recited a poem written by my illustrious friend and internationally known breast authority, Lou Bracato. The same Lou Bracato who was fond of saying "Look at the chick on those tits," and once observed, "Nice boobs for a blind girl," at an advertising league softball game.

"Too much breast below the nipple.
All that flesh and not a ripple."

"And what is that supposed to mean?" she asked, with no indication she was amused.

"It means you would be turning those beautiful works of God into ugly works of man. It's a terrible idea."

She reached over and kissed me lightly on the lips. "Good answer," she said. "You know I really wouldn't do such a thing, don't you?"

"Yes. I know," I said, even though I had never given it any thought.

And then, without another word spoken, just for old time's sake, we made love again on the sofa.

46

At 7:15, after a long and wonderful hot-and-cold shower together, Eva was dressed and ready to leave. She had things to do back at the hotel in preparation for a late morning meeting at a potential location. As we walked down the stairs, I could sense that something was wrong; something was definitely troubling her. At the bottom of the stairs, I stopped her, put my hands on her shoulders and asked her about it.

"What is it, Emm? You seem edgy."

She turned her eyes away, then brought them back, locked onto mine.

"Pete," she said sheepishly, "I'm sure this is unnecessary and it's kind of too late to do anything anyway, but I have to ask you about what we did last night."

"You mean you don't know what we were doing? My God! You were there."

Her grin blossomed into a full smile, ending in a soft chuckle. "This is really awkward," she said. "I'm talking about, you know, vener ... "

It suddenly hit me. Eva had told me she started taking the pill just for her visit. So, it wasn't getting pregnant she was worried about. It was the fact we hadn't used those little latex devices sold for the prevention of disease only.

"VD," I interrupted. "AIDS, gonorrhea, herpes, and let's not forget chlamydia."

Her face reddened slightly. "Well, it's just a reality of the times."

"You're right," I reassured her. "I didn't mean to sound sarcastic. Uh, how about you?"

I thought for a moment she was going to cry. But she fought it off, and with her lips trembling ever so slightly, she answered.

"You may find this hard to believe, Pete," she said bravely, "but it's true. I haven't been with another man for two years."

"Terrific!" I smiled. "Neither have I."

47

I had every reason in the world to be totally exhausted. But, it was with an exhilarating smile that I pulled into Vassili's parking lot. Seeing Eva again, being with her, had put me into a euphoric mood that transcended the need for sleep. I was realistic enough to know it would catch up with me later; I only hoped it wouldn't be until well after my meeting with Emily Bradshaw.

On the way to Vassili's back-door entrance, I noticed Harvey's unmarked sedan across the already crowded lot. It was one of those big, generic looking jobs. If you couldn't read the nameplate, you wouldn't know which one of the Big Three was responsible. Seeing it was no surprise; Harvey is rarely late for a meeting. Especially when food is involved. And it was virtually a given that I would be picking up the tab.

Chris greeted me near the cash register and pointed me over to where Harvey was seated, his head buried in the *Wall Street Journal.* He was wearing shiny black wing tips with a rumpled tan suit. The effect was as conspicuous as green olives topping an ice cream sundae. The suit was by his favorite designers, Polly and Ester. Which meant it was also out of season. He looked up as I sat down.

"Morning, Pete," he said cheerfully. "Hope you don't mind, but I got here a little early, so I already ate." He gestured to the empty bowl in front of him.

"Not at all," I said. "How is the oatmeal today?"

"It's good. Damn good. Good for you too."

"Hmm. Think I'll stick with eggs," I said. "And some coffee," I added as Chris set a cup down in front of me.

Harvey shrugged, and then made a show of folding his *Journal* and placing it on the floor under his chair. He had a look of smug satisfaction.

"So," I asked, "did you have a big day in the market?"

"Not exactly," he replied, "but my IBM is up a point and a quarter."

"Your what?" I was surprised.

"My IBM. Big Blue. The bellwether of the Big Board."

"Harvey, you've been watching Wall Street Week too much."

Harvey sounded a little perturbed. "What the hell are you talking about?"

"How many shares of IBM do you have? Fifty? Sixty? A hundred?"

"I've got seventy two and a half shares. What's your point?"

"What's IBM going for? About 147?"

"151 and 3/4. So what?"

I pulled out a pencil and did some quick figuring on my placemat. "So you've got eleven grand tied up in a stock that has to go up 14 bucks a share for you to make another thousand, which is about a 9% return on the principal."

"Hey, I'm planning for my retirement," Harvey said, defensively. "I need safety."

"Horseshit," I retorted. "You need money. And you aren't going to get it that way."

Harvey took a deep breath and sipped on his coffee as Chris, without my ever ordering, set a breakfast special down in front of me. Then Harv set his cup down and nodded his head. I could see him struggling for self-control.

"All right, all right," he finally said. "I'm a new man. I'm not gonna get belligerent. I'm just gonna stay calm and listen to what my friendly investment advisor has to say."

I shrugged. "It's obvious. Buy cheaper stocks. Stocks that, if they go up a buck or two, are giving you a 5, 10, 20 percent return."

"Yeah? Like what?"

"Hey, Harv," I said, "I'm only licensed to give general advice, not specific."

Harvey must have thought that was funny, because he did something he rarely does. He laughed. A big, loud belly laugh that eventually diminished to a guffaw and finally subsided to a guttural chuckle. "That's pretty good, Pete," he said. "But, seriously, what sort of stocks do you own?"

"Well, first of all," I cautioned him, "I don't recommend that you take the kind of risks I take. What you said a few minutes ago has a lot of validity. I mean, you're not that far from retirement and you don't want to throw away everything you've saved. But I'll tell you something – and this is just for your ears, Harv. For the past 3 years, I haven't bought a stock that cost more than $10 a share. Over that period of time, I've averaged a profit of more than $40,000 a year."

"Jesus Christ," Harv said, obviously impressed, "that's not a hell of a lot less than my fucking salary!"

"That's just the last three years, Harv," I told him. "It took me a while to develop my strategy. And I had plenty of bad years along the way."

"Sounds like you've made up for it, though," he said, waving his empty coffee cup at Chris. "Uh, what kind of risks do you think a guy in my shoes should take?"

"Strategy-wise, you should do it the same way I do. Buy a cheap stock, try to ride it for a double, then sell half. If you only get 30, 40 percent or so, before your patience runs out, sell it all and take the profit. What I'd do differently in your case is up my limit to maybe $12 or $20 stocks. Although that obviously makes it harder for the stock to double."

Harvey was taking notes on his placemat. He looked up when I stopped talking. "That sounds easy enough," he said," but what if the stock goes down? And how do you know which stocks to pick?"

"Hey, there's always the downside risk, Harv. Just set a limit, then sell if it goes down. I'm sure your broker handles trailing stops. As for picking stocks, just read, read and read some more. Look for companies with new products or services that get you excited, or have universal appeal. Then make educated guesses. Hey, you're a cop. You have pretty good instinct. Use it."

Harv pursed his lips, pensively. "What percentage are we talking here? For the downside sell signal, I mean?"

"Depends," I told him. "A $10 stock, you might go 15, 20%; a $5 stock, maybe up to 25%. But I'd set a dollar limit, not a percentage. For example, I bought a stock a few years back that cost 5/32. That's 15.625 cents. If it goes down just 1/32, which it did, you're already off 20%. In that instance, I was prepared to ride it to zero, but that's why I like to set a number limit instead of a percentage."

"Five fucking thirty seconds?" Harv scoffed. "You have to be an idiot to buy a stock that cheap."

"Not necessarily," I interjected. "I read about this stock in more than one place. *Personal Finance. The Penny Stock News.* A couple of other advisory services I was subscribing to. The thing that caught my eye was the yield. It was in the high twenties."

Harv's eyes bulged. "You're kidding! What the hell's the name of this stock?"

"Telefonos de Mexico. The Mexican Telephone Company. I bought 50,000 shares at 5/32, eventually sold 50,000 at 13/16 for an after-commission profit of around $30,000, and I still have more than 12,000 shares left because the bulk of the dividend was in stock."

"Incredible!" was all Harvey could say.

"And lucky, too," I admitted. Then, looking at my watch, "Harv, I could talk about stocks all day. But right now, we've both got some people out in Belleville to talk to, so we'd better get going. What do you say?"

He said, "Thanks for breakfast, my friend."

And handed me the check.

Interlude

Kay Kimberly set the Bible down and went into the kitchen. The water would be boiling any minute and the teabag was already in the cup. Just as it began to whistle, the doorbell rang. Turning off the stove, she went back into the living room and peered out the window.

The caller's back was to the door, right arm down and holding a black valise that looked for all the world like a doctor's case! Now who could that be, Kay thought? A doctor making a house call in this day and age? She smiled at such a preposterous notion.

The figure on the porch had already opened the screen door, so when Kay opened the inner door she was quite startled when she was forcibly shoved backwards.

"Good afternoon, Kay. Are you surprised to see me?"

"Oh my God. What's going on? What are you doing here? What do you want?

Kay stood frozen in shock as the intruder gave the room a cursory glance and spotted what he was looking for.

"I've heard so much about your beautiful candlesticks, I just wanted to see them for myself.

"Candlesticks?" Those are nothing special, they're from a garage sale."

"Oh, but you're wrong Kay," he said, picking one up. "They're very special. This one in particular. See?"

Suddenly the heavy silver stick arced through the air striking Kimberly flush on the left temple, knocking her to the floor. After a few more whacks for good measure, he dragged the body into the kitchen and stripped it naked. Reaching into the black bag, he pulled out some discardable needles and several bottles of pills.

When he was finished, he noticed something out on the back porch, hanging on a post.

"Perfect," he thought. "Why didn't I think of that in the first place?"

48

"Okay, here's the plan," Harvey was saying as we leaned against his car. "You follow me. Might as well just go right down Southfield to I-94. Take it to the Rawsonville Road exit. Head south, and just past Huron River Drive, there's a donut shop. We'll leave your car there and go to Ypsilanti in mine. That's where two of 'em live. The third one, the housekeeper, lives in Rawsonville. If you got the time when we get back, you can go with me to see her. If not, hop in your car and go see the Bradshaw dame. S'alright?"

Rawsonville Road, I thought to myself. Why did I think we'd be getting off at Belleville Road? I hoped Harvey wouldn't remember that I had said it would only take 35 minutes. He had a way of rubbing little mistakes like that back in your face.

"Sounds fine to me," was all I said.

"Good. Then let's get go ... shit, wait a minute," he yelled as he ran back into Vassili's. A minute later he came out smiling. He folded the placemat he had taken notes on and put it in the inside pocket of his suit jacket. "I'll take any help I can get," he said, almost meekly.

I laughed and walked over to my Saab. As I got in, Harvey gave me the final touch of his plan.

"Pete! One more thing," he shouted. "If we should get separated, I'll wait for you inside the donut shop."

49

We didn't get separated until just before Detroit Metro Airport. Harvey managed to get behind a slow haul-away full of shiny new Detroit-built family sedans. By the time I was a good two hundred yards ahead, he still hadn't emerged from behind it. I didn't stick around to see when – or if – he did. I was at the donut shop for seven minutes before he arrived. I walked up to his car with two large styrofoam cups of coffee, tops on for highway drinking.

"Ah, good morning monsieur," I said in my inadequately best French accent. "You ordered the cafe blanc, did you not?"

"If that means black, I'll take it," he growled.

I pulled back the one I had proffered and handed him the other cup, black. "That would be this one, then," I said. "And because of my faux pas, there will be no charge for monsieur."

"Thanks, frog ass," he said, grabbing the cup.

I walked around to the passenger side and got in. Harvey was ripping a semi-circle out of the edge of his top. A nifty trick for minimizing leg-scalding coffee spills on the open road. Minimizing, not eliminating. I did the same as Harv headed us back toward I-94.

"You were determined to make it in 35 minutes, weren't you?" Harvey gave me a sour look.

"Or else you were determined to take 45 minutes," I shot back at him. "Actually, I was wrong," I added. "My timing was to Belleville Road. I didn't realize we were going as far as Rawsonville. I guess I just assumed Mrs. Bradshaw's employees lived in Belleville, too. My mistake. Please accept my humble apologies, monsieur."

He turned to say something, then saw that I was holding out a nutty donut wrapped in wax paper. I had hidden it in my jacket pocket.

"Ooh! Don't mind if I do." Harvey accepted the donut eagerly and made it disappear in five and a half bites. "By the way," he mumbled with the half bite still in his mouth, "Mrs. Bradshaw doesn't live in Belleville. That's just the mailing address. She lives outside the city limits, between Belleville and Rawsonville. Had a hell of a time finding it the other day. It's on a private drive off Lakeview Drive, right in a clump of woods between Belleville Lake and the freeway. Big fucking joint. Pretty isolated."

"You'll have to show me how to get there when we're done," I suggested.

"Sure. It's easy. You just have to go over the same bridge three times and ask directions at five different gas stations. No problem."

I nodded, smiling, and took a sip of my coffee. Then I closed my eyes and leaned back to enjoy Harvey's leisurely driving pace.

50

Harvey's voice woke me up. "Jesus Christ. What the hell is going on here?"

I shook off the grogginess and looked around. We were in a sparsely populated residential area; somewhere in Ypsilanti, I assumed. The scattered houses were half a football field apart. The one nearest us, a small shingle-sided ranch set back about 30 feet from the gravel road, had five cars in and around the driveway. Two black-and-white Ypsilanti police cars, a dark blue Washtenaw County sheriff's car, a rusty old Toyota and a plain brown sedan that instinct told me belonged to the coroner. Instinct and the sight of a distinguished-looking gentleman in a grey suit and topcoat talking somberly to the assembled officers, one of them also wearing a suit.

"Where are we?" I asked Harv.

"We're at the home of Ms. Kay Kimberly, part-time nurse to Emily Bradshaw. The late Ms. Kimberly from the looks of it. Let's check it out."

Harv pulled into the drive behind the cars. Only when I got out did I realize that the front of my pants were wet from spilled coffee. Shit. There was nothing I could do now. Tying my jacket around my waist would be more embarrassing as far as I was concerned.

The group of men stopped talking and one of the uniformed policemen moved to come toward us. Harv cut him short with a wave of his open wallet. "Lieutenant Harvey Steinberg, Homicide, Southfield Police," he said.

"You're a little bit out of your jurisdiction, aren't you, Lieutenant?" the suit said.

"They're just looking for a place to go to the bathroom," one of the cops piped in. "Looks like that one's a little late, though. Ha ha." It was the one who had started to come toward us. He was pointing to my crotch and his laughter brought a round of snickers from the others.

"Maybe I'm just happy to see you, handsome," I lisped. " Is there someplace inside where we can go dance?" My lisp isn't much better than my French. Still, it brought a renewed round of laughter. From everyone but the man I had pegged as the coroner.

"Gentlemen, please!" he said. "There's been a murder in the house and we're out here laughing."

"Shit!" Harvey cursed. "Is it Kay Kimberly?"

"That's who it is," the other suit said. "I'm Detective Toaz. Brad Toaz, Ypsilanti Police, Homicide. Which explains why I'm here. How about you?"

Harvey sketched out the story of George and Janny and the missing Mr. Bradshaw. He also introduced me and explained that I was under retainer to Mrs. Bradshaw, hired to look for her long-absent husband. He didn't mention the names of the gardener or housekeeper; or the fact that we planned to go see them.

"Holy Christ," Toaz said when Harv had finished. "You mean to tell me we now have three deaths that are somehow tied to these Bradshaws?"

"Maybe four," I added.

"Four? Oh. You mean that Mr. Bradshaw might be dead too. Yeah, I suppose so." Toaz's initial hint of hostility had dissipated. He was all business now. I decided I liked him.

"I wonder if we could have a look at the body," Harvey said to no one in particular.

"I'm afraid not," Toaz replied.

"Why not? I thought we had established a little spirit of cooperation here." Harv was obviously surprised.

"Oh, we have," Toaz assured him. "It's just that the body is gone. Believe me, you wouldn't have wanted to see it anyway."

"Maybe I can be of some assistance," the distinguished gentleman said. "I'm Jack Kotwica, Washtenaw County Coroner. If you were looking to establish some commonality in the killings, I'd have to say, from what you've told us about the others, that you've got it. Cause of death was a blow – several blows, actually – to the head with a heavy, blunt instrument. There were some candlesticks inside, one of which appears to be the murder weapon. They're on their way to the lab now. As for other similarities, well, there was some minor mutilation. A dozen discardable hypodermics were stuck into the breasts and abdomen; the mouth was full of assorted pills and capsules; and a large thermometer was removed from the rectum."

Somehow, I appreciated Kotwica's use of the impersonal "the," instead of the pronoun "her." It showed me a sense of compassion, a bit of humanity.

"I'm inferring that the body was nude," I said to him.

"That's correct, Mr. Pepper."

"Christ! I was wondering how you spotted a thermometer up her as-er, uh, rectum," Harvey blurted out.

"Well, as a matter of fact," Kotwica told him, "that was easy. It wasn't a medical thermometer. It was the kind you keep outside to tell the ambient temperature. It was a glass cylinder mounted on a rectangular piece of metal. And it was fourteen inches long."

Harvey didn't say a word. His red face was enough.

"Uh, do you have a positive I.D. on the body?" I interjected quickly to cut short Harv's embarrassment.

"Affirmative," Toaz said. "She's inside the house with a paramedic right now. Some lady that comes around every Tuesday and discusses the Bible with Kimberly. Used to, that is. Apparently, the old lady was a former patient; in-house care, that sort of thing. She said there was no answer when she knocked, but the car was there, so she knew Kay was home. Tried the door and it opened. She found the body in the kitchen. Coroner said she'd been dead about a week. Poor old lady was hysterical, so the medic stayed to calm her down."

"Anything suspicious about her?" Harv wanted to know.

"The old lady? No. Not a chance. I'd let you go talk to her, but I think she might be under sedation by now. You'd be wasting your time anyway." Then Toaz turned to the group of cops, "Hey, one of you guys go check on the medic. You gotta give him a ride back. And see if the lady needs a ride too."

"Is that her car over there?" Harvey pointed to the rusty Toyota.

"The old lady? Nah, she walked here. Lives about a quarter of a mile away. That's the deceased's car," Toaz said.

"That's who I meant," Harv said. "Mind if I look at it?"

"Be my guest," Toaz shrugged, gesturing to the car.

Harv went over to the Toyota, looked in, walked around it, looked under it, and then got in.

"Lieutenant Steinberg is famous for his quick solutions," I explained to Toaz. "He's already formulated and discarded thirty or forty theories. If he doesn't come back with a working scenario, I'll be surprised."

Harvey surprised me. "The whole thing's got me stumped," he said when he returned. "If it weren't for the Bradshaw connection, I'd say it was a different killer. The needles, the pills and the thermometer. What purpose did they serve? Just some whacko, the way I see it. A random, senseless killing."

"Well, that's certainly possible," Toaz said, smiling in my direction.

I didn't know if Harv's speech qualified as a scenario or not. Apparently, Toaz thought it did. We spent another ten minutes talking; Harvey making arrangements to exchange information with Toaz. He gave Toaz the name of Captain Trezona of the Troy Police, who was technically in charge of the investigation of George's murder since the body was found in Troy. Toaz had friends in the Ann Arbor Police Department and promised to pass on anything important from the Vandever investigation.

I exchanged business cards with Toaz and Kotwica, and then we shook hands all around and left. As we approached Harvey's car, the cop who I had done the routine on yelled over, "Hey, why don't you give *me* your card, sweetheart? I might want to call you and go dancing sometime!"

This brought a few gut rumbles from his buddies, and I had to smile, too, as we drove away. I was in an unusually cheerful mood for a guy who had been awake all night and at the scene of three murders in the last four days.

Interlude

Ralph Spaulding was near tears as he looked sadly at the beech tree he had just cut down. So young, he thought, as he kneeled and examined the tree, riddled with beech bark disease. Resigned to the tree's fate, he revved up his chain saw, cut the trunk into two-foot sections and carried them to the woodpile next to his main shed.

After returning the chainsaw to its shelf, he grabbed a couple of shovels and headed back to dig out the stump. In spite of the cool weather, Spaulding was sweating profusely as, half an hour later, he managed to pull the stump out and drag it back behind the shed.

Deciding to complete the job, he returned to fill in the hole. Two minutes later he stopped suddenly as a canvas shopping bag landed with a thunk next to his feet and a can of paint rolled out. Startled, he looked up to see a figure reaching down to pick up the extra shovel he had brought.

"Here, Ralph, let me help you dig that hole," Zachary Bradshaw said.

"I'm not digging the hole. I'm filling it in," Spaulding protested.

Before he could say another word, Bradshaw swung the shovel with all his might and crashed it against the side of Spaulding's head.

"Yes, Ralph,' he said. "That's exactly what you're doing."

51

"What the hell kind of name is Toaz?" Harvey wanted to know, as we drove west toward the house of Ralph Spaulding.

"I don't know," I said. "Maybe Aztec." I had other things on my mind.

"Aztec? That ain't a nationality, is it?"

"Not any more. If I had to guess, though, I'd say his name has been shortened. Maybe Avtoazian, or something like that. Armenian. He reminded me a little, physically, of an Armenian guy I knew named Mike Torosian."

"Hmm," was all Harvey said as he consulted a little hand-drawn map he pulled out of his door pocket.

"I've got a better question," I said. "Why didn't you mention Spaulding and Pringham to Toaz?"

"At the time, I wasn't sure how cooperative they were gonna be. Afterward, I figured we should get first crack at asking some questions. I mention the gardener and housekeeper and, next thing you know, Toaz and his boys beat us to the punch."

"That's probably true," I agreed, "but don't you think those two may be in danger? Toaz and his boys could also offer them some protection."

"Danger? No, it never entered my mind that they were in danger. You think they're in danger?"

"I hate to say it, Harv, but right now, I'd lay you even money that they're both dead."

"Dead?" Now, why the hell do you say that?" I could see Harv's hands gripping the wheel harder.

"Think about it. Right now, we know of at least three murder victims directly connected to either Zachary or Emily Bradshaw. Four if Zachary's dead too. That doesn't bode well, in my opinion, for anybody who's associated with either one of the Bradshaws."

"I think you're letting your imagination run away," Harv opined. "You been reading more of those detective books again?"

"You mean Raymond Chandler? No, I've already read everything he ever wrote. At least twice. It's got nothing to do with that. Just a gut feeling I have."

"Right. We're gonna find Spaulding laying on top of a rose bush, with a Garden Weasel raked across his balls, a mouthful of seeds and bulbs and a shovel handle up his ass. Give me a break."

In spite of his brusqueness, I could tell Harvey was at least a little worried. It was in his eyes. We drove on in silence for about five minutes, until Harvey turned down a gravel side street and into a neighborhood that looked remarkably like the area where Kay Kimberly lived. And died.

"This be the street," Harv said, a little too nonchalantly.

Four blocks up, he pulled over in front of a house that belonged on the cover of House and Garden. The big country-style mailbox had Ralph Spaulding written on it in a typeface I knew was called Olde English from hanging around Lou at the ad agency. Flamboyant. But it didn't light a candle to the house and grounds. The house was more of a cottage, made of fieldstone. It was set back a good thirty yards from the street, and a winding walk made of the same stone as the house undulated its way up to a porch that ran the length of the cottage. Two large black stone lions stood guard at either side of the steps. The rest of the porch was covered with half barrels, full of wild, riotous foliage. I was surprised to see so much color this late in the season. The grounds surrounding the cottage were covered with at least two semesters worth of botany lessons. Spaulding was obviously a man who loved his work.

"Jesus Christ," Harv said as we got out and headed for the cottage, "this sonofabitch is making some kind of statement, isn't he? Problem is, I have no idea what the hell he's saying."

"He's telling the world he can afford a huge water bill," I joked.

"Yeah, that's for damn sure," Harv agreed.

As we reached the steps, I stopped Harv with a hand on the shoulder. "You go check the rose bushes," I told him. "I'll see if anybody's home."

Harv didn't cotton to being the butt of a joke. "Fuck you," he said, slapping my hand off his shoulder.

"Jesus, Harv, lighten up. I'm just kidding. Philip Marlowe always used humor to loosen things up in tense situations."

"Yeah, yeah. Sorry. Guess I am a little tense."

I rang the doorbell and we waited for a minute. No response. Harv zigzagged his way around barrels, made it to the window and looked in. I kept ringing.

"Don't see anybody," Harv said, after peering through the window for a few seconds.

"Was that one word or two?" I asked.

"Huh? Oh. Anybody. Any body. Very funny."

I tried the door, but it was locked. "Let's go 'round back," I suggested.

We did. There was no doorbell in back. I tried the door, but it was locked too. So I knocked, long and loud. Harv was wandering around in the back yard, which was at least as expansive as the front, and with an equal amount of flora, some of which looked like it had been imported from another galaxy.

Maybe that would explain how there could be so much stuff in bloom so late in the season. I jumped off the back porch and walked toward Harvey to see if he wanted me to get us into the cottage.

As he disappeared around a large, thick evergreen, I heard a noise that sounded like someone had hit him in the stomach. "Oh my God!" Harv gasped. "Jesus Christ Almighty! No, no!"

When I got around the tree, Harv was sitting on the ground, his head buried in his hands. Three feet away, a man's naked body, Ralph Spaulding, no doubt, was sticking out of the dirt. It was buried almost to the waist, with the face down and feet up. The legs were tied together and to a long wooden stake. And the penis was painted green.

52

"It's fucking obscene," Brad Toaz was saying. "What the hell kind of sick monster could do a thing like this?" His intense reaction to such an incredibly heinous murder had far outstripped his anger at Harvey for not mentioning the gardener and housekeeper. Toaz had insisted, when Harv used my cell phone to report on Spaulding, that he would accompany us to Edith Pringham's house. But first, he wanted to meet us at Spaulding's.

A couple of crime scene guys were carefully digging the body out of the soil, which had been pretty well packed down. Kotwica and an assistant were standing by with a body bag.

"I assume that's a rhetorical question," I said to Toaz, not knowing what else to say.

He ignored me, not out of rudeness, but because he was deep in thought. "What the hell does it mean?" he said. "It's like someone is making a mockery of their professions. A nurse is defiled with needles, pills and a thermometer. A gardener is "planted," and given a green penis, probably a sick parody of a green thumb. And this Gianotti guy. You say he was mutilated, but I can't connect any of the mutilation with the legal profession." He shook his head.

"Maybe the killer just didn't like lawyers," Harv offered.

"Could be," I said. "Like cutting out the tongue and eyes was symbolically keeping him from speaking and seeing again. But, I think in George's case, Brad, the mutilation was strictly to make the body difficult to identify. A subterfuge. In fact, for awhile, Harv and I considered that the body wasn't George's; that maybe George was even the murderer, and planted a ringer."

"And what about the girl? Vandever. There was no profession-related mutilation with her," Harvey offered. "Of course, she was mainly a retail clerk. What could you do? Cut her up and put her on the shelves?"

Toaz whirled and shot a long, cold stare at Harvey. He looked at him for a full thirty seconds; Harvey standing in baffled amazement. Finally, Toaz broke eye contact and his body visibly relaxed. He spoke in a low voice. "There was mutilation with the Vandever girl," he said. "Of a sort. I talked to Ann Arbor while you boys were sightseeing. Three rolls of quarters were removed from her vagina."

I thought Harvey was going to cry. His face went pale and his lips quivered. But he gutted it out. "Christ. I didn't know," he said. "Look, Toaz, I'm sorry."

"Forget it," Brad told him. "I've been doing this long enough to know you have to keep a sense of humor if you want to keep your sanity. You weren't out of line, Harvey. I mean it." And he walked over and patted Harvey on the back.

"So that's three profession-related mutilations," I said. What could the significance possibly be? *Is* there any significance?

"I only know one thing," Toaz said. "I'd hate to be the Bradshaw family mohel."

Harvey responded with a soft chuckle. I just smiled knowingly and nodded my head, even though I had no idea what Toaz meant. In any event, our sanity appeared to be preserved.

Interlude

Edith Pringham put on her slippers, tied her robe and scooted into the kitchen. The slippers were so old and worn that she had to slide her feet; if she picked them up, the slippers would just fall off. Oh well, she thought, maybe when I hit the lottery, I'll buy a new pair.

She smiled at her own joke as she put on the coffee and tried to decide what to have for breakfast. Was she in the mood for oatmeal? No, she had oatmeal two days ago and pancakes yesterday. An omelet. That's what I'll have! An omelet with ham and cheese.

Edith set the ingredients on the counter, put her iron skillet on the stove and pulled a bottle of olive oil down from her overhead cabinet. Deciding to have coffee before cooking, she poured a cup and sat down at the kitchen table.

"Do you have a cup for me?"

Startled, Edith looked up and screamed. "Oh my God! How did you get in here? What are you doing here?"

"Edith, relax," Zachary Bradshaw said. "Nobody's going to hurt you." He walked over the stove, picked up the skillet and made a show of examining it. Then he turned and strode toward Edith, skillet raised and intentions clear. "Except me."

Too late, Edith attempted to rise from her chair, only to be stopped by the skillet crashing down on the top of her head.

Zachary went to the kitchen counter, opened a drawer, closed it, then opened another. Reaching in, he pulled out a very large knife.

53

Edith Pringham's house was small, just like the others. But the neighborhood was more conventional. Cookie-cutter bungalows, twelve feet apart, fifteen or twenty houses to the block. A detached garage was at the rear of the fenced-in backyard.

Nobody answered the door, so we walked around to the back. Harvey had jogged over to the garage and reported there was a car in it. Some neighbors were gathering out front on the sidewalk, speculating on who we were and what we were doing.

The thought struck me that all three of Emily Bradshaw's employees lived alone. But what it meant, if anything, eluded me.

"All the shades are drawn," Brad observed. "Can't see in."

"How about the window on the door?" Harvey asked. "No shade on that."

I walked up the two steps to the small, square porch and looked in. All I saw was a landing and a flight of stairs heading down to a darkened basement. To the right, as I looked in, was another door, half open. I could make out some cabinets and a table, but the angle of the door obscured seventy five percent of the room, obviously the kitchen.

"Nothing," I said. "Can't see a thing." I turned to Harvey and Brad, still standing on the lawn. Harvey was making eyes at me, his eyebrows jumping perceptibly. I got the message.

"Brad," Harvey said, "come over to the garage for a second. I want to show you something."

"Huh? Oh, sure," Brad answered. He didn't appear to suspect anything. No reason he should. When they returned from the garage, I was sitting on the steps, my picks safely returned to my pocket.

" ... over in the corner like that," Harv was saying, "it could have been a body."

"Yeah. I've often mistaken a bag of fertilizer for a distant cousin," Brad replied.

Harvey cleared his throat. "So what do we do now? Go?"

"I guess so," Toaz said. Then, turning to me, "Hey, Pete, why don't you try the door? Maybe it isn't locked."

"Hey, good idea," I said, lamely. I sprang up, stepped to the door, turned the knob and opened it. Then pulled it shut just as quickly. The incredible stench that assaulted me made the smell when I found Janny seem like $50 an ounce perfume. Instinctively, my hand shot up and covered my nose and mouth.

"Pete! What is it?" Harvey yelled.

Brad looked at him. "Christ, you couldn't smell it? I sure as hell could." Then he joined me on the porch. "I'm going in," he said. "You want to come, come on. But hold your breath."

"I'm with you," I said, following on his heels.

"What the hell is it?" I heard Harvey screaming from the back yard as Brad threw the door open. "What the hell is it?"

54

Two steps into the landing, I crashed into Brad, pushing him against the half-open kitchen door. We almost went down, but something was keeping the kitchen door from opening all the way, and the door kept us upright. We untangled and I stepped back. The stench was overpowering; I reached in my hip pocket for my handkerchief and tied it over my mouth and nose. It didn't do much good. Brad signaled me to follow as he eased through the door sideways. I did and banged into him again. He had stopped in his tracks just inside the kitchen. Together, we saw what was keeping the door from opening.

It was Edith Pringham, on the floor, dead. Very, very dead. She was wearing a light blue, quilted robe, the kind you get on special at K-Mart. Wearing wasn't exactly the right word; it was pulled off her shoulders, the sash tying her arms behind her back. She wore only panties underneath. A pair of well-worn terry cloth slippers were halfway across the room, their nubby whiteness a stark contrast to the brownish red pools and smudges of dried blood that covered the floor.

She apparently had been lifted, forcefully, off her feet. From her face, which was frozen in a mask of terror, I guessed her to be about 60 or 65 years old. I didn't have to guess what scared her. The killer (killers?) had hit her viciously on the head, and then neatly sliced her open from breast to crotch. At least, I hoped she was dead or unconscious before she was sliced.

Edith Pringham was disemboweled, her internal organs spilled into and around a large metal mop bucket that had been placed on the floor between her legs. I was vaguely aware of a large piece of rancid meat in a frying pan on the stove, just beyond the body. The thought occurred that she must have been cooking dinner when she was killed. And there seemed to be more meat than she would have prepared just for herself. Had she been expecting company? Could the company have been the murderer?

All this registered instantaneously, because I'm sure we weren't in the house for more than twenty or thirty seconds. But it seemed like we stood there for an eternity. Strangely, I wasn't shocked or enraged. I was in the spell of a morbid fascination. A scene from my past flashed through my mind. A weekend visit to Ann Arbor, of all places, to see a friend in med school. His name was Gary Watnick and he was blithely showing me cadavers in a lab. His incredibly casual attitude around a roomful of dead winos, bag ladies and the occasional "normal" corpse, made it impossible for me to act anything but normal. It would have been out of place. I would have been embarrassed not to keep a straight face and nod with interest (which was genuine), whenever he pointed out some of the more unsavory aspects of dissection.

Now, as I looked down at the cadaver on the floor, I found myself identifying organs. Ileum, jejunum, duodenum. No, it was the other way around. The duodenum came out of the stomach. The ileum joined the cecum. And there, caught on the handle of the bucket. Was that the ascending colon? And where was the transverse colon? In the bucket?

I wanted to get on my hands and knees to look, but the next thing I remember was being shaken violently. Strong hands were gripping my shoulders, hurting me. A distant voice was calling me. Then it got closer, closer, and I realized it was calling my name.

"Pete! Pete! Are you alright?"

Slowly I became aware that it was Brad and we were back outside. Harvey was standing a little off to the side, looking very concerned. Brad handed me my handkerchief; it was wrinkled and damp. It must have come off when he brought me out. I suddenly realized my eyes were full of tears. Whether it was from crying or natural tearing triggered by the powerful stench, I didn't know. I dabbed my eyes and brushed my cheeks with the wet hanky, not caring.

" ... in a trance in there." Brad was talking again. "Are you sure you're alright?"

"I'm fine," I said, hopefully with at least some assurance. "But I've got to get out of here. I just remembered I have a lunch date."

Harv strode over and grabbed my arm. "Come on, kid, I'll take you to your car. Christ, you had me scared there for a minute." Then, turning to Brad, he asked, "Can you handle this end okay?"

"Yeah. No problem. I'll radio the situation in to HQ from my cruiser. I sure as hell don't want to go in there again. Just take care of Pete. Make sure he's okay before you let him drive anywhere. I'll get a hold of you tonight or tomorrow, Harv. Fill in the blanks. Or, you can come back here if you want. As much as I'd like to pay a visit to Mrs. Bradshaw, it looks like I'll be around here for a good while. If she's not in danger, she might at least have some answers that could shed a little light on this mess."

"I'll call Mrs. Bradshaw and warn her," I offered. "Hell, I'm on her dime. Not a stretch to consider all this part of my investigation of Zachary Bradshaw."

"Yeah, and I just might head right back here after I drop Pete off," Harv said. "Even if I had a lunch date, I sure as hell ain't in any kind of mood to eat."

Brad grunted assent and walked away mumbling, "So much to do, so little time."

Neither Harvey nor I bothered to mention who I was seeing for lunch.

55

In my eight years as a private investigator, I have done and seen a lot of unusual things. But, for most of those years, four and a half, to be exact, I was an investigator with the Oakland County Prosecutor's office. I wasn't officially partnered with a deputy prosecuting attorney named Harold Shyman, but it just turned out that I worked almost exclusively for the guy. The pay wasn't great, but the experience was priceless. Besides, I was supplementing my income fairly well at Hazel Park even back then Shyman didn't pursue many murder cases. His specialty was pinching hookers. Figuratively, not literally. As I said, it was very interesting work. I would do things like befriending pimps, getting the working girls to proposition me, and then testifying against them in court.

Once, I uncovered a high-priced call girl ring operating out of a chain of barbershops. Unfortunately, the operators, five enterprising Sicilians with no apparent mob connections, discovered me. And made the proverbial offer I couldn't refuse: my life for my silence. Partly because of that, and partly because after four and a half years, I began to feel like a whore myself, I ended my association with the prosecutor's office and hung out my own shingle.

Why do I mention all this? Simply because, in all that time I had seen, up close and personal, exactly one corpse. That was a dead john in a motel room with a hysterical hooker. A smiling, happy, peaceful dead john. So it was hardly what you would call unnerving.

Now, in a period of a few days, I had seen four victims of horrible violence; been on the scene of another murder, Kay Kimberly's; and possibly close to a sixth, if Zachary Bradshaw turned up dead, as I suspected he would. It finally got to me.

And, while displaying machismo has never been one of my major concerns, I was a little embarrassed as Harvey dropped me off at the donut shop.

We had driven in total silence. I think Harvey, for once, was at a loss for words. But, as I got out, he said, "Look Pete, why don't you skip the lunch bit and go home. See the Bradshaw dame some other time. Okay?"

"I'm alright, Harvey," I told him. "Really. Maybe I'll stop inside, have a coffee and wash up a bit first."

He just looked at me and shook his head a few times. As he got in his car, I realized there was cigarette clenched tightly between his lips. He must have gotten it from Toaz. I smiled grimly at the realization that Harvey was more than a little shaken too. Because he hated cigarettes; and it was the first time I had ever seen him smoke.

56

Harvey's record for disorientation was in no danger of being broken. I only crossed the bridge once and asked for directions at one gas station. But I did miss the private drive the first time by. It wasn't until I saw an address on a neighbor's mailbox that I realized I had gone too far.

The driveway cut through a dense stand of trees. When I emerged, the house was still a good eighty yards away. It was enormous. In my old neighborhood in Melvindale, it probably would have taken up one-fourth of the block. The drive was blacktop; the grass as green and clean as any I had ever seen, including the eighteenth green at Dearborn Hills Golf Club. Huge boulders were scattered randomly about the grounds. The word "erratics" came to mind, dredged up from somewhere deep in my academic subconscious. Erratics, if I remembered correctly, were rocks deposited by glaciers in places where you wouldn't expect them to be. I was pretty sure Michigan had glaciers; wasn't that how the Great Lakes were formed?

I drove past the mansion and parked in front of a garage that could have housed a couple of airplanes. Then I walked back around to the front and climbed three steps to a black wrought-iron-railed porch adorned with plants only slightly more modest than Ralph Spaulding's personal display. There was a huge elephant head knocker on the heavy door that could have been gold, but was more likely brass. I banged the trunk a few times and waited.

Almost immediately, a young and extremely attractive woman wearing a short black skirt with black nylons and a lacy white apron opened the door. My mouth went slack; I couldn't believe what I was seeing. The woman, in her late twenties, had red hair. And, without much of a stretch, she could have been the girl I had dreamed about the night of George's fateful call.

I quickly suppressed my surprise and smiled. "You couldn't possibly be Mrs. Bradshaw," I said.

She smiled back and showed teeth that belonged on the poster for National Fluoride Week. "No," she said. "But you're Pete Pepper. Come on in, we've been expecting you."

I followed her in and found myself in a marble-tiled foyer that ran from the front all the way to the rear of the house. It was more like a great hall than a foyer, adorned with statuary, antique chairs and artwork. It seemed big enough to play basketball in. Full court.

"In here," the redhead said, her flats clack-clacking against the floor. I was a little disappointed that she wasn't wearing heels. They would have been far more apropos for the costume, albeit totally inappropriate for sweeping and dusting. I followed her through an archway that led to a sumptuous sunroom decked out in glass and rattan, with a liberal sprinkling of leather.

She stopped suddenly and turned around. My stop was less sudden and we bumped together, face to face.

She stood her ground, smiled as though amused. "I'll tell Mrs. Bradshaw you're here," she said. "I'm sure you can make yourself comfortable."

I resisted the temptation to tell her how comfortable she felt. "Sure. Just like home," I replied.

Then I stepped back, walked around her and plopped down on an overstuffed brown leather sofa as she turned and made an exit. I watched her buttocks strain against the material of her flimsy skirt, bouncing like two large watermelons in a small silk bag. It couldn't have been her natural walk. Which meant, I thought with some pleasure, she was probably showing off for me.

After five minutes, she still hadn't returned, so I got up and stretched my legs. There wasn't much to see but the furniture. Two walls were floor-to-ceiling windows with partially opened drapes; the other two were essentially bare, except that one featured an enormous fireplace and a large oval mirror with a gilded frame. There was nothing else on the walls, not even a picture of grandma. Several pieces of furniture were evenly spaced around the room, backs to the wall and about ten feet in. The most prominent was a magnificent armoire that might have spent time in King Arthur's great room.

Walking back toward the sofa, I reached into my pocket and pulled out the change. Two quarters, three dimes, two nickels and four pennies. It wasn't the total of ninety-four cents that mattered; nor was it the number of coins. Eleven of any coin is a piece of cake when you've practiced as long as I have. My personal record was thirty dimes, but sometimes catching coins of four different sizes could be tricky. And I liked to keep in practice just in case Lou ever decided to accept the challenge.

I stacked the coins – quarters, nickels, pennies, dimes – on my bent right elbow, my curled right hand behind my ear. Suddenly my hand flashed, a graceful blur that neatly caught the coins before gravity could overcome inertia. I smiled as I sat back down and routinely, though unnecessarily, counted the change before returning it to my pocket. There was only eighty-four cents! I couldn't believe it. I had missed a dime!

Humbled, I got up and looked around. I hadn't heard anything, but a dime landing on the plush slate-grey carpet wouldn't have made any noise. I got down on my hands and knees and looked around. Nothing. I gave up and tried the sofa, putting my hands down behind the thick cushions. I was rewarded with an old pack of matches and two pieces of popcorn. But no dime. I moved on to the next cushion and struck pay dirt. A quarter! But not my dime.

As I slid my hand behind the third cushion, a voice interrupted me. "Did you lose something, Mr. Pepper?"

I recognized it immediately as Emily Bradshaw's. I got up and faced her, slipping the booty into my shirt pocket before I turned around. "I dropped some change," I said, a little sheepishly.

She smiled. "Well, no matter. Just let it go. Perhaps this will compensate in some small way." She handed me a check made out to Pete Pepper for the sum of five thousand dollars.

"Yes," I smiled back. "It certainly will." I folded the check in half, put it with the quarter, popcorn and matches, and then offered my hand. "Pleased to meet you, Mrs. Bradshaw," I said.

Emily Bradshaw was not an attractive woman. Nor was she exactly homely. Unusual looking was the best way I could describe her. She was tall, around five feet, eight, and a bit on the chunky side. I pegged her at about 160 pounds. Her hair was black, short and had a slight curl. She had the kind of eyebrows Lou would hate – they looked painted on. The kind you see on a lot of old ladies. Not that Emily looked old. She could have been anywhere from her late fifties to mid-sixties. I couldn't call it any closer.

One reason was that she used too much makeup. I couldn't see her real complexion. The almost-fire-engine-red lipstick she was wearing was incredibly conspicuous. Maybe it was intentional, meant to take the attention away from her eyes, which were too close together, and her nose, which angled downward from between her eyes and stopped about an inch above her painted lips. It was unusually thin, too, a visual non-sequitir to the largeness of both her head and body. Or maybe I was just expecting the nose to be red, bulbous and veined, the stereotypical nose of an alcoholic.

None of it mattered, though. Her appearance notwithstanding, Emily Bradshaw was an eminently likeable woman. She had a presence, an aura of confidence. She emanated friendliness.

She took my hand and shook it. Firmly. I liked that in a woman. It showed self-confidence – or a good upbringing. I guessed that Emily Bradshaw had a pretty good relationship with her father. Probably not too unusual when your father was a multi-millionaire.

"My pleasure," she said, letting go. "But let's get one thing straight right off. I'm Emily and you're Pete."

"And I'm Ramona," the redhead said, hovering behind Emily.

"Oh, forgive me!" Emily said. "I assumed you two had introduced yourselves. I'm sorry."

"Actually, I should apologize," I said. "I forgot to thank you for the check. Thank you, Emily."

"You're welcome, Pete. Ramona, see if Pete wants a drink before lunch. I'll have iced tea."

Ramona cocked her head in my direction and widened her eyes. Mine had to struggle to stay off the curves of her long, slender black-nylon-clad legs.

"Uh, you wouldn't happen to have any Canfield's Chocolate Fudge Soda, would you?"

"Regular or diet?"

"Diet."

"Nope."

"Regular?"

"All out." She smiled, teasingly.

"Make it two iced teas, then." I was amused by her game, but, surprisingly, disappointed that she didn't have any Canfield's.

Emily interrupted my self-appraisal. "Shall we get down to business, Pete? Although I'm afraid there isn't much I can tell you."

We sat down. I took the sofa; Emily chose a curved-back rattan chair with a thin, pale pink pillow on the seat. I had already decided not to say anything about Kimberly, Spaulding and Pringham. Not at first, anyway. I didn't want to upset her before I extracted any information.

I rubbed my chin thoughtfully and looked her in the eye. "Well, if you can't tell me much, Emily, we're in big trouble." Then I softened. "But, I'm sure there's plenty you can tell me. Things you might think are insignificant or unimportant could be very meaningful to a savvy professional like me."

She laughed her husky laugh. "Okay, then, Pete. Shoot." She leaned back in the chair, eyebrows raised in anticipation.

"Well, when, exactly, was the last time you saw Mr. Bradshaw?"

She looked down at her hands, clasped together in her lap. "I'm not exactly sure," she said. "We were together on the Fourth of July. After that, I don't know. I think he may have been here for awhile." She looked down at her hands again.

"I don't ... " I started to say, and then realized what she meant. "Oh. You were ... "

"On a binge. A real humdinger," she said softly.

"Alright then, what you're saying is that Zachary may have been gone since July fourth, maybe a few days later." I chose not to query more about the duration of the binge.

"That's right."

"Almost three months. That's longer than I thought. But, you say in his business, he was often away for long periods?"

"Never this long. Usually just a few weeks; occasionally as long as a month. But not three months."

"Okay. I guess the next logical question is why did you wait so long to report it?"

"Mr. Pepper," she said, forgetting her own first-name rule, "I'm not sure if I conveyed this to you during our phone conversation, but mine was not a happy marriage. I was not a particularly attractive young woman, nor was Zachary dashingly handsome. But my father was determined to see me married before he died. When Zachary proposed, I accepted, although I knew his love of money was far greater than any emotions he had for me. He was younger than I, also. But I didn't care. I didn't love him, either. I did love my father, though. Very much. He died happy. And I have lived unhappily ever since. What I'm saying, Pete," she paused for a brief smile to underscore the re-use of my first name, "is that I don't much care if I ever see Zachary again."

"I have written him out of my will and I would just as soon write him out of my life. When I finally decided to call you and hire you to find him, it was more out of my sense of wifely duty. And maybe a little bit of curiosity. And, for your information, I have *never* reported Zachary missing. Not to the police, I mean."

I took a minute to absorb what she had said, and to consider my own next words. I couldn't admonish her for not reporting her husband's disappearance to the police. It wasn't against the law. Besides, if she had,

I'd be out five thousand dollars. She wouldn't have needed me. Nor could I pass judgment on her for marrying someone she didn't love. Thousands of people do it. Maybe millions. And it was none of my business, anyway.

I was still deciding whether to comment or move on, when a question came out of my mouth that caught us both by surprise. "Emily, are you an agoraphobic?"

She almost fielded it cleanly. But she stiffened for the briefest instant, before turning the move into a stretching motion. It was obviously a question she wasn't expecting, but I didn't think it would cause her any unease. She completed her stretch, rubbing her hands along the sides of her chair. "Do you know what agoraphobia is, Pete?"

"It's the fear of leaving one's house, I believe."

"Not precisely," she said. "It's the fear of open spaces. If I were an agoraphobic, do you think I would live out here? Have you seen our grounds? Nothing but wide, open spaces. And I often take walks down to the lake." Her smile seemed a little forced.

"So, you're saying you don't suffer from agoraphobia?"

"I am, indeed. Oh, it's true that I rarely, if ever, leave my house. But it's of my own choosing. And certainly not based on any fears. George often tried to get me out, but I always refused. I think it turned into a game. The harder he tried, the more adamant I became. It was he who kept referring to me as an agoraphobic."

"I see. So, if I asked you if we could go out for lunch instead of eating here, you'd go?"

"I could go, but, no, I wouldn't. I choose not to. Besides, Ramona has already prepared a perfectly fine lunch for us. You'll see."

"Okay." I smiled, a little embarrassed. "Look, let's get back on the subject. I don't know why I asked you that. But I guess it was from George – that is, through his wife – that I had heard you were agoraphobic. I'm sorry. I didn't mean to upset you."

"Upset? Not at all!" she replied quickly. Which meant, of course, that she was.

"So, what can you tell me about Zachary's friends, his interests, his business?"

"His friends? It would surprise me if he had any. His interests? He was essentially interested in Zachary Bradshaw and obtaining as much physical pleasure as possible. And his business? Well, it was just that. His business. None of mine."

I had to laugh, in spite of the situation. "Emily, do I detect a note of bitterness?"

She joined me, unabashedly. "Oh, Pete! George was right. You are good!"

When we both settled down, I continued. "Uh, let's go over this again. You don't know the names of any of his friends? His business associates?"

"Honestly, Pete. I don't. We didn't really communicate much. When my father died, neither of us saw any need to carry on the charade. And that was nearly twenty years ago. I do know he was involved with some trade commission. I think it had to do with the county and international trade. You might be able to get information on that somewhere."

"It was a Tri-County Commission," I told her. "That was the group that went to China, when Zachary brought back bricks from the Great Wall."

"Yes. Yes, you're right. I believe there are still some of those infernal rocks up in his bedroom. And, this time, let me say in earnest, that I'm impressed by the fact that you've very obviously already done some homework."

"Just trying to earn my keep, ma'am," I smiled, patting the check in my pocket.

"Well, you are. In fact, I'm sure you could tell me some things about Zachary that I'm not aware of."

"I'm afraid I've used all my ammunition. But, what's this about physical pleasure? Are we talking about, uh, young ladies?"

"Ladies of all ages, I suspect. Zachary didn't actually tell me about his escapades. But he made little attempt to conceal the fact that he had taken several paramours. He frequently came home late at night reeking of perfume."

"Hmmm. Have you ever been to his store or his warehouse in Ann Arbor?"

She gave me a wicked smile. "I chose not to go."

It was very apparent that Emily couldn't or wouldn't be much more help. That, in itself, didn't bother me. I was confident I had enough information to pick up old Zach's trail. What did bother me was the possibility that "wouldn't" was the correct word. It bordered on the incredible that she knew so little about her husband's actions. But, looking at her, she seemed perfectly honest and innocent. And if she wanted to hide something, why hire me in the first place?

"What about his accountant?" I blurted out. "Surely you must know who his accountant is?"

"His accountant?"

I had caught her off guard again. Her face seemed to redden slightly. Or maybe it was just the bad makeup job.

"Let's see. Uh, yes, he has mentioned the name once or twice. It's a firm here in Belleville, Sutton and Wasyl. I don't know the name of the individual he dealt with."

Before I could pursue the matter any further, Ramona wheeled in a teacart with drinks and lunch.

"Who had the tea?" she joked, holding one in each hand.

I took them both and walked over to hand one to Emily.

"Do you mind if we just eat lunch in here?" she asked, accepting the tea.

"Fine by me," I said.

"Me, too," Ramona added, grabbing a sandwich and plopping down on the sofa.

"Why don't you join us, Ramona?" Emily smiled. "I believe Pete and I have finished our business, haven't we?"

"Just one more thing," I said. "Do you have a picture of Zachary? I may accidentally walk by him in the street and not even know it."

Emily shook her head. "I'm sorry, Pete. I don't even own a camera. The only picture of that scoundrel I have is our wedding picture. But you're certainly welcome to take it."

"Oh no. I couldn't do that. But I would like to have a look at it. Would it be alright if Ramona ran up and got it for me?"

"Is that okay, Mrs. B?" Ramona asked.

"Certainly dear. It's in one of the bedrooms on the third floor."

"Do you know which one?"

"No, just check them all. It should be on a dresser. And be sure to close all the doors."

57

We sat around, idly talking and eating our sandwiches, for about fifteen minutes. Zachary's picture wasn't much help. He looked like he was barely out of his teens. He had a pencil-thin mustache, which Emily said he had long since shaved off. Emily's face in the picture was partly hidden by a veil, but not quite enough to hide that she wasn't smiling. It was a marked contrast to the Emily of the here and now; laughing, ebullient, happy. She was, well, bragging I guess, about the informal ship she ran. How she wanted Ramona to be a friend, not an employee. I think she thought I was surprised that she was eating lunch with us. I wasn't at all. But I was surprised to see her drinking a Budweiser. If it didn't bother Emily, though, it didn't bother me. I wanted to tell Emily about her ex-employees, but wasn't sure how. I finally settled on the indirectly direct method.

"You're new here, aren't you?" I said to Ramona.

She pulled the can away from her mouth, licked a few droplets off her lip and said, "Started three days ago. How'd you know?"

Emily joined in, as I had hoped. "Yes, how did you know, Pete?"

"Because I thought Edith Pringham did your cooking and cleaning." I was lingering on the indirect.

"Edith? Well, she mostly cleaned. Not the whole house, of course. Most of it is closed off. And she only cooked once in awhile, usually just lunch for herself." Emily registered no surprise at the mention of Pringham's name, and I didn't attach any significance to the fact.

"Was that every day?" I asked.

"Oh no. Edith only came in twice a week. Poor dear. She was getting old. Her rheumatism, as she called it, was really causing her a lot of pain."

"You used the past tense. You said she *came* twice a week, not she comes."

"That's because she did. Now I have Ramona. Ramona 's full-time. She lives here."

"You let Edith go?"

"Of course not! It was a mutual agreement. She really didn't want to work anymore."

"What about Kay Kimberly? Is she still in your employ?"

"Well, yes and no." Again, no surprise.

"Meaning?"

"I'm paying Edith and Kay through the end of the year. But neither of them work for me any longer."

"Kay was a nurse, wasn't she? Does Ramona have medical credentials too?"

"No. But Kay can still come if or when I have need. She was more or less on a retainer. She nursed me, oh, four years ago when I broke my hip. We got on so well, I asked her to come on a regular basis. She occasionally ran errands for me; grocery shopping and such. She's such a sweet girl; I just wanted to help her out. We mostly just sat around and talked and played gin rummy."

"You paid her just to play gin rummy?"

"And for companionship, Pete. You see, as long as I'm content, or at least occupied in some fashion, I ... "

"Christ! I'm sorry, Emily. I should have figured that out. I apologize."

"Accepted. But why all the questions? I feel like I'm being investigated, not Zachary."

"I apologize for that, too, but please bear with me for a few minutes, okay? Then I'll tell you what this is all about."

"Well ... okay."

I smiled and nodded at her, but it didn't seem to bring her any comfort.

"Emily, when did you let Kay go?"

"Oh, but I didn't. That was her choice. She's going back to school to get a Master's degree. In Ann Arbor."

"Oh. Well, when was the last time she was here?"

"A week ago Wednesday as I recall. I whipped her good. Gin rummy, of course."

"How about Ralph Spaulding? When did he, uh, stop working here?"

"Ralph?" Finally, a hint of surprise. "But he still works here. At least he has been. Does the yard look like it needs mowing?"

"No, I didn't mean that. Exactly what is your arrangement with Spaulding?"

"Well, first of all, it's Zachary's arrangement. He hired Ralph. I just write the checks. And Ralph just comes when the lawn and gardens need work, which is actually quite often, the grounds being so large. Most of the time, though, it's not Ralph. It's his employees. College kids from Eastern Michigan University, I believe. Come to think of it, Ralph hasn't been around for a good while. He used to stop in for a cup of coffee now and then, but not lately."

"I see," I said, deciding I couldn't put it off any longer. "Emily, I'm afraid I have some terrible news for you. Extremely terrible."

She stiffened quite noticeably this time, and grabbed the arms of her chair. Hard. Apprehension was painted on her face thicker than the makeup.

"What ... what is it? she asked, almost a whisper.

"Edith, Kay, Ralph. They're all dead. They've been murdered. All very brutally, I'm afraid. I'm sorry to have to tell you this way."

"What?! No! No! That's impossible! Edith? Kay? But I just saw her last week! I don't believe it!"

"I'm sorry, Emily." My expression convinced her of my sincerity.

She let out a wail that would have scared a banshee. "Oooh nooo! Oh my God, nooo! No. No. No." Then she broke into an all-out cry, her body heaving with each sob.

I went over to comfort her, but she stood up and fended me off.

"Please, I'm alright. I, I just want to be alone, now. Ramona will see you out. I'll talk to you later."

I called after her as she started to leave the room. "But, Emily, you don't understand! Zachary may be dead too. You may be in danger. At least call a private security service."

She stopped and turned around. " Ramona, take care of it, will you please? I'm sure Mr. Pepper can recommend someone." Then she walked out, dabbing her eyes with a handkerchief that had mysteriously appeared in her hands.

58

I was a bit surprised at how calm Ramona was throughout the scene with Emily. Like hearing about murders was an everyday occurrence. She was sucking down another Budweiser as she readied to write the name I had given her.

"How do you spell that?" she asked.

"C-a-s-h-w-e-l-l," I told her.

"Right. And how about the rest of it?"

I spelled out the rest of Cashwell Security Services for her and suddenly realized the reason for her lack of reaction to the news of the murders. She just wasn't too bright. It disappointed me. My earlier impression was that she was witty. Hell, she *was* witty. Maybe you don't have to be smart to be funny. I made a note to exclude Ramona from my future social calendar. Not that I needed to make new female friends. If things went as I hoped with Eva, I planned to be a one-woman man for a long time.

"Be sure to call as soon as I leave," I urged Ramona, almost wistfully.

"I will," she promised, plopping back down on the sofa. "Right after I have a cigarette. Want one?" she asked, holding out a pack of True Menthol 100s.

"Oh, those are diet. I smoke regular."

"Huh?" she asked, confirming my recent assessment of her mental agility.

"No thanks," I said, waving the smokes away. "Just kidding. I don't smoke cigarettes. What I could go for, though, is a nice big, fat cigar."

"Hey, no problem!" she said, jumping back up. "I saw some this morning when I was dusting." She ran over to the armoire and took a cigar out of a humidor and ran back. I was surprised I hadn't noticed the humidor before. It's my job to notice things. It made me wonder what else I might have missed. Like maybe some evidence of George's demise. I hadn't noticed anything out of the ordinary, but nights without sleep aren't conducive to first-rate sleuthing.

"I guess Mr. B. must've smoked them," she said, handing me the cigar.

I looked it over; it was wrapped in cellophane, no band. I knew immediately it was an expensive one. Handmade, all tobacco, long filler. And possibly Cuban, but probably Honduran. I smiled. Now I had another lead. My friend Maxie over at Maxie's Humidor in Bloomfield Hills could undoubtedly tell me the manufacturer. From there, I could possibly determine the retailer. And that meant I would be able to talk to someone that knew something about Zachary Bradshaw.

On the other hand, I really did feel like a good smoke. I turned on the charm and solved the dilemma. "Say, Ramona, do you think I could have another one of these? It's a long drive back to Southfield."

She smiled, ran back to the armoire and returned with a handful. "Why not?" she winked. "It doesn't look like he's gonna be smoking them any time soon."

59

The late afternoon sun cast a heatless glow low in the sky toward Ann Arbor as I walked to my car. Ramona was waving goodbye from the enormous porch as I blew a tasty mouthful of smoke heavenward. I waved back, smiling. Weird. In the past two hours I had seen one old woman horribly disemboweled and had just put another one through a cruel inquisition, shattered her happiness with some horrible news, and sent her sobbing to her room. Yet, as I walked, shielding my eyes from the day's last rays slanting through the leafless branches of the trees, I found myself in an unusually, if not inappropriately, good mood.

Should I have been disturbed? I wasn't sure. Emily Bradshaw's answers had been very pat, almost rehearsed. On the other hand, they seemed to be true and could easily be checked out. Something I was sure Toaz would do. If Emily Bradshaw was somehow connected to the murder of her own employees, which I doubted, it was Toaz's job to find out. I had been hired to find her husband.

It didn't stop me from thinking about Emily, though. Her reaction when I told her of the deaths appeared to be absolutely genuine. Either that, or she was one hell of an actress. But the clincher, for me, was that she had a built-in alibi and refused to use it. An agoraphobic couldn't have committed the murders. All Emily had to do was admit she was agoraphobic and she'd be eliminated from the possible suspect list. Of course, it may have never entered her mind that she could even be considered a suspect. But she denied being agoraphobic, so maybe she isn't. In which case she could be a suspect. Using that logic, she theoretically made herself a suspect even though she could have avoided it. Hmm. I was thinking too much. But I was pretty sure Emily was agoraphobic and wondered why she denied it.

I shrugged and took another long drag on the cigar. At least I had some places to start. Maxie's for one. Plus the Tri-County International Trade Commission and the offices of the accountants, Sutton and Wasyl. I noticed absent mindedly as I got in the car, that the grass could tolerate a mowing.

60

It was another junk-mail-only day. I sighed, stubbed out the butt of my cigar and threw the unsolicited mail into the wastebasket. Then I went to the kitchen, grabbed a can of Point, and sat at my desk to check for phone messages. Eva had called and said she'd call back. Harv called to see how I was doing and to report that he had stuck around with Toaz until Edith Pringham's remains were taken away. He hadn't heard anything further from Brad.

The last message on the tape was a nasty one from Nematotta.

"Good afternoon, Pietro," he said. "I know it's only Tuesday, but I really expected you to call me by now. I hope you haven't forgotten about our meeting, which, by the way, will be tomorrow morning at my office in Travelers Tower. Suite 615 on the sixth floor. But I'm sure you would have figured that out, wouldn't you?" He laughed an ugly, sarcastic laugh before continuing. "Be there, amico! No ifs, ands or buts. Be there at ten o'clock, capisce? Be there, or be very, very sorry! Ciao."

The "ciao" was warm and friendly, dragged out into two syllables, a distinct contrast to his tone for the rest of the message.

Wonderful. There was no way I could get to Nematotta's meeting. I had to pick Maria up in the morning for George's funeral. It looked like I was going to be very, very sorry.

61

I've always disliked funerals. And not just because I don't own a black suit. Fact is, I don't own any suits. Just a handful of sport coats, some of which could probably be called loud; and maybe a dozen pairs of dress slacks, all solids, in grey, black, blue, brown and various shadings in between. But I felt fairly comfortable in a pair of grey slacks and the only funeral-worthy topper I had for it, a two-button blue blazer. I'd have been even more comfortable in jeans and a pullover, but I followed protocol and wore a light blue button-down dress shirt with a tie that every banker owns: yellow with a pattern of little black encircled bugles running diagonally across it. Club ties, I think they're called.

But it wasn't getting dressed up that I disliked about funerals. It was the incredible feeling of inadequacy I had for never knowing what to say. At least I wasn't alone in this. From my limited experience at funerals, nobody knows what to say. Which is why, I guess, very little is ever said.

I was feeling edgy about Maria, too. Did she have in mind what I thought she had in mind? Would I be able to accommodate her? I tried not to think about it as I checked my tie in the mirror, tightened the knot and straightened it out. I could never figure out why the skinny part of the tie, underneath, was always backwards. I stuck it through the label so it would stay put, and nobody would ever know.

On the way out, I picked up the phone, and on an impulse, called Eva at the Michigan Inn. She answered, still groggy, and accepted my invitation for dinner at Giovanni's. I asked her to make reservations and told her I'd pick her up at 7:30.

62

Maria was waiting at the door; a little surprising because I was ten minutes early. She was wearing a black dress, just like you'd expect of the widow. But you'd never expect her to wear one quite this tight. Her little over jacket, black gloves, hat and clutch purse toned down the effect somewhat. Still, she looked so incredibly inviting that I blushed as she grabbed my arm and we walked, stiffly, to my car.

Other than a feeble "Thank you" when I opened the door, she didn't say a word all the way to the church in Royal Oak, a drive of about ten miles. In spite of my apprehension over Maria and the solemnity of the occasion, I had to hide a smile as we pulled into the parking lot, for fear that Maria would see. The name of the church was Immaculate Conception, probably one of the top five most frequently used names in Roman Catholic history, an observation that once prompted my friend Lou Bracato to say. "Immaculate Conception. That's a franchise, isn't it?"

On the way up the steps, I spotted Harvey, motioning madly for me to come over. I was amused to see that good old Harv had no compunctions about wearing loud sport coats to funerals. It was the first time I had ever seen burgundy and green together. I told Maria I'd meet her inside and excused myself. She continued in like a zombie.

"Are you ready for this?" Harv asked. I couldn't quite put an adjective to his tone of voice.

"For the funeral service?" I asked back.

"No! For what I'm about to tell you, for Christ's sake. You know that meat in the frying pan at old lady Pringham's house? It was a piece of her own liver. Can you imagine that? Her own fucking liver! Holy shit!"

"Jesus, Harv, not so loud," I admonished, looking around to see if anyone was within earshot. Nobody seemed to be. I was shocked by the revelation, and thankful that I hadn't eaten any breakfast.

"Christ," I said, barely above a whisper, "when did you find out?"

"This morning, just after eight. Toaz called."

"Did he tell you anything else?"

"Nah. Not much news yet. They'll be sifting through all three scenes pretty good today. Hope to get some prints, hairs, fibers, the usual stuff.

Oh! He did say one of Pringham's neighbors saw a woman on her porch one evening last week. Didn't see a face and wasn't even sure what day it was."

"That doesn't sound like much."

"Yeah, that's what I just said."

"Right. Well, I'm going to head in and find Maria. You going in?"

"No," Harv shook his head, "I feel a little uncomfortable inside churches."

"I can understand that," I told him," you being Jewish, I mean." I was embarrassed immediately. I could actually feel my face heat up and turn red like a left-on back burner.

If Harv was offended, it sure didn't show. He put his arm on my shoulder and looked at me with an unreadable expression.

"No, you don't understand," he said. "I feel the same way about synagogues.

63

The service and subsequent interment at White Chapel Cemetery were every bit as uncomfortable as I expected them to be. People stood around, not knowing what to say, until they somehow came up with inspired thoughts like, "He was so young," and, "What a shame, there are so few really good lawyers."

At least they said something. Maria didn't. Nor did I. Every once in awhile, you'd hear a sob or someone blowing their nose into a hanky. A lot of people were red eyed or wet cheeked, I noticed, as we all walked to our cars, parked on a winding blacktop lane that wound around throughout the grounds with no apparent pattern. Maria's face, by contrast, was as smooth and unmarked as the flip side of a tombstone.

64

The drive home was as eventful as the drive out. Once again, I opened the door and Maria said "Thanks," as she got out. Perfect symmetry.

We walked into the house and she pointed to a chair. "Wait here," she said, and went to the kitchen. She returned, handed me a can of Canfield's and walked the other way, toward the bedroom. I popped the top, took a long slug, and waited.

After about five minutes, I realized Maria was saying something. The problem was, she was saying it as though I were standing next to her, not two rooms away. I got up and walked toward the bedroom so I could hear.

"Come in here," she was saying, over and over.

So I did.

What happened next is something I'll remember until the day I die. And it won't exactly be a pleasant memory.

Maria was standing beside the bed, a big four poster that could have slept the Brady Bunch. The spread and black satin sheet were folded down. If I had had any doubts about her intentions, they were dispelled now.

She had changed out of her mourning garb and into her evening garb. A clingy, translucent pink peignoir that clung and hung in all the right places. I found myself instantly aroused, in spite of the circumstances.

"Take your clothes off," she said.

So I did.

And as I slid off my briefs, she shook, and her peignoir fell silently to the soft, cut-pile carpet. I stood there and stared at one of the most magnificent bodies I have ever seen. Like a goddess, clichéd as it may be, didn't do full justice in describing her beauty. Her shining black hair, unencumbered by the hat, cascaded to her shoulders. Her face, still expressionless, nevertheless held the soft innocence of a little girl. Her breasts were large and round and proud, the nipples dark brown and rigid, pointing to the heavens from whence they came. Her stomach was flat, well muscled; the hips flared into perfect thighs. Her pubic hair was as black as the hair on her head, thicker than any I have ever seen. It started no more than three inches below her navel and curled its way down past her pudenda, ending in ringlets on her inner thighs; the quintessential isosceles triangle.

If Maria had lived in the times of Michelangelo, she'd be immortal today. She was the kind of girl that would prompt Lou to utter another of his favorite lines, "I'd crawl naked through a mile of crushed glass just to kiss her shadow."

Maria stood and watched me watching her, registering no emotion at all. Finally, she moved to the bed, crawled in, and said, "Make love to me."

So I did.

But it wasn't love.

It was a mindless and emotionless act, taking place for no apparent reason. She was a robot and I was her slave.

I entered her freely, to no response. I worked my hips, thrusting in and out, and soon began sweating heavily. Maria was silent, motionless. I squeezed her breasts, gently rolling the nipples between my index finger and thumb. Maria stared, sightless, at the ceiling.

I don't know how long I went through the charade. Five minutes? Fifteen? However long it was, nothing I did elicited any response from her. An inflatable doll would have had more fun. Finally, thankfully, I climaxed, collapsing on the bed next to her, exhausted.

I hadn't taken two breaths before she said, "You should go now."

I got up and dressed without a word; she remained on the bed, unmoving. I felt ashamed. Pete Pepper, the righteous, moral hypocrite. The man who refuses to touch Marianne, his brother's widow. Yet jumps at the chance to screw – and screw is the right word – his dead friend's widow. I suddenly felt pity for Maria, maybe to lessen my own self-contempt. I fought the urge to reach in my wallet and throw a hundred dollars on the bed.

But, no. It was wrong to blame Maria. Show some compassion, Pepper. And don't be so hard on yourself, either. What you did was wrong, but, for whatever reason, it was something Maria wanted. Needed.

Only slightly ameliorated, I left the bedroom, not looking back.

As I walked through the living room on the way to the front door, I grabbed the half-full can of Canfield's. I poured the rest out on the front lawn and tossed the empty into my back seat.

65

I went home, got out of my funeral clothes for the second time in an hour, and took a hot shower. It didn't make me feel cleaner.

The mail hadn't come yet and there were no messages on the machine. I called Harv's office, but he was out. Only when I hung up did it strike me that I didn't see him at the cemetery. And he wouldn't have been hard to spot.

I grabbed the *Free Press* and looked over the Hazel Park entries and results. There was one going in the fourth I liked. A five-year-old mare named Whistlin' Dixie. She was moving up off a claim and the new trainer's brother was a pharmacist. I called Lou to see if he could go out, but Irene informed me he was off to the West Coast to accept some kind of advertising award. There was no way to reach Lef, so I called Fluff and put down a hundred to win and place and wheeled her in the exacta for twenty bucks.

I knew Fluff would lay the bet off with some other bookie or at the track. It would drive the price down, because he'd pass it on to his friends as well. But it was the best I could do; I had plans for the evening.

Thinking about dinner reminded me I hadn't put anything into my stomach all day. Nothing but half a can of Canfield's. On the other hand, I didn't want to eat too much. I like to be real hungry when I go to Giovanni's.

I opened my desk drawer, grabbed the check from Emily Bradshaw and one of Zack's cigars. It was one thirty. Six hours before I had to pick up Eva. And plenty of time for what I had to do.

My first stop was the library. I made a Xerox copy of the check for my records. The Internal Revenue boys had given me a lot of trouble with my racetrack winnings in the past. It got me in the habit of accounting for every dollar I earned.

Then I stopped at the bank, putting $2,500 into savings, $2,000 into checking and $500 in my pocket.

My plan was to grab something light on the way out to Maxie's Humidor in Bloomfield Hills. I took Civic Center Drive across to Telegraph Road, and the solution to my dilemma loomed up on the left almost immediately. Bob Evans' Farm Restaurant. A bowl of gravy and biscuits was just what I needed. Not too much in the way of volume, but plenty substantial to quell the uprising in my stomach. Quite filling, most delicious and certainly among the tastiest breakfast dishes I've ever eaten.

After my third cup of coffee, I hit the road, heading north on Telegraph. Maxie's was in a strip mall set back off Maple Road, just west of Telegraph.

I pulled into a parking spot right in front, grabbing a slot just vacated by a sleek Mercedes diesel.

Maxie Burke is a short, stocky, bald-headed elf of a man, somewhere in his sixties. He was born with a cigar in his mouth. As I walked in, he was holding a smoldering stub in his left hand, talking animatedly to an amused customer. I stood back and listened; Maxie hadn't spotted me.

" ... Tiger Stadium, for Chrissakes," he was saying. "I mean it's outside, for crying out loud. So this guy comes up to me and he says, `excuse me sir, your cigar is bothering my wife, is there any way you could put it out?, and I say, without missing a beat, `Sure, I could dip it in a bucket of water!`"

The customer chuckled loudly, said adios and left. I approached Maxie, holding out the cigar from Zack. Before I could say a word, he grabbed it out of my hand, looked at it and said, "That'll be 4.00 please."

"Wait a minute, Maxie," I said, surprised. "I brought that in with me."

"Sorry," he shot back through the butt clamped between his teeth, "we don't do refunds."

I couldn't help laughing. "Maxie," I told him," this isn't one of yours. It belongs to a friend. In fact, it's a piece of evidence in a case I'm working on. I thought maybe you could tell me something about it."

"What? About the case? What the hell do I know about your case?" Then he winked and grabbed the cigar. "Oh, you mean about the cigar. Let's take a look."

He removed the cigar from the cellophane, rolled it in his fingers, smelled it, and scrutinized it closely, turning it end over end.

"Yeah. I was right," he said. "About four bucks."

"I wasn't trying to establish the value," I said. "What can you tell me about the cigar?"

He took the butt out of his mouth, flipped it toward an ashtray on the counter next to the cash register. It hit the edge, bounced up in the air a few inches and fell in.

"Two points," he shouted, shooting his right arm straight up with two fingers extended. Then he got serious. "It's handmade, all tobacco, probably Honduran, but maybe Canary Islands." Then, to my surprise, he snapped it in half and continued.

"The wrapper is Colorado. That doesn't mean it comes from Colorado; that's the color. Some manufacturers call it natural or E.M.S., which stands for English Market Selection. It's got a leaf binder, which, if you couldn't tell otherwise, is proof that it's handmade. Machine made cigars use a big homogenized sheet for binding. And it's got long filler, which makes it more expensive. Cheaper handmades use short filler, usually scraps from cutting the long filler."

I kept nodding like I understood everything he was saying. Actually, I did follow most of it, but my true expertise in the tobacco field was limited to lighting up.

"That's very impressive, Maxie," I said, "but I was hoping maybe you could tell me who made it. Or where it was sold."

"Shit. Who do you think I am? Sherlock Holmes? You get the box or bundle it came in; I could probably tell you where it was made, but not who sold it. Of course, if you knew the manufacturer, you could get a list of all the wholesalers. Then you could contact all the wholesalers and get a list of all the retailers. But if you took that cigar to all the retailers that sell that kind of cigar, even they couldn't tell you for sure that they sold that particular cigar, and certainly not to whom." He made a point of emphasizing the "m."

Maxie could see I was disappointed.

"Wait a minute," he said. "There is another angle. Could be that cigar wasn't made by one of the name manufacturers. There's a lot of little independent factories, some of 'em one-man shops. They get the tobacco, make 'em right on the premises."

I brightened a little. "Any around here you know of? Or, better yet, in the Ypsilanti or Ann Arbor area?"

"No, not really. Used to be a place out Michigan Avenue by the stadium. La Dorado. Something like that. Been closed maybe fifteen years. Most of the ones I know are in Florida. Tampa. A few on the West Coast too."

"Well, how could this particular cigar be one of those, then?"

"Mail order. How do you think?"

"Oh. Right."

"So. What else can I do for you? I got a special on Jamaican bundles. Maduro. Fifty-nine ninety-five for a bundle of twenty-five. A steal."

"No thanks, Maxie. I still have a couple of those bargains left in my humidor. Back from when they were fifty-four ninety-five."

Maxie shrugged. "Okay. See you around. Sorry I couldn't be more help."

As I turned to leave, he stopped me. "Hey, you want this back? He had the broken cigar in his hand.

"No. Thanks. I have a couple of those at home too. Just throw it out."

But Maxie didn't throw the two halves away. By the time I reached the door, one of them had found a new home. Clenched between Maxie's teeth, grey smoke curling from its tip.

66

I picked up Eva at 7:00 in front of the Michigan Inn. A light rain was falling, adding a chill to the autumn air. She shivered as she got in and settled down.

"I don't know how you can stand this weather," she said, from the depths of her heavy coat. "It never gets like this in California."

I was wearing only a thin jacket over my sport shirt. "Italians are impervious to cold," I told her. "We have a natural grease layer."

"Ooh, maybe you can grease *me* up later." She winked.

"You never know." I smiled back at her. But I knew I wouldn't. Not after Maria.

We got to Giovanni's ten minutes early, keeping my punctuality record for the day intact. Frances, the owner/hostess, greeted us inside.

"Pietro! Welcome! I'm even more delighted than usual to see you!" She held up a rectangular piece of paper. It was the check from my interrupted visit the week before.

I blushed a little as I reached for it. "Oh," I said. "I was wondering about that."

But before I could grab it, she pulled it away and ripped it up. "Pietro! I'm teasing you! I was so embarrassed when that man took you out of here. That's no way to show hospitality to my good friend. It's on the house with my apologies. Besides, you didn't get to eat much, anyway."

She laughed a rich, deep, wonderful Italian laugh so reminiscent of my grandmother's I almost teared up.

I mumbled thanks as Frances grabbed my arm. "Come on, your table's ready." She took us over to a table in the corner, under a big poster that said something in Italian. I was able to decipher 'drink' and 'wine'.

"Here, you kids make yourselves comfortable. When you're ready to order, I'll send Carlo over." She excused herself and went to greet some new customers, probably from California, by the looks of their overcoats.

We sat and chatted idly; Eva delighted that she had successfully secured three locations for her film.

After a few minutes, Carlo, not waiting for a signal, ambled over with wine and a big basket of hot, crusty bread.

"Pietro, mi amico! Buona sera! And to you, too, bella donna," he added for Eva.

Carlo, whose last name was Garofanini was the stereotypical Italian waiter. He was a true Italian, from a little town called Cosenza in the province of Reggio Calabria in southern Italy. Because my grandfather had come from an even smaller town, near Cosenza, he considered me blood. We were both Calabrese.

He poured wine for Eva and me, not bothering to offer a taste first. This was a manifestation of his trueness. I'm serving the wine, buddy. Therefore, it's good. You don't need to sample it. Don't insult me. He smiled warmly as Eva took a drink and nodded her unnecessary approval.

"Magnifico," he said. "Tonight, my little capo negro, you don't need a menu. Carlo will take care of everything." Then he looked at me and asked, uncharacteristically, "Is alright?"

"Ma certo!" I said, enthusiastically, showing off a little for Eva.

Carlo circled his thumb and forefinger, turned abruptly and walked away.

I had been doing some thinking after my unpleasant episode with Maria. About Eva. About how it might be time for me to go legit. As we sat there sipping wine and chewing the crusty hot bread, I decided it was time to voice my thoughts.

" Eva," I said, looking at her lovely face, "how would you like to get married?"

She stopped in mid-chew, her eyes widening perceptibly. "What was that?" she managed through the crust.

"I said, wouldn't you like to be a Pepper too?" stealing a line from a recent soft drink commercial. At the moment I started speaking, I thought she might think it was clever, but before I finished I was afraid it was a little bit lame.

She laughed.

"I'm sorry. I didn't mean it to be funny." I was a little hurt.

She reached over and grabbed my hand. "Oh, Pete. My darling Pete. I wasn't laughing at you. It was just such a funny way to ask. Clever funny, I mean."

"So?" Maybe not too lame.

"Well, it's so sudden. You caught me by surprise."

"That sounds like a no to me."

"No. It's not a no. It's ... oh, Pete, I don't know. After Monday night, I did a lot of thinking about us. One thing I know for sure is that I do love you. But, I'm just not sure that I'm ready yet. My career ... " And her voice trailed off.

"Okay, I understand. Let's not ruin the evening."

"Pete, I'm not sure you do understand. I want to marry you, with all my heart. I want to spend the rest of my life with you. The way I feel, now at least, is that I'd never marry anyone but you. But, not yet."

"Alright. You've given me the right of first refusal. I'll settle for that for now."

She looked up at me, a sad smile on her face. "Oh, Pete, can't you ever be serious? It's killing me. It's eating me up inside. I truly want to be your wife."

Then she got up and ran to the ladies' room, tears streaming down her cheeks.

At the instant she disappeared through the door, Frances screamed from across the room.

"Pietro! It's him again! Run! Get out the back!"

I looked up in time to see Stu Gotts moving toward me. Fast. I stood up to defend myself, knowing I'd be hard pressed to handle a man of Stu's size and strength. He had fists as big as an Easter ham.

Stu slowed down as he neared the table. He pulled out Eva 's vacated chair and sat down.

"We gotta talk, Pete," he said, breathing hard. "It's Nematotta. He's gonna do something crazy."

67

I eased back into my chair and stared at Stu, totally confused. My emotions ran through a spectrum that began with astonishment and ended with relief. My mouth was nowhere near ready to voice the wild thoughts bouncing around in my mind. But that didn't stop it from moving.

"What are you talking about? What the hell's going on here?"

Stu was still panting like he had been running behind my car all the way from the Michigan Inn.

"You didn't show up for your meeting with Nematotta," he explained. "He's pissed. I mean he is really pissed. I ain't never seen him so mad. He was smashing stuff up like he was Godzilla in one of them Japanese movies."

"Where? What stuff?"

"In his office. I mean his new office in the Travelers Tower. Which he only just had decorated last week."

"Well, tell Mr. Lorenzo Nematotta that I had to bury a friend today. Once again, he dictated the time for our so-called meeting, without giving me the opportunity to change or confirm it. Tell him I might have time in my schedule to see him tomorrow."

"It's too late. I can't tell him nothing now."

"What do you mean too late?"

"I mean he flipped out. It's past the point of talking now. He said he was just gonna have to write you off. Teach you a lesson for not taking him serious. He's crazy enough to do something too. I seen what he's done to other people. I even done some of it myself. So you better watch out, Pete."

I sat listening intently, trying to ignore Stu's atrocious grammar, and concentrate on the message and its implications. Finally my mind crystallized on the cause of my confusion. I felt stupid that it took so long.

"Wait a minute, Stu. Last week, you dragged me out of here; you were ready to beat the hell out of me. Now, you're sitting here like we're lifelong friends, warning me that I might be in danger. What did you do, have a conscience transplant? I don't get it."

Stu gave me a pleading look and bowed his head. I read the gesture as embarrassment.

"That's the other reason I can't tell Nematotta nothing," he said, still studying the silverware. "I don't work for him no more."

With great effort, I kept the surprise out of my voice.

"What did he do, fire you?" I asked casually.

"No. I quit. When I seen him tear up that office, destroying all them expensive things, it made me sick. Not sick of him. Sick of me. I'm tired of being on the shady side. I think I'm ready to turn over some new leaves."

I smiled at him as he finally got the courage to look up again.

"You got anything in mind?" I asked him.

"Yeah. I was hoping maybe I could work with you. Be your assistant. Do legwork. Provide muscle. Stuff like that."

I laughed out loud.

"We don't use that kind of muscle here on the sunny side," I told him. "I'm sorry, Stu. I'm used to working alone. Besides, my business isn't that booming. I don't really need an assistant." Actually, business was great.

"It wouldn't have to be full time," he protested. "Just whenever you needed help. You know, things come up once in awhile. You can't do it, give me a call."

I caught a movement out of the corner of my eye; it was Eva. I motioned for her to stay put. She nodded and went back into the ladies' room.

"Alright," I said to Stu. "Let me think about it."

Stu sighed loudly, like I had just taken a great weight off his enormous shoulders.

"Thanks, Pete. I won't let you down. You'll see."

"Hey, no promises," I told him. "By the way," I added, suddenly aware of more mental crystallization, "how did you know I was here?"

"I was following the girl. I knew she'd lead me to you sooner or later."

I was suddenly furious. And thankful I had kept Eva away from the table.

"What the hell gives you the right to follow my girlfriend?" I spat out, loud enough to attract stares from diners five tables away. "How did you even know about her?"

"I heard Nematotta tell one of his other boys to keep an eye on her. See if you was doing something with her this morning when you shoulda been meeting with him."

"Shit. Nematotta knows about Eva? Damn it. Who's the guy watching her? What's his name?"

"Rico Tallerico. They call him Rico-Rico. He's Nematotta's best man. Now that I'm not with him no more," he added with a sly grin.

"Stu," I asked smoothly, my mind now fully in focus, "why did you tail the girl instead of me?"

"By the time I got to your place, you was gone."

"How did you know Eva was at the Michigan Inn?"

"I didn't"

"You didn't?"

"No. Nematotta musta known, though. 'Cause I hung around outside Bruno's. That's the restaurant where Rico eats breakfast every day. I tailed Rico right straight to the Michigan Inn. The girl never left the hotel all day, but I seen her eating in the coffee shop. Rico was eye-balling her from three tables away."

"Christ! You mean this Rico character followed us here to Giovanni's?"

"No. He left about ten after three. I seen him make a call from a lobby phone, to Nematotta, I guess. Then he left."

I sighed the same kind of sigh Stu had just sighed.

"Stu," I told him, "I'm impressed with your work. Not to mention your initiative. You showed me you have something besides a lot of muscle."

"Well thanks, Pete," he said. "I appreciate that." Now he was being the smooth one. "But before you get too, uh, happy," he went on, "I oughta tell you the other reason I was watching the girl."

"What do you mean?"

"I mean I think Nematotta would just as soon rough her up as you. In fact, he'd enjoy it a lot more. I just wanted to make sure nothing happened to her before I got a chance to warn you."

"Christ! That never entered my mind. Stu, I've thought about it long enough. I've got your first assignment for you. Second, actually. You've already handled your first on your own – and I'm going to pay you for it. But here's what I want you to do now. Keep an eye on Eva until she goes back to California this weekend. At the first sign she's being followed by Tallerico, or any of Nematotta's men, you let me know. Don't move in unless you have to; unless they make a move on her. Use your own judgement. Do you have a cell phone?"

Stu nodded, an intense look in his eyes. I got his number and hand-ed him my card.

"Starting tomorrow morning at nine, I want you to call my office every half hour. If I'm not there, leave a message. I'll check in every half hour. Got it?"

"Got it. You gonna tell the girl? Or should I stay out of sight?"

"I haven't decided yet. About telling her, I mean. For now, let's keep her in the dark."

"Check."

I don't know why, but I felt incredibly confident that Eva would be safe with Stu watching her. Probably safer than if I had chosen to tail her myself. Something I would do under ordinary circumstances. But I had other things to take care of, like an obligation to one Emily Bradshaw. A $5,000 obligation. Thinking of that brought up another thought. I stood and got out my wallet.

"Stu," I said, there are two more things I want you to do. Where do you live?"

"Oak Park," he said, with obvious curiosity.

The way he scrunched his forehead made the two-inch scar with its still visible perpendicular suture marks stick out like a centipede on a stick of butter. The scar I had caused.

"They have Adult Evening Classes at Oak Park High, don't they?"

"Yeah. I guess so."

I handed Stu $500. "Consider this an advance," I told him. "Tomorrow morning I want you to rent a car. Nematotta's boys might spot you too easily in your car."

"Good idea," he agreed. "But it don't cost no five hundred smackers to rent a car."

"I said I had two things," I reminded him. "The second one you do at your convenience. I want you to take a night class at Oak Park High. English. If we're going to be partners, I want you to be more schooled in the social graces. You know? Like talking. And don't be offended, okay?"

"Hey! No offense taken. I'm just delighted I can be of service to you; that we can work together," he said with uncharacteristic aplomb. "And I gotta tell you something. I had a feeling all along that it would work out this way."

I let that sink in as Stu smiled and walked out. He was right. Under the circumstances, which he had been aware of all along, it made a lot of sense for me to enlist his aid. I smiled, too, as I realized what had just happened. How I had, in fact, been manipulated. I might be sending Stu Gotts back to high school, but he sure wasn't no dummy!

68

Dinner was spectacular. Carlo brought out a scrumptious array of antipasti that gave me heartburn long before the main course arrived. I, of course, had my usual prosciutto and melon, but Carlo surprised me with a platter of stuffed sweet peppers he called Peperone all'Amalfitana. With a name like that, how could I refuse? Eva nibbled on this and that, but gave most of her attention to Carlo's Carciofo Villa Romana. Artichokes. You have to expect that from a Californian, even a transplanted one.

For the entree, we were both brought veal dishes. I had Costoletta di Vitello alla Marescialla, which is veal rib on the bone, breaded and sautéed in hazelnut butter. Lef had it once and called it the world's most expensive chicken fried steak. Eva had Scallopine di Vitello in Barchetta, veal with mushrooms, ham and shallots. Lots of shallots.

And, while the food was delicious, the ambience around our table was a little chilly, at least for a while. The subject of my proposal was never mentioned again. Fine by me. But Eva was also upset that I wouldn't tell her who Stu was or why he was at Giovanni's. She didn't buy my story that he was a freelancer who did occasional legwork for me and that he'd stopped by to drop off information and get further instructions. A real shame. It was the most perfectly truthful lie I had ever told.

By the time our third bottle of Valpolicella was nearly empty, though, she had loosened up and found everything I said remarkably amusing.

The drive home was quite difficult. She had her hands all over me, mostly below the waist. Somehow I managed to get us to the Michigan Inn, where she asked me in. I begged off, citing exhaustion and an early morning appointment. She accepted those lies without question.

I parked and walked her to the elevator, though, and gave her a lingering, onion-flavored goodnight kiss. Before she went up, I asked her what she planned for tomorrow and was pleased to hear she had a lot more phone work to do. That explained why she hadn't left the hotel all day.

I drove home feeling pretty good except for my gastrointestinal discordance. The only phone messages were from Harvey and Marianne. Both said it could wait until tomorrow. That was good; so could I.

I went upstairs, undressed and punched out my famous Twin Killers medley on the Wurlitzer. These were records that had great songs on both sides, not to be confused with two-sided hits, because most of my Twin Killers were obscure. Like "Tonight Is Just Another Night" and "Unknown Love" by the Martiniques, and "Misery" and "I'm The Man" by the Dynamics. To my knowledge, only Bobby Day's classics, "Rockin' Robin" and "Over And Over" and Richie Valens' only hit record, the two-sided "Donna" and "La Bamba" had ever received significant airplay.

I plopped down on the sofa and soared to the skies on wings of song. The colorful lights of the jukebox illuminated the room, and I felt like I was glowing too.

A little after eleven thirty and three trips to the john, my blood alcohol level was down pretty close to non-violation of the Volstead Act. I jumped up and ran to the telephone and dialed my favorite 976- number, The Racing Hotline.

Whistlin' Dixie had won, paying $3.60 and $2.80 to win and place. Old Fluff had sent the odds down, all right. But what he couldn't have known was that a longshot filly named DimeADance would run second and key a perfecta worth $92 even. That made my total return on a $340 investment $1,240. Who says you can't win 'em all?

I went to the fridge and fished around on the bottom shelf, finally finding a cold can of Walter's I had forgotten was there. I popped the tab and took half the can in one long slug. Why not? The Volstead Act had been repealed in 1933, along with the Eighteenth Amendment.

69

A loud noise roused me out of a deep sleep. My first reaction was one of panic. Something heavy was on my chest and my head felt like somebody had been playing soccer with my brain. The noise didn't let up, each recurring blast sending stabbing lances of pain through my eyeballs. Groggily, I tried to get up, rolling over instinctively to check my clock radio for the time. But the clock wasn't there and I crashed to the floor as something sharp raked my chest open and an inhuman scream flew by my ear.

Stunned and confused, I sat up – and realized I had fallen asleep on the sofa. The heavy weight on my chest was Nehi. My sudden movement must have startled him and his claws ripped my shirt and opened a neat cut across my right pectoral when he jumped. Blood was oozing out, staining the already ruined shirt. My head still throbbing and my chest in pain, it finally dawned on me that the phone was ringing. That's what had awakened me.

I made my way to the wall phone in the kitchen, pulled out a chair and sat before I answered. It was Stu Gotts, my trusty employee.

"Pete. Stu here. Everything's fine. No sign of Nematotta's men yet. The girl ain't left the hotel." His remarkably cheery tone compounded my own misery.

"Yeah. That's great, Stu. Keep watching." I hung up before he could say anything else. Then I went to the refrigerator and got out my blue jar of Brioschi, the Italian wonder medicine. I fixed a tall glass, pouring in two heaping lids of the white crystals. It took me three minutes to force it all down. That was a sure sign I was in major hangover territory. Usually I can slug down a glass in seven seconds. For me, Brioschi wasn't just an antacid; under ordinary circumstances it was a pleasure drink.

I lumbered back to the sofa, cursing myself for not drinking a few glasses last night. I knew better. I read somewhere that dehydration is a major cause of hangovers. And anytime I drink what, for me, is an excessive amount, I always try to drink at least two glasses of water before I go to bed. Come to think of it, I never did make it to bed. Maybe that's why I forgot.

I forgave myself, cursed the wine instead, and fell back asleep.

True Blue Stu woke me again at 9:30. Amazingly, I felt much better. No doubt the Brioschi.

"They're here," Stu said, sounding like the little girl in the Poltergeist promos.

"They? How many?"

"Just two. Rico-Rico and some guy I don't recognize. Must be one of his buddies. Ain't one of the Toad's regulars."

"Where are they? What are they doing?"

"They each came in their own car. One parked with a view of the front entrance; one by the side. The guy I don't know is sitting in his car, reading a newspaper. I think it's the *Racing Form*. Rico just went for a walk. My guess is he's heading for the Big Boy to get some breakfast."

"Why would he go there when he could eat at the coffee shop in the hotel?"

"You seen the prices on the menu? Anything Rico can do to save a buck, he does it."

"All right. Keep me posted. I don't think they'd try anything in broad daylight, but you never know. I'd have to say this confirms your suspicion that they might try to snatch her. It scares me."

"Don't worry, Pete. I won't let nothing happen to her."

"Right. Thanks, Stu." I hung up, hoping his double negative wasn't an omen.

70

One day, back when I was a teenager and visiting my grandmother in West Virginia, I decided to fry some eggs for breakfast. I was a big fan of sunny-side up back then. While the eggs were frying, I went to the breadbox for some bread and found it empty. It was a disaster. I couldn't eat fried eggs without toast to dip into the yolk. So, without thinking, I grabbed the spatula and attacked the half-fried eggs in the big iron skillet. I swirled the spatula furiously, scrambling the hell out of 'em right in the pan. To my surprise, the result was delicious. In fact, they were the best tasting scrambled eggs I had ever eaten, with big flecks of white scattered throughout the yellow.

I whipped up a batch of those same eggs, hoping I'd be able to keep them down. The Brioschi had helped my head, but I was still a bit queasy in the stomach.

I showered and dressed after Stu's second call. The cut on my chest wasn't as bad as it felt. After swabbing it with alcohol and cleaning the blood away, I could see that it was shallow. Stitches would definitely be unnecessary; it was already starting to scab over.

Stu called at ten, just as I finished the eggs. He reported that Rico had returned with coffee and donuts and didn't give any to his buddy. Of course, Stu said "none" instead of "any."

After that call, I felt strong enough to venture downstairs and outside to pick up the *Free Press*. I was glancing at the Hazel Park entries when Stu's 10:30 call came. He was beginning to irritate me. But he had good news. Rico left and his buddy remained in his car. It made me feel confident that they were just watching her; that no move was imminent. With any luck, Eva would stay in her room all day. Or maybe go no farther than the coffee shop. My spirits somewhat buoyed, I told Stu he only had to call me every hour unless something changed drastically.

A loud rumbling emanated from my stomach, a noise, according to my wordsmith friend Lou Bracato, called borborygmus. It was the eggs, but it was more peaceful than threatening. It made me wonder if Stu had eaten anything yet. So I offered to relieve him if he wanted to go grab some lunch later.

"Don't bother," he said. "I brang lunch with me."

71

Half an hour later I was downstairs in my office, catching up on one of my personal projects. I should have been out tracking down Zachary Bradshaw, but I was still feeling a little queasy. Maybe after noon, I'd feel up to it.

I had a stack of old 45-rpm records on my desk that I was in the process of cataloging. My custom-built cabinet was more of a bookcase with vertical wooden dividers. There were twenty-two compartments, one for each letter of the alphabet except P and Q which shared the same slot, and W, X, Y and Z, also slotted together. I had the records arranged alphabetically, by group or artist. My intent was to feed all the data into my computer and get a printout of every record in my collection. I was up to the J compartment, which meant I was averaging about five letters a year. Not because I had so many records; I just didn't get around to doing it very often.

There was also the problem of learning how to work the computer program that took raw data and alphabetized it. That's why I was writing everything down using pen and paper. I had just catalogued "Jennie Lee," an early rocker by Jan & Arnie on that unforgettable pink and black Arwin label, when the phone rang.

My heart raced. It wasn't time for Stu to call again, unless something had gone wrong.

Harvey Steinberg spoke before I could even say hello. "Are you sitting down, Pete?" His tone was almost smug.

"As a matter of fact, I am."

"Good, my friend. Because I think we have George Gianotti's murderer."

"You're kidding! Who? Where is he? How did you get him?"

"Whoa. Whoa. Slow down. I'm about to tell you. Actually, we don't have him; we just know who he is. But let me start from the start."

I sighed. "Okay, Harv." He was basking in the double pleasure of making me squirm and embarking on another tale of his magnificent exploits.

"Well, this morning, I'm over at Broder, Lerner, Roth, the law firm where George worked."

"And Calabrese," I interrupted.

"What?"

"Calabrese. The name of the law firm is Broder, Lerner, Roth and Calabrese. I might even be related to Calabrese."

Harv ignored my familial speculation. "Oh yeah. Calabrese. The token gentile." He broke into a chuckle and I joined him. Harv is probably the least racist person I've ever met.

"Anyway," he continued, "I'm just nosing around, asking questions here and there. You know, routine. Nobody in the whole joint could think of a single enemy George might have had. So then I ask Broder if I can look at George's files on the Bradshaw business and he says no. But after a little pleading and hemming and hawing, he finally said that, under the circumstances, he'd look the other way if I happened to glance through the file. So I spent about twenty minutes looking through the stuff, but I didn't spot anything that gave me a clue. I was about to leave when this guy comes up and asks if he can talk to me in private. His name was Stan Shapiro, young guy, kind of a loud dresser. So we went into his office and he closed the door and he said he had some information that might be important."

"Seems that last week, Shapiro thinks it's on a Wednesday, but he can't be sure, he came back from lunch and saw some guy hanging around outside the office entrance. A little guy, kinda wimpy, you know, bald headed and wire rim glasses. So Shapiro asked if he could help him and the guy said he wanted to talk to George Gianotti. Next thing you know, the guy started sobbing. Shapiro calmed him down, brought him into his office and let him wait because George was still out to lunch."

"So now Shapiro is feeling bad for the guy, so he asks if there was anything he could do. The guy asked for a cup of coffee, so Shapiro got him one. Then the guy sat down, took a few sips and proceeded to tell Shapiro a very interesting story."

"The guy's name is Randy Sharpe, by the way, and his wife – you guessed it – his wife is the secretary for Roth, one of the partners."

"No, Harv. I didn't guess it."

"Will you shut the fuck up and let me finish."

"Sorry."

"Anyway, according to Sharpe, Ramona, that's the wife, is having an affair with George Gianotti. He knows it for a fact because he followed them to a motel one day during lunch hour, not that lawyers take just an hour."

"Ramona, huh? That's the same name as Emily Bradshaw's new housekeeper."

"Will you stop interrupting me. There's a lot of women named Ramona. Anyway, Shapiro was surprised because this Ramona is kinda the shy, quiet type, not someone you'd expect to be screwing around. Although he did say she could be real attractive if she didn't dress so plain and if she used a little makeup. But he played it cool and asked Sharpe what he had in mind with George. Sharpe said he didn't really know; that he wanted to meet George face to face. Maybe just talk to him. Then he broke down crying again and said 'Who the hell does Gianotti think he is, ruining my life like this?'"

"Then Shapiro comforts him some more, but inside he was a little worried for George. So he excused himself, pretending to go get some more coffee, but really to see if George was back so he could warn him. George was still gone and when Shapiro got back to his office, Sharpe was gone too."

A long pause told me that Harvey's story was over. He was waiting for my reaction. While I was mulling it over, he got tired of waiting.

"So what do you think, for Christ's sake?" he shouted.

"I don't think you have enough to convict him."

"I know that! Jesus! But wait 'til we find this Sharpe character. There isn't any doubt in my mind. He's the killer."

"Yeah? How do you tie him to Vandever and Kimberly and Spaulding and Pringham?"

"That's just it. I don't. I think we've been laboring under false pretenses. I think Gianotti's murder was an isolated case. Not related to the others at all. We just assumed that it was. And we assumed wrong. Plus, I always felt that considering Gianott'e mutilation to be occupation related was questionable."

"Hey, Harv, it's possible. You could be right. But I think the jury's still out. We need more evidence."

"Sure we do. But I think you're forgetting a major piece of evidence we already have." Harvey was approaching smugness again. "Evidence gathered by one Pete Pepper himself!"

"What are you talking about?"

"Something that George said to you, on the night – the morning, that is – he was murdered. 'Her ... husband ... killed ...' "

Wham! It hit me like a ton of bricks from the Great Wall of China. "Holy Christ, Harv."

Harv interrupted my speechlessness with a chuckle. "So, Old Lieutenant Steinberg's theory isn't so farfetched after all, eh?"

I was still stunned, possibilities racing through my mind faster than I could keep track.

"So you're speculating that Sharpe somehow followed George out to the Bradshaw mansion, snuck in and killed George while Emily was sleeping off a bender?

"Why not? He followed his wife to a motel with George."

"I guess. What about Sharpe? Where is he? And what about his wife? Ramona?"

"Interesting little situation, there," Harv replied. "She resigned the next day. Friday. The day George was killed, only nobody knew it yet. Didn't give the usual two weeks. Just up and left. She hasn't been seen since. And we can't locate Mr. Sharpe, either."

"Wait a minute! You said she resigned the next day. Friday. Is that exactly what Shapiro said?"

"I think so. Why?"

"Because if it was the next day, that means Sharpe was at George's office on a Thursday, not a Wednesday. And that particular Thursday was the day George drove out to Belleville and got himself killed. Randy Sharpe just could have hung around the law office and followed George to Emily Bradshaw's house."

"You got that right, my friend!" Harv was excited. "I gotta run. I'm gonna go see Shapiro and see if we can't get these days straightened out."

"Right. And let me know if either of the Sharpes turns up too."

"Will do. Later."

72

It made sense. Maybe Harv was right. George's demise at the Bradshaw house, if that was where he was killed, could have been a wild coincidence, totally unrelated to the other grisly killings. His mutilation wasn't as obviously profession related as the others had been. Could the removal of his eyes, teeth and fingerprints have anything to do with the legal profession? The jury was out on that too.

I wanted to endorse Harvey's theory wholeheartedly. But I couldn't. George's murder was just too much like the others for me to accept coincidence. Every victim, for example, had been dealt a heavy blow to the head. Wait! I didn't know if that were true in Spaulding's case. I'd have to ask Toaz about that.

But let's try another argument. Suppose Randy Sharpe did kill George, who definitely had been hit on the head. Could a small wimp, as Harv (or was it Shapiro?) had called him, remove George's body without a trace from the Bradshaw house? Then transport it some thirty or forty miles to George's own apartment, up the stairs and into his bedroom? George wasn't especially heavy, maybe 140 or 150 pounds, tops. Still, that would have meant that Sharpe had to lift him bodily, because dragging him surely would have left some sort of evidence, both at the Bradshaw house and in George's apartment. Evidence that I saw no sign of. No, it just didn't play. I couldn't convince myself that Sharpe was our man.

I gathered up my "J" records and returned them to their proper slot. I had too much on my mind to do any more cataloging.

Stu's 11:30 call interrupted my speculating. Everything was status quo at the Michigan Inn. Good. One problem was enough to deal with right now.

I was trying to decide what to do next: Look for Sharpe, look for Zachary or lie down and recuperate some more. The decision was made when my doorbell rang. I answered it.

A slight man wearing a white poplin jacket was on my porch. He was glancing around furtively. Like he was afraid of being spotted.

"Are you Pete Pepper?" he asked in a surprisingly calm and deep voice.

"Just like the sign says," I told him.

"My name is Randy Sharpe," he said. "I have to talk to you."

73

With his jacket off, it was apparent that my quick impression of Sharpe – as well as Shapiro's – was way off base. He was small, yes; about five seven. But he was certainly no wimp. He was in superb shape; his musculature solid whipcord. The way he moved would have made a cat salivate.

He was agile and graceful, and in spite of his stature, he looked powerful. I pegged him for a weightlifter or an ex-wrestler, college level. But could he have hefted George's body around? Yeah. I think he could have. There's a wrestling maneuver called the fireman's carry. My guess was that Sharpe could pull it off with ease.

Sharpe wasn't exactly baldheaded, either, as Harvey had reported. Another dubious Shapiro observation. His hairline was about a half inch more receded than Lou's and I could see that there was a telltale circle starting to thin at the crown. A quick glance might render the bald verdict, but Sharpe basically just had a close-cropped haircut. At least Shapiro got one thing right. Sharpe was wearing wire-rimmed glasses.

I surprised him a little when I told him I knew why he was here. I brought him upstairs, whipped up a quick pot of coffee and got us settled down in the living room before I let him talk at length.

"I didn't do it," were the first words out of his mouth after he drained half a cup in one gulp.

I looked at him with pursed lips. His eyes were clear, his expression calm, his demeanor much more relaxed than when he had been on the porch. I believed him and I think he sensed as much. But I wasn't ready to play good cop yet.

"Innocent men don't run and hide," I said.

"Yeah. That's easy to say as long as you aren't the innocent man being chased."

"How do you know someone's after you?"

"I'm an eyewitness. Earlier this morning I took a chance and drove by my house. Not directly past it, you can see it from the side street. There was a guy knocking on my door. Not in a uniform, but I guess I know an unmarked car when I see one."

"That explains why you're hiding now. What about for the past week?"

"I haven't been hiding for a week. Just since I got back from Ohio. Look, when I confronted Ramona, she kinda had a nervous breakdown. Guilt, I guess. She went back home to her family. In Wilmington, Ohio."

"Wilmington? Hey, that's horse country. Lots of trotters and pacers bred down that way."

"Yeah. Could we talk about that some other time? What the hell am I going to do now?"

"Let's just talk some more, Randy. Tell me about what you did on the Thursday you stopped by to visit George at his office. It was a Thursday, wasn't it?"

"Yeah, it was a Thursday. But it sounds like you already know what I did."

"I mean after you left. And why did you leave so suddenly?"

"Impulse. I had a feeling that slick lawyer type who took me into his office was going to stir up some trouble. I didn't really know what I was going to say to George – uh, I assume you know that he was screwing my wife?"

"So I've heard."

"Anyway, I had second thoughts about the whole thing. I thought maybe chances of patching things up with Ramona would be better if I never saw the guy. Christ, who knows what I was thinking. I just panicked and left. When the clotheshorse said he was going to get more coffee, I just slipped out. Speaking of which, do you have any more coffee?"

I took our cups to the kitchen and refilled them, keeping an eye on Sharpe all the while. Not that I expected him to sneak away.

"All right," I said, returning. "Where did you slip out to?"

"This is the part you won't believe," he said sadly, "but it's God's truth. "I just drove around. I tried to clear my head, but instead I wound up in a bar and totally fucked it up."

"The bar?"

"My head."

"Oh. So then what happened?"

"I eventually went home. I don't know what time it was; well after dark, for sure. Probably close to midnight. Ramona wasn't there. So I just crashed on the bed. Didn't even take off my clothes. The next morning I noticed a note on top of the TV. Ramona said she was spending the night with a girlfriend. Don't worry, it said. She also mentioned that she was ashamed and didn't know if she could ever face me again."

"Do you have the note?"

"Right here," he said, reaching into his wallet and handing me some scraps of paper. He had obviously ripped the note up.

"I want to keep this," I told him.

"Fine."

I smoothed out the strips of paper and pieced them together. It said essentially what he told me. I went to the kitchen, dug through my junk drawer, and returned with some tape and the coffee pot. After topping off Sharpe's cup, I taped the note together and put it into my own wallet.

"Please go on," I urged him.

"Well, after I read the note, I cried myself through a bottle of whiskey. Then I guess I passed out. Sometime later, in the afternoon, Ramona came home. We had a scene. We were both yelling and crying. She packed up a few things and said she was going to Wilmington. I tried to stop her, but she left anyway."

The memory was painful for Sharpe. His voice began cracking when Ramona re-entered the scene. Now he let loose and started sobbing. I did my best to comfort him but my soothing tones didn't do the job.

"You don't understand," he choked out. "I hit her. I fucking hit her. Knocked her to the floor. Christ, Pete. Never, ever in my life have I hit a woman. I don't care if she was fucking the whole world, I didn't have any right to hit her. Not Ramona. Oh, God, what am I going to do?"

The phone dictated my next move. I excused myself and took Stu's call in the bedroom. Still no action at the Inn.

When I returned, Sharpe had regained his composure. My heart felt for him. For a second, I had to fight off sympathetic tears myself. More important, my instinct told me that a man this remorseful over striking a woman would not likely have struck a deathblow to the skull of George Gianotti.

"Do you feel up to talking some more? I asked.

"Yeah. I'm sorry, Pete. But it's so tough."

"Don't apologize. It's not necessary. I understand. Just tell me what happened after she left."

"I just sulked around the house. One minute I was in anguish, the next I was pissed off. I fixed something to eat; I hadn't eaten for more than twenty-four hours. Then for some reason, my thoughts turned to George again. I called information and got his home number. I called and his wife answered. Maria."

"Yes, I know her. George was my friend."

"I know that. Maria told me about you. That's why I decided to come here. She said you were there earlier that day asking about George."

"Really? Why would she offer information like that?"

"She didn't, at first. But I wasn't necessarily looking for George. I was just looking to get even. He screwed up my life; I wanted to mess his up too. The reason I called was to let Gianotti's wife know that he was having an affair. I squealed on him. And I still won't apologize for that."

"You told Maria that George was playing around with your wife?"

"You're fucking-A right I did."

"How did she react?"

"She didn't believe it at first. But I gave her dates and times and motel names. Not to mention Ramona's name. Finally, she believed me. She said it explained why he was so willing to move out. Then she reacted the same way I did. Erratic. From sad to mad and back again."

"Wait a minute. When you called, you didn't know George had moved out."

"No way. How would I possibly know that?"

"So you were prepared for the possibility that he might have answered. What would you have done?"

Sharpe shrugged. "I would have asked for Maria. He doesn't know my voice."

"That's true," I said with an 'I should have thought of that' look. In fact, I was sneaking in a trick question. When Sharpe called Maria on Friday evening, George had already been dead for several hours. The naturalness of his response, the very fact that he had a contingency plan, such as it was, was proof enough for me that he didn't know that George was dead. And therefore, couldn't have been the killer. I voiced this opinion to Randy.

"Hey, Pete," he said, "I didn't find out Gianotti was dead until the following Monday. After I spoke to Maria, after I found out that George was missing, my immediate thought was that he was with Ramona; that she didn't go to Wilmington at all. So I killed another bottle of whiskey and contemplated killing myself."

"The next day, Saturday, I drove down to Wilmington and she was there. Had been since late Friday night. That smoothed me out a little and we talked sensibly for a while. But she made me stay in a motel. I did my best to apologize for hitting her and tried to reconcile, but she said she needed some time alone. Maybe we could patch things up eventually. On Monday, she called a girlfriend at work and found out George was dead. She got hysterical and locked herself in her bedroom. I haven't seen or talked to her since."

"You came back then?"

"No. I stuck around for a few more days, hoping to see Ramona again. It didn't happen. Then I drove back here. I knew that I'd be a suspect under the circumstances. Hell, Shapiro is a lawyer. There wasn't any question that he'd implicate me. But I had to come back and see if I could somehow clear my name. That's why I'm here. Problem is, I don't have much money. Ramona cleaned out the savings account, which is fine. But most of the loose cash I have went for meals on the road. And my credit card is maxed out from motel bills."

My caseload was suddenly getting overloaded. And the only paying job was getting the least attention.

"I'll do what I can, Randy," I told him. "As for the money, don't worry about it. Unofficially, I'm semi-investigating George's murder. For Maria. Clearing you is a natural consequence of finding the real killer. What I'm saying is that I believe you. But you're aware that I can check out your story."

"Pete, I want you to check it out."

"Well, maybe I'll just give Maria a call to corroborate a few of the more salient points."

I didn't bother to go to the bedroom. I used the kitchen phone, in earshot of Sharpe. After a few rings, a familiar voice came on the line. Not Maria's. It was a recording that said the number had been disconnected. I hung up, surprised. And a moment later I was utterly stunned by a sudden realization.

My God! My God! My God! I was so attentive to Randy's story that it didn't even dawn on me at first. But now it exploded in my mind, and I reeled and fell hard onto the seat of a kitchen chair.

Maria's mysterious behavior after George's funeral. Her seduction of a bewildered, but strangely willing private investigator. Could there be any other explanation? It was her own misguided way of getting even with George for being unfaithful to her!

For getting himself killed.

74

Until I could figure out what to do with Randy, I thought it made sense to let him stay at my place. If it turned out to be more than a brief arrangement, he could sleep downstairs on the sofa in my office. We took his car to the covered parking structure at Prudential Town Center, a huge office complex near my office. Then I dropped him back at my place and drove off alone in search of Maria Gianotti.

75

It was nearly two o'clock as I approached Maria's house. It was a cool afternoon and several pre-school kids were playing in their yards, most without jackets. A shapely neighbor was watering big pots of fading fall flowers on her front porch, two houses down from Maria's. It stirred up memories of Ralph Spaulding. As I pulled into the driveway, I was surprised to see a for sale sign in the front yard. I should have noticed it sooner, but the neighbor had a momentary monopoly on my attention. The sign could certainly explain the disconnected phone, but there was no "sold" sticker pasted across it. And would Maria have moved out before it sold? Or discontinued her utilities before she moved out?

I got out and rang the doorbell. There was no answer. Fighting a sudden panic, I walked around and looked in through the picture window. There was a small opening in the drapes that let me take in the living room and part of the adjacent dining room. There was no sign of any activity. But, with most of the furniture covered with sheets, I shouldn't have expected any. The house was clearly vacated. Maria was gone. Still, a terrifying image of Maria's dead body under one of those sheets flashed through my mind.

"Can I help you with something?" A husky woman's voice interrupted my vision. It was the neighbor and she wasn't friendly.

"Huh? No. I, uh, I was just looking for Maria Gianotti. You wouldn't happen to know where she is, would you?"

"If I did, why would I tell you?"

She was quickly becoming less attractive. "Because I'm a friend," I told her. "I was doing some work for Maria, investigating her husband's murder."

"Friends don't go around peeping in a friend's window."

"Like I said, I'm a private investigator. We peep wherever and whenever we have to. Especially when we fear a friend may be in danger."

"Maria in danger? From who?"

She didn't pronounce the "m."

"From whomever killed George, and very likely four or five other people. Look, my name is Pete Pepper. I went to college with George. I just came across some new information and wanted to tell Maria about it."

I handed her my identification.

She took it and scrutinized it carefully, scowling all the while. "How would I know if this is real or not?" she asked, handing it back.

"I guess you wouldn't. But if you're a friend of Maria's, it's important that you help me get in touch with her. You don't have to tell me anything directly. Just call her yourself, and let her know that I need to ask, uh, talk to her."

My miscue brought a slight crack to the neighbor's scowl; almost a smile. "So, is Maria a suspect?"

"No, no. Not at all. It's just that there is a suspect now, even though he probably shouldn't be. Anyway, we discovered that this guy, the suspect, spoke to Maria shortly after George was killed, and I just wanted to get her impressions of the conversation."

I didn't bother to mention that the guy in question was George's lover's husband. If the neighbor didn't already know about George's indiscretions, she wasn't going to find out from me.

"Pete Pepper. I remember you now. From the funeral. You sat next to Maria, didn't you? You look a lot different when you're dressed up."

She gestured to my jeans and sweatshirt; a smile had definitely found its way to her lips.

"Hey, I'm not a corporate executive. I like to dress casual, and most of the time, my job lets me."

"I'm Jane Broder," she said, wiping off and offering her hand. "My husband is, er was, one of George's law partners."

"Right! And you're the one who brings the Canfield's back from Chicago!"

Her lips parted and the smile became a laugh. It sounded a little like Emily Bradshaw's. "That's right! My gosh! Maria told you that!"

"She even gave me a six pack. There's an empty can in my back seat right now."

"Oh my goodness!"

"Hey, I told you we were friends. So, can you help me here, or not?"

"I'm afraid not," she said, suddenly becoming serious. "I mean, I would if I could. All I know is that she moved. Quite suddenly, as you're well aware. But I don't know where. I do know she was very upset, and she said she'd call me eventually. So, all I can do for you is tell her you want to speak with her. Assuming she ever does call."

"Well, that's all I can ask for. I appreciate it."

"No problem," she smiled, accepting the card I proffered. "See you around, Pete."

I thanked her again and walked back to my car. On the way home, it dawned on me that I hadn't gotten a call from Stu for more than an hour. Had he called after I left? And if I didn't answer, why hadn't he tried my cell phone? Damn! I had instructed Randy not to answer the phone. Impulsively, I called home on my cell, not expecting Sharpe to answer and not overly concerned. But he did answer. On the first ring.

"Randy, it's Pete. Has a Stu Go ..."

"Get here fast, Pete!" he interrupted. "Stu called not long after you left. He was hysterical. Kept saying the same thing over and over: 'They got the girl. They got the girl.'"

76

Somehow, I kept my composure. I couldn't believe Nematotta would actually harm Eva. It was just his way of making a point. Of punishing me for not taking him more seriously. And forcing me to finally meet with him.

I didn't go home. Instead I pulled into a supermarket parking lot and called Stu. He answered after three rings.

"Pete, is that you?"

"Yeah, Stu. What happened?" I was careful not to sound angry or panicky.

"I'm sorry, Pete. I'm sorry. I guess instead of me watching them, they mighta been watching me too." Stu wasn't hiding his panic.

"How'd they pull it off, Stu?"

"There was three of 'em, not two, having breakfast in the coffee shop. I was pretending to read the paper in the lobby, but I could see them through the window. When they finished, two of 'em went out the front and Rico headed around toward the side door. I didn't see the girl nowhere, so I walked over and watched the two guys get into a car, but they didn't drive away. When I went back to get my paper, here comes Rico out of the elevator with the girl."

"Stu, the girl's name is Eva."

"Right. So Eva looks scared but she ain't struggling, so I don't know what Rico told her or how he got her out of her room. Anyway, I hung back and watched 'em go out the front door. That's when I called you, but someone else answered, and I just said tell Pete they got the girl.

Eva. Then I ran out and saw them getting in to Rico's car, which was in the second row. He helped her into the front passenger seat. Then as he was walking around to the driver's side, I ran up and yelled 'Stop Rico!'"

"He turned and looked at me and just smiled. Next thing I know, there's a gun in my side and his two buddies march me over to my car, which somehow they knew where it was. They put me in the back seat and one of 'em zapped me with a stun gun or something. I only came to a few minutes ago and I still feel groggy. I'm sorry Pete. I really let you down."

"No Stu. You didn't. I don't know what more you could have done. Besides, I don't think the Toad means to harm Eva. He's just using her to lure me in. Trying to teach me a lesson."

"You're gonna go meet him?"

"I have no choice. Where do you suppose they've taken her, Stu?"

"Probly his new office in Travelers Tower."

"The one on the sixth floor. Yeah, that's what I'm thinking too. Listen, Stu, I want you to go home and take it easy. You were probably Tasered. Don't drive until you're sure you have your senses. Maybe you should go in and have a coffee first. But promise me you'll just go home and relax until you hear from me."

"Okay Pete. I promise."

I felt bad that Stu felt he let me down. And even worse that he got Tasered. At least that explained why he hadn't called my cell. On the way to Travelers Tower, I called home again. Sharpe answered and I told him I had some business to take care of and didn't know how long it would take.

"It may be past dinnertime when I get home," I said, "so feel free to help yourself to whatever food you find. I'm pretty well stocked. And plan on crashing at my place at least until tomorrow when we get things straightened out with the police. You can sleep on the sofa downstairs. It's a pull-out bed."

"Pete, you're unbelievable," he almost sobbed. "I'm a complete stranger and you're ... listen, if there's anything I can do to help you. Anything."

"Not necessary, Randy. There's really nothing you can ... no, wait a minute! Yes there is."

"Like I said, Pete. Anything."

"If I'm not back by six, feed my cats."

77

I remembered that Nemnatotta's new office was on the sixth floor, but I didn't recall the number. I should have checked the directory on the ground floor, but my mind was racing with thoughts about Eva.

The layout consisted of one long hall running the length of the building, with two shorter halls intersecting it, effectively dividing the floor into thirds. Or sixths, if you were a math stickler.

I walked past every office door and saw nothing that said Nematotta.

So I took another tour and literally slapped my forehead when I saw it: Lorenzo & Associates. More professional sounding than Toad & Toadies, I suppose.

The door was solid, no way to see inside. But it was unlocked, so I guessed the Toad was in business. I opened it and walked into semi-darkness. The blinds were drawn and the place was eerily silent. I spotted what looked like a body in the doorway of an interior office. God, please! Not another corpse.

Was this a trap? Was the Toad playing some kind of sick game? Only one way to find out. I stepped back to the entrance, felt the wall for a light switch and flipped it on.

Stu wasn't kidding when he said the place was trashed. Filing cabinets were turned over, lamps were broken, art was ripped off the walls and paper was scattered all over the place. What I feared was a body was an overturned coat rack with an overcoat still on it. If Nematotta was planning on consolidating all his operations in one location, he still had a lot of work ahead of him.

Just to be sure there was no one around – dead or alive – I checked inside the three interior offices and the half dozen workstations on the opposite wall. No sign of Eva. No sign of anybody.

Son of a bitch. Where do I go now? I ran through the options on the elevator ride down. And realized there was only one that made any sense.

78

I drove past Giovanni's and parked across the street from the Toad's call center, the office that Stu had dragged me into a week earlier. I heard voices as I walked up the stairs, one at a time. The Toad was clearly expecting me.

He sat behind his beat-up wooden desk, with a smug look on his face. Other than a gun, the desktop was empty. Eva was tied to a chair in the middle of the room, wearing only a bra and panties. A couple of thugs came out of a side room and stood on either side of her.

"Well, well. Look who's here," Nematotta spat out. "Do you have an appointment, Pepper?"

"Fuck you, Nematotta. If you harmed a hair on her head, you're dead. Did he hurt you, Eva?"

Eva just shook her head no. She was obviously scared.

"I didn't touch her at all, asshole. In fact, she was polite enough to take off her clothes with minimal, uh, resistance. Right boys?"

The thugs chuckled loudly. "Yeah, boss," one of them said. Probably Rico from the size of him.

The Toad cocked his head toward Eva. "Am I lying, sweetheart?"

"Didn't feel like I had much of a choice," Eva muttered softly.

"See, Pete. I'm not a cruel person. But you don't have an appointment for this afternoon. And, unfortunately, I have some other business to attend to."

He pulled something out of his desk drawer, apparently an appointment book and glanced at it. "Hmmm, I seem to be booked up tomorrow too. Maybe I can fit you in Saturday. Or possibly Monday. You don't mind waiting, do you? Listen boys, I'm gonna go grab something to eat. Finish up today's paperwork, then take care of that, uh, other business. And don't forget to lock up when you leave."

With that, he got up and walked toward the door. As I watched in disbelief, one of the thugs came up behind me and sapped me. Hard. I went down face first on the floor and felt blood gushing from my nose. Nematotta had a few more words for me as I faded into unconsciousness.

"See you later, Pepper. Much later."

79

When I came to, it was pitch dark. I was still face down, with my legs bound and my hands tied behind my back. My nose must have been caked with blood, because I was breathing through my mouth. Head still throbbing, I managed to roll onto my back and sit up. When my eyes adjusted, I could see that Eva was still on the chair, chin on her chest. I hoped she was sleeping, but I couldn't tell. She didn't answer when I croaked her name. The Toad wouldn't have drugged her, would he?

As I slowly scooted my way over to her, I heard footsteps pounding up the stairs. Seconds later, one of the thugs burst through the door and flipped on the light.

"Pete, are you okay?"

It wasn't a thug; it was Stu.

"Stu! Thank God. Quick, check Eva. Then come and untie me."

Eva wasn't drugged. She was exhausted and still shaken, but she was physically okay. Stu looked away as she got dressed and I went into the washroom to clean my face. My nose still hurt, but it didn't seem to be broken.

The only thing broken was Stu's promise to go home and get some rest. Instead, he decided to check out Nematotta's Travelers Tower office, thinking I might need some help there. Then, as I did, he came to the old office, just in time to see Nematotta's thugs leaving. Apparently, their other business was tying me up and maybe getting a little more familiar with an unconscious Eva. I hoped not.

"How did you know there weren't any more of the Toad's thugs in here?" I asked Stu as we left the building.

"I seen the lights go out as I was pulling up," he said. "Last guy out always turns out the lights. Nematotta's rule. Then I seen two of them come out the door."

"And you just happened to have a spare key for this office?"

"Actually I have a couple of 'em at home. But I didn't want to waste time to go get one."

"So, how … "

"Didn't you notice when we left, Pete? I busted the door down."

80

We headed straight for the Michigan Inn and up to Eva's room. Stu promised to go home and get some rest, but that was the least of my worries.

My only concern at the moment was Eva's safety. She hadn't said a word until we walked into her room.

Then, as she sat down on her bed, "I want to go home, Pete. I need to go home."

"I know, baby. I'm so sorry you had to go through all this. I'll never forgive myself. And I want you to go home too."

"I don't blame you, Pete."

"But I do. I should have been more concerned about Nematotta. I never dreamed he would actually kidnap you like that. He was telling the truth, wasn't he? Nobody put a hand on you, did they?"

"I don't think so. To the best of my knowledge, Connie and Libby escaped untouched and unobserved." She managed a weak smile.

I laughed out loud. "Jesus Christ, Eva! How can you make light of what just happened?"

She stood up and walked toward me. "I don't know. I guess it's from hanging around with you so much. And maybe to keep from falling apart."

But then, she did fall apart, hugging me and sobbing on my shoulder.

I held her tight and whispered in her ear, trying to comfort her. After a while, she stopped trembling and we just stood there, neither of us saying a word.

Eventually, Eva broke the silence. "You know, I've accomplished everything I need to for the film, and I have an open return."

"Okay. Let's call the airline and get you on the next flight to L.A. I'll drive you to the airport."

"I have a rental car, Pete. I have to return it."

"What rental company?"

"Enterprise."

"There's an Enterprise lot right here in Southfield. We'll return it there. I'll follow you in my car and then drive you to the airport."

"If that's what you want, Pete."

"What I want is to go with you and spend the rest of my life with you and never let you out of my sight. But that can't happen. Yet."

"I love you, Pete. I'll always love you."

"Someday, Emm. Someday we'll be together. Because I love you and I promise there will never be another woman in my life. Only you."

"She pushed me away and laughed. "Pete Pepper, did you do that on purpose?"

"What?" I had no idea what she meant.

"In such a profound and sincere sounding statement, you managed to get in the title of two songs!"

"I did?"

"Yes! "Someday We'll Be Together" and "Only You"."

"No. That was from the heart. It wasn't intentional. It just came out and I meant it. Honestly."

Eva broke into a broad smile that became a giggle. "Oh, Pete. No wonder I love you so much."

"And for you to catch that? I love you more now than I did two minutes ago."

We embraced. We kissed. We got undressed. We made love. And then we called the airport.

81

By the time I saw Eva off and headed home, it was almost 2:30, Friday afternoon. We were lucky and got Eva on a 1:45 flight on United. First class, no less. We said our goodbyes and I promised to fly out and visit her the first chance I got. Who knew when that might be?

I did know that I had to call Harvey about Sharpe, but it could wait until I got home. I was just too tired and shaken at the moment. I needed a nap. Yes, it could wait.

Sharpe opened the door before I had a chance to.

"Pete. How'd it go? Is the girl safe? When you didn't come home last night, I didn't know what to think, what to do."

I told Sharpe that she was fine and on the way home and filled him in on as much as he needed to know. Which was basically that she was safe.

"Let's go upstairs, Randy. I'm going to make some coffee and call Lieutenant Steinberg. Set him straight about your situation."

I put on a pot and called Harv from the kitchen phone.

"Steinberg."

"Harvey. It's Pete."

"Well, good afternoon. Where've you been, Private Eye?"

"Hang on a minute, Harv."

I turned to Sharpe, who was pouring himself a coffee, and asked him to go into the living room.

"Sure thing, Pete."

Then, "Okay Harv, I'm back."

"I'm all ears."

I gave Harvey a much more detailed account of the events of the last several hours. At that point, I didn't much care if Sharpe overheard. In a way, he was instrumental in Eva's rescue.

"So, we got Nematotta on a kidnapping charge," Harv replied. "Good. I mean, I'm sorry about your girlfriend, but maybe some good can come out of it.

"I don't know, Harv. The victim is on a plane back to Los Angeles as we speak."

"Doesn't matter. You're a witness, Pete. In fact, you're a victim too. Maybe not kidnapping, but assault for sure."

He was right. "Harv, there's another witness too. Stu Gotts. He saw everything. The aftermath, anyway.

"Hmmm. Wouldn't that be something? Gotts testifying against his own boss."

"Ex-boss," I said. I didn't remember if I had told Harv about Gotts working for me.

"Well, whatever. I'll get hold of Stuart and see where his loyalty lies. Good work, Pete. This is good news."

"Wait, Harv. That's not why I called. It's about Randy Sharpe."

"Ahh, yes. Mr. Sharpe. No sign of him yet, but we've got a BOLO out on his ass."

"You can call of the dogs, Harv. Sharpe is with me right now, having a cup of coffee."

"What the fuck? Pepper, you never cease to amaze me. Did he turn himself in?"

"Yes and no. He came here willingly. And I can prove that he's not guilty."

"Really? I don't suppose he'd be willing to turn himself in to me for questioning?"

"Actually, I think he's looking forward to it."

"Then I'll send a car right over."

"Good. We'll be waiting."

I hung up and turned around as Sharpe walked into the kitchen. He was holding his arms out as if to be cuffed.

"Not guilty, as charged," he said, a smile on his face.

When the squad car came, I saw Randy off then went upstairs. I had second thoughts about the coffee and poured it into the sink. Then I took off my clothes and plopped on my bed. I still needed a nap.

The phone woke me up a little after eight. Five hours of sleep had me feeling refreshed. Lou's voice confirmed it.

"Pete-Sa, whatcha got planned for tomorrow? Lef and I are meeting for lunch. Wanna join us?"

"I thought you were on the coast."

"I am, but I'm taking the red eye back tonight. We're going to Leroy's. You in?"

"Yeah, sure. I guess so. I could use a little fun and relaxation after what I've been through the last 24 hours."

"Wanna tell me about it?"

"I'll fill you in tomorrow. Hey, what's this about you winning some kind of advertising award?"

"Ahh, it was nothing. A public service ad for safe sex. No big deal. It was a KMA. The agency doesn't get any money for it."

"Wow! Lou Bracato actually being modest?"

"I'm being serious. There's a reason the Public Service Awards are referred to as the Pussies."

"Alright, Mr. Humility. What time tomorrow?"

"Noon. It's lunch . And, by the way, the Michigan Colt Stakes are tomorrow night at Hazel. Lef and I plan to go."

"Damn! I totally forgot about it. Count me in. I can use the diversion. And the money."

"Cool. Why don't you pick up some programs on the way to Leroy's."

"I always do."

I hung up and went to the bathroom to splash some water on my face.

While I was drying off, the phone rang again. It was Marianne.

"Hi Marianne. What's up?"

"Hi Pete. Listen, I have a big favor to ask. I know it's short notice, but do you think you could watch Gianni for a couple hours on Sunday? I have something important to do. It's, uh, personal."

Personal, huh? I guess that was supposed to arouse my curiosity. It didn't.

"Sunday? What time?" It didn't matter. I had no specific plans and I was always happy to spend some time with Gianni.

"My, uh, meeting is after the 12 o'clock Mass, so probably around 1:30 or so."

"That'll be fine. Come by any time after noon."

"Thanks Pete. You're a sweetheart. I'll see you then. Bye."

A sweetheart? Yes, I am. But not yours.

In my bedroom, something on my dresser caught my eye. It was the pack of matches I had pocketed from Emily's sofa. It said: Palette Club. *Come and be yourself.* It had a downtown Detroit address, but I never heard of the place.

I pulled out my cell phone and started to dial the number, but when I noticed it was the old style, two letters followed by five numbers, I stopped. I heard weird electronic noises as I disconnected. From the apparent age of the matchbook, chances were that the Palette Club had been closed for years. Still, it struck me that, if the matches were Zachary's, they might somehow lead to someone who knew something about him. I made a mental note to take it with me and show it to the guys at lunch tomorrow.

I grabbed an old paperback science fiction book from my bookshelf,

A Trace of Memory by Keith Laumer. Then I pulled two cans of Grain Belt from my fridge and settled down in my easy chair for an evening of quiet entertainment. I was no longer tired, but after a few cans of brew, I would probably be ready for sleep again by midnight. Considering recent events, I couldn't have been in a better mood.

82

The ongoing joke at Leroy's Home Cooking was that Leroy was rarely around. Customers in the know would ask an employee, "Where's Leroy?" and the response was, "Leroy's home cooking!"

Then everyone in the place would break into laughter. Actually, it was true. Leroy DeBroussard, a Baton Rouge transplant, cooked many of the menu items at home, brought them to the restaurant, then went home and cooked some more. His specialties were Louisiana Andouille Sausage Jambalaya and corn bread, and both were the best I had ever tasted.

Lou Bracato, known to some for his keen wit, kept the joke going.

"Hey DeVaughn, where's Leroy?

"What's that you say?"

"I said, where's Leroy?"

"Why, Leroy's home cooking. That's where."

It was worth asking just to hear DeVaughn laugh, a loud, raucous roar that drowned out all the other laughers in the house.

The laughter gradually subsided as we took our seats. Lou was the first to speak after we placed our orders.

"It happened again last night, on the national news."

"What? Another robbery in Detroit?" I think Lef was being facetious, but it was a legitimate question.

"No! Another gross misuse of the English language. The talking head said new-kew-ler instead of nuclear. Where the hell do they get these guys? You'd think they'd have to pass a literacy test to pull down four or five million a year."

Wordsmith that he is, Lou actually keeps a journal of mispronounced and misused words and phrases. Another gross misuse, as he calls them; one of the most frequent violations, is the non-word intrical that many have used when they really meant integral. What Lou plans to do with his list, I have no idea.

"Yeah, they should at least have good pronounciation," Lef said, intentionally mispronouncing pronunciation. At least, I think it was intentional, judging from the smile on his face.

Lou grunted assent, "Yeah. Well anyway, I have to tell you guys about my latest meet-and-greet caper," he continued. "A masterpiece if I do say so myself."

"Do tell," Lef smiled again as he urged him on.

"Yeah, let's hear it," I said.

"All right," he started, as though beginning a presentation for some ad campaign. "I was at Parlovecchio's Deli last week, a few days before I flew to L.A., and I spotted an incredibly gorgeous redhead."

He paused for effect, looking me straight in the eyes, knowing I had a certain fondness for redheads. I just gestured for him to continue.

"Great face. Fabulous body. And, best of all, she was alone. So I kept a close watch and managed to finish my meatball sub just about the same time she finished her lunch."

"What was she having?"

"Huh? I don't know, Pete. Some kind of pasta salad or something. What does it matter?"

"Well, what a woman eats might tell you something about her."

"That's true," Lef concurred.

"Yeah. Well, this time, it told me she likes pasta salad."

"Or something," I pointed out.

"Do you wanna hear this or not?" His glare was accompanied by a middle finger.

"I do. Sorry."

"Me too." Lef again.

"So, anyway, I casually arrive at the cash register right after she does. And after she pays, she does exactly what I hoped she would do. She puts her business card in the glass bowl where you can get picked for a free lunch. She leaves, I pay my tab and pull out my own business card. With my back blocking the view, I reach in and pretend to put my card in the bowl, but I'm actually grabbing hers and a few others."

"How do you know you got hers?"

"Because I watched very carefully and saw exactly what it looked like and where it landed."

"So why did you grab the other ones?"

"A key part of the plan. Shut up and you'll find out."

"Okay." I made the zip my mouth shut motion and he gave me a very insincere smile.

"So I take the cards home and give it some time. This morning, I called her and said it was Parlovecchio's and that her card was drawn for a free lunch next Saturday at noon. She's thrilled. She says great I'll be there and Oh my God, I've never won anything before!"

"What about the other cards? Lef persisted.

Now Lef got a glare. "Then I call the names on three more cards," Lou continued. "And two of those lucky winners will be there too."

"Why just two?" I asked.

"Because the third one never answered the fucking phone. It didn't matter."

"The plan still sounds iffy."

"The plan is simplicity itself. The four of us show up and find out there's been some kind of mix-up. We didn't win at all. Then I say as long as we're all here, why don't we just have lunch anyway? My treat."

"Seems like a pretty complicated way to meet a woman. And what if the other two lunch guests are, dare I say it, more charming than you?"

"Pete. Lef. Come on. Do I look like a *buffo*? I'll be the only guy."

Just then, DeVaughn appeared and set our food down. He looked at Lou and said. "Sounds like a good plan to me."

Lou stood up and gave him a high five. "Thanks, DeVaughn. Your support will be reflected in my tip." Then he sat down, a cocky smile spreading across his face.

"Hey, while you're in a good mood, I brought you something," Lef said, reaching into his pocket and pulling out a piece of folded paper. "It's a poem. A sequel to your poem about boobs."

"What? You can't write a sequel to my poem. Besides, it isn't a poem; it's just a couplet. Too much breast below the nipple. All that flesh and not a ripple. That's two lines. A couplet."

"Well then, my sequel is a couplet too. I call it *Titties, Part Two*."

"Who said I named it *Titties Part One*? You can't do that."

"Hey. I wrote it, I get to name it. Now sit back and relax. I think you're gonna like it. You ready?"

Lou sighed and sat back. "Alright. Go ahead."

Lef cleared his throat, unfolded the paper and read: "It ain't the number, it's the letter. If it's double, even better."

Lou was silent for a few seconds, and then nodded his head. "Good. I like it. I like it a lot. But, Jesus Christ, Lef. Did you have to read it? You can't remember two fucking lines?"

"It was for the dramatic effect."

Lou laughed. "Well, whatever. But I think I will now officially call my couplet *Titties, Part One*. With a tip of the cap to Lefkowitz Turner".

"Or we could put 'em together and just call it *Titties*." Lef actually sounded excited at the thought.

"That would increase our chances of getting published." Lou was neither excited nor serious.

"Hey, before you guys launch your literary careers, I want to show you something." I reached into my shirt pocket, pulled out the match-book and tossed it on the table.

Lef picked it up. "Palette Club. Never heard of it." He handed it to Lou.

"Come and be yourself. What the hell does that mean?" Then he threw the matches over to me. "Where'd you get 'em?" he asked.

"And what's the significance?" Lef added.

"I found them behind a sofa cushion at the Bradshaw mansion out in Belleville. I thought it might produce a lead as to the whereabouts of the husband. Zachary. It's not much, but I don't have a hell of a lot more."

"Sorry. Can't help," Lou said.

"But I know someone who might be able to," Lef offered. "You know him too, Lou."

"Huh? I do?"

"Yeah, Ralston Rackford. Rack's working for the mayor downtown. Has been for five or six years now. Got himself some kinda gig helping troubled teenagers get on the straight and narrow. Hell, he's head of the whole department, the Action Coalition for the Rehabilitation of Negro Youth Militants."

"Oh yeah. ACRONYM. I remember reading about that," Lou said. "You mean to tell me Rack's running the show? Damn!"

"Oh yeah. Rack's always been a charmer. And Pete, even if he doesn't know anything about the Palette Club, he might be able to put you in touch with someone that does. Gotta be some old timers still working for the city. Want me to try to set up a meeting?"

"Sure. Why not? It's a long shot, but it's billable hours. And I'll finally get to meet the famous Ralston Rackford."

"Good. I'll give him a call."

"And speaking of long shots," Lou interjected, "who do you like in the big race tonight?"

Actually, there were several big races on the card, but I knew he meant the Three-Year-Old Colt Stakes. Its $350,000 purse made it one of the biggest ever for Michigan breds.

"Well, I have a good feeling about Hymie Bonaducci, but anything can happen with young horses. He should pay a decent price if the morning line holds at 4-1. I'm hoping to have a word with his trainer before the race."

"Farley Chederman? The Big Cheese?"

"Yeah. Farley Chederman. I've been talking to him about maybe buying a horse sometime. He's a straight shooter. He might have some insight into the race."

"Hmm. I'd be interested in what he has to say," Lou said. But I'll tell you right now, I don't think anyone's got a chance against Major Domo."

"Don't be so sure, Lou," Lef added his two cents. "Hymie's from the Kosher-Pizza Stables and they've got some really good nags. They rule the California tracks"

"That's right. And they *keep* the good ones in California. I know because I went to Los Alamitos when I was out there. And I cashed a few tickets on one of their mares, Gina Greenbaum."

The "they" Lou was referring to were Sol Adelson and Gino Altobelli,

a couple of successful ad execs that became equally successful in the harness racing business. All their horses had names that were half Jewish and half Italian. I thought it was a clever gimmick.

"Let me guess. You met one of them at the track."

"No. I met them both at the Pussies Awards Banquet. We talked horses quite a bit and they didn't say a word about Hymie Bonaducci, even when I told them I'd probably be going to the track tonight. And I don't think they'd have a less than A-list trainer handling one of their horses if they thought he was a top contender."

"Cheese may not be on *your* A-list, Lou, but he's been one of the top two or three trainers on the Michigan circuit for years."

"Well, it's going to take a hell of a training job to win out of the number eight post. Major Domo's got the three hole."

I didn't argue. I just opened my program to the eighth race and took another long look. Major Domo was definitely going to be the favorite.

83

We were all having a pretty good night. In the fifth race, we took a flyer on a two-year-old named Pirouette in the Filly Stakes and she danced home to the tune of $22.60. Comfortably ahead, we decided to bide our time until the eighth race, the Michigan Three-Year-Old Colt Stakes.

We had met in the grandstand and decided to forego $1.00 Hot Dog Night and have a leisurely dinner in the clubhouse instead. As per our custom, the biggest winner would pick up the tab. We did enjoy a couple of $2.00 beers before we headed up.

Lef and I had finished our dinners and Lou was still picking at his prime rib, meticulously trimming the fat from the meat.

"Hey Lou, you seemed to be reluctant to talk about your prize winning ad campaign yesterday," I said. "What was that all about?"

"It wasn't a campaign; it was an ad *for* a campaign. On safe sex."

"So what was the ad?"

"Nothing fancy. There wasn't even any visual. Just type. The headline was Abstinence. The *moral* contraceptive."

"Neat. A little word play on *oral* contraception."

"I can think of a better way to practice oral contraception besides abstinence," Lef said. "Two ways, in fact."

"Lef, be nice. Don't insult the wordsmith. I think it's pretty clever, Lou."

"Clever enough to win a Pussy I guess."

"That must have been hard for you, Lou," Lef observed. "Promoting abstinence, I mean. But then, you could be the poster boy for abstinence. Although you don't abstain by choice. It's been quite a while since your Gainsboroughs got some action, hasn't it?"

"Gainsboroughs? What the hell are his Gainsboroughs? I asked Lef.

"His blue boys. Just hanging down there doing nothing."

"I thought you guys got some action with a couple of babes from the Iron Cage a week or so ago."

"We partied and Lou did a little groping, but there was no penetration of any kind. Hell, I think the last time Lou had an orgasm with a woman in the room was three months ago. And she didn't even know it."

"Good thing you drove tonight, Lef. Or you'd be walking home."

I knew the ribbing was good-natured, but I decided to change the subject just in case. "Hey Lou, what's a moe-ell?"

"Huh? How do you spell it?"

"No idea. Pretty sure it starts with an m."

"You probably mean m-o-h-e-l, also spelled with a y instead of an h. I've seen it both ways. Where did you hear it?"

"One of the cops at a crime scene said he'd hate to be the Bradshaw family mohel. What's that mean?"

"I think our friend Lef can answer that better, being at least part Jewish. Lef?"

"Uh, I don't actually practice Judaism so much these days, but I did take part in the particular ceremony that involves a mohel. He's the guy who separates the foreskin from the penis at circumcisions. It requires a very deft hand. And in my case, of course, it took quite a while"

"Is that a veiled allegation regarding the size of your member? Lou asked.

"You wouldn't say that if you ever saw the unveiling." Lef was very pleased with his rejoinder.

"I don't remember being overly impressed in the showers after basketball games in high school."

"You have a short memory." Lef chided.

"That *is* my memory, " Lou shot back. "It was short."

The boys were going at it again, but this time I was enjoying it too much to change the subject.

"Well, let me remind you of something, my little Italian water boy. I'm sure you've heard the phrase, 'Once you go black, you'll never go back'?"

"Yes, I have," Lou admitted.

"Well, you're looking at the man who very likely inspired that saying."

"Hmph. It may be that the brothers go to great lengths, but it's the Italians who are the world leaders in circumference. And you're looking at the man who inspired another saying, widely known and acknowledged by the sexual elite."

"Oh yeah? What's that?"

"Once you go white, you'll never be tight. I can't tell you how many times I've said that to women of color."

"I can," Lef laughed. "Zero. But I have heard some of them say that what you lacked in size, you made up for in speed."

They both broke out laughing and gave each other high fives.

"Okay, guys, enough dicking around." I said, laughing along with them. "Lef, thanks for the moyel information. I'll have to mention my newfound knowledge to Brad Toaz next time I see him. But right now, I'm going to wander downstairs and see if I can gather some intelligence from Farley Chederman."

"Good luck with that," Lou said.

Lef jumped out of his chair. "I'm going with you. Do you mind?"

"Be my guest."

It took us only a few minutes to spot the Cheese. He was leaning against a post, scrutinizing his program. He saw us approach and waved us over.

"Hey Pete. You ready to buy a horse yet?"

"Actually, I am. Maybe we can talk more about it next week. Don't want to bother you now with the big race coming up."

"Yeah, this is the biggest race I've ever been a part of. Gonna be tough to beat Major Domo, though, considering the post positions."

"You got a shot, though. Right?" Lef asked.

"Hey, anything can happen with three year olds."

"That's what Pete said."

"He's right. Listen, I'd like to stay and chat, but the owners are in town and I need to go see them about last minute instructions." And with that, he walked toward the stable area,

Lef was clearly disappointed. "Well, I guess that was fruitless," he said. "He didn't give us anything at all."

"Oh, but he did," I replied.

"Huh? What?"

"He said the owners were in town. They didn't fly in from California to see their horse lose."

"Oh. Ohhh! That's a good thing, right?"

"A very good thing."

"Well, uh, I'm gonna go and bet now."

"I'll see you back up in the clubhouse. And Lef ... "

"Yeah?"

"Don't feel obligated to tell Lou."

"The horses are entering the track for the eighth race, the Michigan Colt Stakes for three year old pacers, with a purse of $350,000. Number one, Pardon My Dust ... "

The track announcer faded into the background as we eagerly awaited the big moment. Unfortunately, the moment didn't exactly go as I hoped.

Major Domo was indeed the favorite, with odds of 3-2. Hymie was only the fourth choice, a surprising 9-2 flashing next to his number on the tote board. It was a bigger payoff than I expected, but the bettors apparently knew better. Post position was definitely a factor. Major Domo got a sweet trip, never leaving the rail. Hymie was parked on the outside every step of the way and was forced to go four wide entering the home stretch. Nearly eight lengths back, he flew down the stretch and was beaten by a nose in a photo finish.

Lou jumped up waving his tickets and screaming. I was happy for him, but I didn't hesitate handing him the dinner tab, $87 plus tip. He didn't seem to mind.

"You were right, Paesan," I told him. "Well done." What I didn't tell him was that I boxed the Major and Hymie in the perfecta, which paid $36.60. My $20 ticket netted me $346 and my winnings for the night were just north of $700. I hoped he had made at least that much.

84

The unseasonably cold weather convinced me to get away from my scrambled eggs habit and have some hot oatmeal for breakfast instead. I rinsed out the bowl, grabbed my third cup of coffee and settled down in my easy chair with the *Sunday Free Press*.

As always, the sports page was my first stop. The Lions were at home, three point underdogs to the Cleveland Browns who had beaten them by two touchdowns earlier in the season at Cleveland. I decided not to bet the game. I was still pleased with last night's winnings at the track. I had now set aside just over $12,000 in my horse fund. I'd be seeing a man about a horse real soon.

A few hours later, after I scoured the business and entertainment sections, the doorbell rang. 12:45. Was Marianne early?

She was.

"I'm sorry, Pete. I know it's earlier than you said, but my plans changed a bit."

"Hey that's alright. Gianni's welcome any time."

She blushed noticeably, apparently catching that I didn't include her name. I'm not even sure I left her out intentionally.

"Well, uh, okay. I shouldn't be more than a few hours. I really appreciate this Pete."

"Any time, Marianne. And take as long as you need to." I leaned over and gave her a hug, feeling a bit guilty about the slight, intentional or not.

"Thanks again, Pete. Bye." I thought I saw a tear in her eye.

"You got the Sunday funnies, Uncle Pete?"

"I set 'em aside just for you, little man. Let's go up."

He raced up the stairs and was already reading the funnies by the time I made it to the top.

"You want something to drink, Sport?"

"What flavors do you got?" It was a line from a soft drink commercial, one of Broderick and Stanley's accounts.

"Hang on, I'll check."

I looked in the fridge. Assorted soft drinks, including two cans of Canfield's Diet Chocolate Soda. It wouldn't be right to serve diet pop to a kid, would it? Of course not.

"You like beer?" I yelled.

"No. It tastes terrible. Don't you have any pop?"

"Uh, Vernor's and Seven Up."

"Vernor's. I'll have Vernor's."

I popped the tab and took it in to him, along with a Canfield's for myself. I just sat there and watched him reading and giggling. After a few minutes, he folded the paper.

"Can I go on the computer, Uncle Pete?"

"Of course. You don't have to ask. Il mio ufficio e il vostro ufficio."

"Huh? Is that Italian Uncle Pete?""

"Si. My office is your office."

" Well, did you remember to get some more paper for the printer?"

"Darn it Gianni. I forgot. Again. I'm sorry."

"That's okay. I'll just play some games or maybe do some drawing. Call me when it's time for lunch."

I decided to take care of some long overdue housecleaning. By the time I remembered to turn on the Lions game, it was almost halftime. The score was 10-10. A little later, as I was dragging the vacuum out of my storage closet, Gianni came running upstairs, waving a sheet of paper.

"Look Uncle Pete. I drew a picture of you!"

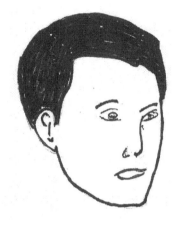

I looked. You could tell it was supposed to be a man, but it wasn't like looking in a mirror. "Hey! Awesome, Gianni. Thank you. It's great. Can I keep it?"

"Not yet."

He grabbed the picture from me and ran back downstairs. He was clearly up to something, but I would just have to wait to find out what. I vacuumed the living room and bedroom and cleaned the bathroom. Maybe I'd clean my office later, but that was enough for now.

Midway through the third quarter, the Lions were suddenly trailing, 17-13. I realized it was nearly three o'clock. Marianne was late, but I told her to take as long as she wanted. I decided to put on a pot of coffee and ask her to stay for a while when she did get back. Gianni came into the kitchen and handed me another sheet of paper.

"What do you think, Uncle Pete?"

I was momentarily speechless. It was the same drawing as before, only now, it had long hair.

"It's my mom!" Gianni said.

"Uh, it looks like the same picture, Gianni."

"Oh, you noticed. But there wasn't any more paper. I had to use the same sheet."

"Oh gosh. I'm sorry, Gianni. I promise I'll get more paper tomorrow. But it looks great. Nice job. Your mom will be proud."

"Okay." He grabbed it back again and headed downstairs just as the doorbell rang.

Marianne didn't stay for coffee. But she did give me a warm hug and a kiss on the cheek. She seemed a lot more cheerful than I felt.

85

The week of Monday, October 30 was not overly productive. Other than setting up some appointments for the following week, I didn't make much headway on The Case of the Missing Husband.

As of Monday morning, the cold spell was still in full swing, so I turned the thermostat up to a comfortable 70 degrees and settled down in my easy chair with a cup of coffee and the morning *Free Press*. The trotters and pacers were switching over to Northville Downs, a half-mile track about 20 miles west and a little south of Pete Pepper Investigations. It was actually my favorite track because I knew the secret of handicapping a half-miler. But I liked to have the horses get in a few races before I got too involved. I glanced at the entries and saw a lot of new names. But, as always, I'd wait until just before Thanksgiving before I ventured out.

After my third cup of coffee, I decided to have breakfast at Vassili's.

Then I picked up a couple bags of mini candy bars for Halloween and a ream of computer paper. Gianni would be pleased on both counts, since my Halloween turnout was almost non-existent and he would get the leftover Paydays and Snickers.

At mid afternoon, as I was listening to my Weekday Medley, featuring "Monday, Monday" by the Mamas and Papas, "Tuesday Afternoon" by the Moody Blues, "Friday on My Mind" by the Easybeats and "Saturday Night" by the Bay City Rollers, the doorbell rang. It was the UPS guy with a package for Pete Pepper.

I was surprised because I hadn't ordered anything. I went upstairs and opened it on my kitchen table. It was a box of cigars with a hand-written note.

Pete,

Thanks for your help. You went way above and beyond. Please accept this small token of my appreciation. I hope you like this brand. The guy at the store (Maxie's) said he was sure you would. Anyway, smoke them in good health.
Randy

I liked them alright. Macanudos. One of the better brands in my self-imposed price range. I could afford better, but I am definitely not sophisticated enough to tell the difference between a $5 cigar and a $10 cigar. My sense of taste and smell pretty much peaks at the $2 range. And I rarely pay even that much. Anyway, I took the cigars into the living room to transfer them into my $30 cedar-lined, humidity-controlled humidor. It's not automatic, of course, you have to submerge a little perforated metal gizmo into water every week or so, then pop it back in place inside the lid. Lou once referred to it as being hygroscopic. I took his word for it.

When I opened the humidor lid, I realized I hadn't been keeping up with the submersion procedure. There were only two cigars left and one of them was pretty dried out. Strangely, the second one seemed fairly fresh. I puzzled over the discrepancy for a minute, and then realized that one of them was from my own supply and the other was the last of the handful Ramona gave me from Zachary Bradshaw's humidor. But which was which? For a second I thought it didn't matter; then it struck me that it did.

I was pretty sure the fresh one was Zachary's. For two reasons. First, the ones I had already smoked at Bradshaw's were definitely fresh. And second, I couldn't remember the last time I watered my gizmo.

The reason it mattered was that someone was keeping Zachary's cigars fresh. And I was pretty sure it wasn't Emily or Ramona. Which strongly suggested that Zachary had been home relatively recently. Certainly more recently than a few months ago.

I transferred the Macanudos into the humidor, put the other two on top, soaked the gizmo in water and closed the humidor. Then I called Emily Bradshaw.

Ramona answered. "Bradshaw residence. Ramona speaking."

"Ramona, it's Pete Pepper."

"Oh, hi Pete. How you doing?"

"Good, thanks. Listen, Ramona. I need to speak to Emily. Is she in?"

"No. She left about an hour ago. Took the Cadillac. Didn't say where she was going."

"Hmmm. So Emily is definitely not agoraphobic."

I didn't mean to say it out loud, but I must have, because Ramona said, "Agger-what?"

"Huh? Oh, nothing. Just thinking out loud. Listen, Ramona, are you in the room where Zachary keeps his cigars?"

"Actually, I am. Vacuuming. Why?"

"Can you check and see if there are still some cigars in the humidor?"

"Why? Do you want some more?"

"No. No. Just check for me, would you please?"

"Only 'cause you said please."

Fifteen seconds later, she reported back. "Yep. I'd say there's about ten or so."

"Alright. Good. Now would you say that's more or less or about the same as what was in the humidor the day you gave me some?"

"Huh? Geez, I don't know. I just reached in and grabbed a few. I didn't really look inside and count 'em. Probably about the same though. Why is it so important?"

"Oh. It's probably nothing. Just let Emily know I called, would you?

I need to speak to her about the case." I didn't think Ramona needed to know of my suspicion. And it was only a suspicion, after all.

"I'll tell her as soon as she gets back. Speaking of which, when are you coming back out here?"

"Oh, I'm sure I'll be out there many times over the next several weeks."

"Yeah, well maybe one evening we can go out for dinner or something. I'm free after six o'clock."

"Yeah, that sounds like fun. Talk to you later. Bye."

"Bye now."

A few weeks ago, I might have been tempted. But after the ordeal with Eva, there would never be anyone else. Not even casual. Sorry, Ramona. Not gonna happen.

Half an hour later, as I was deciding what to play on the jukebox, my onomatomaniac friend called.

"Hey Pete, what would you say is the plural of hard-on? Hards on or hard-ons?

"Huh? Jesus, Lou. What kind of question is that?"

"Seriously. I need your opinion."

"Well, let's see. Uh, well, you've got cupsful instead of cupfuls, but in that case cup is a noun and ful is a suffix, I guess. But with hard-on, the whole phrase is the noun. Hard just by itself would be an adjective, and on isn't a noun. So I guess I'd have to say hard-ons."

"Yeah, that's what I thought. Couple of proofreaders over here say it should be hards on. But I think the way you explained it makes more sense."

"Yeah, thanks. But you know, you could avoid any controversy just by saying boners."

"Could have, but that wasn't the bone of contention. It was a grammar issue. Pun intended, by the way."

I couldn't help but laugh. "By the way, while we're on the topic of words, you're wrong about the definition of onomatomaniac. I looked it up."

"Oh yeah?"

"Yeah. It isn't someone who's crazy about words. It's someone who's obsessed with a certain word and uses it repeatedly."

"I know what it means. Actually, the word is onomatomania; no 'c' at the end."

"I thought you said it meant crazy about words. Like someone who uses big words all the time. You know, a wordsmith. Like you."

"You must have misunderstood me. Your definition is the right one."

"Well then, of what word are you so enamored that you use it repeatedly?" I hoped he noticed my proper grammar.

"Tits."

Somehow, I didn't think that qualified. But I couldn't disagree.

"Goodbye Lou."

By the time I hit the sack, I had finished *A Trace of Memory* and three cans of Leinenkugel. And Emily hadn't called back.

86

Just after breakfast Tuesday morning, she did call.

"Good morning, Pete. I hope I didn't wake you up."

"Gosh no, Emily. I already had breakfast and put the dishes in the sink."

"Well that's nice," she chuckled. "Now tell me what this concern over Zachary's cigars is all about. Ramona said it sounded like you thought it was important, but then sort of pooh-poohed it."

"Yes. Well I didn't want to raise any alarm with her, but I think it's possible that you may be in danger. I think Zachary has been in your house."

"Really? And why is that?" She definitely wasn't shocked.

I explained to her about the cigars and how they were still fresh and if she or Ramona wasn't keeping them that way, it had to be Zachary.

"I meant why do you think I may be in danger?"

"Because Zachary has likely been in your house, and if so, he's being sneaky about it."

"Hmmm. Well, at this point, it's his house too, Pete. I think if I were in danger from Zachary, the danger would have struck by now."

"It doesn't concern you that he's been around without you knowing?"

"That would be nothing new. It's pretty much how we existed for several years. He lived his life and I lived mine. I believe I mentioned that it wasn't unusual for him to disappear for days at a time."

"So you're saying even when he was gone, he may have actually been around and you didn't know it?"

"It's a big house, as you call it, Pete. His living quarters were in a wing that I've since closed off. Believe me, I have no fear that Zachary wants to harm me."

"I do believe you. If you were concerned, you would have called me back yesterday."

"I didn't call you yesterday because I didn't get home until this morning. I was at the Holiday Inn lounge in Ypsilanti. The bartender suggested that I shouldn't drive home, so I got a room. I certainly was in no condition to disagree. I called you as soon as Ramona informed me of your call."

She didn't sound even slightly embarrassed by the admission, but I was. "I'm sorry, Emily. I didn't mean to pry. That's none of my business."

"Forget it, Pete. I've told you that I make no apologies for my alcoholism. So let's move on. Now that you've established that Zachary is snooping around in secret, what's your next step in the investigation? Any progress to report?"

"Not a lot, Emily. The only possible lead I have so far is a place called the Palette Club."

A good five seconds elapsed before she responded. "The Palette Club? Is that one of those topless bars?" Was her voice shaky, or did I just imagine it?

"I don't know. Never heard of the place. But I'm going to meet someone that might know something about it. At least I hope I'm going to meet him."

"Well, if you never heard of it, how on earth did you ever come up with the name?"

"Remember when we first met and you walked into the room and I was fumbling with your sofa cushions? Well, I found a pack of matches there from the Palette Club. And if you've never heard of it, the matches were probably Zachary's."

"Well, I'll be. Good work, Pete. Let me know if anything comes of it, okay?" Now she sounded just a bit too upbeat.

"Of course. I want to earn my pay, Emily. You were very generous in that regard. And I have some other appointments I'm trying to line up. I'll keep you apprised of them as well."

"Excellent. Thank you, Pete."

"Oh wait, Emily. Can I ask you one more thing?"

"Certainly."

"The night of your meeting with George Gianotti, the meeting that never happened. Were you about to file for divorce or maybe change your will?"

"My goodness! Where did that question come from?"

"A few minutes ago when I mentioned that Zachary might be snooping around your house, you said "at this point it's his house too.' That suggests that maybe the situation was going to change."

"Wow! Very impressive, Pete. I have hired myself a remarkable investigator. And the answer is yes. I was in the process of changing my will."

"Were you going to cut Zachary out?"

"Yes, as a matter of fact I was. I intended to leave the bulk of my estate to various charities, but also a substantial amount to my employees."

"Who are now all dead."

"Yes."

"Do you think that might have been motive for Zachary to eliminate them?"

"Oh my God! No. No, I don't think so. I never even thought of that. Zachary wouldn't do such a thing. I mean, he had accumulated a substantial amount through his own business. It was quite lucrative. I don't know, Pete. I just don't know. But I certainly don't think so."

"I'm sorry Emily. I didn't mean to upset you. It's just that I have to consider all the angles. It could explain why he's in hiding."

"I, I suppose so. It does seem that he doesn't want to be found. Please keep me informed." And then she hung up.

Since it was Halloween, I decided to do some paperwork down in my office. I wanted to be close to the front door in case any trick-or-treaters showed up. I had the porch light on and a plastic pumpkin on my stoop just in case. By 7:30, nobody had come, but both bags of candy were open and a few pieces were missing from each. Since no kids had rung my doorbell, I must have been the one who ate them. Absent mindedly, of course. I didn't think Gianni would mind.

The picture he had drawn was pinned to the corkboard on my wall. Cute. At nine, I re-papered the printer and printed out my notes. There weren't many. Then I shut down and headed upstairs after grabbing one more Snickers for the road. Just as I finished chewing it, the phone rang. It was Lef.

"Yo, Pete. I just got off the phone with Rack and he said he could meet you either this Friday afternoon or next Monday morning."

"Great. Either one works for me."

"Well, just so you know, Lou wants to go with you and he said Monday works best for him."

"You called Lou before you called me?"

"No. He's here at my place."

"Oh. Okay, Monday's fine. What time?"

"Rack said to show up anytime; his schedule's wide open. Lou said he'd drive and he'll pick you up around nine."

"Great. Hey, ask him if he wants to grab breakfast first. He can fill me in on his lunch with the redhead at Parlovecchio's. That's this Saturday, right?"

"Yeah, it's Saturday. He's geeked. That's all he's been talking about." Then aside, "Hey Lou! You want to have breakfast with Pete Monday morning before you go see Ralston?" And back to me, "He said yes, but then he'll pick you up about a quarter to."

" Tell him I'll be ready. See you later."

"Wait! Don't hang up," Rack yelled. "I almost forgot. Rack said he *has* heard of the Palette Club."

"Terrific! I'm looking forward to meeting him. And finding out what he knows."

87

_Call Jane Broder/See if husband can
help re: will/possible divorce
_Visit Sutton & Wasyl Accountants
_Check with Tri-County Trade Commission
(a more recent photo of Zach?)
_Call Harvey/get bank records of both
Emily and Zach
_Meet w/ Ralston Rackford re: Palette Club

After breakfast Wednesday morning, I poured my third cup of coffee, sat at the kitchen table and studied the list I had printed out Halloween night. Something was off about Emily and I couldn't quite put my finger on it. Her reaction to the possible presence of Zachary in her house, as I call it, didn't make sense to me. Even if she didn't fear him, I would have expected at least a mild display of surprise. And her reaction to the mention of the Palette Club was, well, she did appear to be shocked by that. So I decided to make her a part of my investigation too. Theoretically, at least, checking up and keeping an eye on her could very possibly lead to locating Zachary.

The items on my to-do list weren't in any particular order of urgency and I didn't necessarily know what I might discover, but any of them might provide some kind of breakthrough. Since the meeting with Rackford was already on the docket, I decided to start at the top.

Jane Broder answered on the third ring.

"Hello?"

"Jane? It's Pete Pepper, Maria's friend."

"Of course! What can I do for you Pete?"

"Oh boy, this is awkward, but I want to ask you about your husband."

"Cal? What about him?"

"Well, his name for starters, but you just told me that."

"It's actually Calhoun on his business card, but he much prefers just plain Cal. Why are you asking?"

"I was hoping to talk to him about Emily Bradshaw's will. George Gianotti was working on it when he was murdered. I wondered if that might be something he'd help me with, especially if he and George were friends. Of course, I wouldn't want him to do anything illegal or unethical."

"Hmm. Well I'm sure he wouldn't do that. But I'm also sure he'd help you if he can. He and George were great friends. They played golf together at Knollwood quite often. You know Pete, you could have just called him directly. You must have his firm's number if you're a friend of George's."

"I do. And, of course, I considered that. But … "

"But what?"

"But I would feel much more comfortable asking *you* about your supply of Canfield's Diet Chocolate Fudge Soda."

I could hear her laughing even though she clearly dropped the phone. A few seconds later she replied.

"Sorry about that," she said, still stifling a laugh. "Uh, it just so happens I have a couple of cases in the basement. I'm sure I could free up a six-pack or two if you want to come by and get them. Just give me a call in advance. And not Cal!" Then she laughed some more.

"See, now you know why I said this was awkward. I will come by, maybe later this week. And I'll only call Cal at his office."

"Tell you what, Pete. I'll be talking to Cal later. I'll mention the will thing to him and he'll call you back. If that's okay with you."

"Absolutely. I'd rather he called at his convenience instead of me interrupting his day."

"Consider it done. Pete, you've made my day. See you later."

"Yes, you will. Goodbye Jane."

Item number one on my list was only halfway home, but it was still a very productive call.

88

Items number two and three were not quite as productive. Neither Mr. Sutton nor Mr. Wasyl were in this week, but the receptionist said they'd both be back next week. Feel free to walk in any time during business hours since their schedules were very light and she and a couple of admins did most of the work anyway. Their office was actually in Belleville. A long drive, but I penciled it in for Tuesday.

The Tri-County Trade Commission, on the other hand, was apparently out of commission. At least, the phone number was no longer in service. So I went down to my computer to do a little cyber investigating.

There wasn't much to investigate. Although the Commission had been de-funded two years ago, in 1993, a small part of it still existed. A Mr. Herman Kaplan to be exact. He provided oversight for the few programs that the Commission had started and for the meager funds that were still in the Commission's coffers. There was, however, a current phone number.

Herman sounded eager to help.

"Why yes, Mr. Pepper, I do remember that trip to China, although I personally wasn't allowed to go. And I recall Zachary Bradshaw very well too. In fact, I took several of the publicity photos of that particular boondoggle. I'm also sort of the unofficial archivist for Commission projects. Exactly what is it you're looking for?"

Did I detect a bit of bitterness in Herman's voice? "Actually, Mr. Kaplan, I'm just trying to locate a recent photo of Zachary."

"Well, you've come to the right place. Unfortunately, those files are in storage at another location in Oak Park."

"That's fine. I'm right next door in Southfield. Would it be convenient to meet you there? Perhaps tomorrow?"

"Well, yes to your first question, but no to the second. I'm leaving this evening for a conference in Toronto. But I'll be back next week. I'd be happy to accommodate you then. I'll give you a call."

"Well, okay. I'll talk to you then. I gave him my cell number and added, "Enjoy your trip."

"I will. Thank you."

Herman was clearly making up for lost boondoggles. I glanced at Gianni's picture on my wall and smiled. Why did I keep looking at it? Because your nephew drew it for you, dummy. Why else?

I shrugged and headed upstairs to call Harvey.

89

It was just after lunch and Harvey was in a good mood. "Pete, my boy. What's new and exciting in your life?"

"Just thrilled to have friends like you, Harv."

"As well you should be. But then, I'm fortunate to have friends like you too." Harvey was in a *really* good mood!

"Wow, Harvey, what did you have for lunch?"

"A Big Apple pancake at the Original Pancake House. But that's not why I'm so ebullient."

"Ebullient? Have you been hanging with Lou Bracato?"

"Not lately. No, I have some good news for you, my friend. Thanks to you, I'm close to arresting that scumbag, Lorenzo Nematotta. Your buddy Stuart has agreed to testify against him. On several counts."

"Great. That is good news. I hope Stu's getting some kind of immunity. I mean …"

"Mr. Gottschalk hasn't been charged with anything. He doesn't need immunity. Oh, and by the way, Randy Sharpe was also very cooperative. His story checked out and he's a free man."

"Free in body, maybe, but not in soul. The poor guy is an emotional wreck over the situation with his wife. I hope things work out for him. I really like him."

"I liked him too. Did you get the cigars?"

"Huh? How'd you know about that?"

"Heh heh. When he said he wanted to thank you, I suggested a box of cigars. I take it he came through."

"Macanudos. A whole box. I guess I should thank you too Harv."

"That'll be easy. Just send a couple of those beauties my way."

"You got it. How's the Gianotti investigation going? You been in touch with Toaz?"

"Just a couple of times. He's busy enough with all the other murders to spend time helping me with Gianotti. At least he's got crime scenes. We can't confirm that Gianotti was killed in Belleville, Pete."

"Trust me, Harv. He was."

"That may be. But the ball's in my court now."

"So Toaz isn't making any headway on the other cases, huh?"

"I can tell you that no arrest is imminent. Whoever did it – and it's a pretty safe assumption that it was the same person – didn't leave any prints, which is surprising because there was a lot of activity at every scene.

"No surprise if he wore gloves."

"Yeah. But it's out of my jurisdiction. I hope Toaz can figure it out. Clearly there was a connection between the victims; they all worked for Emily Bradshaw. Except the Vandever girl, of course; she worked for Zachary. Toaz is even stumped for a motive."

"Harvey, that connection *is* the motive. Emily's four employees, I mean. They were all going to be added to Emily's will. And Zachary was going to be cut out."

"And you know that because … "

"Emily told me. And it seems to me that the one person who would want to stop the will from being changed is Zachary."

"Has it been changed?"

"I don't know. I'm getting mixed messages. I hope to find out soon. From Cal Broder, George's partner.

"So, here's what I don't understand. If he kills the four employees, what good would it be for him to be the sole beneficiary if he's serving a life imprisonment sentence? And what about Vandever and Gianotti? They weren't in the will. It doesn't make sense, Pete."

"I didn't say it made sense."

"Well, I'll pass that information on to Toaz anyway. He might want to talk to Emily some more."

"Hey, speaking of Toaz, did he happen to mention if Ralph Spaulding was hit on the head? Like the others?"

"As a matter of fact, he was. And they found a shovel in Spaulding's shed with blood on it. Presumably his."

"I thought that would be the case. Listen, Harv, I called for another reason. I have a favor to ask."

"Yeah?"

"I need to get hold of the bank records for both Emily and Zachary."

"Really? And how am I supposed to do that. I'm not part of that investigation, remember?"

"No, but Toaz is. Do you think you could ask him – when you call with the news about Emily's will?"

"I can ask, but why do you want 'em?"

"I want to see who Zachary has been writing checks to. If I can get an idea of where he shops or eats or whatever, I might have a chance of finding him. And in the case of Emily, I'm really confused about whether she's agoraphobic or not. George told Maria she was. That's why he went out to Belleville for the meeting. And I know for a fact that Emily has been out and about. I'm hoping to find some evidence that she was seeing a shrink."

"Okay, I'll ask. Maybe in the spirit of interdepartmental cooperation, he'll do it for you."

"Thanks, Harv. I really appreciate it."

"And I really appreciate the Macanudos you're gonna give me."

90

I was in my office when Calhoun Broder called late Thursday morning.

"Pete Pepper Investigations."

"Pete Pepper, it's Cal Broder."

"Thanks for the quick response, Cal. I was hoping to get a look at Emily Bradshaw's file. I'm ..."

"Yes, I know. Jane told me about your request. As you're probably aware, it would be a violation of the client/lawyer privilege for me to divulge the contents of any of George Gianotti's files."

"Oh. I'm sorry to hear that."

"However, since George is no longer available, his clients have been divided up among the partners. And, as it happens, Emily Bradshaw is now my client, until such time she deems otherwise."

"But it would still be a violation for me to look at the files."

"That's correct. But I *have* looked at the files, specifically regarding the information in which Jane said you were interested."

"And you're willing to share it?"

"Do you really think it could lead to finding the vicious reprobate who killed George?"

"Yes, Cal. I really do."

"Then fuck confidentiality. What do you want to know?"

What! Where did that come from? Cal sounded like an erudite, mild-mannered, straight-laced gentleman. I restrained my surprise and responded as though it were perfectly normal.

"Just a confirmation that the will was being changed and whether or not Emily was filing for divorce."

"First of all, Emily's estate is worth just under $17 million. The previous will, which was drawn up in 1960 and is still the existing will, by the way, left 75% to Zachary and the rest to various charities. The mansion was included in Zachary's 75%. The in-progress will, which was never signed and therefore is not yet valid, left 20% each to Kay Kimberly, Ralph Spaulding and Edith Pringham. The remaining 40% was earmarked for charity, with the bulk going to the Salvation Army."

I hastily jotted down the numbers.

"And what about any divorce proceedings?"

"Well, they never proceeded. Emily has not filed for divorce. I did notice in George's notes, however, that she was considering filing and he was to check back with her after the first of the year."

"Wow! Thanks Cal. I really appreciate your help. And, believe me, this is very helpful."

"Well, like I said, Pete, if there's anything I can do to help find George's murderer, I'll do it."

"I appreciate that, Cal. And if there's any way I can thank you … "

"There is. Since I haven't yet met Emily, or even informed her of my taking over for George, you might want to say a few words on my behalf the next time you speak to her."

"Cal, I would have done that without you asking, believe me."

"I do. And, Pete, the next time you're in the neighborhood, please stop in for a drink."

"You mean at your office?"

"Yes."

"I will."

"Good. There's usually a six-pack of Canfield's in my office fridge."

"Great. Thanks again, Cal."

"Oh, Pete. One more thing. It probably won't come into play and if it were to, I wouldn't deny divulging any information in Emily's will, but I'd appreciate it if you didn't name me as the source until or unless you're under oath."

"Cal, how could I have gotten it from you?   We've never even met."

I hung up without mentioning to Cal that I knew he had already broken client/lawyer confidentiality when he passed on information to Harvey.

91

The conversation with Cal concluded my short list. I got my answers regarding Emily's will; had a meeting with Ralston Rackford set for Monday; would visit Sutton and Wasyl on Tuesday; had a happy-to-help-you-week-after-next promise from Herman Kaplan; and Harvey was going to try to get the Bradshaws' bank records from Toaz.

There really wasn't much for me to do on the case until Monday morning. So, on an impulse, I called Eva and booked an afternoon flight to LAX.

I was going to drive to Detroit Metro when it dawned on me that I hadn't spoken to my employee for a while. I figured it was time to give Stu another little job. Two jobs actually. The first, of course, was driving me to the airport. On the way, I told him that we should have a sit down when I got back to finalize the terms of his employment. It would be beneficial for him to have something down in writing. And beneficial to me to make his salary deductible. I really did like to play it straight with the IRS. The second job was to feed Nehi and Nesbitt.

The flight to LA was uneventful, although someone within a two-aisle radius had clearly eaten cabbage for lunch. I cabbed it from the airport to Eva's one-story bungalow in Hermosa Beach, a 20-minute ride in surprisingly light traffic. I wasn't sure how she would react, but she welcomed me with open arms. She was completely over the psychological trauma of the previous week. I knew, because when I rang the doorbell, she said it was unlocked and come on in.

So I did. And found her sitting on a folding chair in front of the door wearing nothing but a bra and panties. Her hands were behind her back as though they were tied. I stood there speechless for a few seconds, then when she broke out laughing, I followed suit.

"I thought you might get a kick out of that," she said. And then led me into her bedroom where we reaffirmed our commitment to each other. I think I set a personal record for unhooking her bra.

One of the perks of her job was the ability to occasionally work from home and she could have done so on Friday. But, being a very honest and conscientious person, she called in and took a personal day off. Just one of the many reasons I love her.

We had a wonderful three days, from Thursday afternoon through Sunday afternoon. She cooked dinner for me Thursday night, but we ate out on Friday and Saturday. My favorite meal, though, wasn't at an expensive restaurant. Lunch on Saturday was at El Pollo Loco and Foster's Freeze; the best fast-food chicken and milkshake I've ever devoured. And devoured is the right word.

Most of the time we just sat and talked at her place; playing old 45-rpm records on her ancient turntable or holding hands while watching all the Godfather movies.

I'm a light packer and I didn't pack many clothes. If I was concerned about not bringing enough, I shouldn't have been. As it turned out, there were a few occasions when I didn't need any at all.

I took a noon flight home on Sunday. Eva tried to talk me into taking the redeye Sunday evening, but I wanted to be plenty rested for Monday morning. I had a big week ahead.

92

"Lou, you have egg on your face."

"Huh?"

"Looks like you did some dripping when you were dipping your sunny-side-ups."

"Oh." He pulled out a wrinkled handkerchief and wiped all around his mouth. "Did I get it?"

"Yep, you got it." We were waiting in the lobby of the Griswold Building, headquarters of the Action Coalition for the Rehabilitation of Negro Youth Militants, as well as several other City of Detroit governmental departments.

Minutes later, we were approached by a slender, smartly dressed young black man. His nametag proclaimed: *Melvin Lackey, Asst. to the Director* in a typeface Lou later identified as Times New Roman, Italic.

"You the gentlemen here to see Mr. Rackford?" Not surprisingly, he had a rather high-pitched voice and actually looked a little like Eddie Kendricks of the Temptations. I wondered if he could sing.

"That's us," Lou replied.

"Follow me."

We rode an elevator up to the fifteenth floor, walked down a well-lit corridor to a door marked ACRONYM. It led to another small lobby with a desk I presumed was Melvin Lackey's. The door to the right of his desk had Ralston Rackford, Director in bold, gold letters stenciled on opaque glass. Lackey led us in.

Modest is not a word I would use to describe Ralston Rackford's office. It was rectangular and fairly large, maybe twenty feet by thirty feet. But it wasn't what I would consider overly lavish, either. Yes, the furniture looked expensive. The first thing you saw when you walked in was an oversized desk facing out from the back wall. It appeared to be solid oak, as did the framework of the leather desk chair. A matching leather sofa with an oak coffee table was to the right as we entered and a leather love seat with an end table to the left. A slate-top wet bar graced the wall to our left and plush, floor-to ceiling burgundy draperies covered the wall to our right.

But the décor wasn't the reason I wouldn't call the office modest. It was the display behind Rackford's desk. For lack of a better term, it was a trophy case. It was not only filled with trophies of all sizes, but also dozens of framed pictures of Ralston Rackford, some in football gear, some in basketball gear and some shaking hands with smiling men in suits. Plus a dozen or so footballs and basketballs painted with names and dates.

While Lou and I were taking all this in, Lackey coughed politely and said, "Mr. Rackford will be right with you."

As if on cue, he was right with us, striding into his office with a smile and a bag of potato chips. "Sorry guys, suddenly got the munchies."

Then, turning to Lou, he screamed, "Water Boy!"

Lou advanced toward him to shake hands, but Rackford hugged him and literally lifted him two feet off the ground. Rackford was tall, probably six-feet four, but Lou is stocky, and easily 170 pounds. I was impressed.

"Damn, man! How long has it been?"

"I wasn't the water boy. I was the equipment manager."

"Did you bring me water during time outs?"

"That was part of my job."

"Then you *was* the water boy, man! Ain't nothing to be ashamed of. Damn, Luigi. Don't be so sensitive. So, how long has it been?"

"Uh, about six years I think. The last time I remember us seeing each other was at the 10-year reunion in '89." I don't recall ever seeing Lou quite so subdued.

While they were re-connecting, I took a good look at Rackford. When I was going to Michigan State, I had summer jobs at the Ford Rouge Plant as a production burner in the Basic Oxygen Plant. I was teamed up with an older black man named Silver Ragland. Old Silver was in his early sixties and I was nineteen or twenty, but we got to be pretty close. The work we did with oxygen torches was hard, hot and dangerous, but much of the time we were just on call.

One night as we were sitting around chatting, Rags, as he was also called, was describing to me what it was like to be black. One thing he said that I found interesting was that there was sort of a class system based on the degree of blackness. Very light-skinned blacks were referred to as high yellow.

Obviously, I'm no expert, but I'm pretty sure that Rackford would be considered high yellow. And I had to reconsider my assessment that he was ostentatious because he was wearing Levi's, a Wayne State sweatshirt and black, high-top gym shoes.

"Pete!" It was Lou. Pete, wake up and say hello to Ralston Rackford."

I stuck out my hand and he shook it. Firmly. "Hi Ralston."

"Hi Pete. I'd like to say I've heard a lot of good things about you, but I never even heard *of* you until just the other day." Then he smiled broadly and broke into a laugh. "Just kidding," he said.

"Well, I have heard a lot about you and I'm pleased to finally meet you."

"My pleasure too. I noticed you was looking at the trophy case over there."

"Yes. Very impressive."

"Well, that's the idea. It's supposed to impress the teenagers that come here. I like to think of myself as a modest man, but sometimes all that bling helps me persuade them to better their lives."

"What is it exactly that you do to guide them, Ralston?"

"Rack. Call me Rack, like all my friends."

"Sorry. Rack."

"Actually, I like what I do and I'm pretty good at it. Uh, why don't we go and sit down first. And, where's my manners? Lackey, go get these gentlemen something to drink. What'll it be, guys?"

"Water," we both said, simultaneously.

Lackey headed out and Rack continued, "There's a lot of poverty in this town, 'specially 'round the inner city, but I work with kids from all over. Kids that don't have a chance for a decent shot at life. Every one of the kids that comes here is high school dropouts. I try to convince them to go back and get they degree."

"Interesting," I said.

"So, how many teenagers do you see in a typical, let's say, month?" Lou asked.

"Oh, thirty, forty, fifty. It varies."

"And what's your success rate? Lou continued.

"That varies too, but on average, I'd say about twenty percent."

"I'm confused," I interjected. Why do you refer to these teenagers as militants?"

Rack laughed. "Because it starts with an M," he said. "I thought it would be cool to have an acronym that really was ACRONYM and that it would attract a lot of attention. It did too. We got tons of coverage in the news. On television and in the newspapers. And the fact is, almost all the kids that come here have somewhat of an anti-authority attitude. And a goodly number of 'em have juvenile records too. I got some resistance, but the mayor said I was the man for the job and if I wanted to use militants then that's the way it's gonna be. Come here, I wanna show you something."

He walked over to the drapes and opened them. "See that building over there," he said, pointing to what appeared to a six- or seven-story building about a quarter mile away. It was hard to tell in the late morning haze, but it looked to be brownish grey to me.

"That's Cass Tech," Rack continued.

"Everybody knows Cass Tech,' Lou said.

"That's right. One of the best academic high schools around."

"Also well known," Lou concurred.

"Yeah, but did you know that I placed six boys on their football team? All of 'em starters too. And I got two of the starting five on the basketball team as well. Some of them boys is gonna get scholarships to college.

Better to spend four years in college than ten to twenty somewhere else, if you know what I mean. I want them to have the opportunity I got through athletics. You understand?"

"Absolutely!" I was impressed again. "How about girls, Rack? Do any young females come to ACRONYM?"

"Oh, not nearly as many as I'd like. Most of them aren't athletes, but I still get a lot of 'em placed here and there. One girl I got into Mumford, though, she was All State in track. High jumper. Really long legs. Hey, speaking of jumpers, Lou, you ever hear from Hanger?"

"No, not a thing. I don't think he was at the tenth reunion either."

"Rudy Zahn. Boy that little sumbitch could really jump. Couldn't have been more that 5-foot-seven and he could leap up and hang on to that rim for five minutes. Me and him made quite a backcourt. I wonder if he ever went on to play college ball?"

"Not a clue, Rack. Totally lost track of him."

"Me too."

"Hey, how about Purina, Rack? How's she doing?"

"She doing fine. Got married right after high school; had herself some twins. A boy and a girl just like me and her."

"Man, I'll never forget that game against Denby. That was something else. Hey, tell Pete about it, Rack."

"Come on, Lou. Really?"

"Really. I think Pete will get a kick out of it." Then, turning to me, "It involves Purina, Pete."

"Alright, I guess." Rack's reluctance must have been feigned because he told the story with a lot of enthusiasm.

"It was the state quarterfinals in 1978, my junior year. We was one point down, 67-66 with ten seconds to go. We didn't have no time outs left, so I got the in-bounds pass real quick and dribbled all the way down the floor and drove in for a lay up just before the buzzer. The ball went in, but the ref blew his whistle for a foul before the shot. So now, I had to go to the free throw line to shoot two free throws. I can still hear the announcer saying 'Stepping to the line for the Knights, Ralston Rackford. Two shots.' Just as I'm taking aim, one of the Denby players comes over and whispers in my ear. I just stared at him, turned to the hoop and swish, shish. Sank 'em both. The crowd went crazy and stormed onto the floor. Just then, Water Boy here comes running up and asks what the dude said. He said 'Your sister gives great blow jobs,' I told him and he says, 'Holy shit, that didn't bother you?' and I said, 'I knew the dude was lying, man. She got no technique at all.'"

I didn't know if it was appropriate to laugh or not, but I couldn't help myself. I roared. Lou and Rack did too.

Then Rack added, "But you gotta understand man, I was just trying to be funny. I would never do anything like that with my sister. And I made damn sure nobody else ever touched her either."

"Rack! I never thought for a minute that you and Purina actually did anything."

"And I never thought you did think that. If I had of, I woulda dumped that water bucket right on your head."

Just then, Lackey returned with two bottles of water. Or had he been standing there listening to Rack's story? Rack didn't seem to care, so I didn't either.

"Thanks, Melvin. You can go back to your desk now."

I figured it was about time to get to the reason we were there. "So, Rack. What can you tell us about the Palette Club?"

"Actually, not much. I know it closed down about five years ago."

"Oh, I thought Lef Turner said you knew something about it."

"I told him I heard of it, not that I knew about it." Before the disappointment registered on my face, he quickly added, "But I found someone who can probably tell you everything you want to know."

He walked over to his desk and pressed a button on the intercom. "Lackey, go get Shalise Porter and bring her in here." Then he looked at me and smiled.

Shalise Porter looked to be about Emily Bradshaw's age, somewhere in her fifties or sixties. The Palette Club, she told us, was a hangout for gays, lesbians, cross dressers and so forth. It was one of a handful of places around town where they could gather and not be harassed. It was very popular among that particular demographic, my words, not hers, and was always crowded, especially on weekends. As society became a bit more accepting, the patrons began frequenting so-called straight establishments.

Eventually, the club's popularity waned and its doors were closed.

We thanked Shalise, who I was fairly certain had spent many evenings at the Palette Club. She nodded meekly and Lackey ushered her out.

Then we thanked Rack, shook hands, slapped backs and made our own exit.

"I don't know quite what to think of Rack," I told Lou as we walked to his car.

"What do you mean?"

"Well, I can see he's sincere about his work. He's very outgoing, and as Lef said at the track, a real charmer. But, he just didn't strike me as being overly intelligent. Not that there's anything wrong with that."

"You mean because he said time outs instead of times out?"

"Ah, so you caught that, huh?"

"Of course I caught that."

"That was probably the least offensive of his grammatical miscues. He was pretty spotty from start to finish."

"Pete, you have to consider his clientele. He has to talk like they talk to get through to them. I'm sure it's easy to slip in and out of street talk."

"I suppose so. I'd have to agree that he's eminently qualified for his job."

"And he was obviously familiar with the word 'acronym.'"

"That's a plus."

"Definitely. And he had a 4.7 at Wayne State, you know."

"Really? When I was at Michigan State, we were on a 4.0 marking system. I think Purdue was on a 5.0, though."

"Uh, that wasn't his grade point average, Pete."

"Huh? What was it?"

"Yards per carry."

93

Lou dropped me off at my place and headed over to Lef's, who, conveniently, also had the day off. We agreed to meet at Vassili's for dinner at 7:00. I went upstairs, grabbed a can of Walter's and settled in my easy chair to assess the new information.

The assessment didn't take long. And while it was inconclusive, I guessed it was also probably irrelevant. The Palette Club had been closed for years, so it was a dead end as far as getting some kind of lead on Zachary. There was no way of knowing if the matchbook was even his. The Bradshaws certainly had done some entertaining over the years; anyone might have dropped it behind the cushion. The only real conclusion I could draw was that Ramona was not a very thorough housecleaner.

I suddenly realized that I had been fighting jet lag and decided to take a nap before I met the guys at Vassili's.

Emily called me just before six.

"Hello."

"Pete, it's Emily Bradshaw. You sound tired."

"I'm fine, Emily. Just dozed off in my easy chair. I'm glad you woke me up, though. I have a dinner meeting at 7:00."

"Well, I won't keep you. I was just wondering if you found out anything regarding the Palette Club?"

"As a matter of fact, I did. I'm afraid it was a dead end. Turns out it was a gay bar and it's been closed for years. Not likely it had anything to do with Zachary, and even if it did, there's no real way I could follow up."

"Oh. Well I'm sorry to hear that. Just keep me posted on any further developments, okay?"

"That's what you're paying me for."

"Speaking of which, how are we doing money wise? Is my retainer holding up or do I owe you more?"

"Oh, not even close, Emily. Maybe I'm half way through it. And I haven't been very productive so far."

"Well, in my opinion, you're doing a fine job. You've already shown me how instinctive and intelligent you are. So don't hesitate to let me know when I should write another check."

"Will do, Emily. But that's a ways off."

"Alright then. Goodbye Pete."

"Bye Emily."

Hmmm. Strange call. Why did Emily seem so interested in the Palette Club? Was there a hint of relief when I suggested it was a dead end? I couldn't be sure. But I wondered if it might be wise to reassess my assessment. Only time would tell.

94

"Oh yeah, I remember Purina Rackford," Lef said through a mouthful of chicken stir-fry. "She was red hot. *Her* nickname should have been rack, if you know what I mean."

Lou had been relating the events of our meeting with Rackford.

"Well, Ralston is a good looking guy," I said. "And they're twins. Stands to reason she'd be attractive too,"

"She wasn't just attractive," Lou piped in. "She was drop dead gorgeous. I really had a thing for her. Even wrote a song about her to the tune of "Corrina, Corrina" by Ray Price."

"Ray Peterson," I corrected.

"You sure?"

"Lou, don't argue with the authority," Lef admonished.

"Yeah. Anyway, we had a few classes together and I think I flunked every one because all I could do was stare at her and dream."

"Say what?" Lef sounded surprised . "If you were so hot for her, how come you never asked her out?

"Why do you think?"

"Because she was black and you were a coward."

"You're half right. I was a coward. Skin color had nothing to do with it. It was because she was a lot taller than me. Than I? Damn. I'm not sure."

Lef still had his doubts. "You mean to tell me you would have asked her out if you were taller or she was shorter, even though the two of you were salt and pepper?"

"Damn right I would have."

"Hmph."

"Tell me this, Lou," I said. "Have you ever dated a black girl? No wait, have you ever had sex with a black girl?"

"Sure. Lots of times."

"He means for free, Lou," Lef pointed out.

"Oh. In that case, no."

95

Traffic was light on westbound I-94 at 10 am on Tuesday. I took the Belleville Road exit and had no trouble finding the offices of Sutton & Wasyl. It was right on Belleville Road, in a one-story stand-alone building adjacent to a strip mall populated with the usual auto insurance firms, dance studios and tattoo parlors.

I didn't know what to make of the sign in front of their office.

SUTTON & WASYL
Certified Public Accountants
Numbers don't lie?
Give us a try!

I introduced myself to the receptionist and she told me that Mr. Wasyl wasn't in yet and Mr. Sutton was in a meeting, but she was sure he'd be with me in a few minutes.

I took a seat on a sofa that Emily Bradshaw would have thrown in the trash ten years ago. The most recent magazine in the rack was a three-year-old copy of Esquire. I picked it up and flipped to an illustrated article of the ten best-dressed celebrities of 1992. As I was about to assuage my curiosity, I heard a distinct toilet flush and a middle-aged gentleman emerged from a door I hadn't even noticed. The way he was dressed might have qualified him to be in the article. Had he been a celebrity, of course.

"Mr. Sutton, this is Mr. Pete Pepper, a private investigator," the receptionist announced. "He called last week about meeting with you and I told him you'd be fairly open this week and he could just walk in. Uh, I don't think he said what it was about."

"Yes, Mary," Sutton replied. "I vaguely recall that you did mention that." Then to me, "Mr. Pepper. Steven Sutton. Pleased to meet you."

He offered his hand and I shook it reluctantly. I didn't recall hearing any water running after the toilet flush.

"My pleasure, Steven. I hope this isn't a bad time."

"Not at all. How can I help you?"

"I'm looking into the disappearance of Zachary Bradshaw. To be honest, I haven't gotten anywhere so far. I thought maybe you could tell me something about him. The last time you saw him, for example. Anything at all you know about him. Favorite restaurants. Who he associates with … "

"Oh my God! You say Zachary is missing?"

"For about three months."

"Hmm. Let's go into my office."

The office was not quite as ostentatious as Sutton's sense of fashion. But there were clues. The desk and furniture looked to be standard Steelcase.

Various diplomas adorned the wall behind the desk. All the walls were otherwise hung with rows of hats, from baseball caps to fedoras and deerslayers to top hats. There was even a couple of what Lef would have referred to as stingy brims. Sutton noticed my staring. It would have been hard not to.

"Yes, I collect hats, Pete. May I call you Pete?"

"Of course. I just called you Steven."

"Yes, so you did. Anyway, there's a story behind every one of those hats. That Detroit Tigers cap, for example, was worn by Kirk Gibson in the 1984 World Series. But I'm sure you don't have time for a rundown."

"Actually, I think it would be fascinating. But you're right. I'd rather get to Zachary Bradshaw."

"Yes, of course. And the answer to your first question is that I last saw Zachary this past June. His business wasn't going very well and he had run up some significant debt. It was just a routine meeting to go over his finances. See if we could work in some tax breaks, et cetera."

I had to laugh.

"Did I say something funny, Pete?"

"No, no. I was just thinking about your sign out front."

"Oh that. That's tongue in cheek, Pete. It gets people's attention and it definitely has gotten us some business. But we would never suggest anything illegal to our clients."

"Oh, I never … "

"We might get caught," he cut me off. Then he laughed too, and I think he winked at me.

"Well, I can tell you, it definitely got my attention."

"You see? It works. Anyway, as for your other questions, I can tell you that he likes to entertain at the Rathskeller in Ann Arbor and the Holiday Inn in Ypsilanti. I suppose I could check his returns and get the names of some of his guests."

"That would be great. You think I might get an actual copy of one of his returns?"

"Oh no. I couldn't do that. Sorry. Just the names. And that might even be stretching legal boundaries."

"Of course. I understand. But, how about something not so confidential. Like maybe something with his signature on it?"

"Possibly." Then he buzzed the front desk. "Mary, could you please bring me Zachary Bradshaw's file? Just the last year will do."

Half an hour later, I left with a copy of a handwritten note signed by Zachary Bradshaw and the names of three of Zachary's business lunch guests. One of them was Herman Kaplan.

When I got home, I brought in the mail. I was especially interested in a large manila envelope from Brad Toaz. Inside were about forty pages of Xerox copies of checks written by both Emily and Zachary. A funny idea was bouncing around in my head and I thought the signatures might confirm it. But first, I had to call Harvey.

96

Harvey beat me to the punch.

"Pete, good news. I talked to Toaz the other day and he said he'd get you the bank information. He was happy to help with anything that might break the cases. His case and yours, that is."

"Harv, better news. I already got an envelope from Toaz with copies of checks written by both Emily and Zachary. About forty pages worth, with four checks per page. Just got it in the mail. I was wondering if you might have access to a handwriting analyst?"

"No, not here. But the county has a guy they use. What's this all about, Pete?"

"There's just something not right about Emily. Can't put my finger on it, but she's acting funny. I want to compare Emily's signature on the checks Toaz sent me to the signature on the check Emily wrote to me."

"Seriously? Why?"

I wasn't ready to say that I thought Emily Bradshaw might not be Emily Bradshaw. "I don't know, Harv. Just a feeling I have. Come on, go with me on this. Please."

"Okay, sure. I've learned to trust your hunches from time to time. Why don't you bring the checks over and I'll have the signatures analyzed. Better yet, why don't we meet at Vassili's? You can return the favor by buying me dinner."

Right now?"

"Let's say six o'clock."

As usual, Harvey got there first. I ordered the chicken stir-fry. Watching Lef wolf his down the other day reminded me how much I like it. Harv was polite enough to keep the bill down by opting for a burger and fries. Totally out of character.

After, as we were nursing our decaf coffees, Harv looked through the checks Emily wrote. I only brought half of the sheets of Emily's checks and none of the ones Zachary had written. I wanted those for another reason.

When he saw the copy of the check Emily wrote to me, he almost spit out a mouthful of coffee. I wondered if the plural was mouthsful or mouthfuls. Or should that be were, not was? Probably.

"Five thousand dollars! She paid you five thousand up front? Holy shit! That's as much as I make in a month."

"I didn't ask for it, Harv. That's what she offered."

"Damn, maybe I should quit the force and hang my own shingle. Five thousand dollars. Jesus!"

"Well, if it makes you feel any better, go ahead and order dessert. I am buying."

"Thanks, I'll pass. I gotta do some paperwork back at the office anyway." Then, "Here, let me pick up those checks." He scooped them up, stood up and then handed them to me.

"What did you think I meant?" he said with a smile.

I just accepted them and smiled back.

"Hey, listen Pete. I don't mean to sound bitter. You're good at what you do and you deserve all you can get. I'll try to put a rush on this for you. Call you when I have something." Then he left.

97

I spent the better part of Wednesday morning going through the checks Emily wrote, making sure that I kept at least one copy written to each recipient. There were several duplicates, especially the ones made out to the recently deceased. But five of them were made out to doctors or medical facilities. Those were the ones I was interested in.

Surprisingly, all five of them were psychologists or psychiatrists. Or maybe it wasn't surprising. I noticed that the phone numbers of a Dr. Kerk Roberts, with an e not an i, and Sunrise Psychiatric Services were identical except for the last digit. I thought I'd have a better chance of reaching Kerk if I called what I figured was his direct line.

I was wrong.

"Sunrise Psychiatric, Dr, Roberts' office."

"Hello, my name is Pete Pepper. I'm a private investigator and I was hoping I might speak to Dr. Roberts about one of his patients. Emily Bradshaw. Is he available?"

"Uh, yes he's here, but I don't think he'd want to discuss anything about his patients. Certainly not over the phone."

"Please. It's very important. In fact, it's regarding an investigation that Emily hired me for."

"I don't know. This is highly irregular."

"Could you please just ask him? I won't need more than a minute of his time."

"Well, I suppose I could ask. Hang on please."

Thirty seconds later, Kerk picked up his phone.

"This is Dr. Roberts. What's this about Emily Bradshaw? Is she all right?"

I quickly switched into my lying mode. "Well, I'm not sure. She actually hired me to find her husband Zachary. He's been missing for several months."

"Hmm. Well you know, Emily is no longer my patient. I haven't seen her for several months. She called in one day and said she didn't need my services anymore. I was surprised because I thought we were making good progress. Three years of therapy and then, boom, she ended it. I had grown very fond of Emily. She was a wonderful woman."

"Yes, I think so too."

"Exactly what is it you want to know?"

"Just one thing. Is she agoraphobic?"

"I'm afraid I can't talk about her condition. Confidentiality, you know."

"Yes, doctor, I do know. But it's very important. I have a confidentiality issue as well. I can't give you the details, but knowing that she's agoraphobic could prove her innocence in her husband's disappearance."

"Oh my God. You mean she's a suspect? Then why would she hire you?"

"Good question. But some of my friends on the police force think it might be a good way to throw off suspicion."

" No, I can't believe Emily would be involved in something like that."

"So you can't help me?"

"Mr. Pepper. I can't divulge anything in her files."

"I understand … "

"But I can tell you this. As I said, I was and am very fond of Emily and I made a rare exception in her case."

"Yes?"

"She is the only patient for whom I have ever made house calls."

"I see."

"I'm sorry I couldn't be of any help, Mr. Pepper. But please, if you would, let me know that Emily is okay."

"You can count on it, Doctor. Thank you for your time."

"You're welcome. Goodbye."

So. Either Emily was lying about being agoraphobic. Or she wasn't Emily. I was hungry, but I skipped lunch and drove to Ypsilanti.

98

The Holiday Inn lounge wasn't very crowded, not that I expected it to be at two in the afternoon. Only a handful of tables were occupied, but the bar was fairly well attended.

I walked over and got the bartender's attention.

"Can I help you Buddy?"

"I hope so. By any chance, were you here a week ago Monday? It would have been October the thirtieth."

"I'm here every day, Monday through Friday. So, yeah. Why do you want to know?"

"Do you remember a woman, maybe in her late fifties, that had too much to drink? It would have been later, maybe seven or eight."

"Buddy, there's almost always a fifty-year-old woman in here that's had too much to drink. But I get off at five, so I don't think I saw the one you're looking for."

"Okay. Thanks."

"Any time."

I went to the front desk where a thin, shaggy haired kid was leaning on his elbows. He could have been Spike Davis' brother.

"Help you, man?"

"Yes, my Aunt Emily checked in here a couple weeks ago for an extended stay. I think it was Monday the thirtieth. She flew in from California and was going to visit several friends, including me, her nephew. Funny thing is, she never called me. Now my Uncle Paul, her husband, he did call and he hasn't heard from her either."

I casually handed him a twenty, which he eagerly accepted. He didn't even look around to see if anyone noticed.

"Anyway, I was wondering if you could confirm that she's still here."

"Piece a cake. What's the last name?"

"Bradshaw. Emily Bradshaw."

"Be right back."

He went over to a computer terminal, fumbled with the keyboard for a minute, and then returned.

"Bad news, mister. She checked in all right. But she checked out the next morning."

"Oh no!"

"Sorry. Hope you find her."

"Thanks. Thanks for your help." And as I walked away, "What am I going to tell Uncle Paul?"

That confirmed it. Emily was not agoraphobic. But it didn't confirm whether she was lying for some unknown reason, or whether she was an impostor.

99

I walked over to a quiet corner of the lobby and called the Bradshaw residence. It was on my way home and I wanted to stop by for a chat.

Ramona answered the phone.

"Ramona! Hey, it's Pete. Is Emily around? I'm sort of in the neighborhood and I was hoping I could stop by for a minute."

"Aw, gee. *I* was hoping you were calling to ask me out."

"Sorry. Not tonight."

"Well, hang on a minute. She's right here."

"Yes, Pete. What's on your mind?"

"Hi Emily. I'm sorry to call you at dinnertime, but I'm on the way back from Ann Arbor and there's something I really need to talk to you about. I was hoping to stop by."

"Certainly Pete. Have you eaten yet? Ramona's making beef stew. It smells delicious. Why don't you join us for dinner?"

Have I eaten yet? Yeah. Breakfast. I was so hungry I could smell the stew. "Gee, I don't want to impose, Emily, but that sounds pretty good to me."

"Not at all. She made plenty. How soon can you get here?"

"Half an hour or so."

"Excellent! We'll have a nice meal and then discuss whatever it is you're so eager to talk about. See you soon."

Was it because I was starving or was it really the best beef stew I had ever tasted. Ramona wasn't just good looking.

After dinner, Emily and I retired to the sunroom that was really a great room. We hadn't been seated for thirty seconds when Ramona wheeled in a cart loaded with cookies and handed me a chilled can of Canfield's.

"Oh my God! Where did you get that?" I was shocked.

"I have a cousin in Chicago. She drove in the other day and I asked her to bring me a case."

"Awesome. Thanks Ramona. That's very thoughtful of you."

"I think she's hitting on you Pete," Emily said.

"I know I am," Ramona confirmed.

I couldn't think of anything clever to say, but fortunately, Emily saved me.

"Maybe some other time, Ramona. You run along, now. Pete and I have some business to attend to."

Ramona put the tray of cookies on a coffee table and wheeled away.

"So, what do you want to talk about Pete?"

I had already prepared my lie. "This is awkward, Emily. I don't want you to think I don't believe you, but I got a call from Lieutenant Steinberg the other day. In the course of investigating George Gianotti's murder, he got access to George's files. He said there were notes George had written that clearly stated that you *are* agoraphobic. The lieutenant also had a statement from a Dr. Robertson who confirmed it. I'm guessing that's why George came out here instead of you going there."

"I see. And you, on the other hand, know that I'm *not* agoraphobic, if for no other reason, because I drove to Ypsilanti last week." She didn't sound even a bit concerned.

"Well, yes."

"Pete, I told you before that I wasn't. It was just a little game I played. It was a matter of convenience. I've always been a homebody. I like it here and if I can get people to come to me instead of me going to them, well, that's what I do. I have to confess, though, there were times when

Zachary was out of the country that I did sneak out here and there. You know, to do a little shopping."

She gave me a knowing nod.

I gave her back a blank stare.

"For liquor! My goodness. You couldn't figure that out?"

I laughed in spite of myself. "Oh Emily. You're right. And you thought I was a good investigator. I'm sorry I doubted you, but Harvey, Lieutenant Steinberg that is, asked me to follow up."

"Well, there you go. You *were* being a good investigator."

"I guess so."

"Listen Pete, I usually head up to my room about this time of night. So, if there's nothing else … "

"Actually, there is something else," I said.

"What is it, Columbo?" she asked with a smile. It was a reference to the annoyingly persistent detective from the television show. In fact, I was being persistent, but not in a particularly annoying fashion.

"Mmm. This is awkward too, Emily. And you don't have to answer if you don't want to. It's just that I can't let go of the notion that Zachary might somehow be involved in the deaths of your employees. I mean, he had a lot to gain with them out of your will."

I didn't mention that I had found out from Steven Sutton that old Zach's business was suffering.

"I don't agree with you at all, but go ahead."

"Well, it's none of my business like I said, but the money you were going to leave to Kay and Ralph and Edith. Was it a significant amount?"

"You're right," she said abruptly. " It isn't any of your business, but I hired you to do a job and I can see you think it's important. So I don't mind telling you at all." The she softened noticeably. "The fact is, I haven't really decided."

"Oh!" I feigned mild surprise. "So there's no way Zachary would have known."

"That's right, Pete."

"Well, I'm glad we cleared that up. Thanks for seeing me Emily. And thank Ramona for a truly delicious meal. And the Canfield's."

"Oh, I will."

She walked up the stairs to her room as I headed for the front door.

Ramona was waiting for me there. "If you really wanted to thank me, you'd rip off my clothes right here and now."

"Ramona, I think you are extremely attractive and I would love to ravage your magnificent body, but I'm really tired and I'm sort of in a committed relationship."

She just gave me a come hither look and dropped the bodice of her uniform. She was braless and her breasts were all I imagined and more. Lou would have fainted on the spot.

"Do you still feel tired?"

"Ramona. Please. Be content with knowing that I *do* want you. I truly do. But I just can't have you."

She leaned forward so that her breasts were almost touching me.

"Just two little kisses?" she offered.

"You're going to have to settle for one." I leaned over, felt my chest brushing against her bare breasts and kissed her on the forehead. It took great willpower for me not to slide down.

"Goodbye Ramona. You are a very beautiful woman."

"Aw, dammit! Take these anyway." She reached into her apron pockets and pulled a can of Canfield's out from each.

I took them and leaned over again, this time giving her a light kiss on the lips. She tried to linger, but I pulled away and she let go.

"And that's two," I said.

She was clearly fighting back tears as she softly said, "Goodbye Pete. I'm sorry."

"Goodbye Ramona. I'm not."

An interesting visit. And despite the convenient story, it confirmed to me that the woman I was talking to was not agoraphobic. *She* wasn't. But the real Emily was. The fake Emily, whoever she might be, didn't correct me when I said Dr. Robertson instead of Dr. Roberts. That wasn't necessarily incriminating. She could have just misheard me. But then she said she hadn't decided how much she was going to leave to her help. That's not what Cal Broder said. And he had a document that proved otherwise. I was growing more confident that my farfetched speculation wasn't so farfetched after all.

I couldn't wait to tell Harvey Steinberg.

100

It wasn't until morning that I finally reached him. Three calls to Harvey Wednesday night netted zero responses. Could it be one of those rare occasions when Harv took the Mrs. out for dinner and a movie? I had only seen Esther Steinberg on a few occasions and she was a very pleasant, likeable woman. Certainly deserving of a night out just for putting up with Harvey.

I caught him at his office just before noon.

"Harvey, It's Pete. Emily Bradshaw isn't Emily Bradshaw. She's an impostor!" I couldn't contain my excitement.

"What? Wait a minute. Slow down. What are you talking about?"

I told him about the conversation with Kerk Roberts that proved the real Emily was agoraphobic and the woman we thought was Emily clearly was not. And how the impostor claimed she hadn't decided how much money she was going to leave to Kimberly, Spaulding and Pringham, but the real Emily already had it in her new will.

"Jesus Christ! Then who the hell is she?"

"I don't know. A friend of the family? A relative? Does she have any sisters? Cousins?"

"I have to let Toaz know about this immediately. He'll want to check it out."

"Harv, you can check it out too. That woman, whoever she is, also has to be a suspect in George's murder. That's your case. You are still involved, aren't you? Working with the Troy police?"

"Right, right." Then, "Holy shit. There's a good chance she might have knocked off the real Emily. And Zachary too."

"That's my guess."

"All right. Thanks, Pete. I'll give Toaz a call now. Keep me informed of any other blockbusters you come up with."

"Will do."

I hung up, feeling more than just a little pleased with myself.

101

I had almost forgotten about Herman Kaplan's promise to call me back. He said he was returning this week and this week was almost over.

He finally kept his word Thursday afternoon.

"Mr. Pepper, it's Herman Kaplan."

"Herman. Thanks for calling. I take it you're back in town."

"No, I'm afraid not. I've been delayed."

"Oh. I'm sorry to hear that. The conference didn't go well?"

"Uh, well, yes. Everything went as planned. It's just that, um, well uh, the Red Wings are playing Toronto on Saturday and I'm a huge fan. I've managed to get a ticket for the game, so I won't be returning until next week."

"I see. Well, can we set a definite date to meet? Things are moving fast here and I really would like to get that picture of Zachary."

"Most definitely. Let's say Wednesday morning at eleven. We can meet right at the office building where my files are stored."

He gave me the address and I jotted it down.

"Okay then," Herman said. "If there's nothing else ... "

"Actually, there is, Herman. Do you recall having lunch with Zachary Bradshaw at the Rathskeller in Ann Arbor? It would have been a few months ago. Maybe May or June?" I felt like Columbo again.

"I've had lunch or dinner with Zachary at the Rathskeller on a few occasions. It was one of his favorite places to eat. Do you have a specific date in mind? I'd have to check my calendar."

"No. I just wanted to confirm that you did meet him there. Thanks for your help."

"You're quite welcome. Until next week then?"

"Until next week."

I hung up, wondering who would be auditing Herman's expense account. More than likely, it would be Herman himself.

102

I was in my office Friday afternoon when Harvey called.

"Are you sitting down, Pete?"

"Yep."

"The handwriting analysis just came in. Keep in mind we just sent copies of the checks, but there's 80 percent likelihood that the two signatures are *not* the same person. The Emily who wrote the check to you is not the Emily who wrote the checks to her employees."

"I'm not surprised, Harv. I pretty much had that figured out. But who is the impostor? Did you or Toaz come up with anything?"

"Emily Bradshaw was an only child. Both of her parents were only children. No known living relatives."

"Interesting," I said. "Very interesting. But what about Zachary? It could be one of his relatives as well."

"Same story as Emily. No known living relatives. Maybe it's one of their acquaintances. That could be a bear trying to track down."

I glanced at the picture Gianni drew hanging on my corkboard and suddenly realized why I kept looking at it.

"Do me a favor Harv," I said. "I'm going to bring over a copy of the checks Zachary wrote. I want you to compare them to the check Emily wrote to me."

There was a pause. "Are you thinking … ?"

"That's exactly what I'm thinking."

"Sounds crazy, but it's worth a shot."

"It would explain everything, Harv."

"Yes, I suppose it would. But listen, don't bother to bring any more checks over."

"Why not?"

"I already have some. The checks you gave me that Emily wrote? There were a couple sheets of checks that Zachary wrote stuck in with them."

"Oh. That was unintentional, but good."

"Yes. Very fortuitous."

Fortuitous? Lou would have been impressed.

103

Was it possible? Could Zachary Bradshaw be masquerading as Emily? Clearly he had motive. But, if so, what an incredibly elaborate and risky scheme. I mean he/she *was* a woman. I had little doubt of that. Which could only mean one thing. I called the Bradshaw residence, hoping that Ramona would answer.

She did. "Bradshaw residence. Ramona speaking."

"Ramona, it's Pete.

"Pete. I wasn't sure I would ever hear from you again. You must think I'm a slut."

"No. No, Ramona. Not at all." The thought had never entered my mind.

"Well, the way I threw myself at you. I don't know what else you'd think."

I wasn't sure how to put her mind at ease, but I gave it a try.

"Listen Ramona, you have to understand how a guy's mind works. When a woman makes it obvious that she wants to be intimate with a man, it's because she finds him attractive and desirable. That's exactly how a guy wants to think of himself. It's a compliment."

"I do find you desirable."

"Yes, I understand, and I find you desirable too. Believe me. But then, say the next day, you hit on some other guy. *That* would make you a slut. To the first guy, that is. Not the second guy. He'd see it as a compliment. Does that make any sense?"

"I think so. But I'm still very embarrassed. And disappointed."

"Well, don't be embarrassed, because I'm very flattered."

"Is that why you called? To make me feel better?"

"Yes. That's one reason. But there's another."

"What?" She sounded a little pouty.

"This is going to sound crazy, Ramona, but have you ever seen Emily without any clothes on?"

"What?!" Total shock.

"Have you seen Emily naked?"

"No, but you've seen me naked."

"Half naked. And I was very impressed."

"Now you're flattering me."

"You deserve it Ramona. Really. Anyway, I'm at least glad we've got our situation straightened out a bit."

"I suppose. Anyway, I'm sorry I've never seen Emily naked, although I'm *not* sorry, if you know what I mean."

"Yes, I'm sure I do."

"Actually, I really don't see much of Emily at all. She has a pretty regular routine. I serve her breakfast in the morning, lunch around one – unless she goes out somewhere – and dinner around six. After dinner, she usually goes up to her bedroom. Sometimes we play Scrabble or gin rummy after dinner, but she's always upstairs around nine or so."

"And she's fully clothed all the while?"

"Huh? Oh, you're joking."

"Sorry about that. I thought it was amusing. Anyway, thanks for the information. I'll see you … "

"Pete! Wait a minute."

"What?"

"There was one time she was taking a bath and I took her a towel. But it was a bubble bath and she was pretty much covered up."

"So you couldn't see if she had breasts?"

"No, but I can assure you they would be nothing compared to mine."

"Oh, I've had firsthand proof of that. Well, first *eye* proof. My hands never came into play."

She laughed at the unintentional joke.

"No, but I sure wanted them to come and play," she joked back. Then seriously, "Pete, why are you so interested in Emily's boobs?"

"Just a crazy theory I'm investigating. But I'm not interested in her boobs, per se. Just trying to determine if she has boobs."

"Crazy theory? That's an understatement. But I can tell you this. I didn't see her boobs, but when I took her the towel, there was a bra on the floor next to the hamper."

"Well, I guess that would support the boobs theory. Listen, Ramona, you've been a big help. And I'd appreciate it if you didn't say anything about this to Emily."

"Pete, there is no way I would get into a conversation with Emily about her boobs. Don't give it a second thought."

"Thanks, Ramona. When this investigation is all over, I owe you a dinner."

"Oh, sounds good. And whenever that may be, I can assure you that I *will* be hungry."

"Goodbye Ramona."

"Bye Pete. Hope you find Zachary soon."

I had no response for that. But I was quite certain I already had found him.

104

Saturday morning I went to the Southfield Library. Ruth Abraham looked up from *The Jewish News* as I walked by the front desk.

"Morning, Mr. Pepper. What brings you to the lie-berry?"

"Oh, morning Ruth. What do you know about sex change operations?"

"We call it transsexualism here at the lie-berry." Ruth was in a funny mood. Fairly rare for her.

"Well, what can you tell me about it?"

"I'm surprised you don't know, Pete. It's when a man has an operation to become a woman. Or a woman has one to become a man."

"Oh, thanks. Guess I'll be leaving now." I turned around and pretended to walk out. I could play her game.

She pointed to the stairs.

"Second floor, southwest corner. Medical Sciences, 610 in the Dewey Decimal System. You might try 612, Human Physiology or 617, Surgery. But I'm sure it's in there somewhere."

"Damn, you did that without even looking it up?" I turned to thank her, but she was already face deep in her newspaper.

I spent the next few hours looking through several volumes that dealt with the topic. I found out quite a few interesting things.

The first known sex reassignment surgery (SRS), as it is called in medical circles, took place in Germany in 1930. The subject was a man named Einar Wegener who was a successful artist. Interestingly, the reference book used the term 'presented.' Einar was presented as a man. Apparently, even as a youth, he enjoyed wearing women's clothing.

Anyway, Einar eventually married another artist, a woman named Gerda Gottlieb, a lesbian. The marriage was mutually beneficial because it allowed Einar to live openly as a woman (Lili Elbe), and Gerda to practice lesbianism. They lived together for many years; Lili often posing as a model for Gerda, and the public unaware that she was a man.

As she approached the age of 50, Lili/Einar decided she wanted to have a child. The sex change procedure required five surgeries. The first was to remove the testicles and the second to remove the penis and transplant ovaries. I made a note of the term 'penectomy', and looked forward to using it on Lou. Third and fourth surgeries were necessary to remove the ovaries, which Lili's body rejected. Unfortunately, she died after her fifth surgery, which was for the transplantation of a uterus.

Christine Jorgenson was probably the most publicized case of SRS, although tennis player Renee Richards also received a lot of press. Neither of the surgeries was performed in the Unites States. Jorgenson's surgery was done in Denmark in 1952, and while my reference didn't mention where Richards' took place, it wasn't relevant to my case.

It wasn't until 1966 that the first male-to-female SRS was performed in the United States. A Dr. Elmer Belt at the Johns Hopkins Medical Center was the surgeon. The reference didn't mention the name of the recipient, but again, it wasn't relevant. I was more interested in the legality and the timeframe of the transition. Could anyone get an SRS? And how long did it take?

The answers were "maybe" and "indeterminate." Different countries had different laws and guidelines. Apparently, Scandinavia was more liberal in both regards. At least initially.

True transsexuals, one reference said, really felt they belonged to the other sex and wanted to function as such. Did Zachary fit in that category? There was no way I could answer that one. I never met the man.

The term transsexual was rooted in psychology. The preferred term was transgender, because the underlying condition is a matter of gender, not sexuality. Some countries required intensive psychological screening before permitting a sex change. In others, you just had to ask for one. Interesting, but still not helpful.

Then I found a case history of an actual SRS patient. I'm glad it wasn't illustrated. The testicles are removed and the skin of the foreskin and penis is inverted to form a vagina. Some other surgical things are done to make the vagina viable and functional. There were no complications in this particular case and, to my surprise, the entire procedure took only four hours.

After that, the transgender can choose to have more surgeries, including facial feminization, breast augmentation and voice feminization. I wasn't sure how much of that Zachary had undergone, but I did notice that his voice was a bit on the husky side. Transgender, by the way, is a noun referring to the person. Transsexual is considered more of an adjective, although it is often misused as a noun. At least, according to some.

Bottom line, Zachary could easily have pulled everything off without Emily being any the wiser. His travel schedule and their lifestyle made it a piece of cake. And I wondered if the cost of his SRS might be part of the reason why he was having financial difficulties.

Ruth spotted me on the way out.

"Did you find what you needed, Pete?"

"Right where you said."

"So have you decided to go through with the operation?"

"Oh, that research wasn't for me," I responded, doing my best to lisp. "It was for a friend."

105

On the short trip home, Stu called. I pulled into a strip mall parking lot and answered. He said he was in the neighborhood and wondered if we might meet at my place, so I invited him over for a late lunch.

After devouring six Buitoni individual pizzas, two for me and four for Stu, we each popped open our second can of Grain Belt and settled in the living room.

"So how is night school coming, Stu?"

"Very well, thank you," he said with a proud smile. "It isn't as difficult as I thought it would be. I think I've mastered most parts of speech and I'm quite proficient at diagramming sentences, although I have no idea how that particular skill will ever serve me."

I laughed at his surprising erudition. "Damn, Stu, that was an impressive answer. You *are* doing well."

"My instructor says I'm a fast learner, but I have to confess, I practiced that answer. I figured you'd be asking me about night school sooner or later."

That response brought another loud laugh.

"Well, let's get down to business. I want to establish the ground rules for our working relationship. I think you're aware that I can't pay you on a full-time basis, so it's going to have to be some kind of part-time arrangement."

"That's fine with me, Pete."

"But I want to make it worth your while, of course. You've already proven your value. How does $20 per hour sound? I call you when I need you and pay you when the job is done."

"I'm amenable to that. Especially since I already got a pretty regular job." Stu's vocabulary was obviously coming along well too.

"Really? What kind of job?"

"Uh, sort of a driver/bodyguard for a retired executive. That's on an as-needed basis too. But it's been three or four days a week so far."

"Hmm. Anybody I'd know?"

"Oh, you'd know the name, alright, but I'm not supposed to say. Sorry, Pete, but you know I'd be discreet for you too."

"I'm sure you would."

"Yeah. So I was wondering, do you think you could pay me under the table?"

"I don't know, Stu. I like to keep things straight with the IRS boys.

At this point, there's no way of knowing how much you'll earn in a year. Tell you what, I'll just write you a check each time you do something for me, but if it turns out to be a sizeable amount, I'm going to have to claim a deduction when I file my tax return. That means I'll be issuing you a 1099 and you're obligated to claim the income when you file."

"That's fine. I'll take my chances."

"By the way, I haven't paid you for the trip to the airport. How many hours are we talking?"

"Oh, that's on me. There's a restaurant out by the airport that I like, so I went there after I dropped you off. I wouldn't feel right charging you for what turned out to be a personal trip."

"If you say so, Stu. What's the name of the restaurant? Maybe I'll try it some time."

Stu's face turned red. "Uh, the Runway Club. It's a topless place. And sometimes, it's more than topless, if you know what I mean."

I wondered if Lou knew about the place. It sounded like their policy was very similar to the Iron Cage's. "Oh," was all I could say.

"Gee, Pete, I hope you don't think I'm a bad person because of that."

"Not at all, Stu. Some of my best friends like to frequent strip clubs. In fact, I'm meeting them tomorrow at Ken's Bar over in Dearborn. On Michigan Avenue. You know the place?"

"I've drove by it."

I didn't bother to point out Stu's grammatical error. After all, my good friend Lou has often said that the past participle and past perfect tense are the most frequently misunderstood and misused.

"So are you free to join us tomorrow? Two o'clock. And I'm buying."

"Sure. I'm off tomorrow. From my other job, I mean."

"Excellent. Shall I pick you up?"

"No. I'll meet you there. Two o'clock."

"Actually, do me a little favor. Show up about fifteen minutes late."

Before Stu left, I wrote down another short speech I wanted him to learn. I had a little surprise in store for Lou.

After he left, I pulled out my cell phone and called my little Italian buddy. I hoped I wasn't premature in telling Stu I was meeting friends for lunch on Sunday. My friends knew nothing about it.

"Luigi, it's Pietro."

"Hey, Pete. What's up?"

"Lunch. Tomorrow at Ken's Bar. Two o'clock. I'm buying. You in?"

"Hell yeah. Can I bring Lef?"

"Please do. By the way, have you ever heard of a place called the Runway Club?"

"Heard of it? Lef and I closed the place last night. He's crashed on my sofa right now."

I guess I shouldn't have been surprised. "Uh, right," I stammered. "See you guys tomorrow then."

106

I woke up Sunday morning full of optimism that I was about to close the Zachary Bradshaw case. To me, the evidence was already overwhelming, but I had another idea I wanted to check out. I was pretty sure the second handwriting analysis would confirm that Emily's signature on my check was the same as Zachary's signature on his checks. Then, there was the meeting with Kaplan on Wednesday. I was really looking forward to seeing a picture of the real Zachary. The one thing I hadn't figured out yet was how I was going to approach him/her.

I ate a light breakfast and just glanced through the *Free Press*. It was freezing outside, but since I hadn't been there for a while, I bundled up and went to the 10 o'clock Mass at St. Luke's. I'm not sure what motivated me to go. Maybe it was a preemptive act of contrition for all the alcohol I knew I'd be drinking at lunch. It was the Sabbath, after all.

Whatever the reason, it turned out to be a big mistake.

Father Wong was happy to see me, of course. And so was Marianne.

But she wasn't content to just say 'Nice to see your face again, Pete' like the Father. Oh no. She had something else in mind.

"Pete, I have something to ask you."

"Sure, what?"

"Gianni's spending Friday night at a friend's. I want you to come over for dinner. I'm making fettucine with clam sauce. Hand cut fettucine, not store bought."

"Oh, uh, that sounds nice." As soon as I said it, I sensed it wasn't a very enthusiastic response.

"You don't sound very enthusiastic." I was right.

"No, really. I *love* fettucine with clam sauce." At least that was sincere.

"That's not what I mean. You sound like you don't want to have anything to do with me."

"Marianne, I'm nearing the end of a very important case. I don't know if I'll even be free Friday night."

She shook her head and gave me a pleading look. "Pete, you know how I feel about you. If you love me, you'll be there, case or no case."

Apparently she either didn't understand or was unwilling to accept how I felt about her. "Look, Marianne. I can't promise, but I'll try to be there. That's the best I can give you right now. Okay?"

She repeated, "If you love me, you'll be there." Then she turned and walked away.

When I got to Ken's Bar, Lou and Lef were already seated at a four-top. A half empty pitcher of beer indicated they had been there for a while. For all I knew, it was their second or third pitcher. Knowing that the boys would not have attended church beforehand, I had stopped home and changed into casual clothes. Even so, I felt overdressed next to them.

Lou gave a magnanimous gesture and said, "Pull up a chair, oh gracious benefactor."

"Huh?"

"What he means," Lef explained, "is that there *is* such a thing as a free lunch."

"Right. I suppose you boys parted with more than a few thousand lira last night."

"Worth every dinaro," Lou confirmed. Then, "Hey, we thought of another great nickname last night."

I recalled our nickname discussion after Lef's announcement of the Oak Park High starting five at Hazel Park. "Oh yeah?" What?"

"Billy Weingarden. Remember him? Nofux."

"I didn't go to Oak Park High, guys. So, no, I don't think I know him. What's the significance of Nofux?"

"He was an egghead," Lef said. "Got straight A's. He wanted to be cool like the jocks, but he would never say fuck."

I looked around to see if anyone was listening. "You might want to keep it down, guys. The customers might overhear you."

"Fuck the customers," Lou said, followed by a loud guffaw from Lef.

"Anyway," Lou continued, "Nofux would say things like fother mucker and fut the wuck. You know, switching letters, so in his mind, it wasn't swearing."

"Actually, I know a few people like that," I said. "And I like the nickname. But I can't imagine you called him that in front of other people, you know, like adults."

"Yeah," Lou said. "But then we'd pronounce it like noffix, with the accent on the first syllable."

"And while we were reminiscing," Lef said, "it brought to mind a fascinating philosophical question."

"Which is?"

"When did being a mother fucker become a derogatory term?"

"Always has been, as far as I know. Why would it not be?"

"Because," Lef explained, 'if it wasn't for mother fuckers, everyone would be an only child."

I had to laugh, but Lou jumped up, a scared look on his face. I immediately saw why. Stu Gotts was walking toward us.

"Guys, you know Stu, I believe."

"Oh yeah," Lou replied.

Stu took the empty chair and smiled. "Afternoon guys."

Lef reached out and shook hands, but Lou just let out a weak, "Hi, Stu."

"Lou, relax," I said. "We're friends now. Stu works for me."

"That's easy for you to say. He's never chased after you looking for money I owed the Toad. Hey, that rhymes!"

"No, but he's chased me for other reasons."

"Oh yean. Right. Sorry, Stu. Guess that was just an instinctive reaction. Good to see you."

"Likewise."

We ordered hamburgers around and two more pitchers of beer, and then settled into relaxed conversation. I was waiting for the opportunity for Stu to unleash the line I had written for him. Lef finally gave it to me.

"So, Stu, Pete tells me you've been going to night school. How's it going?"

Stu glanced at me, and I nodded. Then he recited so perfectly I could hardly believe it. He even embellished it a bit.

"Quite well. Thanks for asking. I must say that, even though I'm a neophyte at such academic endeavors, I find matriculating at my age to be quite fulfilling and I suspect it's awakened a sesquipedalian bent I never knew I had."

Lou literally fell off his chair, laughing. "No fucking way," he said. "That has to be a setup. Pete, you put him up to this. Don't deny it."

By then, we were all laughing so loud that the entire room was looking at us. When we finally settled down, Stu looked at Lou and said, "Yes, Pete did have me rehearse that line. And it's a good thing for you that it was a setup."

"Why is that?" Lou wanted to know.

"Because if it was for real and you laughed at me, I'd have to break your face."

There was a brief silence until Stu's stern look became a smile, followed by a loud laugh. Lef and I joined in immediately. It took Lou a few seconds longer.

Before we left, Lou mentioned that he and Lef were thinking of going to Northville Downs on Friday night and wondered if I could join them.

"I don't think so," I said. "I might have dinner plans."

107

The problem with drinking beer from a pitcher is that it's much harder to keep track of how much you've consumed. At least with cans or bottles, you can line them up and count them. And then decide when to stop.

I felt fine when I got home from lunch. I certainly didn't feel drunk. In fact, I don't recall ever being inebriated; not since my college days, anyway. And I would never even think of driving if I felt out of control. But later last night, while I was trying to read an old Harlan Ellison anthology, the room started spinning. When I woke up Monday morning, it had slowed down, but only a bit.

Fortunately, everything came into focus around three in the afternoon and I was in the kitchen trying to decide between oatmeal and scrambled eggs when Harvey called.

"Theory confirmed," he said, as though it were his theory.

"The handwriting?"

"Yes indeed. According to the analysis, there's almost a hundred percent likelihood that the same person signed those checks. And we both know who that person is,"

"Zachary Bradshaw."

"Currently masquerading as Emily Bradshaw."

"So, what's next, Harvey?"

"That's what I was going to ask you."

"Well, I want to confront Zachary, of course. I'm just trying to figure out the best way to go about it."

"You think it could be dangerous?"

"Not if I do it right. But I am licensed to carry, you know. It's just that I don't like to."

"Yeah, well you know I have to pass this information on to Toaz, right?"

"Of course. Do you think that's sufficient evidence for him to make an arrest?"

"Maybe. Maybe not. That's Toaz's call."

"So, when are you going to tell him?"

"Any reason why it shouldn't be today?"

"What if I could get you more evidence?"

"You got something in mind?"

"Just something I want to check out at the Bradshaw mansion. Without Emily's knowledge, of course."

"You're gonna go snooping around her place? Kind of risky, don't you think?"

"Not necessarily. Emily usually goes up to her room after dinner. I'll wait until late at night. Plus, I have an informant on the inside."

"Oh, you mean that little red headed maid. What was her name? Mona?"

"Close. Ra-mona."

"Yeah, Ramona. Very lovely young lady. Remarkable body."

"You have no idea." Harv didn't react to my implication, which was fine. I hadn't intended for it to slip out. It just did.

"So what do you expect to find?"

"Whatever's there. Hopefully something that will link Zachary to one or more of the crime scenes."

"Hmmm. Well, I should let Toaz know as soon as possible, but I suppose I could wait until tomorrow."

"I don't plan to go out there until tomorrow night, Harv. I really don't feel very well today. I'm thinking maybe I got food poisoning yesterday."

He sighed. "Alright, Pepper. I guess I can wait until Wednesday."

"Actually, I'll have even more evidence Wednesday morning, Harv. Something that could be the real clincher."

"Then I'll wait 'til Wednesday afternoon."

"Good."

You gonna tell me what the evidence is?"

"No. I'm going to hand it over to you Wednesday afternoon. At lunch. At Vassili's. And then I'm going to try to convince you not to call Toaz until Thursday."

There was a long pause. Then, "Nice talking to you, Pete. I'll be sure to let you know when that handwriting analysis comes in." His voice was noticeably louder than before, but not unnaturally so. I assumed there were people within earshot. And he wanted them to hear.

"Thanks, Harvey."

"You're welcome. Oh! And one more thing. If you're planning on going out tomorrow night, you know, like to the racetrack or something? Be sure to bundle up good. I heard on the radio that the temperature is gonna be in the teens."

108

The radio was right. I don't usually wear hats, but tonight I was wearing the only one I own that had earflaps. And my ears were still cold. Too bad I didn't have access to Steven Sutton's wall display. I was also bundled up in an old winter coat and wearing my best driving gloves. Traffic was light and I made good time. It helped that I had committed the route to memory.

A light snow started to fall as I turned off my headlights and I pulled into Bradshaw's long driveway. I took it past the house and stopped about ten yards in front of the garage, a rather large structure with not one, but three garage doors.

Just as I got out and pointed my flashlight toward the garage, another flashlight pointed at me. Shit! If it was Emily, I was screwed. I was definitely exceeding the bounds of what she would consider good investigating.

"Hold it right there, Buddy," a voice said. It wasn't Emily's. "Mind telling me what the hell you're doing here?"

A large man approached me and aimed the light in my face.

"Pete? Is that you?"

"Uh, yeah. Who are you?" I had instinctively raised my arms as the memory of the first meeting with Lef ran through my mind. But, of course, it wasn't him.

"It's me. Bob Hawkins," the man said as he shone the light toward his own face.

I let out a sigh of relief. "Bob, of course. What are you doing here?"

"Are you kidding? You're the guy who got me this gig."

"Oh. Right." Bob was one of the owners of Cashwell Security, the company I had recommended to Emily. "You just took me by surprise."

"So I take it this isn't a social call."

"No. Emily hired me to find her missing husband and I'm just following up on a lead." I didn't think it was necessary to tell him that Emily and Zachary were one and the same.

"So what are you looking for exactly?"

"Something in the garage. I'll know it when I see it."

"Hmph. Okay, let's go take a look."

We entered the garage through a side door, unlocked. From the outside, I couldn't tell exactly how big the garage was. I recalled thinking "airplane hangar" when I saw it in daylight, the first time I visited Emily. I was right. Inside, it was enormous. I couldn't even see the back wall. For all I knew, there really might be a small airplane back there in the darkness.

Immediately visible, though, were a 1995 Cadillac and an old Ford pickup, a big F150. Shelves along the left wall were filled with the kind of stuff you'd expect to find in a garage. I was more interested in the truck.

"Want me to turn on the light?" Bob asked.

"No. No, please don't. Just bring your flashlight over here."

We walked over to the bed of the truck, which was covered in a heavy tarp, reminiscent of the one that covered Janny Vandever's body. I pulled it back and we both flashed our lights. What I initially saw wasn't necessarily suspicious: a couple of shovels and other garden implements, a rolled-up garden hose and a few buckets. I wondered if it might be Ralph Spaulding's truck or maybe one that he used on occasion.

On the other hand, any truck might have shovels and garden implements in its bed. Then I flashed the light back a bit farther and saw something you wouldn't expect: a small black valise, like the kind doctors used to carry when they made house calls. I had no idea what that was about. But the object next to the valise made my heart skip a beat. It was a small can of paint. I reached in and picked it up for a closer look and I immediately knew I had hit pay dirt. The label said Forest Green.

"This is what I was looking for," I told Bob.

"A can of paint? Why, are you gonna do some redecorating?" He could have been joking, but he sounded sincere.

"Something like that," I said, hiding the truth for no particular reason.

"Do you mind if I take this?"

"Be my guest."

"Listen, Bob. I'm sure Emily wouldn't mind, but let's just keep this between you and me, okay?"

"Mum's the word, Pete."

I wondered if Ralph Spaulding's body was still in the morgue and if there was any way to match the paint on his penis to the paint in the can. Actually, at this point, I didn't really think it mattered.

109

The building looked like it might be abandoned. It was one of those old two-story office plazas that gave way to the high-rise revolution that took over Oakland County back in the eighties. The address said 3027 Greenfield, just like Kaplan said. A big sign in front offered office space for just $100 a month.

There was only one car in the pot-holed, asphalt speckled parking lot, a shiny red, late-model Camaro. I figured it had to be Kaplan's. There were two entrances, so I took the one nearest me, walked past the steps leading to the second floor and came to a long hallway that ran the length of the building. The paint on the walls was chipped, the carpet was badly worn and there were no lights. Down the hallway to my right, toward the other entrance, I spotted the only hint of light in the building.

I headed toward it and saw it was coming from an open door. I approached the door and walked through, into a roughly 10-by-10-foot office with one small desk and maybe a dozen filing cabinets. Kaplan was leaned over one, shuffling through some files.

"Herman, good morning," I greeted him.

"Oh, good morning, Mr. Pepper. I thought I'd get here a bit early and have the photos ready for you." He walked toward me and plopped a file on top of a few that were already on the desk.

"I found several shots of Zachary. Are you looking for anything in particular?"

"Just the most recent you've got."

"Ah, that would be in here." He pulled out the bottom file, opened it and handed me a photo. It was a smiling Zachary holding what had to be a piece of the Great Wall of China. I studied the face carefully. It wasn't a dead ringer for Emily, but it didn't take an expert to see the similarity. Zachary apparently did have a little feminization surgery done, but not enough to conceal the fact that he was, without much doubt, Emily.

"Do you mind if I take this, Herman?"

"Not at all. I have plenty more."

"Thanks, I really appreciate it."

On the way out, I stopped and turned as Kaplan was putting files back into one of the cabinets. "By the way, Herman," I said, "that's a nice car you've got out there. Very nice."

"Oh, that isn't mine," he replied. "It belongs to the Commission."

110

Harvey was already seated when I got to Vassili's. There's something about a free meal that seems to jumpstart his promptness mechanism.

"Afternoon, Pete. I assume that's the new evidence you have in that envelope there."

I plopped it down on the table. "Yeah. Take a look."

He pulled the picture out and stared at it for about twenty seconds, then looked over at me. "Sure looks like it's Emily to me. But what the hell is that in his hand?"

"A piece of the Great Wall of China. He imported it a few years ago when the Chinese were making repairs. I'm pretty sure that's what he used to kill Janny Vandever."

"Son of a bitch. That very piece?"

"No, no. He brought in several pieces, all different sizes. Maybe a thousand pounds or more, I don't know. But apparently there's still some in the Bradshaw Enterprises warehouse in Ann Arbor. If that even matters."

"I don't see how it would."

"Right. But I have something that probably does matter out in my car."

"Oh yeah? What's that?"

"A can of green paint. I found it in the bed of Emily's truck last night.

And I'm betting it matches the paint that was on Ralph Spaulding's penis. Do you think they can still make a comparison?"

"No idea. I'll check with Toaz about the disposition of the body. But if they can't, the paint is only circumstantial, you know. Plus, how you gonna prove you got it from Emily's truck?"

"Witness. Bob Hawkins from Cashwell Security. He was with me when we entered the garage last night."

"Excellent. Good thinking."

"So what's next, Harv?" I didn't bother to tell him that it wasn't my idea to have Bob there.

"Call Toaz. Get the photo and paint to him."

"Yeah. When are you going to call him?"

"When I get back to the office. Right after lunch."

"About that, Harv. I need a little more time. Can you hold off until tomorrow morning?"

"What do you have in mind, Pete?"

"I want to go see Emily. Tonight."

"You're asking me to withhold evidence in a multiple murder case?"

"Not at all. It's evidence I discovered in a missing person's case. I deserve to confront my client with evidence I found. I'm not obligated to share it with Toaz. At least not yet. Hell, I didn't even have to share it with you."

"That may be. But if I knowingly keep this evidence from Toaz, my ass is on the line."

"Okay. Let me ask you this. Who knows about the picture and the paint?"

"You, me and anyone else you may have told."

"I haven't told anyone else, Harvey. Herman Kaplan knows about the picture and Bob Hawkins knows about the paint. But neither of them knows anything about evidence in a murder case."

"Yeah, so what's your point?"

"Only you and I know about both, Harvey. And, as of now, only I know. Because I'm not giving you the picture or the paint until tomorrow. Does that take your ass off the line?"

"Uh, yes, I guess it does. But I'm not sure about your ass."

"I'll take my chances. The picture is evidence in my investigation to find Zachary Bradshaw. I intend to share it with Toaz, but not just yet."

"Okay, but what about the paint?"

"The paint? I didn't find the paint until tonight when I go to Bradshaw's."

Harv just looked at me and shrugged. "Let's order lunch," he said.

We ate in relative silence, not even looking at each other except for an occasional quick glance. The chicken stir-fry at Vassili's is that good.

111

Emily/Zachary answered when I called. No formalities. She just said, "Hello."

"Hello Emily. It's Pete Pepper. I was hoping we could meet sometime later this afternoon or evening. I have an update on Zachary and I think it would be best if we talked in person."

"Ohmygod! Did you find him? He isn't dead, is he?"

Wow! What a great piece of impromptu acting. I had to stop myself from complimenting him. "No, Emily. I didn't find him. And he's not dead. At least, I don't think so. I just want to share some information I got from Brad Toaz, the detective who's investigating the death of Janny Vandver and the others."

"Oh, I see. Well uh, okay. Would seven o'clock work for you?"

"Seven o'clock? Sure. See you then."

"I'd invite you for dinner, but I gave Ramona a few days off – the whole weekend, in fact. She's going to visit some friends Downriver.

Trenton, I think she said. I'll probably just pop a chicken pot pie in the oven. Actually, if you like pot pies … ?"

"Thanks, Emily. I do, but I have some leftover pasta I want to finish before I have to throw it out. Thanks for the offer, though."

"Okay then, I'll see you around seven tonight."

112

I didn't anticipate any trouble, but when I lowered the boom on Zachary, as I intended to do, there was no telling what might happen. I doubted very much that he would be armed; there was no reason for him to be suspicious that I knew the truth. At least I didn't think so.

Nonetheless, I *was* going to be armed. I 'm not ashamed to admit that I don't like guns and my expertise with 45s is limited to records, not guns. Nonetheless, I was packing an old Colt 45 Revolver that had belonged to my brother Domenic. I adjusted my shoulder holster as I banged the elephant- trunk knocker against the pad on the front door. It opened about twenty seconds later.

"Pete. You're a little early. Come on in."

"Yeah, the traffic was lighter than I expected. Guess I made pretty good time."

"Let's go into the sunroom."

Still the sunroom, eh? Maybe that's what she called it, but I considered it to be what a real estate salesman would definitely call a great room. A very large great room. Anyway, we both got comfortable, me on the sofa and Emily on her chair. Just like the first time we met.

"So, what's this information you have for me from Detective Toaz, Pete?" She rubbed her hands with anticipation that definitely wasn't feigned.

"I'm afraid it's not good news, Emily. He says he has DNA evidence that puts Zachary at the murder scene of both Janny Vandever and Edith Pringham."

"What!" There was no faking his shocked look. But was it feigned shock over the likelihood that Zachary was a killer or real shock at the possibility he had left DNA at either scene. Since he already knew he was a killer, I was pretty sure the shock was real.

"I, I can't believe it. That's horrible." This time, it was definitely an act. Then, "I wonder how Toaz got Zachary's DNA? Did he say?"

"Actually, he didn't. But I assume it had something to do with the Tri-County Trade Commission. He must have had a physical or maybe some sort of inoculations before he went to China. I'm not sure." Of course, I was sure, since I made up the whole story and had no idea if Toaz had samples or found any unidentified DNA at any of the murder scenes.

There was a noticeable pause; probably Zachary trying to recall if the Commission somehow had his DNA on record or if he had inadvertently left any at the scenes. He finally shook his head and said, "This is all so hard to take. So hard to believe."

"I'm sorry, Emily. I know this has to be a shock for you. But I think Zachary had motive and that would also explain the situation with George Gianotti."

"What do you mean?"

"Well, I never doubted that George was killed here, maybe even in this room. I was on the phone with him when I believe it happened. And since you were, you know, indisposed upstairs, Zachary being the killer is the only plausible explanation I can come up with."

He buried his face in his hands and uttered a muffled, "Oh my god, Zachary, what have you done?" Then, looking at me, "But you haven't found him yet?"

"No, but I think I'm close. Very close."

He looked in my eyes and I think at that moment he knew that I knew.

"How close, Pete?"

"About five feet, Zachary."

He actually smiled as he shook his head. "Well, it was worth a shot," he said. There was no apparent panic, just resignation.

It took me by surprise. "Really? It was worth brutally murdering six people?"

"Six people? It was only five." He sounded indignant, as though one less murder really made a difference.

"Emily, George, Janny, Kay, Edith and Ralph," I reminded him.

"I didn't kill Emily," he protested.

"What? You mean you've got her hidden away somewhere? Sedated or something?"

"No. Emily died. She must have been dead two or three days when I found her in her bed. Probably a stroke or heart attack. I merely disposed of the body."

"And the other five?"

"It had to be done. Emily was agoraphobic, as you no doubt found out from your visit with her shrink. They were the only people she had any contact with for the last few years, which means they could identify me. Or at least know that I wasn't Emily. For my plan to work, they had to go."

I marveled at his callousness. "But why so brutally, Zach? Do you mind if I call you Zach?" Now, why the hell did I ask that? I guess I meant Zach instead of Emily.

He smiled again. "Not at all. All my friends call me Zach. The reason I killed them the way I did was to throw off the police," he continued. "I tried to make it look like it was a serial killer, which, I suppose I am. I guess I got the idea from watching some cop shows on television. Making the murders look like they were related to the various professions was a stroke of genius. I must admit it became a creative challenge to make them all look that way. I hope it kept the profilers scratching their heads."

I just looked at him and shook my head in disbelief, but he continued on.

"Of course, I was going to kill Emily too. But after I disposed of the help, she died. At that point, I didn't know for sure if she had officially changed her will. Too bad. As it turned out, the will was still in the process. If I had done nothing, everything would have been mine anyway. But it was too late. Once I put my plan in motion, Janny and George had to go too. Janny, I'm pretty sure, recognized me at the warehouse. And George, of course, knew I wasn't really Emily."

"About George, we still can't figure out the logistics of that one. How did you pull it off? An even bigger question is how did you get George to come to your house? Didn't he recognize that your voice wasn't Emily's?"

"Ah, yes. That was a stroke of luck. I was trying desperately to figure out how to kill him. Then, out of the blue, he showed up at my door that evening. It was a scheduled meeting with Emily and, of course, I had no knowledge of it. When I opened the door and realized it was George, I quickly turned my face away and grabbed an umbrella from the stand. The minute he crossed the threshold, I whacked him across the face. He was startled, of course, and put up his hands, but I kept whacking and he finally fell to the floor unconscious."

I found his continued matter-of-factness to be totally unnerving, but he went on as though he were reading me a bedtime story.

"His coming to me was fortuitous, but there was also a downside. It left me with the problem of how to get rid of his body when I eventually killed him. The others were no problem. So, I tied him up and went into my study, poured myself another drink and considered my options."

"I must have dozed off; I often do when I've been drinking. I'm an alcoholic too, you know. Emily and I actually met at an AA meeting. Anyway, later on during the night, I heard noises from the foyer, where I had left him. When I got there, he had somehow gotten loose and had the phone in his hand. I grabbed a vase and bashed him. He was mumbling something I couldn't make out, so I hit him again and he dropped the phone and collapsed on the floor. I made sure he was dead and carried him out to the garage and did some cosmetic work on his face and fingers. Then I came back to the house to further ponder the situation."

By now, I was mesmerized in spite of the brutality. "So how did you resolve the situation, as you call it, Zach?"

"Yes, I did manage, as you're well aware. Another stroke of genius, if I do say so myself."

"I'm listening."

"After I made breakfast, I drove George's car back to his apartment. His keys were in his coat pocket. It took me a while, but I finally located his building and parked in his assigned space. Then I went inside and checked out the lay of the land. It was important that I knew what I was facing ahead of time. Then I drove over to his office building and parked his car there. I went inside the lobby and used my cell phone to order a town car, which brought me back here."

"Unbelievable," was all I could say.

"Yes, well after midnight, I put his body in the passenger seat of my truck and drove back to the apartment. About two in the morning, when no one was around, I carried him in and put him on his bed. I had to unlock the outer door, but I had left his apartment unlocked. Then I just drove home."

"George must have been a heavy load for you to carry."

"I used what's called a fireman's carry; it was relatively easy."

"I have to admit, Zach, you certainly carried it off. What about the others? Was Janny your first victim?"

"No, she was the fourth. Edith Pringham was first. Then Kay and Ralph. I had to wait for Janny to go to the warehouse. I couldn't very well have dispensed with her at the store. And she lived right on campus. Too many people around. You know how college students are always wandering about."

I sat in stunned silence for a minute, then asked Zach another question. "But your plan, Zach. Wasn't it kind of extreme to have a sex change operation?"

"That? That was something I was in the process of doing anyway." He let out a brief chuckle.

"Why is that funny?

Oh, I was just thinking how Emily used to accuse me of screwing around when I came home smelling of perfume. She had no idea it was me wearing it." This time his chuckle was a loud, long laugh. Then he stood up and started walking toward the armoire across the room.

"Where are you going, Zach? You should know that I'm armed."

"Relax, Pete. I know the jig is up. I'm ready to turn myself in. It's just that I'm fascinated by this conversation so much, I feel like having a cigar. Would you like one?"

Actually, that sounded good. "Uh, yeah. Sure." Now I was the one being matter of fact.

He went to the humidor and came back with two cigars. Davidoffs. Very, very expensive. Funny, the ones Ramona had given me didn't have bands. Zachary had apparently replenished his supply. I watched him closely, although it certainly appeared that he wasn't going to try to get away or do anything crazy.

"Need a light?" he said, as he handed me one, then produced a lighter from somewhere and held it out to me. I rotated the cigar above the flame until it was burning evenly. Zach sat back down and made a show of lighting his.

"Ordinarily, I'd use a wooden match to light a cigar, but I don't know where Ramona put them," he said, apologetically. "A true connoisseur would never use a lighter. Only wood will do."

"I didn't know that."

"It's true." He leaned back and sent a plume of smoke toward the ceiling, a contented look on his face. I was baffled by his casual demeanor and it unsettled me even more.

"Anyway, where were we?" he said, as though we had been discussing last weekend's football game.

"You were wearing perfume and probably a dress and having a good time at the Palette."

"Ah, yes, the Palette. I have such fond memories of that place. I was saddened when they closed it down."

"I bet you were."

"Indeed." He pulled out his lighter and stoked his cigar again. "See? This wouldn't happen with a wooden match."

I couldn't imagine how the source of the flame made any difference, but I didn't pursue it. Somehow, it seemed like he was stalling, but I got the conversation back on track.

"There's something I don't understand, Zach. Why did you hire me?"

"Ah, yes. That turned out not to be such a good idea, didn't it? I wanted to establish that Zachary was missing, you see, although now I'm not so sure why. But for sure, if my plan were going to work, I would have to pass muster as a woman, as Emily. With everyone who could identify me eliminated, what better way than to see if a detective could tell I was transgender?"

"Probably not to hire a detective."

"Yes, as it turns out. But at the time, I thought it would throw off suspicion. Why would the guilty party hire a detective? My thinking was that he wouldn't and therefore would not be a suspect."

"I guess that's logical." In fact, that's exactly what I had suggested to Harvey.

He pulled out the lighter again and looked at his cigar. "Damn! This thing won't stay lit. Maybe it's the cigar and not the lighter. Probably packed too tight. That happens sometimes, even with the good ones. I'll just have to get another one. How's yours Pete?"

"Fine. It's drawing fine."

He walked back to the humidor and a few steps beyond. "Huh? What in the world is this?" he said, sounding quite surprised as he continued on behind the armoire.

It took me a few seconds to realize he wasn't coming back. I jumped up and raced toward the armoire and saw an open door behind it.

Damn! He had been stalling, waiting for a chance to make his move. But where was he going to run?

The moon was out and it was freezing. The snow was falling a little harder now, but I spotted him about twenty-five yards ahead and sprinted after him. I knew I could outrun him. Not just because I was twenty years or so younger, but because I was wearing pants and he was in a dress. I was steadily closing ground when I realized we were headed toward the lake. Was it frozen? Probably. It had been well below freezing for a few days. But was it solid enough?

I don't really know when I left solid ground and hit solid ice, but I suddenly heard the sound of the ice creaking. He was still ten yards ahead.

"Zachary," I yelled. "Come back. It's not safe."

I stopped and he didn't. And he didn't make a sound when the ice gave way and he plunged into the depths.

113

Rather than call Harvey, I felt it would be more appropriate to tell him in person. He was on the phone when I entered his office and he motioned me to sit down. When he hung up, he looked at me with questioning eyes.

"So, do you want the good news or the bad news first? I asked him.

"Son of a bitch. I knew something was up the minute you walked in the door. Just tell me what's going on."

"Okay, the good news first. Zachary Bradshaw confessed to five murders. Gianotti, Vandever, Pringham, Kimberly and Spaulding. He claims that Emily died of natural causes and he just disposed of the body."

"That sounds more like the bad news."

"No. The bad news is that Zachary's dead."

"What the fuck? You killed him?"

"No, no. He killed himself. Sort of."

I recounted the events of my evening visit, not sure how Harvey would react. When I finished, he just stared at me with a look I couldn't read. His response was calmer than I had hoped.

"Well, what's done is done, I guess. I'll meet with Toaz and fill him in. Under the circumstances, I can't imagine he'll be too upset. Hell, he shouldn't be. The murders are solved, after all. And, not that it matters anymore, but I'd like to turn the picture and paint can over to him."

"Right. They're in my car. I'll go get them."

I went home and brooded most of the day. In my heart, I felt I was right, but I couldn't help feeling I'd done something wrong. Around three o'clock I called Lou and asked if he and Lef could meet me for dinner at Vassili's. I needed the company of friends.

114

"Shit, man. You're lucky to be alive," Lou said, through a mouthful of veal parmigiana.

"Damn right," Lef agreed.

"Yeah, I guess so." I later found out that a sand bar extended about thirty yards out from the Belleville Lake shore. The ice was solid enough to support the weight of a running man. But, where the sand bar ended, the water was much deeper and the ice much thinner. Zachary should have known. But under the circumstances ...

"So, you're saying that the pictures Gianni drew gave you the idea about a sex change?" Lou interrupted my thoughts.

"I think subconsciously that may have been the key. But it was a combination of things. The agoraphobia thing, the Palette story and the photograph from Kaplan clinched it, of course."

"And what about the handwriting?" Lef interjected.

"Oh, right. The handwriting analysis was a very important clue."

"You know, I never put much stock in that handwriting analysis stuff," Lou said.

"What do you mean?" Lef asked. "It's completely valid. In fact, I'm somewhat of an expert myself. Go ahead, Lou. Write something down."

Lou pulled out a Sharpie, scribbled something on his napkin and handed it to Lef.

"Uh, could you write something besides 'You're an asshole Lef Turner'? That isn't very nice."

"What for? Writing is writing."

"Please."

"Okay." Lou took the napkin and scrawled again.

"Oh wow, that's much better."

"What did he write, Lef?" I asked.

"You're not an asshole Lef Turner."

"Yeah, just go with it," Lou laughed.

Lef sighed, took the napkin and scrutinized it.

"Uhumm, yep, yeh. Oh yes. Mr. Bracato, I see by your sloppy loops and flamboyant ascenders that you're a frequent masturbator."

"Damn! I was wrong. I never would have guessed handwriting analysis could be so accurate."

We all got a laugh out of that, but Lef wasn't through putting the screws to Lou.

"Hey Lou, tell Pete about your lunch date with the redhead."

"Oh yeah, that was the Saturday I was in LA with Eva. You never said anything about it when we had breakfast Monday before the meeting with Rack, Lou. Damn, I forgot all about it."

I could tell by Lou's expression that things didn't go well.

"What happened? Didn't she show up?"

"She showed up all right. Along with another girl and a guy."

"Wait a minute. I thought you said there were two other girls. Oh my God, don't tell me. One of the so-called girls had a name like Pat or Terry and it was actually a guy."

"No the girl that didn't show up was named Valerie."

"So who was the guy?"

"The redhead's fucking boyfriend."

I left feeling much better than I had all day. My friends didn't let me down.

115

Friday morning, my buoyed spirits had slipped back down into neutral. I was still feeling a bit better about my episode with Zachary; it was the dinner with Marianne that brought me down some. I still didn't know what I was going to do about her invitation.

I spent half an hour halfheartedly glancing through the morning *Free Press* down in my office. Nothing caught my attention. Then I called Harvey to see how things had gone with Toaz, but he wasn't in. More than likely he was in Ypsilanti, bringing Toaz up to date on Zachary's demise. I hoped that turning the evidence over to him might make the news easier to take. I didn't want to think about any other possibility.

For a minute, I considered getting back to the task of cataloging my records. I grabbed a handful off the shelf, and then put them back. I wasn't in a mood to concentrate. Instead, I punched in a medley of slow tunes and went upstairs. I leaned back in my recliner, closed my eyes and listened to the music. I was obviously putting off a decision on dinner with Marianne and I needed to clear my head. The music worked, because halfway through "Smoke Gets In Your Eyes" by the Platters, I drifted off.

The sound of the phone ringing woke me up. Dion was singing "Where Or When," so I couldn't have been out for too long. Before I could get up to answer, the answering machine kicked in. It was Marianne.

"Pete, it's Marianne. I'm just calling to remind you about dinner tonight. Fettucine with clam sauce, your favorite. Don't bother to get all dressed up. Just come as you are. I figure we can eat around seven, seven thirty or so, but you can come earlier if you want."

She was pretty upbeat up to that point, but then her voice took on a note of sadness. "I know you said you might be busy, Pete, but I hope you can make it. I really do. Bye, Pete."

I got up and went to the kitchen to splash some water on my face. What the hell, I thought. I might as well go. But I was too hungry to wait until seven o'clock to eat, so I sliced up some soppressata and fontinella cheese, warmed up some Italian bread in the microwave and had a sandwich. Just enough to hold me, but not so much that I wouldn't be hungry later at Marianne's. I reached for a beer to wash it down, but my better judgment took control of my hand and I poured myself a glass of milk instead. There was a 100% chance that Marianne would be serving wine with dinner. White Zinfandel, more than likely.

I still had several hours, but I decided to pick out what to wear just to kill time. When someone tells me to dress casually, I take them at their word. I set out some clean socks and underwear, an $85 Missoni shirt I got on sale for $35 and the one pair of jeans that I keep ironed just for occasions like this. As I was admiring the sharp crease, the phone rang.

I got it on the third ring. It was Harvey.

"Well, I just got back from meeting with Toaz and I can tell you, he wasn't happy."

"I was afraid of that, Harv. How mad is he? Mad enough to try to make trouble for me?"

"Calm down, my boy. Calm down. He *was* angry when I first gave him the news, but by the time I left, he was happy and smiling and said to thank you."

"You're kidding. What happened?"

"Well, more than anything, I think he felt like he was left out of the loop. You know, the murders pretty much got solved without him. And he did suggest that you were stepping over boundaries by getting involved."

"But, Harv, I wasn't working his cases. I was trying to find Zachary Bradshaw. The cases intersected. What was I supposed to do?"

"Pete, I told you he's happy now. I explained that to him and he sort of backed down. Then when I gave him the picture of Zachary and the can of paint, he was extremely pleased."

"Harv, you should have told him that he could take credit for finding that stuff."

"Well, uh, I think that was implied. For the paint, anyway. Just let your buddy Bob Hawkins know it was Toaz he met the other night, not you."

"Done, Harv. Bob won't have a problem with that. What about the photo?"

"You get the credit for that. You found it in your investigation of Zachary's disappearance and were kind enough to turn it over to Toaz. You're both heroes."

"What about Zachary?"

"They have a team of divers coming in tomorrow. Supposed to be a little warmer, I guess. Toaz already sent some of his guys out there and they marked a spot where there was a big hole in the ice. That's probably where he went in."

"More than likely. Do you think I should be there?"

"I'd let Toaz run the show from here. He said he'd keep me posted."

"Okay. And you'll keep me posted, right?"

"Hey, what am I doing right now?"

"Yeah, right. Thanks Harv. Later."

The closer I got to Marianne's, the more I was having second thoughts. What did I really expect to accomplish? Every scenario I could imagine ended awkwardly. I didn't want to be in the position of controlling her happiness and I felt guilty even thinking that I was in such a position. I didn't want to hurt her feelings, but I didn't want to give her false hope either.

My stomach was churning as I drove slowly past her house, a small two-bedroom bungalow two blocks south of Nine Mile Road in Ferndale.

The kitchen light was on, but the blinds weren't open enough to see in. I circled the block, slowed down, turned off my headlights and pulled into her driveway. I just sat there for a minute, thinking. 'If you love me, you'll come,' she said. I do love you, Marianne. But not the way you want me to love you. And I never will.

I put the car in reverse, backed out of the drive and headed west on Nine Mile. With any luck, I'd make it to Northville Downs in time for the third race.

Postlude

Stuart Gottschalk, aka Stu Gotts, ran up the stairs two at a time, being careful to keep the large pepperoni pizza level so the cheese wouldn't slide off.

"Pizza's here, Pete," he said, setting it down on the kitchen table.

Pete Pepper emerged from his bedroom, wallet in hand. "How much was it, Stu?"

"My treat, Pete."

"You sure, Stu? I invited you here."

"Yeah, I'm sure. You bought the beer and burgers at that bar the other day. It's my turn."

"Okay," he said, with just a hint of reluctance. "Thanks. I'll get us some plates and a couple of beers."

Fifteen minutes later, the pizza was gone and four empty beer cans were lined up next to the sink.

Pepper popped open two more and handed one to Gotts. "The reason I asked you here, Stu was..."

The phone rang and Pepper stopped in mid-sentence. "Just a minute, Stu." Then, picking up the phone, "Pete Pepper Investigations."

"Pete, It's Harvey. Are you sitting down?"

"Actually, I'm standing in the kitchen."

"No matter. It was a rhetorical question. I just got a call from Toaz."

Pepper's heart jumped. "Did they find Zachary's body?"

"They found it, alright. Guess where."

"At the bottom of Belleville Lake."

"Of course, it was at the bottom of the lake. But guess where."

"You got me, Harv. Where?"

"Five feet away from the body of Emily Bradshaw."

From the Song Book of
Luigi "Lou" Bracato

Not Tonight, I've Got A Heartache
I saw him in a club outside of Houston
Knew right off he was trying to catch my eye
He must have thought that I was out there cruisin'
But I was only trying not to cry.

(CHORUS)
Not tonight, I've got a heartache.
New romance is the last thing on my mind
I thought he loved me too
He turned out to be untrue
Don't know how I could have been so blind

He walked right up to me like we were neighbors
Asked me if we hadn't met before
He wanted me to dance
Guess I should have took a chance
But I got up and waltzed right out the door.

(CHORUS)
Not tonight, I've got a heartache.
Don't know if I'll ever love again
But if you give me time
To straighten out this life of mine
Come back and who knows what might happen then.

Now I'm sittin' here alone and thinkin'
Rememberin' that handsome stranger's glance
Did I do what's right?
Or should I have stayed that night?
My heart says it's too soon to take a chance.

(CHORUS)
Not tonight, I've got a heartache
This pain inside is more than I can stand
I hope it goes away
I'm hopin' and I pray
That someday I'll find me a faithful man.

Now I'm sittin here with Johnny Walker
Hopin' that my miseries will drown.
I turned down that dance
Didn't want to take a chance.
And Johnny Walker's never let me down.

(CHORUS)
Not tonight, I've got a heartache
But the pain is starting to subside.
When will it go away?
If ever comes the day
A faithful man will stand here by my side.

(CHORUS)
Not tonight, I've got a heartache.
Don't know if I'll ever love again
I hope it goes away
I'm hopin' and I pray
That someday I'll find me a faithful man.

71741692R00209

Made in the USA
Lexington, KY
24 November 2017